The Seraphim Chronicles

Book 2

Testament

A Novel By

John H. Hamilton

Raven Hall Books
Shelbyville, Kentucky. 40065

johnhamilton00@yahoo.com

ISBN-13: 978-1-7338381-1-5
ISBN-10: 1-7338381-1-2

* * * * * *

Other books by John Hamilton

The Wizard of Raven Hall
Age of Antiquity
Baptism *- Seraphim Chronicles Trilogy — Book 1*

Cover design by John Hamilton
Cover and in-text graphics from *'Starship Concept Art'*

R7

DEDICATION

For my mom and dad,

Mom, for your love, caring, help in showing me the way. Your strong dedication to the family, so artistic and a strong woman in a time when being one wasn't in vogue.

Dad, for being a role model providing examples of leadership, just principles, and knowing right from wrong,

The Seraphim Chronicles

Book 2

Testament

"Testament: Something that serves as a sign or evidence of a specified fact, event, or quality"
John Hamilton

"Of all the branches of men in the forces there is none which shows more devotion and faces grimmer perils than the submariners."
Winston Churchill

"Life, forever dying to be born afresh, forever young and eager, will presently stand upon this Earth as upon a footstool, and stretch out its realm amidst the stars."
H. G. Wells 1866 - 1946

"I don't think the human race will survive the next thousand years, unless we spread into space. There are too many accidents that can befall life on a single planet. But I'm an optimist. We will reach out to the stars."
Stephen Hawking

Seraphim

(A member of the highest order of angels)

Introduction

Ⅰn the small village of people and profound science
called Angels Landing, the time has come. All the
dreams of the amazing scientists that conceived, designed and
built the magnificent vessel sitting quietly in hold-down
cradles, are contained within. It is time to venture out to a
place no-one has ever been before, far beyond all that is
known. The ship is complete. The training of all on board,
finished. The crew is ready. The early missions planned.
Supplies are loaded. Confidence is high, excitement higher.
Hundreds of Angels Landing theme park personnel stand
outside waiting for the moment the hold-down clamps
release. Hundreds... thousands more stand outside the chain
link perimeter fence and closed gates waiting patiently with
cameras in hand for the moment that will surely come.

This moment promises a new age of space exploration and a
new step for all mankind. World-wide, people watch in rapt
fascination as the images on TV screens report in real time
the events happening in a place called Angels Landing in the
desert of Wyoming, USA. A distant sound is heard. It is a
beautiful rendition of the Navy Hymn for submariners,
"Eternal Father" dedicated in reverence to Seraphim, her
captain and brave crew. Slowly, silently, Seraphim begins to
rise from her cradles and move skyward. She may not return
for months, possibly even years. Teary-eyed fans look on in
wonder.

What will they find out there? Will they ever return?

***  ***

Part I
Prologue

Two months earlier

A t the very edge of space, 37 miles above the Earth's surface in the lower mesosphere, two small, unique ships fly north at 5500 miles per hour. With the VASIMR-5 engines shut down and silent, they coast the last 1200 miles through the very thin atmosphere high above Earth. The few air molecules have little effect. The nose and small stubby GMI stabilization wings heat up but remain within limits for the speed. Very little speed is lost to wind drag.

From the shuttle *Raphael*...

"Where are we?" Peregrine answers...

"North end of the Colorado Rockies. Looks like it's overcast all the way to Canada. Let's split apart a little more for the flip." Raphael moves three hundred meters abeam the larger *Peregrine*.

"Standby to flip in 5 – 4 – 3 – 2 – 1 Flip."

As one, powerful maneuvering thrusters flip each ship over backwards, now inverted and facing the direction they had come, the big plasma engines face the line of flight and ready to decelerate the ships.

"Set 7-second at 1/3 thrust. On my mark. 3-2-1 MARK."

Two bright blue horizontal columns of 1,000,000 °C; (1,800,000 °F) plasma light up the early morning sky. The overcast below masks what would look to on-lookers like two meteors entering the atmosphere. As each shuttle slows to 200 mph, and with the plasma engines shut down, the GMI (Planet Generated Gravity and Magnetosphere Interferometry systems) takes over. The maneuvering thrusters flip the ships back facing the direction of flight.

"*Seraphim this is Peregrine flight of two, with Rafael inbound to Angels Landing, over.*"

"*Peregrine flight, this is Seraphim. Welcome back. The visitor gates are closed. Only authorized personnel are on site at this time. Seraphim is on the cradles. Who is in first?*"

"*Peregrine is number one through the airlock.*"

"*Copy that. How was the trip, Lory?*"

"*Uneventful, but useful COB. Is the captain around?*"

"*No, Captain Parish, professors Remington and Hunter, are off site in meetings in Rawlins with top level people from SpaceX, Blue Origin, NASA, JPL and more. Where are you.*"

"*Ten minutes out. Rafael has a stop to make. They will be there in twenty. See you in a bit. Oh, and COB, could you meet us in the hangar.*"

"*Copy that. Will do. See you in ten.*"

On the Seraphim bridge, all is quiet. Most crew members sit in whispered conversation. Others, are reading from a new series of publications from various national and international agencies on the future of humans in space.

An LED light flashes on the tactical panel alerting the duty officer, Lt. David Janssen, that the outer door to the main airlock was opening. He flipped a switch near the base of a video monitor and watches as the shuttle *Peregrine* slowly noses into the airlock tunnel. The alignment sensors along the interior of the airlock, monitor and control the movement of the shuttle keeping it from touching the walls of the tunnel. Once inside the hangar, *Peregrine* moves to its spot among the several utility and personnel carriers.

A few minutes later, having made a stop in Rawlins to drop someone off, the smaller shuttle *Rafael* enters the interior of the main hangar and slowly floats to its assigned parking spot. The rear loading ramps on both vehicles lower and several people exit to the hangar deck. Chief of the Boat

(COB) LCDR Augustus (Augie) Lincoln approaches the pilot of the *Peregrine*, Loretta (Lory) Amundsen as she descends the ramp.

"Hey Lory, how was the trip? Did you get what we needed?"

"Yep. Everything is in there. You're going to need help. Some of that stuff is pretty bulky. We dropped the XO off in Rawlins to join the others in the meeting. Jake Maxwell took over as pilot."

"How did she do in *Rafael*? She doesn't have much time in the shuttles yet."

"No, but she knows what she's doing. The way she handled Seraphim when we were shot at by the deep-space interceptor missile and then the landing back here, proves she has the touch. She was a C-130 Hercules pilot back in the day. We are wondering if all the top-tier bridge officers should be qualified pilots in the shuttles. Redundancy! It was the Captain's suggestion and I concur. Did they drive down to Rawlins?"

"No, they took a *Pocket-Rocket*. Darien Hunter was pilot. Said he had a reason for not taking a car. They parked right in front of the hotel in a visitor parking spot. The thing is so small it easily fits in a parking place between cars."

"Do they have security?"

"Yea. Jerry Dickson and one of the SEALS went along. They were packing some serious heat. They are due back in about an hour."

"OK! Before we move anything, let's wait 'til they get back. I'm going to the head, then to the café for a coffee and Danish."

Establishing Priorities

Having only recently joined the Seraphim crew, Lory Amundsen turned out to be a positive addition. At 5 foot 10 and no more than 141 pounds of pure muscle, she is an imposing figure. She works out daily and even plays Zero-Golf with the scientists. She was an Air Force Academy graduate with 23 years of active service as an F-15E Strike Eagle pilot. Her last assignment was squadron commander before putting in her retirement papers. As a civilian she found work at a fixed base operator (FBO) at an executive airport near her child-hood home outside the Norfolk city limits as an instructor pilot. It was there she met some of the former SEALS and other ex-military now aboard Seraphim. She is well liked among the crew and aggressive in her determination to understand how Seraphim functions and the world the massive ship will be going to. She is being tutored by Seraphim Science Officer, Professor Theo Remington in the theoretical sciences. She challenges him just as I did. He loves it. The men and women aboard Seraphim are among the most capable and intelligent people in their respective positions and bring to Seraphim and her future the best chances for success. It won't be long now... they will prove it.

Earlier, I had stopped at my quarters for a quick power nap and refresh before joining the group of six for a meeting none of us were particularly keen on. This morning's deliberations in Rawlins did go well, overall. It was more about familiarizing them with how we do things. There were a couple of moments it seemed a few of the NASA people felt they should be in charge. I had sat quietly as Darien calmly pushed back when a former Navy Rear Admiral (retired) from the Naval War College in Newport, Rhode Island, and now, a planning coordinator for NASA's future space activities, seemed to look down at us, or least seemed skeptical. Admiral Bascom Holder insisted on being addressed as 'Admiral' in our meeting. A few months ago, we had a meeting aboard Seraphim where we discussed how people outside our world might view us. So, we expected something like this might happen. They saw us as amateurs and should step aside and let the pros do the thinking with us following their lead.

The door opened and XO Jessica Pearson entered. She was just dropped off by one of two returning shuttles to Seraphim. She introduced herself and took a seat to my right. Darien had cast a couple of quick looks my way expecting me to rise up in my inimitable style and deck the Admiral. I didn't, of course. I waited for the right moment, content to demurely sit with a smile, and listen to some mostly good ideas from scientists and engineers. I got the feeling they were not very enamored with the former Admiral either. No matter. We had the hardware... they didn't. They knew it, that's why they were here.

I noticed that the 'other' team occasionally looked at me sitting quietly. They probably had heard the stories and saw the videos. I think they expected a more active participation on my part. It was XO Jessica Pearson that opened that can of worms. She had been a full-bird colonel in the Air Force, a C-130 Hercules pilot and squadron commander back in the day. She had also been around her share of jackasses, too.

"You know..." she began. "We aboard Seraphim don't take kindly to condescending attitudes by administrative types such as yourself... ah... Admiral. We've been out there... in space. Even got in a tussle with some folks who thought they had rights to our technology. Poor judgement on their part. Some were summarily reassigned to the Godly Court just outside the Pearly Gates for all eternity. I wonder what the ruling of the Court was. Have you been in space? No wait, you let little robots do all the work: both mechanical and human. If you and your minions would like to come along with us, command and control is the purview of Seraphim and its bridge crew under the command of Commander Hannah Parish. You **will** take the subordinate position aboard Seraphim and let US do the flying. If that is beyond your capability, Admiral, I suggest you head on home, open a beer and watch the game. I am only the XO. But, if you want a real challenge? You go head to head with her," pointing at me "**... at your peril.**"

Both Theo and Darien had smiles from ear to ear. I continued my quiet observation. I did however stare into the Admiral's eyes with that look that often terrifies people. He became a little fidgety and uncomfortably moved in his seat. He, too, was aware of the potential the captain of the Seraphim had, and also heard the term, *'Most-Bad-Ass-Female-Starship-Captain.'* He became very quiet. Darien broke the moment.

"Well, ladies and gentlemen, I think we made some headway, but for now, we need to get back. Thank you for your consideration. Perhaps we can meet again... hopefully in a more congenial atmosphere. You have considerable experience in Space with your navigation to distant worlds and robot landers. We can learn from that. We, however, have the resources to get humans out there in comfort in much less time and personal risk. I suggest you plan wisely because in short order we will be on our way to someplace far, far away. Join us if you like. Do have a nice day."

The four of us exited the hotel and joined our two-security people standing guard over the vehicle we call a *Pocket-Rocket*. We stood chatting and laughing beside the sleek little ship when we noticed the others from the meeting stood to the side watching us. We stepped back to allow the split clear gull-wing canopy of 1.23-inch thick laminated polycarbonate-acrylic to open on each side allowing entry to the six seats. Darien assumed the position as pilot with Theo beside him. Jessica sat beside me in the second row, security behind. Without a sound the little futuristic soccer-mom vehicle slowly rose straight up, remaining level as if by magic. The gull-wing canopy closed and sealed. We waved as Darien pivoted the little ship northward, advanced the GMI control stick and darted to the north and Angels Landing. What were they thinking, I wonder? Deciding to take the little *Pocket-Rocket* was a good idea instead of taking a car. It had the effect of drawing a clear line in the sand about who had the technology. Some might think we were showing off. I submit, it was a clever strategy. If the arrogant Admiral had something to show off, he would have. But... he had nothing. Darien was right. We did make progress at the meeting and will continue talks as we move to a departure date set six weeks, hence. Now, we have to run through the pre-departure checklists and make sure we have all things right.

I'm always thinking of things, trying not to be left behind when potential problems loom. I had a concern and needed to talk to the people in Engineering. I had Mr.Scott make an appointment with Gus Mayer, Seraphim's First Engineer. I took the elevator up one deck to 9 only long enough to get a coffee from a new *Starbucks style* café. Then it was back on the elevator to deck 4 and the office of LCDR and First Engineer, Gustaf (Gus) Mayer, power-wizard extraordinaire. I stepped to the side on entering as he had three others who seemed agitated over something and the discussion had become heated. I decided it would be best if I waited outside. When they saw the captain leave the room and wait outside, the talk calmed down and seemed to end. I heard some muffled laughter. I didn't recognize any of them but then again, Engineering has the largest single purpose department on Seraphim. They had never met me, and were a bit nervous as they left the room each giving a respectful nod as they passed.

I finished my coffee and deposited the empty cup in the circular waste basket beside the desk as I reentered.

"Hey, Captain. Good to see you. What brings you to the inner sanctum of all things power?"

"Sorry I interrupted, Gus. Sounded serious. I just came down to ask about something that I have been curious about."

"They are engineering-technicians. Good ones, too. They are concerned about some replacement parts we received from a supplier that were not built to our specification. Didn't fit properly. That's all. I called the supplier to find out what happened. They have been very good in the past. They will fix the problem. Now! What do you need, Captain?"

"Remember about a year ago when I was trying to understand the systems and departments on Seraphim, and you wiz-banged me with the science of ACPUs and the like. I asked if they burned a lot of fuel. Then, you went on to explain how they work. You had said that anti-matter was very rare but it was extremely efficient and we use very little of it. Here's the question... actually three. Where do we get it?... Do we have enough for extended missions? ... And, what kind of backup do we have, if any... if we run short?"

"OK! I'm not sure if it would be helpful for you to know this, but, we think we can harvest matter and its brother, antimatter, or rather collect it from free space. I will go this far. Each particle of matter has an exact copy of itself but with an opposite charge: one negative, one positive. They have identical mass and are ubiquitous throughout the universe, although in minute quantities. Scientists believe, both were created during the so-called Big-Bang. When one negative molecule comes in contact with its positive brother, they annihilate each other giving off a huge spike of energy. That's what powers our ACPUs. We believe, and, please understand this is speculation right now, if we create a very special collector, a kind of scoop into which space dust could flow as we move through space, Surrounding the collector, powerful magnets with opposite poles on each of two sides; matter would be drawn to the negative side and collected and stored in a, we call it a magnetic jar, anti-matter would be drawn to the other... and also collected in a magnetic jar. The two provide the fuel for the ACPUs and other needs. It's far more theoretical than hard science but that is the gist of it without delving into the quantum realm. We have been buying small amounts of antimatter from suppliers with big laboratories including the Swiss *Large Hadron Collider*. It is hugely expensive and they don't want to part with it as it is used for a myriad of science studies. Do we have enough? We believe we do. Should be enough to keep us going for a few years, maybe. Well if our quantum scoop works we could be self-sufficient. Keep in mind that going from A to B in space is done with engines mostly off, used only to get up to speed which should only be about 5% of the time. Once at the selected speed, we coast the rest of the way. When we approach the destination, we decelerate by turning the ship around... you call it 'flip' and fire the VASIMRs to slow down. Along the way, we collect space dust, parse the particles and have more fuel. We are now looking into the idea that since nebula clouds are composed mostly of dust, they may have a higher concentration of matter/antimatter particles than open space. We may be able to harvest more by just carefully flying through the nebula. But, the idea is still a work in progress, and again, as it sits right now, is completely hypothetical.

It would be like driving down a highway in a gasoline powered car. The centerline of the road is a narrow ditch in which gasoline freely flows. A small scoop under the car sucks up some of the gasoline and refills the gas tank. Something like that. A poor analogy perhaps, and as I said... purely hypothetical. Anyway, that's the plan."

"Wait, you're messing me up here. If these two particles are of opposite polarity, and are floating around in free space, why don't they just annihilate out there?"

"Only you would ask that but, you're not the first to ask. For some unknown reason... they don't. Ask your science officer. See if he has an answer. Now on to you last question.

We do have a backup. It's not advertised and few know about them, but we have a pair of nuclear reactors nearly identical to the ones in your submarine and other Navy vessels but with our own cooling systems. Navy ships have a lot of cold water around them to cool the reactors. Here, nothing goes to waste, not even heat. We adapted a technology called a thermoelectric generator (TEG), also called a *Seebeck Generator*. It is a solid-state device that converts heat flux (temperature differences) directly into electrical energy through a phenomenon called the Seebeck Effect (a form of thermoelectric effect). Thermoelectric generators function like heat engines, but are less bulky and have no moving parts. So, it does two things: gives us an additional power source and at the same time cools the reactors.

On submarines the nuclear reactor heats water to produce steam for a turbine used to turn the ship's propeller through a gearbox or through an electric generator and motor.

We use only electric power to run our gravity systems and everything else inside Seraphim. Each reactor has enough output to power one VASIMR-9 at low power settings during an emergency, so we can still move and maneuver. The cross-over networks are quite elaborate and complex to meld power from multiple sources.

I hope that answers your questions."

"Why is it that when I come down here to ask a simple question, I always go back to the bridge with a headache. My brain over-heats from synapses firing trying to keep up with your science. And, yes, you answered my questions most adequately proving once again how freakin' smart you folks are down here. All good-to-know stuff. WOW! Well thank you Gus. We should get together for lunch someday."

"Thanks for coming by Hannah. Always good to see you."

I elevated back to Deck 8 and the Captain's Quarters where I plopped onto the bed for a power-nap that lasted all of 37.126 microseconds. *Of course,* there came a knock on the sliding door.

"Come in."

"Hey, Mom. How are things in Medical?"

"Things have really quieted down. All the new hires have taken the mandatory classes. They have been sorted into assignment areas, schooled on med-bay procedures, both normal and emergency. We asked Ship to install hand holds and safety bars in the ceiling and blank walls in the event of gravity loss. The guys down in Engineering designed and built an IV drip pole that uses a very low-pressure pump as a replacement for the gravity bags. It has completely adjustable flow rates that parallel exactly what the older ones do. A modification to the flooring in each bed module provides instant electromagnetic hold down of the bedside tables, and roll-around carts. They have steel plates in the base that make everything still moveable but will not float off in a loss of gravity. All personnel are looking at some new shoes that have plates in the souls that keep us from floating around. The electromagnetic source in the floor shuts down when gravity is restored. I'm told there is still a problem that placing the electro-magnets essentially co-located or near the gravity mats reduce the effectiveness of the gravity mats. They will solve any problems. Those guys in engineering are masters of their craft. It seems we are only limited by our imagination. The idea is catching on elseware. Even the food service areas are thinking of adopting the EM alternative in their plates and utensils. On tables, it is not an issue with gravity mats. If this goes ship-wide, it will be a complicated and work intensive upgrade, but a lot of folks think it could be worth it. The modifications can be continued even as we move off planet. How are you doing, honey?"

"Completely exhausted. I can't get any sleep. People are banging on my door 24/7 it seems."

"Sorry! I just came to invite you to lunch. Maybe a bad time. Rain check then. I'll leave you be. Love you." and the door closed behind her.

I had Mr.Scott send a message to the XO who had the Conn. I told CDR Jessica Pearson that I wanted... no, needed some sleep and not to bother me unless blood was flowing. A quick acknowledgement was received and I pulled back the covers and descended into blissful sleep.

Hours later, Mr.Scott woke me with the subdued sound of harp and cello music. Mom's signature alert.

"Play."

"Hey Honey. Dad and I are making supper, more like breakfast. We would love to have you join us."

I responded: "Be there in 15 minutes." Mr.Scott relayed the message. I got up, took a quick shower, put on civvies and made my way to deck 10. People quizzically looked at me, out of uniform, hair loose to my shoulders, as I walked to the elevator. Just what I needed. A break. Two hours later and after a wonderful evening *breakfast* and visit, and wearing a freshly cleaned uniform, I was on the bridge. Meetings and more meetings. Another meeting Day. Well, I agreed to this job.

The reduced staff of the night crew (B-shift) updated me with reports from all decks. Everything was copacetic and hunky-dory. Did I just use those words? Especially considering they are redundant in the same sentence. Obviously, I'm not quite awake yet. Anyway, I guess I'm ready for the first meeting at 7pm. I will be mostly just an observer. Well... you know me. Not always quiet.

The meeting was a series of reports by department heads reviewing the status of their preparations and logistics needs. Everything seemed in order. Then...

Mr.Scott demanded my attention. I read the message on the small screen and bolted upright, alarmed in my chair. I stood, rereading the text. Everyone was looking at me aware that something serious had just happened.

"I'm sorry to interrupt but I have been made aware that we have some guests that are quite insistent we meet. Some are from Washington and appear to have interesting credentials. One of the them is an old friend of Darien's, Gregory Vasilyevich. The XO correctly called General Quarters-Standby and moved us to DEFCON4. The hangar deck is on alert with all shuttles and Valkyrie on ready-alert.

These visitors are being held in the rotunda by Jerry Dickson's people. Some may NOT be friends of Seraphim. Would Darien Hunter, Theo Remington, Commander Parish please come with me. I also would like both Angels Landing and Seraphim Security prominent at any meetings later on. Tactical is on alert monitoring airspace high and low, terrestrial activity, and has closed the gates. The rest of you, please stand-ready at your duty stations. Anything could happen. This meeting is adjourned."

"Captain on the bridge" called out the XO.

"Call GQ, XO." I responded.

Others that had been off duty came through the Bridge doors on the run, responding to the call to General Quarters and taking their positions. Within 30 seconds all were at their stations. Lt. Francine Calder relieved a junior officer at the comm position that was still in training but kept her close by to watch.

I called...

"**Gravity**: report."

"All at their stations, Captain. Gravity A-OK, Counter-Gravity at station-keeping. All is well, Captain."

"Very well, Carry on.

Navigation: Report."

"All personnel at their duty stations Captain. All is well."

"Very well.

Environment: Report."

"All present and accounted for, Captain. All systems functioning well."

"Mr.Scott have Jerry Dickson call me."

"Message sent, Captain... OK! He is on"

"Jerry. This is Captain Parish. I need to know the number of visitors you are holding. I need names, who they work for, why they are here, and what is their background? And why we should talk with them?"

"Copy all, Captain. Give me a few minutes."

"Take your time. They are authorized to use the corner café and adjacent restroom. They are not allowed on Seraphim or in the theaters. Only the rotunda, copy? Oh, and keep an eye on Gregory Vasilyevich. He is a bad actor and was responsible for the illegal detention of Professors Hunter, Remington and Michaels. He is not a friend of Seraphim."

"Copy all, Captain. Dickson, out."

I turned to the three that stood with me on the raised bridge deck.

"Please come with me to my Day Room. The XO has the Conn. Dad, have Roger Davidson, Donna Singleton, Sam Lonegan join us, please." Within minutes, the seven of us took seats at the multiuse table in the Captain's Day Room. I began...

"At my request, Jerry Dickson is preparing a comprehensive list of the people he is holding in the rotunda. I am suspicious of the reason some of them are here. The thing that casts a shadow over this visit, is the presence of Gregory Vasilyevich. Why is he here? Is he part of the NASA, Boeing and JPL group? I would prefer if he were deemed *persona-non-grata* and removed from the property. Your thoughts."

"We should contact legal and get their take. I can call Susan Richards and by extension our new department near Jerry's office. Is Seraphim ready if we need to bolt?"

"Within minutes of the XOs call to GQ, everyone was at their position and prepared for anything." When I returned, Darien asked,

"Is this how the personnel aboard the Andrew Lindstrom responded to General Quarters?"

"Yes. We drilled on all possible situations until even people who were hot-racking were at their positions in seconds, putting their pants on as they ran. We all took the drills seriously. The captain drove us hard. But that kind of training pays off. Most of the crew on this ship are civilians, never were in the military. Seraphim may not be a naval vessel, nor are we military in this assignment, but proper discipline and training are imperative considering where we are going and the challenges we may face. We have already been tested twice. People who will join us and are not part of ship's crew depend on us to respond to challenges for their safety and well-being. We have families on board, too." Darien looked on pleased that his dream was in safe and responsible hands.

A knock on the door interrupted my mini-lecture.

Meredith Ames from Jerry Dickson's office stood holding a slash folder containing the requested information.

"Come in, Ms. Ames." I introduced her and everyone in the room.

"This is the information you requested, Captain. Again, you were right. There are several nefarious characters among our guests. We asked park visitors to leave the rotunda for a few minutes. They are in the big theater in the converted barn out back watching a new documentary on Black Holes. It should last about 40 minutes."

"Thank you. How are folks holding up down there?"

"Everyone is fine, Ma'am. We have been through this kind of thing before, haven't we? Everyone knows who is in charge and are confident you will resolve this just fine."

I smiled, as did the others.

"Please tell Jerry we will get back to you in a few minutes after we review this. Thank you, Meredith."

She smiled and left.

"OK! Let's take a look."

For the next half hour, we reviewed all the guests' backgrounds and sorted them into three piles: *OK*, *Suspect*, and *Known Problems*. Only three fell into the latter category, with Gregory Vasilyevich topping the list. Those in the 'OK' category were legitimate guests whom we could welcome. Only two fell into the 'suspect' category and required further review. We then decided what to do. I wanted to know how

'Known Problem people' somehow joined the 'OK' people. Did they know each other? The TAE (Tactical Analysis and Evaluation) people went to work. Calls were made to the extended group in and around Washington, DC, and Norfolk, Va. In less than an hour we had the information we needed. Darien was nonplussed and delved into the evaluation process with a fervor I had not seen in him.

"What do you want to do with Vasilyevich?" He asked. I thought for a minute.

"Let's put him in the tricky-room. Let him bounce off walls for a little while. That should soften up any cocky attitude. Then, I would like to interrogate him. Would you like to join me?" He smiled big with overtones of mischievousness.

"OK." I called Jerry.

"Jerry, would you put Gregory Vasilyevich into Briefing Room #4, please?"

"Sure thing, Captain. Who is going in with him?"

"Darien and I"

"Oooooh, I sense a slam dunk."

"Something like that."

Minutes later...

"What's he doing?"

"Just sitting there."

"Did you flip the room?"

"Several times. At first, he looked terrified. Then he settled down a bit. When we stopped flipping the room he sat back down and kind of zoned out."

"Yea, I did that, too. May I have that folder?... thanks."

"Are you ready?" Darien smiled but I could see he was nervous.

"You go in first, sit down but don't say anything. Then I will come in and sit and just read from these files. Let him

simmer. He's never met me but probably knows who I am."
I waited almost a minute then quietly entered and sat down. I
opened the file and studied it. It had some good information.
It was Vasilyevich that spoke first.

"You must be captain. Parish is it?"

"It is." I studied a second page without looking up.

"What is this room?"

"Huh? Oh, it's a prototype for a theme park experience,
kinda like a ride."

"Do you think you are going to intimidate me?"

"Nope, not my intention." I pushed a page over to Darien
for him to read. He remained silent as he browsed through
the text.

"Hmmm! Interesting."

"So... what was it like working for or with Runestone?" I
asked.

"I never worked with them. They are not true
professionals."

"And, you are?"

"I try to be."

"You are not an American citizen. You're Russian."

"I am contractor for Roscosmos and have legitimate
Green Card from U.S. Government. We were sharing
information with Boeing on design development of VASIMR
technologies. We, and Boeing learned that Seraphim has
found the key to creating viable interstellar starship engines
based on VASIMR design. We wanted access to that
documentation but Darien would not provide it."

"So, you got pissed and thought you could extort it out of
him. Whatever good faith you may have developed with the
U.S. was tossed out the window. Then came overt attempts
to take it by force. I would never let that happen and would
meet any attempts with deadly force if necessary."

"It is known." He laughed, "You very effective. After first attempt by Runestone and their failure, I started watching the captain of Seraphim. I thought all along that Darien was person in charge. Then I realized that as smart as you are, Darien, most of how you do things are completely predictable. Then I began to hear stories about new captain and how she is totally unpredictable and comes up with ideas nobody else does, in a tiny bit of second. Then when Seraphim security people rescued Theo Remington and Sarah Michaels, then identified two spies in your 'Council', I knew I couldn't intimidate you into releasing the information I needed. So, I let you go home. The people I work for as contractor not pleased with my lack of success and really angry with my tactics. I think they feared my behavior might damage the rapport they have with NASA and your government. Both countries often work together. We do on ISS. Russia works with NASA to bring Cosmonauts and Astronauts to and from ISS on Soyuz. I thank you for your help recovering and hospitalizing Cosmonaut Sergey Kuznetsov from the ISS. That was bold move. I was told that through NASA, Roscosmos has been invited to some pre-launch briefings for which you are in favor. Is that so?"

"It is. We are new to space flight and would benefit from the wisdom of those who have been doing it for a while. For the record, however, they are aware that sharing some time together does NOT mean we will release classified information of our proprietary technologies. We have far more important considerations as we move into deep space. Some may ride along with us as we do a shakedown cruise... sea-trials, I like to call them. In doing so, they will learn how we do things and will, at least, see the technology at work."

"I messed up." He said and looked downright ashamed. I sensed he wasn't faking.

"I must be old fashioned or something. I really regret I put all of you through that. It was wrong and I apologize."

"There are others you owe an apology, too." Somehow, I believed him. That's why he is here, I thought. He's doing penance.

"If you would like me to leave Angels Landing, I will... and will never come back." He really seemed contrite.

"Oh, you're not getting off that easily. This meeting is over. Come with me." The nearly invisible sliding door opened and the three of us walked out. I stopped and asked Darien to keep an eye on Gregory. He smiled knowing I was offering an olive branch.

I saw Jerry standing in the middle of the rotunda talking with a fairly sizable group. When he saw me standing to the side, he excused himself and walked over.

"How did it go?"

"Went OK. He has a penance to make. We are taken him aboard Seraphim. Don't worry. It will be fine."

"OK! here is a further update on his past. He wasn't in the FSB or the KGB and has no political affiliations. He has no military service other than the 12-month mandatory service when he was much younger. Accept for his treatment of our colleagues, he is otherwise squeaky clean."

"Thanks, Jerry." Then Darien asked...

"Where we going?"

"My quarters, via the bridge."

"WHAT!" then he softened.

"Watch."... I said quietly. I walked ahead, followed by Gregory Vasilyevich, then Darien. I asked Mr.Scott to have the science officer and my executive admin assistant meet me in my quarters if they are not busy. Then Mr.Scott proclaimed.

"They'll be on their way in 20, Captain."

The door to the bridge opened...

"Captain on the bridge."

"Carry on." I replied

I turned to Gregory Vasilyevich and simply said,

"Welcome to my office." And turned away. He was looking around, mouth open in absolute awe. Crew members at all stations remained fixed on their duties.

"Francine, have Paddington Lewis or whoever is working there, set G=0, bridge only, for 10 seconds."

"Copy that."

Both Darien and I grabbed the command island railing.

Suddenly the gravity was gone. I watched as a look of surprise and fear overtook Gregory as he fought to find something to hold on to. Nobody else on the deck seemed ruffled at all. Then slowly, the gravity returned to normal. He looked at me still visibly shaken.

"And you thought the VASIMR engines were something special." I said with a smile. "This way please." We entered my quarters and I directed Gregory to the far side of the table. Darien at the table end, and me the other end. I answered the knock at the door and welcomed Theo and Sarah. They had a look of shock upon seeing Gregory Vasilyevich at the table.

"Please have a seat."

"What the hell is he doing here?" yelled Theo angrily. Sarah just stared with a look of fury. I let the emotions wane a bit before asking if anyone would like some water or something a little stronger. I poured five glasses of water from the fridge and handed them around. I sat down. They just glared at the guest opposite them.

"Before you consider committing homicide, please read these." I handed them the results of Jerry's official inquiries. As they read and exchanged unread pages, surprise replaced the hate in their eyes. Then they looked at the person opposite them whose eyes were downcast and moist with shame. Theo's expression changed again as he understood my motive for this meeting. Sarah looked off as if into the distance. I waited. Then the supposed bad guy, Gregory Vasilyevich spoke...

"I am here to apologize for my stupidity and hurt I put you through. I do not ask for forgiveness. I was wrong. You did not deserve that. I was cruel." His eyes had watered up and visible tears ran down his face. This wasn't an act. He was truly sorry. Theo spoke in a calmer tone.

"What happens now? Between you and Runestone, we were put through hell."

"I had nothing to do with Runestone or anyone else here in U.S. I am simple contractor working for Roscosmos. They no longer want me as contractor. I was fired from job. I have to go back to Russia now and try to find job. I have wife and two daughters. Please believe me when I say how sorry I am. That was not me. I was scared that I would lose job if I didn't find answers they wanted. I had never been in United States before and thought Americans hated Russia and her people. I learned they do not. All of you have been kind and pleasant. I made friends I really like and then I do this to you." Fresh tears wound down his face once more. I grabbed a Kleenex box and placed in front of Gregory. A silence fell over the scene before me. Theo looked at me as I just sat there and let the epiphany wash over everyone. Sarah looked on, too. Only, she had tears that had formed but there was a small knowing smile. Darien hadn't said a word since we came to the bridge. But he too was caught up in the emotional moment. I began...

"I don't believe it is healthy to carry around hatred in our hearts. It is destructive to who we are as people. Especially when we only know part of the story. Let us not carry misplaced ill-will around with us. It is not who we are."

Four sets of eyes looked at another side of the most *Bad-Ass-Female-Starship-Captain.* I guess the moment hit home when... Sarah said...

"I am willing to forgive your actions Gregory. But that's just me. Theo?"

"I'll let it pass, too. Perhaps you were overwhelmed being your first time in the States. By any chance was this your first job with Roscosmos?"

"Yes. I was theoretical scientist at Moscow State University teaching cosmology and astrophysics. But position did not pay well, so when I was approached about contractor position, my wife and I agreed I should take it. Maybe I can get professorship back at Moscow State University or maybe Moscow Institute of Physics and Technology. I hold PHD in Astrophysics."

"What are your plans now?" asked Darien.

"I go back to family, find work and try to forget this. What choice do I have?"

Theo added something that had a new set of possibilities...

"Now that you lost your job with Roscosmos, technically you have to turn in your green card and go home."

"That is understanding, yes. I must go."

Why was I feeling... weird? Here is a person who had emotionally harmed my friends. But he did not physically harm them in any way. He didn't tie them up with a dirty rag stuck in their mouth, in a musty barn somewhere. They were held in nice hotel rooms with services. Was I going soft?

"I have an idea." I said, Theo followed up.

"I have an idea, too" Then Darien,

"Me too."

"What if... " I said. I waited, then said

"I'm going to call the Council into session."

"YES!" said everyone in unison.

Not such a bad guy after all...

Sarah, I would like you to find Mr. Vasilyevich quarters on deck 10. Advise Jerry of this and tell him our guest will be staying with us for a little while. I want a guard posted at the residence to provide security and escort when he leaves the residence. Are you OK with this Gregory?" Surprise dominated his expression. Tears again formed. He looked at me in wonder. He quietly said...

"I think I do not understand Americans. I do wrong thing and yet you listen. When captain came into that room, I thought I was dead. The stories I heard about you. Those other people are terrified of you. You did things, used unbelievable technology and nobody was killed. Well... until that group from your own government tried to take-over of Angels Landing. When I was standing out in that big room with all others, young people in uniforms talked to us, showed us things, invited us to see movies and hear lectures. They had smiles and were really nice. Someone asked about Captain Hannah Parish... they said they all love you. You are their role model, one said. I guess I am naïve in ways of world. I could never imagine this." Theo walked over and...

"Gregory, would you come with me, let's have a talk down in my office."

I wondered what Theo was up to. But I trusted him. Darien stood nearby getting ready to brief the Council and seek some advice. I decided to read some of the proposals that the planning teams from Seraphim, NASA and representatives from National Space Agency, an arm of the U.S. Government... the suits with the money...

. . . and agendas.

We were running out of time. I decided to try to integrate some of the teams. I knew that '*NASA works with partners in other Government agencies, aligned with the principles, goals, and objectives of the National Aeronautics Research and Development Policy and its related National Aeronautics Research and Development Plan, to achieve its missions.*' (That was borrowed from the nasa.gov website.) So, I thought, why not merge the planners with Seraphim navigators to come up with mission profile or profiles that not only satisfies the NASA objectives but focuses key Seraphim technologies to broaden the result potentials. The scientists already resident on board are fully equipped for the actual research, and will support mission objectives as the hands-on element. They will be the ones to don the new space suits from Boeing and shuffle along in the 1/6th gravity of moon dust. Each suit can be used completely independently of a shuttle or the ship with a removeable back-pack unit called a '*Primary Life Support System*'. It can support an astronaut's life for up to 4 hours of moderate activity. Since most of the EVAs will be performed from the shuttles, the shuttles will leave our main airlock purged to whatever indigenous atmosphere the moon or planet has. Special new materials had been adapted into the suits that provide the wearer additional protection from the various radiation dangers in space.

I was provided an update on the *Dragon-Slayer*, the autonomous drone being built in hangar 3. I would really like it to be ready when we head out there. Since its construction and test protocols are already on board, we can proceed with our initial plans for Lunar-only studies. However, I would like it to be functional if we decide on a trip to Mars or the gas-giants' moons. Otherwise, I feared going too fast might put us in danger without it. I explained its function to some folks from JPL that had similar concerns about going very fast. I explained that it will operate as a spearhead, placing itself well ahead of Seraphim along the line of flight during high speed travel through space. Using a new more powerful wide-beam version of the Force-Field Projection emitter, it hopefully will clear the way ahead to prevent Seraphim from a catastrophic collision with an unseen asteroid, comet or any other threat. Distance ahead would be predicated on the speed of Seraphim; from 1 mile to 100 miles. The analogue was an ice-breaker that plowed ahead of tankers and cargo vessels busting up the ice in the arctic.

They seemed impressed and asked questions some of which we were not at liberty to talk about. They understood.

Mr.Scott apprised me that Theo and Gregory were about to have dinner at the Captain's Mess, and would I like to join them?

"Be there in 10." I responded.

We were now down to three weeks until cast off. I couldn't wait. Then... whatever we have done, however prepared we are, comes down to that one defining moment. Now I was hungry. But I wasn't prepared for what happened next.

I entered the Captain's Mess and stopped for a moment to talk to the head steward. I asked if he and the others were planning on staying through first-flight. He said he and the others wouldn't miss it. I heard rustling behind me as I turned to go to the table. Most of the people were guests from the other space agencies at the tables but now, they were all standing. They were looking directly at me and began clapping. I stood for a moment with a genuine smile waiting for them to stop. Why were they doing this? I raised my hands in front of me requesting they stop. They slowly quieted down and sat down. That is, some... not all. As I made my way between tables those that remained standing extended an arm to shake my hand. On their jackets were name tags and who they worked for. Some were JPL, NASA, Blue Origin, SpaceX, Boeing, Lockheed and even Roscosmos. Why? As I approached my table I saw Theo, Darien, Mom and Dad, Gregory and a surprise, Rear-Admiral (retired) Bascom Holder, the project planner from NASA. Even he had a smile on his face. My dad stood, pulled my chair back and, as they say, seated me. It wasn't over. A man I recognized as a charter member of Seraphim's *Symphony*, but I couldn't remember his name, raised his glass and spoke. His voice loud and clear.

"I propose a toast. To one of most remarkable people I have ever had the pleasure of working with. Young, beautiful and charming, and perhaps the most powerful 'Being' in the universe. I salute Commander Hannah Parish, Captain of the Seraphim. And as we all shall soon discover, the most competent leader and protector of those who serve with her and all of us privileged to tag along on Seraphim's maiden voyage. *Oooorah, Seraphim."* And from the crowd... *"Oooorah Hannah Parish."* Hands were high in the Vulcan Salute, now adopted as our official homage to our favorite childhood TV show. I was burying the emotions that were pulling me apart. I was losing that war. Tears came to my eyes that I couldn't stop. Surprisingly... through all this, we actually had dinner. As the stewards were moving about the tables, one came to me and handed me a folded note. He nodded to Darien. I looked up to his smiling face and nodded back. I read the hand-written note.

"Hannah. I was approached by members of the Roscosmos upper management people here in this room. They wanted to talk a bit, which I did. Then they asked if they could meet with you, me, Theo and Gregory Vasilyevich someplace private. I suggested your quarters after the meal. I told them I would pass along the request. Your call.

Darien"

I folded the note into a pocket, picked up a partially eaten buttered roll, and took a bite out of it. Then I looked at Darien while I chewed the roll... and nodded my head. The Captain's Mess guests began to leave. I waited a short time but felt I needed to be in my quarters. As I stood Admiral Holder stood. Old fashioned guy, I guess.

"That's not necessary on my ship." Then he said...

"Not because you're a woman, but because you are the captain."

"Then I accept, thank you." I smiled, pushed in my chair, turned and walked out." I learned later he said...

"Remarkable woman, so young."

My dad added...

"Top of her class at Annapolis. Bridge crew member aboard a hunter-killer Los Angeles class submarine for 3 and ½ years. Was looking for a job. Found one."

"Yes, indeed she has."

Steps Forward

I didn't attend all the meetings but what came out of them was exciting. Guests were given briefings on the technologies aboard Seraphim and tours of appropriate areas. The pièce de résistance was gravity. Our people had cracked the code of Quantum Gravity and the guests were further amazed at how we used it. The idea that if we had plenty of time we could simply release the hold-down clamps and in a few hours, we would be floating in space, moving further and further away without doing a thing, all in the lap of luxury, using no power, was utterly amazing to them.

Per their request, Darien and I met with the Roscosmos leadership team, and with Theo and Gregory Vasilyevich. They wanted to know about Gregory's behavior as a contractor to Boeing. Theo and Darien explained the atmosphere around those meetings. Darien explained...

"I did not have the information you wanted. I am not a propulsion guy. I made it clear that there were many break-through technologies built into Seraphim that are all classified and not shareable. Gregory was afraid that you would not be satisfied with his findings and fire him. You did. Now he does not have a job." Theo added more...

"I learned that Gregory has a PHD in Astrophysics and has tenure in two of your top universities. He only worked for you for just a few months. He understands only the culture of the universities, not the cooperate or government world. Then he was thrust into American society attempting to learn about VASIMR technologies. It was a no-win situation for him. At first, we thought he was some kind of spy. We recently found out he is not a spy but a really nice guy just trying to succeed for his wife and two daughters.

After my one-on-one with Gregory, I sat with Darien Hunter and Captain Parish. We have a proposal. Keep him on your payroll, and make him a Roscosmos liaison to Seraphim. He would live and work right here on Seraphim as your representative. His first assignment might be to work in Engineering with our folks and learn how Seraphim gets its power to Gravity, Environment and other service departments throughout the ship. And, yes work with engineers that are scientists in their own right, about VASIMR, MPDSF and GMI. We won't release detailed proprietary information but maybe from what he does learn you can develop your own version of those technologies. What do you think?"

"That is an intriguing idea and has merit but we must talk to Moscow to get their approval. May we think about this for a day? We are staying in Rawlins at this hotel." Theo was handed a business card.

"We will come back tomorrow. What about Gregory?"

"We have assigned him quarters here." I said. "We await your decision." The Roscosmos people left with escort from security. Gregory remained sitting.

"You do this for me? After what I do to you?" Theo being Theo went philosophical... he was looking at the ceiling as if it were transparent.

"It's a really big place out there. There is room for all of us. This ship was built on the intellectual backs of extraordinary people. None of us knows everything. We base our dreams on science that began thousands of years ago. Names like Isaac Newton, Albert Einstein, Neils Bohr, Louis Pasteur. Galileo Galilei, Antoine Laurent Lavoisie, Johannes Kepler, Nicolaus Copernicus, Werner Heisenberg, Max Planck, Christiaan Huygens, Dmitri Mendeleev, Euclid, Archimedes, Aristotle. And so many others. Their souls are part of this ship. Seraphim is a tribute to them. We will take them to the stars. Come with us. Make your PHD worthy of who you are."

"I will. Thank you for your trust." Then I added...

"If you want to call your wife, we can hook you up through a security patch. Say hi to her for us." I left the room to go to the bridge. As I walked to the door I overheard...

"Theo, who was Mendeleyev?"

"Dmitri Ivanovich Mendeleyev discovered the periodic law and from that, the creation of the periodic table. Using his periodic table, Mendeleev predicted the existence and properties of new chemical elements. When these elements were discovered, his place in the history of science was assured. (CE 1834 to 1907). He is one of my heroes. I have a small picture of him in my office along with many others. I never believed in wasting good minds."

"How do you know all this?"

"Science is my life and my hobby. Like you, I became a teacher, and a professor like Darien. Hannah Parish was my student."

I smiled. Theo is one of the most extraordinary people I have ever met. There is no person on the planet that could ever replace Professor Theodore Benjamin Remington. I continued to the bridge absolutely in love with my job.

I was sitting in the center chair when the XO scooted closer and asked...

"Captain, Seraphim's non-denomination Chaplin, Sandra Davies, would like to hold a gathering in the large theater for those who feel the need for comfort through the scriptures and prayers for everyone's safe return." I turned to her and remembered a moment recently.

"Interesting you should ask. A month ago, I was eating lunch in the Captain's Mess by myself when Chaplin Davies came to my table and asked to sit down. We had a very nice chat about our pending departure into our next big challenge. She asked if she could gather some of the devoted into a prayer service or something, either before lift-off or shortly after we clear the atmosphere.

I told her that it would be fine but cautioned her to keep it ecumenical, speaking to all present without leaving anyone out. Also, to make allowances for those on duty. Perhaps she could hold more than one at a later time. She understood and planned to do just that. I told her it sounds like a great idea. She has my permission."

"Thank you, Captain. She will be notifying the crew using the general message system."

Thinking back... my family did not practice any particular religion but I had attended Sunday School when I was in 2nd and 3rd grade. I suppose we all just drifted away from the spiritual side as each family member became more involved and focused on flying and medicine. At Annapolis, underclassmen were encouraged to attend a service of their faith. I did not, but appreciated and respected those who did. I grew up during my time at Annapolis, I think, surrounded by an atmosphere of integrity, responsibility, respect, and duty. I remember our mission statement:

"To develop Midshipmen morally, mentally and physically and to imbue them with the highest ideals of duty, honor and loyalty in order to graduate leaders who are dedicated to a career of naval service and have potential for future development in mind and character to assume the highest responsibilities of command, citizenship and government."

I hope... I pray, that I carry with me all the precepts from those heady days that turned me from a simple high school girl into the leader I am today. Quite a change. Now we have among us, some of the most literate in the subjects of space and travel through it. We will surely need that.

I have always believed that when people were brought together from disparate backgrounds and education, brilliant ideas could form, much like the group *Symphony* did in the evolution of Seraphim. There was much we can learn from these people. There is much they can learn from us.

Over the next few days, extraordinary smart people met, collaborated, disagreed, agreed, wrestled, argued and raised their voices. From those meetings, programs were designed, destinations pinned on Lunar landscape maps, EVA personnel assignments were handed out. Drills covering safety and protocols for the shuttles exiting and recovering through Seraphim's airlocks were exercised over and over. Shuttle bay Ships' personnel practiced standard and emergency procedures. A rescue backup with a second shuttle in Hangar 2 was implemented, procedures were created and practiced. All systems had performed well on our first singular journey into space and the rescue of ISS stranded Astronauts and Cosmonaut. We even survived an attempt at our destruction by a still unknown group of conspirators using surface to space anti-satellite missiles. However, we still had work to do verifying system reliability and function as well as training all personnel. There is a breathable atmosphere aboard Seraphim... outside there will be nothing. Engineers spent hours verifying proper function of the airlock doors, inspecting everything associated with the primary means of exit and entry. The valving systems which controlled the release of air from the closed airlock interior to a vacuum, and the reverse, refilling the closed bay with ships atmosphere were exercised until all those who were involved were satisfied everything would function as advertised since lives were on the line. All ingress and egress from the main ship's interior to the hangar bays pass through pressure doors that were tested and inspected for function. Newly created protocols required these doors be closed and sealed during EVA operations, isolating the ship from any hull or airlock breaches from the hangars.

An emergency backup to the main airlock was instituted using Hangar 2s airlock system. The *Michael* shuttle and a *Valkyrie* tactical vehicle barely fit into Hangar 2 together, with its shorter airlock and doors located on the port-side of the hull. They were placed there as a rescue and recovery back-up to Hangar 1.

Hangar 3 was filled to near capacity as work continued building, modifying, upgrading and testing all space worthy vehicles. Technicians, engineers and scientists worked side by side preparing for the greatest adventure of their lives.

In Hangar 1, Jake Maxwell was assigned primary pilot with Scott Randal, former ISS Astronaut as co-pilot approved by NASA.

In Hangar 2, Lory Amundsen was backup (rescue) pilot in *Michael* or *Valkyrie with* Richard Daniels former ISS Astronaut as co-pilot. Each of the former (rescued) Astronauts' were qualified pilots in the military and now were qualified in Seraphim's shuttles. They were thrilled and performed their functions skillfully and professionally.

All pilots and EVA personnel were fitted and trained in space suit operation including emergency procedures.

When my own duties allowed, I oversaw some of the hangar bay / airlock procedures. I felt it was incumbent on the Captain to be as knowledgeable as possible if and when the doo-doo hits the blades of an air-circulation device. I watched as people moved about with focused intensity I only witnessed before in the steel confines of a submarine. I wonder what Captain Douglas Freeman would think of this.

Ship's Crew personnel, including Command, sat in flight planning briefings that included establishment of time lines, approach to destination strategies to each of many sites to be explored. Robotic equipment drop-off and initiation by EVA personnel was reviewed and practiced again and again. All equipment was loaded into the shuttles in the order of emplacement on the Lunar surface.

The gravity in the entire Hangar was reduced to 1/6 earth gravity, including inside the shuttles. Everyone wore full space suits on internal air as they experienced for the first time what they would experience on the Lunar surface. The NASA, JPL and other people were crazy-happy watching the activity below from their position looking through the pressure windows separating the ship's interior and the hangar. The potential for deep space exploration in the very near future was so tantalizing, planners back in Houston and Los Angeles and all over, watched real-time video, the activity inside the ship called Seraphim. The day before the launch date, the hangars were reset to normal. Spacesuits were returned to lockers, tools were tucked away in tool boxes and wall cabinets. The decks were cleaned of dripped liquids. All was ready for the big moment. All personnel returned to their duty stations. A quiet aura of peace and personal reflection flowed over the people aboard Seraphim. Nervousness was accompanied by confidence that their training and ability would carry them through. I walked among them as they performed their duties, asking questions along the way, realizing once again how complex this world is that we will soon become part of. But this ship... this Starship had the best, most capable people I have ever seen. Confidence was at its highest. I think the awe was getting to me. Yes! For the first time... I was frightened. Frightened I would miss something. I retired to the sanctity of my quarters.

Countdown to liftoff was only minutes away.

A knock on my door rousted me from a daze as I sat in the comfortable reading chair in the private part of the Captain's Quarters.

"Come in." I responded, but remained seated.

"Hey, Darien."

"Hey, Hannah. May I?" ... pointing to the other reading chair.

"Yes, of course."

"What are you drinking?"

"Tea. Earl Grey... with lemon. Want some? There is plenty in the pot. Still hot." I moved to get up.

"Please stay. I'll get it." He went into the diminutive space optimistically called a kitchen and poured a cup, added a pinch of sugar and a squeeze of the lemon I had cut for the purpose. With cup in hand, he sat looking steadily at the hot mist that rose from the cup with its bergamot and lemon nose.

"I love this stuff."

"Me, too. Thanks for the introduction."

"What's that music? It sounds familiar."

"That's the Soundtrack from the movie *Crimson Tide*, starring Denzel Washington and Gene Hackman – music by Hans Zimmer."

"That was a submarine movie."

"Yes. It has a beautiful rendition of the Navy Hymn for submariners, *"Eternal Father"*. When I hear it, I get a little melancholy thinking about all the men and women who served aboard submarines and other ships of the Navy who never made it home... whose burial was at sea. Will we share a similar fate?"

"No! We will not." ... a moment passed. "You've changed, Hannah."

"Have I?"

"Yes... you have. But in a lot of ways, for the better. You are calmer" Another moment passed.

"So, have you."

We sat quietly sipping our tea just looking into each other's eyes, both smiling slightly, but, in deep thought. He looked at his watch.

"Almost time."

"Yes, it is."

"They are all waiting for the captain of the Seraphim. Hannah, are you ready for this?"

"Yes, I am. Sometimes I have doubts. But not this moment. Are you? This is your dream. Are we doing this the way your dream thought we would?"

"It has been my dream for over forty years. It began long before we formed *Symphony*. I would have had my doubts, too. But, if it weren't for the emergence of the true captain of the Seraphim. I am now ready. And, so are you. Yes, we are doing the right thing." He got up and put his cup in the sink.

"I'll wait on the bridge."

The door closed behind him. I was alone as I listened to the final bars of *Eternal Father* play out in a long *Amen*. I shut off the music player with my remote and sat for one more minute.

"How is this possible?... Me?... Doing this? People all over the world are waiting for my word. I'm just a kid from Norfolk, Virginia who couldn't find a job. A tear rolled down my cheek. I rose from the chair, put on my dress jacket, grabbed a tissue and mopped my tear. I looked into the mirror, refit my ponytail, straightened my uniform and walked to the door, hesitated, then placed my hand on the button...

The door hissed open...

Slipping the Surly Bonds of Earth

By John Gillespie Magee, Jr

Oh! I have slipped the surly bonds of earth,
And danced the skies on laughter-silvered wings;
Sunward I've climbed, and joined the tumbling mirth
Of sun-split clouds, --and done a hundred things
You have not dreamed of --Wheeled and soared and swung
High in the sunlit silence. Hov'ring there
I've chased the shouting wind along, and flung
My eager craft through footless halls of air...
Up, up the long, delirious, burning blue
I've topped the wind-swept heights with easy grace
Where never lark or even eagle flew --
And, while with silent lifting mind I've trod
The high untrespassed sanctity of space,
Put out my hand, and touched the face of God.

"Captain on the bridge." ... called the XO. This time I didn't respond. I stopped in the middle of the main deck of the bridge and just looked around at all the faces looking expectantly at me... waiting for their captain to give the word.

To the side stood a group. Representatives from around the world. Scientists, who have been working for years on their own projects, wait in wonder as Seraphim promises to close the gap between theory and reality. The moment is now. The tension was at its highest.

There wasn't a sound. I moved up the three steps of the raised command island and looked at the center seat... the seat of the captain... my seat. I turned while standing in front of it.

"XO: Report"

"All departments report ready. The crew is ready, Seraphim is ready. Captain... Give the word."

"**Helm**: report."

"Initial heading laid in, all gravity systems ready, power is ready. GMI and VASIMR at station-keeping."

"Very well. Main screen view-ahead. Let's see what's in the heavens." I froze for a moment as a chill raced through my body.

In homage to my Navy background, I began with...

"*Cast off all lines fore and aft*, release hold-down clamps, float the boat to 500 feet AGL. Report clear of all objects."

"Clear, Captain."

"ENGAGE GMI, climb to 5-0 thousand feet, Set Initial heading. Report at our egress point."

"Coming up on egress point in 20 seconds, Captain."

"Point her to the stars Mr. Whitmore. Shutdown GMI. With VASIMRs 1, 2, 3 and 4... all ahead 2/3. Standby to engage on my mark." The ship was now vertical, pointing to the stars and the infinite abyss known as the Universe.

"ENGAGE"

In the background someone turned on music.
The Navy Hymn, *'Eternal Father'*, played once again, this time for all to hear.

Our beloved ship, Seraphim, bolted into the heavens atop four bright blue streams of plasma from the largest VASIMR engines ever built. The dream of so many is now realized. We all looked on in wonder.

Part II
The Adventure Begins.

Seraphim's four mighty electro-plasma rocket motors shut down precisely as programmed by the Nav computer. Seraphim coasted toward an exact point on the moon's ecliptic. In 13 minutes, we would be there. The moon grew larger and larger as the minutes passed. I walked off the raised bridge island and walked to the helm position.

"Helm! Where is our turn?"

"Coming up, Captain. We need a flip to slow down. By your command. The Nav computer will control the maneuver."

"Do you have the coordinates for the turn?" He nodded.

"Copy that. Flip the ship." The MPDSF-5 retro rockets kicked Seraphim over 180°.

"With VASIMRs 1 and 2, at 1/3 power. Engage, Reduce speed to 800 knots Lunar reference."

"Aye! Parameters set in. Here we go." In minutes...

"OK... stable at 800 knots relative."

"Very well. Flip the ship to normal configuration." Seraphim half-tumbled once again returning the nose forward.

"Using the MPDSF-5s from now on, take us to the moon, nose first, final altitude 1000 feet AGL."

"Copy that. We're coming in on a tangent. Will arrive at tangential point-alpha at 1000' AGL in 7 minutes 15 seconds... mark."

"Copy that. Let's get the scientists up here. Comm, make the call."

"Aye, Captain... Most are already here, the rest on their way."

"Very well. Helm, keep it smooth. Follow protocol, Initiate Auto-pilot."

"Engaged, Captain. Auto-helm is making minor corrections to our flight profile. Setting speed control to Auto, controlling via the small maneuvering thrusters. OK! We're locked. Coming around the dark side. We should see Earth in 45 seconds." The surface of the moon was closing to 1000 feet, sliding past in silent dignity, the utter blackness of the universe lay beyond with only specs of light from billions of stars. Then...

"Their she is."

A glorious moment as all watched Earth-Rise, the 'Blue Marble' as some have called it. The moment was stunning as the moon passing to our right, seemed to move away like a theater curtain exposing our home, our planet. It was seen by everyone onboard, on video screens in Angels Landing, Houston and a hundred other places. The elegance of this moment caused unintended physical reactions: Flowing tears, involuntary choking as breaths were held, too long. Some had to sit as overwhelming feelings of awe affected stability.

Of all the planets long known and new... none are as beautiful as our home world, home to 7.7 billion human beings and a myriad of amazing plants and animals. The moment lingered as all would remember this vision forever.

Sadly... I had to get back to business...

"Nav, show us a plot superimposed over the forward view with distance to Point-Bravo and ETA. Mr. Whitmore lock auto-helm onto Nav plot. Report engaged."

"Auto-helm locked. Forward thrusters firing. First stop 108 miles at our 12 O'clock. Reducing altitude to 100 feet AGL and speed to 120 knots over the surface. We'll overshoot and take pictures of the site. Then we'll stop, backup and hover." We coasted along, smoothly and in complete silence.

"Easy does it, Josh. Role the ship to port, make the horizontal orientation of the ship parallel to the lunar surface. Maintain 100 feet AGL." Seraphim silently rolled 90° to port.

"There's the site, 2 miles ahead, Captain. Slowing to 30 knots."

"Copy that. ease her down. This area has irregular topography so watch the keel line. Make your altitude 100 feet above highest surface feature. Once in a hover and locked to the side of the site, test the GMI for function. It probably won't work very well, if at all. Use the maneuvering thrusters to remain at station-keeping."

"Aye, Captain. Slowing... Stopping.   In position and holding."

"Very well. Tactical do a 360°, full hemisphere mapping and sweep of the frontier."

"Aye Captain. No targets. The sky is clear."

"Very well. Nav, split screen with topographical map of Lunar surface from our altitude. Overlay Point Bravo with rifle-scope-like cross-hairs and lock on target.

Gravity, reduce counter gravity, bridge only to 90%. I want to feel any motion. Seat of the pants."

"Aye, captain. Counter gravity set to 90%, bridge only."

"Very well. Where are the collars set?"

"Both collars set at mid-point captain. Essentially zero wave-function and Interferometry is neutral."

The 'Lunar Explorer' team from Houston watched fascinated at how simple our arrival at the first site was. No fuss, no bother. Everyone was enjoying their first space flight and Lunar insertion with no feeling of acceleration and nice comfortable 1.000 Gs throughout the ship. Once hovering just 100 feet above the surface, the Nav computer put us in a fixed position. The GMI was engaged and as expected, there was very little control since the moon had a fraction of Earth's gravity and almost zero magnetosphere. The small thrusters automatically corrected position errors when GMI wasn't able to. Thirty minutes later... I hailed Jake in *Raphael*.

"Jake, you have the honors. You are cleared for Site-1 departure and deployment of Seraphim's 1st official contribution to science."

Everyone watched on video screens with nervous fascination as shuttle *Raphael* moved slowly to the airlock. Once inside, the inner pressure door was closed and sealed. Inside *Raphael* space-suit wearing Jake Maxwell, Scott Randal, and a NASA crew of seven performed pre-vacuum check lists of their suits. With both inner and outer airlock doors closed and sealed, the shuttle's loading ramp was opened 10 degrees following protocol. The loud sound of air rushing through large conduits could be heard until the inside of the shuttle and the airlock air pressure dissipated to... nothing. And with it... all sound disappeared except the sound of breathing in the pressurized masks. When the air pressure was zero, the outer airlock door began to silently open. On monitors in Seraphim, Angels Landing, Houston, Cape Canaveral, Washington DC, and thousands of TV sets around the world, people watched enraptured as the shuttle craft *Raphael* smoothly and silently exited the Seraphim into a world few would ever see in person. Slowly Jake maneuvered to the spot identified by the coordinates sent from Seraphim, set down with barely any dust within 1 meter of the intended location. The GMI seemed to be working but at a highly reduced level, yet it still provided some control of the vehicle albeit in slow motion. Seraphim was able to reach and hold station-keeping with the on-board GMI. So far, once in position, the small maneuvering thrusters were not needed but were ready in an instant. The rear loading ramp on *Raphael* extended stopping one foot from the Lunar surface. Seven of the NASA crew stared out the back of the shuttle looking at the bright, barren landscape they had all dreamed about. Ensconced inside 7 space suits, 5 men and 2 women just stared... emotions raging through each. None expected to ever see this. The moment passed all too quickly as duty interrupted their emotions. They turned and lifted the 125 pound (750 Pounds on Earth) Autonomous Lunar Rover onto the surface for a geological study of the area. About the size of the original Lunar Roving Vehicle (LRV) that ferried two Astronauts around on earlier missions, this version carried only cutting-edge scientific equipment; some of the most sophisticated robotic high-tech investigation gadgetry ever placed on an extraterrestrial planet or moon. Powered by a *Multi-Mission Radioisotope Thermoelectric Generator* without need of batteries other than for backup, it waited, asleep, for the power switch to be turned on. There were no seats. The team shuffled back to *Raphael,* getting used to the lower gravity and its effect on their inner ear vestibular system. They learned to move slowly and not turn quickly.

The crew off-loaded and emplaced the permanent Autonomous *Communications Transfer Station* (CTS) which included a *Data Collection Forwarding System* (DCFS). The radiation protected shed about the size of a small garden shed included a large parabolic dish antenna. The aliens in blue suits from the planet Earth aligned the dish pointing it at the nearby planet's center mass. On each side of the shed, large solar panels were unfolded and aligned perpendicular to the lunar ecliptic, essentially north-south, but parallel to the lunar surface. Once emplaced, sensors located the sun's position and precessed the solar array to collect the most rays of sunshine to power the equipment and also charge the batteries inside the shed for the 15 or so days the sun would be on the other side of the moon, a 'new-moon' to people on the blue marble. Since the moon faces Earth from this location all the time and rotates on a sidereal axis of 29.32 days, it would soon be dark. Called *Tidal Lock*, there were still several days of sunlight until the night terminator would shut the lights out. Then the morning terminator would bring forth the sun in approximately 15 days. The position of the solar array would re-orient to the morning position with the passing of the night terminator and darkness. With that, lunar observations could continue 24/7.

The rover was given a walk around: wheels checked for freedom of movement, a large antenna complex was raised to vertical, power turned on and checked. A system self-check reported all systems functional. The blue earthman pressed several buttons on a computer key pad initiating a series of test signals to verify the comm. A chirp emanated from the CTS to the comm systems in each EVA Helmet and earth receiving stations. Nineteen seconds later a series of beeps sounded from the rover's comm verifying that earth stations received the test signals and sent back confirmation. Finally, the protective cover on special hinges was lowered and sealed to protect the human-computer interface and control panel from dust intrusion. The tech stepped in front of the rover and gave a thumbs-up to the camera with scientists on earth observing via video link. He then stepped to the side. Thirty-two seconds later, a command was received from mission control in Houston. The rover's wheels silently dug into the grey chalky dust and was on its way.

Equipped with several experiment packages that read data from its many exploration tools, the rover immediately began sending data to the DCFS for relay to Earth receiving stations.

Over the next two hours, using its robotic arm, the rover placed five multi-function seismometers in pre-determined locations inside the crater which also began sending data to the DCFS. They reminded me of a similar technology the author of my now finished book used when the science teams dropped their version from aircraft into seismic and volcanically active areas of earth's northern frontiers. A merging of contemporary science.

So far, the mission was proving successful. *Raphael* and its intrepid Lunar mariners returned to Seraphim. Once inside, the crew disembarked and made their way to change into their 'street' clothes, to be replaced by a different crew.

Hangar crews began post flight analysis that would include pilot debriefings, shuttle systems checks and visual inspection of the craft. Boeing techs in charge of the EVA suits checked each individually as the wearer removed the protective high-tech garment replacing it with his or her daily wear. *Raphael's* on-board flight computer up-loaded all flight and performance data wirelessly to the hangar terminal for review and storage. The interior of the shuttle was then cleaned of any dust or dirt that might have been tracked in. The oxygen (actually normal air) pressurized tanks were topped-off although not much had been used. With the help of low-G loaders, several more equipment modules destined for emplacement at the next location were placed aboard and arranged according to the drop-off sequence. The hangar had never been so busy. People watched from behind thick pressure-proof windows overlooking the hangar. The main Exit/Entry doors from the ships interior to the Hangar were sealed per safety protocol. Small utility rooms off the main hangar area, contained small airlocks where suited personnel could enter Seraphim or the hangar through sealable pressure doors at each end, isolating the interior from loss of air pressure during an EVA. These doors were interlocked to preclude opening both at the same time. Among these utility rooms were personal equipment rooms and lockers where space suits and helmets were stored. Each locker contained suits unique to the assigned authorized person. Specially trained technicians from Boeing's Millennium Space Systems, were on-hand with an Environmental Test Engineer over-seeing all aspects of the Boeing suit's usage in the real lunar environment. Their purpose was two-fold: to support the mission on the moon, and keep a running record of the performance and ease of use while performing the mission requirements. A Log book stayed with each suit and functioned much like log books for aircraft. All parameters were monitored. This provided feedback to the designers at Boeing, siting possible needed areas of improvement in design and function. The team routinely performed checks and tests for suit integrity, oxygen system functionality, electronics (comm equipment, various radiation dosimeter alert systems), air usage, suit temperature and visor clarity following each EVA. Each suit included an Extravehicular Mobility Unit (EMU), a back-pack that contained the oxygen tanks, cooling system, environmental protection, mobility, life support monitoring, including vital sign telemetry, radiation dosimeter values and communications systems for each suit.

I was sitting in my chair on the raised deck on the bridge watching the activity mere feet outside the hull on the moon. When they recovered into the comfort of the ship, new coordinates were selected from the prepared list of stops we were to make. I was alerted to move to Site-2. I verified that all access to the outside was closed and sealed. Air was balanced throughout the hangar spaces and airlocks.

"Helm, confirm Site-2 coordinates set in and ready."

"Set in and GMI at station keeping. We'll see if GMI is reliable."

"Copy that. But standby the maneuvering thrusters in case GMI isn't up to the task. Be prepared to go manual."

"Aye, Captain. We'll be ready."

"Comm, shoot the ship." She nodded.

"This is the captain. We have completed the first of our stops and preparing to move to Site-2. All departments, if you're prepared, hit your Go-Flight button or Hold button."

"Captain, we are green across the board. All departments report ready."

"Very well. On GMI, float to 500 feet AGL, upon reaching, steer to new heading to Site-2. Let's see it on the screen."

Minutes later we arrived at Site-2, the shuttle was again deployed with another drop off and a new deployment team. A smaller version of the rover was sent on its way doing different studies. So far this was moving along as smooth as silk. Everyone with hands-on in the deployment, inside and outside performed flawlessly. I had stepped off the command island and moved to a position behind Helm and Tactical. My level of concentration had never been higher. I was watching everything, every nuance of ship motion, listening to chatter between departments. I was scanning the many video screens watching for any variation from normal function, watching indicator lamps come on and go off as AI monitored what I was seeing and responding quickly with programmed efficiency. I stood watching while nursing a now just-barely-warm cup of coffee.

Our guests just shook their heads in amazement and how relaxed the bridge seemed. Little did they know the amount of focus each of the ship's personnel applied to their work.

With cup in hand, I walked over to Science officer Remington's position.

"Hey Theo. What's up in the Universe?"

"It's still there. And... still moving. Never stops."

"You have a bunch of new stuff. Looks complicated."

"It is. It took me awhile to understand how it all works. But I seem to have access to pretty much anything. JPL and Lockheed helped out. Some of this stuff they provided. I would ask them a question, sort of like you did with your 'What-If' questions, and they would show me how the equipment can find out stuff I've never heard of. It's quite remarkable. I haven't had so much fun since I joined this project 24 year ago. I also feel like I am contributing something. It's amazing how many people have come by with questions. The Quantum world is a big part of the questions. I think I am learning more than I'm teaching."

"I'm glad you're enjoying it. I feel more comfortable with you close by. As you become more knowledgeable and get your 'seat-of-the-pants' feel for this, please remember that the science officer back-checks the captain's decisions and offers suggestions, cautions, as we swim in shark infested waters. I need you just as Captain Kirk needed Mr. Spock."

"You know, Hannah, everyone is watching you. They see you move around the bridge, through other departments, the hangers, everywhere. They are amazed at your attention to detail. Some have said they have never seen that level of responsibility exercised by anyone in their experience. We are doing something no-one in the history of human endeavor has ever done before, and yet they feel secure and safe, even out here. Darien told me about his visit just prior to lift off. He said you were very quiet and introspective. But he also said there was nobody on our planet that he feels more confident about, with you in the middle chair. A lot of people feel the same way."

"Thank you. Obviously, I have never done anything like this, Theo. The intensity of the responsibility levels are beginning to take their toll, I fear. If you see me waver, hit me with a chair."

"Hannah, nobody throughout the history of mankind has ever done anything like this. You stand alone with that achievement. But, really, you are not alone. There are a huge number of genius-level people backing you up."

"Tell me, Theo. Seeing what we are doing and watching it in a kind of reality TV, do you ever feel like putting on one of those blue suits and taking a walk outside?"

"Actually, I have thought about it."

"Me, too."

"Do you know why?" asked my favorite smart person... "because, in this ship... I feel cooped up inside the box. Someone once told me... *maybe you and I should take a walk outside the box. You would be surprised at the revelations you can find there.*' I'll never forget that.' Now... even out here, I pine for that opportunity."

"It's possible, you know?" I smiled and he smiled.

Site-2 went off as easily as the Site-1 drop-off. It was in an adjacent crater. I don't remember the name. It was in Latin.

Three days later...

The team from NASA and the rest finished deploying the last of seven science packages in just three days. Everyone, from Hanger personnel, to shuttle crews to scientists and everyone aboard began to relax as their respective jobs became more routine. Occasionally I cautioned against complacency. *"Always follow the checklists,"* I would say. During the down-time as we waited to see what the next activity would be, many of the guests learned to play Zero-Golf, watched movies in the theater, enjoyed really good meals in the small variety of restaurants on board. Although I enjoyed the challenge, I didn't get much down time. No rest for the captain. I did make time for my exercise regimen. Here we were, the ships keel just 100 feet above the Lunar surface, hovering. They loved the Seraphim and were amazed at how quickly and easily they accomplished their missions. Living on board this ship was like magic to them. The science packages that were emplaced at the seven sites were transmitting data back to the receiving points on Earth faster than the various receiving laboratories could collate them, never mind study them.

I went back to my quarters, de-corked a bottle of a chilled California Cabernet, then filled a stemmed water glass halfway, and with a bowl of lightly salted peanuts in hand, retired to my favorite reading chair and matching ottoman. I opened a book left on the small side table by Admiral Holder that he thought I might like. I guess I didn't have the same taste in literature that flag officers have. A supposed true story of a Cherokee family leading up to the Battle of Chickamauga in 1863. I think I liked volcanos better. My eyelids were heavy. Two hours later with a still half full wine glass, I was awakened by a knock on the door.

"C'mon in."

Paul Conway Chairman, Executive Committee peeked in.

"Oops! Sorry, didn't mean to wake you, Captain. Just some information. The shuttle *Gabriel* just left for the south pole to set up camp and will begin the science studies as soon as *Raphael* brings the rest of the gear. They were asking if *Peregrine* could join them and provide logistics support and a place to rest. Two medics and three engineers volunteered to go along but will remain on *Peregrine* unless needed. They have their suits but not zipped up."

"Copy that. Cleared as requested with one caveat. I know Peregrine is capable of fairly long term in-space living, but I'm not comfortable with that in this case. I want all three shuttles to return to Seraphim each late afternoon. Begin again tomorrow morning. Anything else?"

"No, Ma'am." ... he quietly closed the door.

Soon we would have to return to our home in Wyoming. I must say I wasn't actually looking forward to it. We have been in Space now for over a month. Not a long time compared to the crews aboard the ISS, but this was only a sea-trial. All systems were functioning perfectly. The crew found that the training they had received was "spot-on", as one put it. There were no surprises. But even while sitting so close to the Lunar surface I continued with drills as I thought of them. Submarine captains never let up in the training of his or her crew, and they are among the best crews in the world (Me? Biased... not a chance. LOL). As part of the drills, someone suggested we practice proper deployment and recovery of the shuttles and Sentinels, strictly following the set protocols. I told them they would have to wait since we have been asked to head back home. And... we have a lot to do before we weigh anchor. Plus, I might just have to see if you have forgotten anything... some more drills, maybe?

I had taken a half-hour power nap just as Mr. Remington knocked on the door.

"C-mon in... hey there Theo. I was just trying to get a little shut-eye. What's up?"

"I think everyone is looking forward to our return to Angels Landing. When do you think we can weigh-anchor and turn toward home?" Even Theo began to use Navy jargon.

"I'm ready whenever everyone else is. But we still have a team working the south pole. When they're done, we are. Do me a favor and get a consensus. Will the scientists be leaving everything on the moon , or will we need to go get some of it? We'll move forward from there."

"OK! Sounds good. Get some rest, I'll have something for you within the hour. See you later."

"Yup!"

Lights out.

Blissful sleep.

'Knock, Knock'.

"Hannah, Hannah, it's mom. Wake up honey."

"What... what time is it?"

"0815. You slept for over 13 hours. We are going to the Captains Mess for breakfast in about a half-hour. C'mon. Drag your butt out of bed and join us."

"OK! I'll see you there. I need to wake up under a nice hot shower. I wonder if Pauline Baxter got my uniforms cleaned."

Mom opened the closet and sure enough, all my uniforms had been cleaned and pressed. I do like my little house."

I was late getting up to deck 9 and the Captains Mess. The place was crowded with Ships Crew and scientists. I stopped by the front desk and had a brief conversation with a steward. He pointed to a table on the right side near the wall. Not our usual table. But the place was nearly full. No wonder.

"Good morning everyone." I couldn't help it, I yawned big.

"Good morning sleepy head." Said Mom.

"It looks like you got a good night's sleep."

"Yea! It's been long time coming. Have you ordered yet?"

"No. We were waiting for you." I smiled, then everybody ordered a sumptuous breakfast and engaged in good natured banter. I guess I had been uncharacteristically quiet... sort of lost in my own thoughts. It didn't go unnoticed by the glances made my way. But no one said anything, leaving me alone with my personal thoughts. I guess I was looking forward to arriving home, to my planet after all. Theo, who was sitting to my left got my attention by waving his fork.

"Hannah, the folks in charge of the deployments said they had done some reliability and functional testing of the equipment out on the lunar tundra. Everything was performing optimally and therefore will be left in place. The south team will be going down to the site one more time tomorrow morning to finish a couple of experiments and then will pack up everything into the shuttles and will return around mid-day. I suspect they are going to have to organize the equipment before we move out. Earliest departure could be in two days. They have nothing further that needs to be done on the moon. The rest will be analysis of all the data so far collected."

The shuttles came back as expected and off-loaded their equipment. Hangar personnel began cleaning and servicing the shuttles, scientists huddled around the returned equipment and moved it to the back of the hangar.

"OK! That's good news. When we get back to the bridge, let's review some of our pre-departure check lists."

"Maybe we should convene a meeting of the Council and revue what needs to be done from a departmental point of view. Let's find out if there are any time constraints we are unaware of." offered Porter Williams, Exec Administrator, Science Divisions.

"Let's do that. Except. First, let's bring in Ships-only department heads to allow them time to run whatever system verification and performance tests. Let's simplify the process: from each department, I want a *GO FLIGHT* and *HOLD* lights on the bridge from each department. Any *'Hold'* light puts departure on hold.

Let's go with Tactical first. Verify we can find our way home without being shot at. Include internal security and hangar operations. All vehicles in tactical configuration.

Next would be Gravity. Then Navigation, Environment, Power, and Med Bay.

Then, when they are done, bring in the heads of the scientific divisions. They do not require a Go-NoGo, so, in summary, Ships department heads followed by science divisions. Are we agreed?" all agreed and we moved to leave the Captains Mess.

"I will be addressing the entire ship, and that includes everything from house-keeping to food preparation of our intention to head on home. Sarah, since there is no GO FLIGHT from them, please see to all others; from hydroponics to schools, make sure they are prepared for the trip home.

OK! Let's go to work."

We filed out and dispersed to our respective work areas. I elevated down to 8 and walked the fifty meters to the Bridge.

Following along were Theo, Darien, Admiral Holder, and dad. As we entered the bridge...

"Captain on the bridge."

"As you were." Then I heard Admiral Holder say...

"Tight. Tight. She definitely runs a tight ship. We need more like her in the Navy. I'll be first to admit that my view of women at top leadership positions was way off base and I stand corrected. I'm *'Old Navy'* I guess." My dad simply smiled. I walked around the bridge deck just looking at the activity at each position; responding to an occasional question and asking my own, plus a joke or two along the way. Things were as they should be.

I mounted the raised command platform to the center chair. I looked over at comm and pointed to the ceiling. The new comm specialist who had finished her training, engaged a series of switches then pointed at me. I nodded with a smile.

"Attention all personnel and guests of Seraphim. This is the Captain. I hope you enjoyed our first excursion into space and our lovely natural satellite, the moon. Having completed all the science studies, it appears we are ready to set sail for our home port and the place we call home. I want to thank each and every one of you; Seraphim crew, scientists, engineers, guests, food service personnel, house-keeping, school teachers, religious services, med-bay personnel... and every person on board, how proud I am of your service to this wonderful ship. Never in my experience have I seen such dedication and professional attention to your jobs, inter-departmental cohesion and adherence to the rules that make space travel not only safe, but a model for future generations who will someday join us out here. Today, we go home. Then, in time, with a new assignment, we will journey forth once again to explore the mysteries of the universe. "Ooh-Rah, Seraphim".

Parish out."

"Ooh-Rah, Seraphim", "Ooh-Rah, Captain Parish". Resonated through the ship.

... from CDR Ed Parish's perspective...

"My God. Ed, your daughter is amazing. You should be very proud. I've never seen anyone like her."

"We are proud of her. Seraphim is very lucky. Her mom and I are truly amazed. We have a concern, however. She drives herself so hard, afraid she is going to miss something, resulting in harm to the ship and the people aboard. That's one reason she prioritizes training to such a degree. If command for some reason is not available, every department is so well trained and cognizant of their responsibilities and how each meld with others, they can carry-on without direction. She does sleep better with that in mind. Lorraine is keeping a professional eye on her, from a fitness point of view; watching for anything in her behavior that might affect her decision-making ability. No matter who is captain, Lorraine would do that. But Hannah is smart. She is grooming two other exceptional women who could step in if necessary. One is the XO, Jessica Pearson, former Air Force Colonel, and the other is another former Air Force Colonel, Loretta (Lory) Amundsen. Each has command experience as senior combat pilots and were squadron commanders."

"You were a Navy pilot, too, weren't you?"

"Yes! 32 years. I have a lot of experience in various theatres, but I'm tired. I can't keep up with any of them. I will step in only if I have to. I hope I never have to."

"How old is she?

"Thirty-three, almost thirty-four. Most everybody else is at least ten years older than Hannah. The XO and Lory are in their late forties. It used to be the reverse, top positions were old guys, now it seems the reverse. Of all our command with the highest responsibility level is the youngest, Hannah."

"I'm old!"

"Yea, we both are. But, Lorraine and I are going to help any way we can. She is Seraphim Hospital Administrator, and I'm head of Tactical and Security."

"Commander Ed Parish, report to Tactical CIC, ASAP."

"On my way."

"Can I come?"

"Sure"

"What's going on?"

"I have no idea..."

"Here we are... YOU CALLED!"

Donna Singleton, followed by Ben Crowder, both former Secret Service moved quickly to the two of us standing near the door.

"We just received a secure message from Jerry Dickson, Director of Internal Security at Angels Landing. Something's up. They don't have a handle on it yet. But they received a heads-up from our guys down deep in DC of some kind of activity... planning sessions, they said, from our old pals in the MiB. This time it is funded by middle-eastern fundamentalists. It seems like they want some new hardware. Big bucks involved, possibly trillions. These are seriously bad actors. Through our east coast operatives, we have securely alerted 1600 Pennsylvania avenue."

"Are the White House, NSA and Homeland going to help out this time?"

"Unknown. We may be on our own again. Roger Davidson is briefing the Captain now. She's holding a meeting of the top bridge crew and put us at DEFCON 3... for now. She will call General Quarters if necessary. Can you get the Hangars to outfit the shuttles and Valkyries accordingly?"

"Yes, of course."

"I told Hannah you were in CIC, she'll be here shortly."

"I guess we won't be going home, just yet." considered the Admiral.

"Could be. Let me talk to my guy in the Hangar...

Hey, Jake. Did you get the word? The MiB are looking for a rematch. Do what you can to get our little Space Force ready for another air show. We'll keep you informed. Yes, I know we have three Valkyries, now. Prepare all three of them, please. Oh, and we may have a use for Dragon Slayer. Good work, as always."

... from a distance.

"Captain on the bridge."

"Let's go."

"Hey, Dad... Admiral. Did you get briefed?"

"Yes, we did. I have the hangars on alert and all shuttles and Valkyrie are being moved into tactical position. Dragon Slayer will join us this time... if we can control it."

"We can. Look over there at the bridge tactical console. On the right-hand position do you see that F-16 joystick, rudder pedals underneath and a Mode-2 power quadrant on the left?"

"Where did they come from?"

"Oh! I had a thought one day and went down to hangar 3 to look at the Dragon. An engineer did a walk-around with me as I looked. I asked my usual questions, listened a lot, then came up with an idea. I had those controls installed along with the appropriate hardware and software. It works." ... and pointed to the new tactical position. "We have a new very powerful drone... *Dragon Slayer.*"

"You did that?"

"Yea, Well no... I didn't DO it. I highly recommended that they do the work. Kinda cool, isn't it? Might just get to use it. I also went down to visit my group in Nav. It has been awhile since I was there and I was glad to see them. They had a million questions. So, did I. I asked them to prepare a complete route back home by way of Hawaii, fly north to Alaska, then south through Alberta and down to Angels Landing. All done. However, we don't really have to go home now, do we. We can stay right here. Maybe swing around to the other side, the so-called dark side. The smart guys can explore the region. To my knowledge nobody ever did an EVA over there. Then I had another thought. You're going to love this or hate it. I had Nav plot a course to a landing site on the *Acidalia Planitia* plain. It's all plotted, and ready to go. I ran it by some of our scientists, too. They were giddy with excitement and said they are ready to go."

"What the hell is acid ... planet?" asked the admiral.

Theo had been listening...

"Hannah, are you serious? Acidalia Planitia? You need to get back into your box with all your marbles."

"There is no such thing as the BOX... or misplaced marbles, Theo."

"Not for you, maybe, but... Acidalia Planitia?"

"Well the bad guys would have a bitch of a time finding us, wouldn't they?"

"Theo, what's she talking about?" inquired Donna Singleton. Theo responded...

"It is located between the Tharsis volcanic province and Arabia Terra to the north of Valles Marineris, centered at 49.8°N 339.3°E. Do I have that right, Hannah?"

"Yes."

"Theo, where is Acidalia Planitia?"

"MARS."

From Captain Parish's perspective...

"What? What are you saying?" responded Donna Singleton. Then I added...

"We have a great navigation department. They have the whole thing plotted with more than one actual landing area. We have choices, ladies and gentlemen. For now, we just stay where we are. Let's see what happens in the next few days. If the threat is not as real as initial observations indicate then we may be going home as planned. If it looks like we will stay on here for a bit, I would like some of the non-scientists to have an opportunity to tour part of the moon in the shuttle Peregrine. This may be the only opportunity for some of them. If it's not used for EVA, then occupants don't need space suits. It has a toilet, rest area with bunks, a small galley and food refrigeration. So, it's a pretty good-sized RV. It has the best radiation protection of all the shuttles, second only to Seraphim. Gravity and counter gravity systems are the same as Seraphim. It has a state-of-the-art air recycling system with automated gas level monitoring and refurbishment systems. O2 levels are kept at 21%. CO2 is scrubbed out of the air to a level equal to normal Terran percentages... around 2-3 percent. Long distance space flight is also possible in Peregrine.

There is some thought that if necessary we needed to bring some people back to earth, soon. We could do it in Peregrine. They may have a need to be there for family issues or business considerations. We do have a lot of choices."

Sarah made the announcement that a tour bus, A.K.A, shuttle Peregrine will be available to take up to forty passengers for a one-hour tour of the nearby craters. Within the hour she had 76 people signed up. I watched on a video monitor of hangar 1 as a line of people in single file, walked up the rear loading ramp into our largest shuttle. I waited as the ramp closed and after a 15-minute safety briefing the inner airlock door opened and the shuttle floated in. The inner door closed, the air inside the airlock was evacuated and 40 first time 'quasi-astronauts' floated out into the lunar day.

That's when I gave XO Jessica Pearson the Conn and invited Theo to join me in Hangar-2. He and I both had been fitted for a space suit weeks earlier. Then, to his surprise I ordered the normally reluctant scientist to board Valkyrie-1. Yup! He surprised me by climbing aboard and took the right seat up front. We slowly floated out the port airlock of Hangar 2 with GMI control and speed greatly diminished by the low Lunar gravity. Hangar-1 was being heavily used with *Gabriel, Raphael* and occasionally *Peregrine* coming and going to the south-pole research camp and subbing as a tour-bus. It was decided to exclude *Michael* since it didn't have quite the protective skin the others had. It functioned fine but lacked some of the cosmic and gamma radiation protection. Our suits partly made up for that. That's when *Symphony* decided that *Michael* should have the retrofit to the new standards when we get home.

The huge windscreen on VAL-1 offered an amazing view as we moved along the meteor-pocked surface, silent and effortlessly. Theo was loving this. We had a normal atmosphere and gravity inside so we had raised our face shields. I guess we were about 8 kilometers from Seraphim when something caught my eye. We had just crested the outer rim of a deep crater whose rim was maybe 15 kilometers across.

That was when my best friend, Theo, and I were thrust into a situation beyond our imagination. I slowed the Val to near stop and turned around.

"Pull down your face shield, seal, and pressurize your suit." I did my suit and checked it was all secure. I checked Theo's and he was all set. He seemed apprehensive. We checked comm and it worked both directions. He asked...

"What's going on, Hannah? Why did we stop? Is something wrong?"

"Everything is fine, Theo. There is something that we need to look at. We have to step out for a few minutes. No, there is nothing wrong with the ship, either. I need help understanding it. Besides, you get to walk on the moon."

I depressurized the Valkyrie, extended the landing struts. Felt the ship descend the few remaining feet to the surface drawn by the low lunar gravity. I shut off the artificial and counter-gravity. With our seatbelts unhooked we carefully moved to the door. I stepped out first onto a hard surface without any dust on it. It was like the slickrock found in the western deserts on Earth. Theo stepped down gingerly and stood still, taking a moment getting his equilibrium in the 1/6 gravity.

"Move slowly and don't turn your head fast."

He looked around and up seeing Earth a quarter million miles away. He just stared. The only sound was the air moving through our helmets and our breathing. Standing on the surface of the moon is a very strange experience. It is kinda like being in a theme park ride. It was also a very lonely feeling. Nothing around us moved or was alive. No sounds of life. Nothing moving. Nothing! It was dead! The nearest indigenous life was 239,000 miles away. The only sound came from inside the suit. Nothing from outside. It was creepy.

I moved slowly to a point where the crater walls began their climb. There in front of me was something that raised my 'Holy Crap' alarm to its highest point ever.

"What is it, Hannah?"

"Look here." I was looking down into a perfectly round hole about a 12 to 14 inches in diameter that was very deep and seemed to go on forever.

"Please tell me, that is a natural feature and wasn't drilled on purpose."

Theo was transfixed. I knew the mind of the scientist was hard at work sorting out the myriad thoughts brought on by the revelation before us. He was scared, excited, elated and exuberant. Before he said anything more I shut off my comm and reached over and shut his off, too.

Then we put our helmets against each other.

"Why did you do that?"

"Our communication is monitored on the ship."

He yelled.

"That... was drilled. Hannah. That... was drilled. What's happening?" his voice had a hint of fear.

"I saw two other holes on our flight over here. There may be more. Let's get back to the VAL." We walked slowly, carefully, across the hard rock to the Valkyrie sitting in the airless, low gravity world known simply as 'the moon'. I was always amazed that Earth's moon was the only celestial object that had never been given a proper name. Well, that's not entirely true. There were references to 'Luna', but not as a proper name. All other planets' moons have discreet names. Curious! This celestial body did have a first name, though... *"The"*.

I closed and sealed the entry door and pressurized the interior. Then we flipped up our face shields. Now we could talk. I also turned on both gravity systems. With the thrusters, I brought us up about 100 feet and floated.

"We are not alone." I said.

"That is true. Apparently, we are not alone." He nervously repeated and continued...

"You know, when we were talking about being on the outside of the BOX, you said, *'... You would be surprised at the revelations you can find there.'* But, this goes far beyond revelations. What do we tell them on Seraphim?" I thought a minute then reasoned...

"I suggest we tell them nothing. Not yet. We don't need a panic on board. Some will want to get the hell out of here and go home. Others may want to go hunting. I can't let that happen, Theo. Not yet. We need to think this through before we do anything. In fact, without getting out let's continue our flight for say, another hour, OK?"

After the hour of wandering around, we counted 13 holes exactly like the first. Someone's been digging. And it all seemed to be into the hard surface I was calling slickrock. Very hard stuff indeed.

"You know, Theo, we just answered the age-old question and darling of science fiction writers... *Are we alone?*"

The Firmi Paradox is being answered.

We continued our tour of the area and stopped at a crater with a vertical outcropping in the center. If water poured out the top it might look like a fountain. We both stared at the sight before us. The ugly lifeless nothingness, with chalky rolling hills that made up crater rims and with a black sky and stars in sharp relief was not easily appreciated. Suddenly, though, it became an odd kind of beautiful in an arid, weird, alien sort of way, like a desert seen for the first time in the early evening by someone accustomed to trees and grasses. There was life here, but not indigenous, rather visitors... Us. We are the aliens. I felt a gloved hand on mine and heard the words...

"THANK YOU."

Ethics and Responsibility
(Moral Agency)

I was deeply troubled by the discovery Theo and I made during our latest trip and the profound effect it had on both of us. With it came a philosophical and ethical dilemma I surely was not prepared for. I needed to talk with someone who understood how deeply troubling it was. In the meantime, Theo and I agreed not to tell anyone... not yet anyway. Then we started to laugh. Did you ever start laughing for no apparent reason? A kind of maniacal reaction to something; extreme stress or a profound realization. Maybe it was simply a release of tension. It didn't last long and we resumed our normal behavior, whatever that was.

We both attended planning meetings and carefully suggested alternate exploration sites keeping them clear of the known drill sites. We were concerned other teams might discover what we found and have a different ethical position... one of openness. Bad idea... at least for now.

Theo suggested we find out if there were any philosophers on board that could help us cope. Perhaps a psychologist. On my computer in my quarters and using a filter to search for specific words. I reviewed the backgrounds of personnel aboard or had visited Angels Landing. I found an interesting listing. *Dr. Laurie Zoloth, Ethicist and Dean of the University of Chicago Divinity School in the University of Chicago and Northwestern University.* She had written a treatise called *"The Ethics of Human Spaceflight.* I spent an hour going over her background and papers she wrote.

And guess what? She was on-board Seraphim. I was thrilled. Maybe I had found someone that could make some sense out of our concerns. I sent a message with a request to have a chat with her. I asked if she minded if Professor Theodore Remington came with me. She agreed and we met in her residence on deck 11.

This turned out to be a changing moment for both of us, and as it would turn out, the future of Seraphim and most importantly... her crew.

Dr. Laurie Zoloth was an attractive, elderly, grey haired lady possibly in her late sixties. She had an eager smile and seemed to have great energy. She welcomed us into her "home", offered us tea and asked what brought the Captain and Science officer to see her. I was curious why she chose to come to Seraphim and join us for our first journey. She was introspective and said she had an interest in why we wanted to come to '*THE*' Moon at all. We answered as best we could and she seemed to study our answers. I told her I had read '*The Ethics of Human Spaceflight,*' and, enjoyed the parallel with the Lewis and Clark expedition. She smiled and said,

"Perhaps that is the reason I came along." I looked on in wonder as she continued.

"I was fascinated that a ship of this immensity and capability was commanded by a woman. I read about your adventures and willingness to save Angels Landing and this magnificent ship. And, as I see, a young woman. This appears to be a demographic paradigm. That fascinated me. I have stayed aloof of any publicity preferring to stand in the background and watch. So, now. What is so important that made you discover me on-board, then sought me out and requested a *chat*, as you put it?"

"In '*The Ethics of Human Spaceflight.*' In a topic called ... '*The ethics of encounter.*' You write in part... and here I quote... *"Encounters across serious differences with life forms we cannot know will be a sterling ethical challenge, both ethically and philosophically. We cannot anticipate the range of possibilities, and much of the speculation is outside the range of ethics and into the range of science-fictional scenarios, which have done a credible job in this realm."*

She nodded, thought for a moment then...

"You found something, didn't you?" She didn't move but she had a big smile and looked hopeful.

"Yes, we did. And we don't know how to proceed."

"What are you afraid of?" She studied our faces. Theo answered...

"Are you familiar with the Firmi Paradox? I think we fear the revelation itself. That we are not alone. How will others react to something like that?"

"That you are asking, in itself, tells me something about you. You both are very moral and responsible people. Perhaps you are wondering that as captain, do you have the moral agency to even wonder about the ethics in just knowing we are not alone and how people might react to that knowledge." She waited a moment, and...

"Yes, I am familiar with the Firmi Paradox? Enrico Fermi understood that the universe is unbelievably big, with trillions of stars and even more planets. So... there just has to be life out there, right? But... *where is it?* Do you now wish you hadn't made this discovery?"

"Now that ushers in a mixed answer." I considered, puzzled.

"We certainly would like to know, wouldn't we? Science is groping for answers, spending billions on research and robotic exploratory inter-planetary missions."

"Then, am I to assume the captain and science officer of Seraphim are the only people on board that know about this?"

"That is correct. We haven't shared this with anyone else." She leaned forward searching our eyes.

"What would you like to do? What's your next step? This is a research vessel. Would withholding this information go against the goals and mission of that charter?"

"Yes, I guess it would. I'm curious why you haven't asked what we found."

"Oh! I am curious, but I'm also prepared to wait as you decide what to do."

"Are you afraid to know?" Theo asked. She sat back and considered her answer.

"Heavens, no. Perhaps you should consider an analogue to your dilemma. Consider what was meant by the Federation's Prime Directive?" She had a huge also smile and I sensed our chat was over. We said our goodbyes as I remembered my years as a trekkie.

From the Star Trek Canon: *"The United Federation of Planets has the Prime Directive, aka Starfleet General Order number 1. This prohibits Starfleet personnel from interfering with the internal development of alien civilizations."* There was more, but that was the gist of it.

We retreated to Theo's residence... and talked. I thought a moment then offered,

"What if I convene a council meeting and we run it by them? They are restrained by the Non-Disclosure Agreement to stay quiet."

"I'm not sure that given the gravity of this discovery that an NDA will stop anyone from sharing. This is big stuff. Thousands of years of wonder... 'Are we alone'? This is not something that can easily be hidden. Everyone will want to be part of this find. We would need a plan in place where we could follow up on the reason for the holes and then send science teams to do a real evaluation. Besides, those holes could be very old. Things don't change much on the Moon. They could be thousands... millions of years old. In any event, they were looking for something. It may be important for us to know what that might be." He continued with an extraordinary smile as he studied a live view of Earth on his computer screen...

"You know, Hannah. There are approximately 7.7 billion humans alive on Earth, an estimated 108 billion humans have lived on earth since homo sapiens first came into existence, about 52,000 years ago." He laughed... and giggled...

"Do you realize, you and I are the only human beings out of all of them to KNOW that we are not alone in the universe... that is AWESOME!" His smile was a welcome addition to this pivotal moment, and accompanied by our shared giggles, helped to wash away some of my concerns.

I sent the usual request to Council members for an important meeting. Meanwhile, Theo and I thought up some ideas how to approach the subject obliquely, in a sort of 'What If' way. I also invited Laurie Zoloth with the option she could just 'sit in' and observe, or could join in if she wanted to. I also told her we would approach the subject using a 'What-If' we found evidence of life. What were our options and responsibilities as a research ship? I told her I would understand if she chose not to come.

But she did. Considering her life's work... how could she not?

The Paradox...

The meeting began around three in the afternoon. I opened with questions about their personal experiences since lift-off. They all seemed impressed with the fast arrival to our first Site. There was talk about taking some additional bus tours in *Peregrine* to see what the place is like from only a few feet up. 'Great idea', I said. I introduced our invited guest Laurie Zoloth who said she might write a book on humanity's latest adventure into space. Darien Hunter sat alone in the back of the room watching closely. I think he sensed something was happening. He may not be the most empathetic scientist when it came to human nature, but he was extremely sharp and mindful of the world around him.

One of the Council members said he was disappointed. He didn't see any little green men and the moon was not made of green cheese. Laughing, Theo chimed in...

"Oh! The disappointment." And we all laughed.

"What would you do if you had?" Laurie asked also laughing. And they laughed some more.

"No seriously, what is the protocol if you did find life or evidence of life if not here, maybe Mars or one of the big moons around Jupiter or Saturn?"

I referenced her book '*The Ethics of Human Spaceflight*' and the association of what we are doing to the *Lewis and Clark expedition* book she published in 1996. I was afraid some might attack the premise. But, they didn't. In fact, they inquired why she was interested. She was definitely prepared. They listened as she talked about the seminars and lectures she gave on the track record of western migration and the impact it had on the indigenous populations across America and Africa way back when, and wondered how we would treat whatever we meet in the future. It was a perfect lead in. My turn...

"Seriously, do we even have a consensus or protocols for this?"

People looked around and shook their heads or made body motions that said they didn't know.

"Oh, come on people." Said a frustrated Theo. "Even Captain Kirk's Enterprise was bound by the United Federation of Planets Prime Directive, aka Starfleet General Order number 1. And, that was fiction. We are out here for real... in a Starship. What does Captain Parish do if this question is thrust on her by circumstance?" I remained quiet. Then Laurie popped another question.

"Do you mean to tell me this wasn't part of your planning, that the subject of finding extra-terrestrial life didn't even come up?" She was startled and showed it, also disappointed.

"I guess we never got that far. Everyone knew the Moon could not support life, so we assumed that we needn't worry about it." said one.

"There is no life here... accept us."

I had a quick response...

"People... the last thing we can allow ourselves to do is, *something*, or *nothing*, based simply on 'assumption'. We should not assume anything out here. Doing so could be very dangerous.

I looked at Theo and he just blinked. Then I looked at Laurie. She looked at me, quickly glanced at the others, then back to me, pursed her lips and nodded her head. That meant to me... do it. I thought for a minute and came up with an idea. Darien saw the nuances we exchanged. His attention suddenly peaked as he sat up straight in his chair. He can be very perceptive. His instincts were suddenly moved toward *'Fight or Flight.'* I began...

"What-if..." Theo smiled and nodded his head.

"What if we find an artifact of some kind that was definitely not of Earth origin or indigenous to the moon? What if others from another civilization came here sometime in the past. How does that change your perspective? Is there something we should be doing? Should we then consider creating some guidelines, fitting the 'What-If' scenarios?" I half stood, and for emphasis slammed both hands splayed out in front of me flat on the table, supporting my weight.

"What-If we discover we are not alone?" I scanned the faces, with my own glaring at them as I sought answers from the brilliant minds. How had this NOT come up in their planning?

The dynamic in the room suddenly changed completely. I momentarily forgot Darien was sitting in the back and hadn't spoken since the meeting began. He was looking straight at me wide-eyed with a look of astonishment and realization I could only translate as *'Oh! My God, she's found something'*. He knows me and the way I think. He knows my use of the 'What If...' was never used for fun. He knew I would only use it to explore something 'real'. He said nothing but still continued to stare at me with incredible intensity. I think he figured it out.

I quickly withdrew from the thought and decided we had enough.

"Well... that was exciting. It does however raise an interesting thought, doesn't it? What do you think? Should we get together in a week or so. Perhaps you can think about it. I do not want to be caught in a first-contact situation without some options. That is what this Council was created for, to help the Captain find solutions to dilemmas that require serious consideration. I am asking you for your help. This subject is as serious as it gets, folks. Please think it over.

Beyond the simple 'are we alone?' question, we owe it to every human being on this ship and every person on that blue planet out there to effectively and safely be prepared for any eventuality as we move further out into the universe. If we can't do that... perhaps we aren't ready after all and should call it a day. So... anyway... on that note I think we can close the meeting until another time. Thank you for coming."

As they left the Council Chambers I could see and hear them still talking about my 'What-If'. They also knew I used that kind of tool to get people to think and solve problems. And now Darien Hunter knows we found something. Laurie stopped me in the hallway and thanked me for inviting her. I thanked her for interjecting some concern into the meeting. We said goodnight, and she headed toward the elevator. I turned toward my quarters with Theo beside me when Darien caught up with us.

"Do you have any more Earl Grey?"

"I think so... you want some? How about you, Theo?"

"I think a Diet Coke if you have it. I need something fizzy." We entered my quarters and I commented to Theo...

"There are bottles of diet coke in the door of the fridge. Would you get me one, too, please?"

We sat taking sips of the cold 'fizzy' stuff. The water bubbled in the electric tea maker. There was a knock on the door. I answered it. A serious Laurie Zoloth stood there, eyes sparkling. I stepped aside and she entered, stopped, looked at Theo and Darien, then back to me. I suggested she sit and asked if she would like some tea.

"Earl Grey? Lemon?" asked Darien.

"Sounds lovely, thank you." In minutes we were sipping out respective drinks.

"Darien, please sit down." I said with a kind of authority that really suggested he sit down. He did. Laurie was looking seriously at me without moving. Then, she spoke...

"OK! That got everyone's attention. Now you have my mine. It's been a long time since I had the hair on my arms at full attention and goose-bumps. That was chilling. My curiosity got the better of me. OK, what did you find? Come on, considering what just happened, there's no sense being shy." I looked at the floor uncomfortable in my thoughts. I looked at Theo and saw him nod his head again. I looked at Darien, his tea cup in hand with a steady gaze like I'd never seen him have. I began...

"Theo and I were talking today about how we felt cooped up inside. I asked him if he ever thought he would like to go for a walk outside since others were doing it. He surprised me when he said, yes. I wanted to go, too. So, we went down to hangar 2, put on our pre-fitted full space suits and climbed aboard Valkyrie-1. We exited through the Hangar 2 airlock. Once outside we scooted along the surface using GMI with my hand on the maneuvering thruster controls, just in case. It was slow, but smooth and quiet and had a beautiful view of the Lunar surface. I guess we went about seven or eight kilometers when I noticed something. We slowly stopped. I extended the struts and settled onto a surface of slickrock or whatever it is. We closed our face shields, pressurized the suits, depressurized the ship, opened the door and stepped out onto the slickrock. It took a moment to find our equilibrium in 1/6 gravity. Theo hadn't seen what I saw, but followed me as I walked toward the rim of the crater we had just crossed over. I was looking down as Theo caught up. I shut off both our COMM's, put our helmets together so we could talk without others hearing us. I think I said...

'Please tell me, that is a natural feature and wasn't drilled on purpose', as we stared at a singular hole about a foot or more in diameter, perfectly round and very deep. We could not see the bottom. The hole was drilled through slickrock which is extremely hard. Somebody drilled it. Not us... not anybody from Earth. We left and took a little trip. There were more in different locations. We counted thirteen. All drilled through slickrock. And, they were only in the area we happened to be in. How many more are there around the Moon? Theo noted they could be very old since not much changes in the barren landscape of our only natural satellite. We didn't want to create a panic so we decided not to say anything to anyone. So, we just sat in Theo's residence to figure out what we should do. If those holes were old, there would be no concern. If they were recently drilled, then it would not be a surprise if the drillers came back. I didn't know what to do."

"Nor I" said Theo.

"We needed a new perspective. Something to guide us."

"That's why you sought me out." Said Laurie.

"Yes. You have a unique perspective since you had done a lot of research regarding strangers in a strange land, an allusion to the 1961 science fiction novel by American author Robert A. Heinlein, *Stranger in a Strange Land*,"

"You did the right thing, Hannah." Said Darien. I followed up...

"I suspect they may be miners. These things resemble bore-holes, similar to the ones oil companies drill. But, I don't think they were looking for oil."

"What then?"

"I have no idea." Then Darien inserted...

"Let's get some people together and go out there in a shuttle. Tomorrow. Right now, I'm exhausted. But, this keeps getting better and better. Damn! Hannah. I knew we would find interesting stuff, but this??? Why is this giving me the willies?" I just smiled.

The following day we met again in my quarters. The bridge was quiet and in a kind of automatic mode. Everyone was at their station. Per an earlier request I asked Tactical to keep an active monitor on the black sky from the vertical all the way down to the horizon in all directions. I said something like keeping a weather-eye out for approaching objects... meteors, asteroids or whatever. That diluted the question... why?

Theo had reviewed the crew complement for likely candidates for an away-mission (WOW! I liked using that phrase). He showed us five scientists that not only had the requisite credentials: geology, astrophysics, etc. but also had calm demeaners and demonstrated a curiosity for new things with an open mind. I asked Sarah Michaels to invite only the five to my Day-Room for a meeting. The exception was, and needed to be, Jessica Pearson, the XO. Although she would remain on board. She would be cognizant of our away-mission, but would be alone with the knowledge of its purpose, and would deflect inquiries. She would also have the Conn.

Coincidentally, some scientists with backgrounds in planetary geoscience wanted to set up a mission to explore the Lunar south pole. Recent observations from earth astronomers following pictures from the *Lunar Reconnaissance Orbiter* (LRO) in an eccentric polar mapping orbit made some assumptions that because the craters never see sunlight due to the shadows from the crater's rims, they might support existing water-ice. The sun would cause massive sublimation if it were exposed to water-ice in the crater. The suggestion that water-ice might exist in the always dark and always deep cold of the crater centers at the poles would be a monumental find as we learn what other natural resources might exist here. They would need to bring along powerful work lights to illuminate the crater centers since the sun is never in a position to shine directly into the craters. Although the 'geo-'prefix typically indicates topics of or relating to Earth, planetary geology is named as such for historical and convenience reasons; due to the types of investigations involved, it is closely linked with Earth-based geology. Using ground-penetrating radar to image the subsurface, and with other tools, they hoped to narrow the speculation to prove or disprove the theory of water-ice. Led by an expert in Planetary Geoscience and member of the non-profit Planetary Science Institute (PSI), the team wants to spend upwards of a week exploring parts of the moon not easily seen by an earthbound telescope. A support team with pilots Jake Maxwell and the fully recovered Sergey Kuznetsov, plus a med team of two volunteer adventurous nurses were included. First Engineer Gus Mayer, approved two volunteer engineers to go along with impressive tool kits... just in case.

My guess was they would decide to do the same on the north pole. I decided it would be best if Seraphim remain where she is while there were people outside the ship. I made it clear at an early morning rap session regarding future plans while in the Lunar back yard. We apprised them of other away-missions but did not discuss the particulars. I decided to visit NGE. It had been quite a while. They were still my responsibility as no head for NGE was found. So, it was still mine. I had been thinking that I could raise one the Lieutenants to Lieutenant-Commander and put him or her in charge of either all of NGE or promote three, one for each department. I will think about that: *note to self.*

I walked in and quickly climbed the three stairs to the raised deck and sat down in my 'other' chair.

"Hey, Captain, welcome home." Yelled someone from Environment."

"Hey guys, miss me?"

"Nah!" yelled someone from Gravity. I saw an empty chair in Navigation.

"Where's Mary?"

"Mary Pipkin?"

"Yes!" I saw emotional expressions on their faces.

"She's in Med Bay, Captain."

"What? Why?"

"Don't know but she's been gone several days now."

"I'll be back." ... and ran out to the main corridor and on to Med Bay. I saw Mom at her desk and moved quickly as she saw me coming.

"Hey honey. What do we owe this honor?"

"Hi Mom, I heard Mary Pipkin is here." Her expression changed.

"She's over there. Really sick, I'm afraid. An old cancer seems to be back for another go at her. She's lucid and mobile, and would prefer to be in her residence but we need to be watching her 24/7. The prognosis is not very good. Go over to her. She's awake and feisty as usual which is a good sign. We have her on a new form of chemo that has fewer side effects. We are also looking into some new uses for some of the technology we have on board Seraphim that uses focused quantum particles that replace conventional radiation treatments. One of the doctors that joined us had been working at The *Memorial Sloan Kettering* (MSK) Cancer Center in New York City. He has picked scientists here that have inspired some new ideas that uses quantum physics, an area of study he was not too familiar with. Wouldn't that be something if we, sitting on the surface of the moon, find new treatment protocols for Cancer? I love this place."

"Thanks Mom. Sounds exciting. Do what you can. She is a very special lady that I like very much."

I walked to her bed-cube, deeply concerned.

"Good morning, Mary."

"Hey! Good morning, Captain. What are you doing down here?"

"I came to see you. And for you, it's always Hannah. I'm sorry to hear of your situation. Are Mom and people in Med-Bay taking good care of you? If not, I'll raise hell."

"Oh, no. They're wonderful. The new treatments they are using are so much better than my first bout with cancer, and I think it might be working. Oh, and I have a video screen so I can watch everything. It's amazing isn't it? When you walked out of your quarters onto the bridge just prior to liftoff, it was an electric moment. You could hear a pin drop. I saw an amazing young woman do something never done before and with such grace and determination. That moment is one I will never forget and gave me goosebumps the likes of which I never had before either. I'm so proud of you."

Coming from you, Mary, that is very special. If you feel well enough, perhaps you and I can take one of the Valkyrie ships for a ride over the Lunar surface. Would you like that?"

Mary Pipkin, one of the best Stellar Cartographers in Nav and my friend, looked at me with tear filled eyes and a smile as big as a rainbow.

"Can you do that?"

"I'm the captain. I can do anything... well, almost. So now your job is to get better. I'll be back to visit. Meanwhile... I have to go do captain stuff.

"Go do captain stuff, Hannah. You made my day. Thank you."

I smiled and hoped upon hope she would recover. I waved to Mom as I left Med-Bay for... where am I going? Mr.Scott beeped and a message stated the team was in Hangar-1, *Raphael*. It said also, "Suit-Up"

I went to my locker in Personal Equipment, put on my Space Suit, plugged in the test connection and the automated test set ran a quick series of pressure tests, comm checks and safety monitoring circuits. It checked OK and I walked through the small airlocks into the big hangar. Everyone was already aboard. Some interesting equipment occupied the space behind the seating area. The left seat in the cockpit was empty, all others taken. I guess I was driving. I walked around the others, inspecting their suits and helmets, seat belts fastened, at the same time reminding them that I expected everyone to observe all the requirements and understand that if I give an order, I expect it to be followed to the letter. I did some pre-flight checks and signaled the deck crew we were ready.

The inner door to the airlock opened, the outer one, of course, was closed. GMI was working using Seraphim's artificial gravity.

Raphael managed a slow but controllable entry to the airlock tunnel. I stopped. The inner door closed behind us. Protocol required the outer door remain closed until a final check of shuttle integrity was complete: The airlock interior was emptied of all air. The last check showed no leaks, no faults. I thumbed-up to the camera monitor for the airlock control engineer and the outer door opened. The sun was mostly overhead so we didn't need to lower our helmet pressure visors but did lower the outer sun screen. I turned to the east following the path Theo and I took. I preferred to move slowly across the Lunar surface and at a higher altitude since GMI was lagging my control inputs. I'd rather give myself some control latitude, but again was prepared to revert to maneuvering thrusters should GMI not keep us from burrowing onto the Lunar dust. The shuttle was not as responsive as the Valkyrie. We were approaching the outer rim of the crater. I hoped it was the right one. They all look alike out here. It was the correct crater but we were more south than before. I turned north along the inner rim moving the shuttle slowly. And, there it was, barely visible from our angle of approach. I lowered the struts and set down on the surface about 50 feet further into the crater, shut down artificial gravity with counter-gravity already at station-keeping. I heard a noise from someone that was caught off guard by the sudden loss of 5/6th of the normal gravity. Slowly, each removed their seatbelts and stood slowly so they wouldn't launch themselves into the shuttle ceiling. Bootcamp paid off.

"Drop your visors and seal, pressurize your suits and check others beside you. Function as a team, people. Hold up your hands when ready." Soon, all hands went up.

"First a comm check. Raise your hand if you hear me. Good! Now starting over here, sound off." I pointed to first one, then the next in line clockwise. Each said, "Copy all."

"OK! very good. Now, I'm dumping the air and opening the rear loading door."

Again, there was that moment that takes your breath away as the ultra-bright Lunar surface and ultra-black sky reminded everyone, *'we are not in Kansas anymore.'* Everyone carefully left the shuttle via the extended ramp. They stopped in a kind of ragged group getting used to the weak gravity and its effect on the inner ear balance mechanisms. They looked around to the horizon, each standing alone in their spacesuits without the safety of a space ship. For each the moment was surreal as they took in the view of Earth now so far away. Their homes, their lives, loved ones, were over 239,000 miles away. I understood the profound loneliness and fear felt standing in a place with an absolute lack of any sound or movement when looking out over the quarter million miles from everything that they ever knew and was familiar.

Then slowly, first one, then another turned and approached the curious hole with trepidation. They went to work. Samples of the surrounding dust and rock chips were put in polymer pill sized containers. Pictures were taken. One person had a special sealed and heated video camera and captured everything that was done at the site. Then came the investigation of the hole itself. First, they placed protection mats on the surface around the hole so they could kneel without fear that a rock or something sharp might put a hole in their suits. Measurements were taken and they studied the inside walls of the bore-hole.

"Yup! It was drilled." said a voice in my helmet. "Who-ever, whatever, definitely used a fancy bit. See these striations? We don't have anything like that. This is definitely not from Mother Earth. Another scientist opened a carrier and pulled out a long rope with a small video camera and an LED head-band flashlight on the end he had quickly jury-rigged before we left Seraphim, and fed it into the hole. He ran out of rope without hitting the bottom. We will review the video and images when we get back to the ship. For another 30 minutes they talked among themselves, excited at the prospect that another intelligent species from somewhere other than Earth had been here. And... these holes were a blessing. We would soon find out just how much.

When everyone was back aboard the shuttle, in full 1-G and breathing regular normal air, again. We lifted off and did a search along the inside rim of the entire crater. Everyone had their faces against the two large quarter windows on each side of the shuttle. The crater was larger than I expected and took us well over a ½ hour to make one trip around. We found five additional bore-holes. Each was mapped to be able to find again. Back in Seraphim and with all our personal gear stowed away, we met in the Council Chambers.

We watched the video as the camera with the LED illuminator descended through the so-called slickrock. At 83 feet it gave way to a much darker and shiny rock. We ran out of rope at 100'.

"That's *Obsidian*." Said Jody Lynn Sampson from *Environmental Studies Laboratory*. "Obsidian is a naturally occurring volcanic glass or crystal formed as an extrusive igneous rock. Once upon a time this area must have been highly volcanic. It now seems to have about eighty feet of slickrock. At least that is what we thought. On closer analysis, there is definite stratification in the hard-upper level rock you have been calling slickrock. We are looking at possibly five or more strata layers. It is not the same material as southwest U.S. slickrock but similar. *Slickrock* is a term used to describe outcroppings of smooth, weathered sandstone most prominent in Utah. There is no weathering here... or sandstone. We are doing an analysis of its composition in the lab. Our friends have done us a huge favor by drilling these holes. I'm going to hazard a guess that not all the holes will yield similar results. This is an amazing find." Then Joseph Lindquist, Geologist also from *Environmental Studies Laboratory* added...

"In an informal meeting after we got back from our field trip, we decided, for expedience sake, to split our proposed visit to the south pole and create two groups; the polar research team will continue as planned, and a new team will be created to study the geology of the bore-holes in detail. Captain, it would be very helpful if you can put together some instructors to familiarize the new people who have little experience in this work considering where we are. I was reminded, you require everyone assigned aboard to attend a 'New' boot camp?"

"I do and given what we will be doing... it must be mandatory. It is different from the general 'boot-camp' in that it is tailored to the dynamics of the moon. We will pay close attention to sunlight and radiation issues. With no atmosphere the sun will appear several times brighter than on Earth. When you have selected your teams, we will be ready for them to attend the boot camp available tomorrow. Oh! And they will all need to be fitted for a spacesuit. Training will be done with spacesuits on, in an artificial 1/6th gravity. So please contact Tactical for appointments to be fitted. Oh, and here is something nobody talks about... night time. This side of the moon receives direct sunlight for approximately 15 days a month. The rest of the time it is near absolute darkness. There will be some Earth-light which will help give us a small amount of illumination. Imagine working on earth with only 'moonlight'. Same thing."

"Jesus! You folks don't mess around and have thought of everything."

"I hope so. But, if we do miss something, please let us know. What about your hardware?"

"Our people are designing several instrument packages to be lowered into the bore holes all the way to the bottom. We are prepared to go 1000 feet or to whatever depth each hole is. Each identical package is a cylinder, 9 inches wide and 36 inches long so it should fit. The bottom end has four wheels set vertically 90° apart on the outside. They are spring loaded and will press against the interior walls. They will measure the drill hole's diameter as it is lowered and also keep the cylinder centered. We don't know if the hole diameter is constant for the entire depth. We have 4 identical strips mounted vertically into the sides for each package, also set 90° apart around the cylinder. The strips are being designed and built, as we speak. Each contain 15 unique cameras with appropriate illumination. Each of the cameras looks at the hole walls with different intensities, wavelength and luminosity. Each set of four are being built into the instrument package and provide near microscopic analysis of the hole walls. Other sensors include:

Hall effect transducers: they will measure the magnitude of magnetic fields in the strata.

Gravity sensors: will measure the acceleration effects of the Moon's gravity, it may not always be constant.

Gas Sensors: will determine the presence and amount of a specific *gas* or *gases*, should there be any. Though the moon has no atmosphere, any resident gas would seek the lowest point... even helium gas would fall to the bottom of these holes.

Spectrum analyzer: to determine, by direct observation, the bandwidth of digital or analog electromagnetic signals over a defined band of frequencies.

Seismic Detectors: will detect the acceleration caused by a moonquake or induced vibrations like explosions or impacts.

Horizontal Rock-boring drill: and dust collection for analysis.

Temperature measurement of the wall.

Radiological Geiger counters: will monitor for nuclear radiation should there be any.

EMF: Electromagnetic Field Radiation Detection

Our intention would be to build 10 units, each with its own tri-pod motor driven winch system to be placed at the top over the hole. However, we may not have all the parts necessary for 10 units. We are cannibalizing parts from other projects to finish 7 units. That may have to do. There don't seem to be any Radio Shack or Lowes around here. But even with seven we can deploy several at the same time. Then when each completes its test, we can hop-scotch it to another location. What do you think?" I was impressed.

"Where did you get the spools of wire rope? A thousand feet on each spool?... seven spools? Did you folks bring it? If so, why? You didn't know we would need it for this purpose."

" Actually, you had it. Your engineering folks tell me they were in an off-site storage facility in Wyoming where parts were kitted for building Seraphim and the shuttles. All that stuff was brought into Seraphim following concerns that those operatives would confiscate it. You agreed to do that."

"Yes, I did, didn't I? There was a lot of stuff and it takes up a lot of room in areas of all three hangars. OK! I think it's a workable plan. We will begin focusing on the logistics and transportation. Good talk. But, now I need to stop by Med-Bay and engineering. I will discuss this at length with my staff. We have 4 shuttles. One of which doesn't have the radiation protection the other three have. But since everyone aboard will be wearing spacesuits, the threat will be minimal.

The shuttle is called *Michael.* It will function as our emergency backup and rescue ship if things go sideways. And will be fully staffed with rescue personnel, a doctor and med-techs. It will remain inside Seraphim and launch only if needed and will be on alert status whenever a team leaves Seraphim. I will get back to you tomorrow with a time-certain for the training. I hope this is acceptable."

"Oh yes... it is indeed acceptable. It is amazing that you can improvise so quickly."

"By the way, if any of you not part of an away-team would like to go for a romp through the countryside, you will need the training, too. Now's your chance. I insist on it for all Seraphim personnel using the shuttles. Now I will have to leave you in the capable hands of our scientists and engineers."

I went to Med-Bay. They were not too busy and I stopped by Mom's desk.

"Hi, how's everyone doing? Mom looked up and...

"We have had a few panic attacks. People came up from the observation deck and had looked out at the Lunar surface with the Earth overhead. It looks small which is an indicator of how far away from home we are. I guess some were wondering if they would ever see home again. We have been playing psychologist here. Chaplin Sandra Davies came by and helped by holding a lot of hands. She has held several nonsectarian services in one of the auditoriums. She was wondering in the last several months why she decided to come along with us. To use one of her terms, her choice to stay, turned out to be a blessing to many. She has been working sometimes from 10 to 15 hours a day holding group meetings and visiting families at their residences. She said something recently that brought tears to my eyes. Apparently, everyone, and these are her words, 'thank God for the Captain of Seraphim'. With you in that chair, they know they are being protected and you won't let anything happen to them with God at your side. Even Chaplin Davies, was impressed and found herself sitting with them praying for the crew and their captain. As a family, we have never really followed a religious path, but your dad and I feel as they do."

"Well... I don't know what to say. I would like to think that if God is my co-pilot, I may be doing OK. I'll sleep better. By the way, how is Mary Pipkin doing?"

"You know, when people are sick and their body is fighting a disease, their attitude plays a big role in their recovery. Our treatments seem to be working, slowly of course. But since we started her on this new regimen and your orders to her to get better, her spirits are higher. People from Nav are constantly visiting with her. I think she may make it. I'm praying for her."

"Let's hope all together it helps. I'm going to see her. I'll talk to you later. We have some remarkable things happening and I really would like to share it. See you later."

"Bye, Hannah."

I walked toward Mary's bed cube. There were 4 people from Nav sitting and laughing with her. They saw me coming and got up as if to leave. I raised my hand stopping them.

"Hey, don't leave. It's good you are all here. Hey Mary, how are you doing? You're dressed in real clothes and sitting up, reading. That looks like an improvement. And who are all these people from Nav? AWOL from their posts? Are you ready... . WHAT IF...?" and they all started laughing... "What-if... Mary Pipkin is faking, just so she can escape the Navigator grind and garner attention?"

"Yea! Mary, what about that?" said Pamela Martin, Astrometrics specialist.

"Yea, Mary...?" remarked Aldus Franklin, Senior Astrophysics Professor.

"Is this true? Are you abandoning us?"

"You know that is NOT true." Mary said modestly defending her need to remain in Med Bay.

"We better go. Just in case the captain catches us and sites us for dereliction of duty. We'll be back Mary."

"Love you Mary, bye"

"Yea, Help! We can't do it without you, Mary. Get better. Bye"

"Thanks guys, Bye."

They all left laughing and joking.

"Well, Mary, you have quite a following. Were there more?"

"I'm supposed to be getting more sleep, then they show up. Look, they brought me presents and even smuggled in some candy. Those flowers came from Botanical. You know, Hannah, I have lived most of my life alone. I'm an only child. My parents died in a car crash when I was at Texas A&M. I met my husband there. We didn't have any kids. Then he passed away in '94 from a heart attack. It hasn't been easy. Friends came and went over the years. I tried keeping myself busy working odd jobs as an analyst. Then, a couple of years ago I was on vacation in Yellowstone with some friends when I heard about Angels Landing theme park not far from Yellowstone. We came down on a whim and I fell in love with the concepts. Like you I attended a bunch of seminars and classes. Then I was asked if I would like to see something. That's when I was introduced to the dynamics of space flight. It was fascinating. I heard about a woman who worked for the National Advisory Committee for Aeronautics (NACA) in the Human Computer Project in 1953. Later it became NASA. Her name was Katherine Johnson. She was a mathematician and physicist. Early in her career, she and others were called 'computers', because of their math skills, since back then they didn't have any real working computers with specific programs. With paper and pencil, she verified and calculated trajectories, launch windows and emergency return paths for Project Mercury spaceflights, rendezvous paths for the Apollo Lunar Module and command module on flights to the Moon. She helped NASA put an astronaut into orbit around Earth. Then she helped put a man on the moon.

In 2015, at age 97, President Obama awarded her the Presidential Medal of Freedom, America's highest civilian honor for her work.

I almost didn't come on this trip, but I was so inspired by Katherine Johnson that I applied for a position. Even this late in life, I pushed myself to learn and contribute something at least one more time. Along the way, I now have more friends than anytime or anywhere I have ever been. This whole ship is my family. You told me that in Nav that day when you were feeling overwhelmed in your new position. That's when you said, *I believe what will happen and what I want, is for all of us to work as a family. If anyone feels the need to talk, on whatever subject you want, I will make time to sit with you.* and...

... here you are, and here they are."

"Thank you, Mary. I still believe that, and hope I never forget it. How have the doctors and nurses been treating you?"

"Your mom and the people of Med-Bay are really kind and sweet. The regimen they have me on is nowhere like the old treatments. I met the new team headed by some kind of genius from *Sloan Kettering* (MSK) Cancer Center. I know they can't cure it, but I feel almost normal. Oh! There is some talk going around that you and Theo found something in one of the craters not of this Moon... or Earth."

"Yes, we did. There are some holes drilled in the exposed hard rock all around here. They appear to be bore-holes like geologists use when researching an area for natural resources like oil or coal. They were pulling out rock cores. Listen, I have to go. We will be sending science teams out to study the holes. I think I may know what they are for. I'll be back later to update you and talk about stuff. I'm praying for you."

"I thought you weren't religious."

"I'm not, but a I'll try anything if it helps. Love ya."

"Bye Hannah. Be careful." I smiled and left.

"A Meeting in Council Chambers begins in twenty minutes, Captain. Your presence is requested." Said Mr.Scott.

"Copy that."

I walked in to a standing-room-only gathering of scientists and crew members. The only empty chair was at the head of the table and was, I guess... mine. I sat and in front of me were three piles of recent print-outs. Pile 1, was labelled *Schedules and Sites.* The second, *Equipment Required.* The third was labelled, *Seraphim Support.* I took a few minutes and pawed through each pile looking to see what was being proposed. The rest, talked in muffled tones. When ready, I started...

"OK! Do you believe the holes are just holes or are they borings from which cores were extracted since there are no piles of cuttings around the holes?" Darien responded...

"We believe they were extracting cores. They probably cut down to a predetermined depth, maybe the length of the drill casing itself, cut it off then draw it out and load them on carriers of some sort. We saw no boring dust anywhere. They are taking their cuttings and core samples with them on a vehicle that doesn't touch the surface. There are no wheel tracks or jack marks. They seem to have some comparable technology."

"What is the status of the *Sonobuoys? Cylinders?*"

"Sonobuoy? Were you in the Navy?"

"Yea. Well, it's the only metaphor I could come up with?" One of our engineers responded.

"They are being fabricated as we speak. The integrated science package itself that will be placed into the tubes is being assembled. There are several unique sections from different laboratories that have to be tested separately, then when integrated, must be tested again together as a system. They must be environmentally tested in very cold and zero pressure. The batteries that power the whole integration must be wrapped in special heating blankets to keep the package somewhat warm. Deep cold can shut things down. We use similar technology on our robot missions. We have fifty people down in Hangar 3 busting their chops to build what the teams need." Said the expert from JPL.

"Well, this is what Seraphim was designed for. We have no idea the obstacles and challenges we will face, moving forward. The beauty of Seraphim may lie mostly with the minds on board that invent, consider and build new stuff that prior to this may never have been considered. That's why you're here. I will get you to wherever you want to go. As you push forward in this your first in-space challenge, perhaps you should put together a team that will create a wish-list of things you might need someday. Raw materials: sheet metal, bar stock, tubing, wire, other electronics, etc. We will be going back home when we resolve the bore-hole puzzle. Then you need to carefully plan our next destination like you do for your robotic missions. Once launched, we may not return for a while. Talk to our designers if modifications to Seraphim or the shuttles might need to be made. This is a sea-trial. This adventure has barely begun."

"A couple of days ago, you hosted a small gathering on the subject of 'What-If' they come back? Do you know what you will do to protect Seraphim?"

"Nope. Not yet. That, I intend to play by ear. We don't know what kind of ships they use. But if they become belligerent, I assure you we will be prepared to protect Seraphim. No harm will come to the crew and guests or the ship itself. If we have people off ship, and an emergency alert is sent, all must be prepared to abandon what they are doing instantly and get back aboard a shuttle and return to the ship. No heroes out there. I need to know that you are disciplined enough to instantly follow emergency procedures. If I need to get Seraphim out of here, be assured, I will. Anyone left behind that didn't follow procedure could pay the ultimate price for not doing so. But if the 'Others' do come back I doubt they would want to enter into any kind of conflict. We believe they are miners or geologists. They may be doing the same thing we are. It's highly premature to assume a situation with a society that may be as peace loving as I insist this ship to be. So, let's not get ahead of ourselves. My guess is they have been here, drilled, and came up empty. I submit the possibility they have moved on to other moons or planets. In fact, we are going to do that, too, aren't we? When will be the first away-mission to investigate the bore-holes?" JPL answered...

"We think the first five of the instrument packages will be available following full functional testing in maybe two days."

"How many people at each site? And... would it help if we used two shuttles and doubled the number of people and equipment.?"

"We think four people can get each site set up. We could set up two at a time so that is eight people outside at a time from one shuttle. Then each team would hop aboard the shuttle and move to the next location and emplace the next one and so on. That would mean the shuttle would need to be present inside the crater if needed at all times we have people outside on the... surface. Once the packages are in place, the tripods will automatically descend the package following a preplanned profile, then bring it back up when all the tests are completed or the bottom is reached. The rate of descent is still in discussion. Too fast and we miss things. Should we go down in steps, stopping to run the series of tests? In a kind of last minutes decision, we placed a camera and LED illumination light on the bottom end of each tube. We will be able to see what the bottom looks like before we hit it. When the package has completed all tests, it will return to the surface and send an alert and will stand by until the team returns to retrieve it. The data collected from each site will not be immediately comm-linked to the DCFS and Earth laboratories. It will be stored within laboratories here on Seraphim, only. We will review the data and have some understanding of what these holes are for. Then at an appropriate time the data will be shared. Each instrument package and tripod winch system will be recovered and loaded back in the shuttle where the recorded data will be removed, a new empty memory module installed. It will then be ready for another deployment. It's like a vertical version of the Mars Rover. It's totally automated. As an aside, maybe we could arrange a team to move further out and explore new locations bringing one unit with them. We probably won't see much difference within the same crater but that could change 500 miles from here. Putting down a half dozen... what is it you call them, sonobuoys? ... will not give us all the information. Oh, and at each new location with bore-holes we are going to do a sweep with the ground penetrating radar."

I looked on at these extraordinary people who once only observed previous missions via datalink from a probe out near, or on Titan all the way to Earth. They sat in air-conditioned rooms with many desks and desktop computers.

Yet here, they **are** the probes. They step out into the most alien of environments: no air, very little gravity, in sunshine brighter than they had ever seen. But the enthusiasm was like kids entering through the front gates to Disney World. They would capture more data about the moon in the month we are here than at any time in the history of star-gazing. The scientists on that beautiful blue marble out there are driving themselves crazy collating and studying the data already received from our lunar sending station, the Data Collection Forwarding System (DCFS) at Site-1.

Soon it will be time to share the wealth of knowledge gained with the world. But I needed a consensus first. It was suggested I convene a general Ships Council meeting with the major departments from NASA and affiliates taking part. This was going to be huge. Angels Landing will have all their theaters tied in but will be receive only. All Seraphim personnel will have access through our on-board video comm system. But we will tie in Houston, both audio and video, live (minus the 5 to 10 second delay in the transmission). They will tie in, receive only, other NASA offices and Labs, Boeing Aerospace, SpaceX, Blue Origin, Roscosmos, and many, many others. Call it the first interplanetary comm link ever made. Guglielmo Marconi and Nicola Tesla would be proud.

We will hold the symposium in the large theater auditorium. The high-definition digital movie screen set in back of the small stage would see all other major participant organizations in split screen.

I passed Darien in the hall. It looked like he had been crying.

"What's with the tears?"

"Look around," he said. "This **is** the dream. It is everything and more, that we thought about for over 23 years. It is magnificent. I had forgotten, your job on the submarine was more than just a bridge officer. You and the other women were doing what we are doing here: you were evaluating new science in submarine navigation, doing calibration and comparison studies, verifying its usability for submariners to do their jobs. This is not completely new to you, is it? You are bringing your experience and training forward, adapting what you learned to the new paradigm, and with it, the discipline required to see elements most of us can't. Others see it, too, and have asked how I found you. I told them you stumbled in off the street. One said, 'nobody gets that lucky'. But I guess I... yes, we did. And now, you found the holy grail of space exploration, proof of extraterrestrial life. And this is only our first journey."

"Maybe we just got lucky. I have been thinking about it. I doubt we will ever meet the engineers that drilled those holes. We will probably find out they were drilled eons ago. They came, did what they needed to do, and left. They won't come back. But at least it's a start. For us, they did us a favor. We don't have the tools to do what they did. And now they left us a way of doing some real scientific study of the moon... from the inside. We are very lucky."

"You think the holes are old?"

"I do, yes, but I'm only guessing. Theo made the same observation. He felt they could be even millions of years old. But, we will know soon enough, won't we? We have three of the instrumentation packages ready for deployment and plan to dispatch one shuttle this afternoon. I have never seen scientists, or anyone, for that matter, as excited about this. Scientists all over the world... the ones on that blue marble, are waiting with baited breath for the first data to come in. People are giddy with anticipation. Aren't you excited, Darien?"

"Giddy might be an apt term but I hesitate to use it. Like it's not befitting my station." I laughed and asked,

"You have a station?" and he laughed, too.

"I'd like to think so. I need something to do besides just watching. That is thrilling enough, I suppose, but not full-filling."

"I understand. Maybe you can shift your focus. You are a brilliant physicist and mathematician; this vessel is proof-positive of that. So, I have a thought. Maybe you and the great people in Symphony should put the orchestra back together and consider something totally outside your... BOX??? First,

I actually hope we don't meet up with the hole drillers. I'm not sure if I'm the right person in a first-contact situation. I've been doing a lot of thinking about it and although I have some good ideas, I need them backed up by some other points of view. I had Sarah Michaels make PDF files of part of Laurie Zoloth's book that includes. *The Ethics of Human Spaceflight'*. It's a worthwhile read given possible challenges ahead. It also includes a section called *'The ethics of encounter.'*

Sarah put it on the Seraphim General Information web site so anyone can access it. I would like your appraisal of the ideas Laurie puts forward. Share it with others and let's get a discussion started. I think it would be appropriate to ask for assistance from Laurie Zoloth herself. She has been thinking about this subject for years and her points of view may be helpful."

"I'll do it. I'll give Ms. Zoloth a call and see if she is interested.

"Oh! She will be interested."

It has been a week since Darien and I had that talk. Now everybody aboard Seraphim is aware of our findings. The number of hits on the new Zoloth website had, as they say, gone viral. Over 219 people had already read Laurie's 'book' and the number was growing daily. The spirit of adventure and mystery, although very high anyway, took a surge as the possibility of meeting other life resident somewhere else in the galaxy was exciting beyond our wildest imagination. Laurie offered to hold regular Q and A meetings in one of the smaller auditoriums. At first it was rather rowdy with people talking over one another and chaos ensued. Darien stepped in and organized the meetings. Then someone else stepped forward and offered his help as moderator. With a thorough knowledge of Roberts Rules of Order, Edward Parish, my dad, who was a Past Master of a Masonic Lodge in Norfolk began the arduous task of finding deputies to manage the meetings. Anyone wishing to actively participate in the discussions would need to 'join' the group. Others were free to watch but could not ask questions directly. They could forward written questions to one of the deputies that would be reviewed and included in later Q&As. The first meeting was simply an overview of how the seminars were to be organized. When she saw the amount of interest, Laurie looked incredulously at the numbers of requests to join. The interesting thing was how many requests came from people not on Seraphim. Many were from Angels Landing. So! A live two-way audio/video comm-link was set up with an Angels Landing auditorium going live once a week, orbit permitting. Needless to say, once the word was out, Angels Landing was overwhelmed with visitors, now rivaling Disney's Epcot Center. Our home base was becoming the world-wide Mecca for all things 'Space'. It was no longer just about the science, it now had taken on philosophical overtones. An additional layer of Space Flight consideration was added.

A return date has yet to be decided, but you can bet that it will be monumental as the world crawls all over itself to see Seraphim arrive home and meet its crew. I wondered if the MiB would try again. We did get periodic updates from our associates quietly meandering the halls of power in Washington, sniffing the ground for possible moves to annex our classified systems once again. Our counter-espionage division of Seraphim Tactical is alive and well on the moon and in Angels Landing. I am content in the knowledge that people have our backs.

Meanwhile, Mr.Scott beeped with a message requesting Darien and I join others in the JPL lab on deck 15. I had never been in the upper levels of Seraphim's decks... the so-called restricted areas. JPL's several labs occupied portside amidships space with other companies' labs opposite and along the length of available space on the three decks.

Walking into their entry was like going into NGE for the first time. It was awesome... and busy. We were greeted by Special Projects Manager, Charlie Parker. We had never met but he was the one tasked with designing and building the instrument packages to be lowered into the bore holes... my so-called *Sonobuoys*. He managed the 5 teams in charge of each section and the overall integration into a complete unit.

"Step over here." We followed him to a table where three finished units were laid out for our inspection. To the side were three tripods with the motor driven winch system and huge spool of wire rope. They looked a bit primitive without a proper paint job but who cares about aesthetics out here, as long as they are functional.

"This is all we have for now. We have enough parts to complete a fourth, probably by the end of today. So, we are thinking we can begin the bore hole study immediately. Final planning and training are on-going. We only have about four more days with sunlight. We go dark next Sunday, so says your Navigation department. Then another 15 days until we get the sun back."

"Have you selected the deployment personnel?"

"Yes, they're going over the site selections and deployment order as we speak, and looking at detailed pictures of each site. We are also sitting with your shuttle pilots and hangar folks to get these three instrument packages aboard and ready. All of our people are simulating deployments in 1/6 gravity with suits on, following your training model. It is amazing what we can do out here. On earth, we don't have the ability to truly simulate a Lunar or Martian environment like we can aboard Seraphim. The key dynamic is gravity. We can create a vacuum or lower temperature, but we are stuck with one G. We have a team working closely with other NASA folks organizing a 'wish list', as you put it. Organizers are considering rerouting some launches from big heavy lift rockets to Seraphim if you folks agree to it. Given the tremendous cost of rocket launches, I can assure you that Seraphim and its crew will be highly compensated for your participation. Proposals are being written in big meetings with your council and several NASA organizations. These considerations are looking years into the future, if the people of Seraphim are willing to continue your collaboration and help us."

"That's not up to me. The future is rife with change. A lot can happen that may force a change at a moment's notice. However, Seraphim and her crew stands prepared to meet any obstacle that we are confronted with. Otherwise we would not be here. Now, may we proceed with the deployment? I am going back to the bridge. Let us know when all is ready. By the way. Coming up here I saw a portion of the deck constructed like a vertical air-lock, with a pressure hatch horizontal at the base, and a ladder to the hatch. What is that."

"That leads to a control room and above it from deck 16, through deck 17 to a dorsal location on Seraphim's hull. It contains a very large communications dish stored in a retractable housing. At its inception, it was designed for ultra-long-distance communication to earth. Although it functions fine it has never been used. Perhaps on a longer distance flight, like Mars, we will use it."

"Good to know. I wasn't briefed on that. Thanks for the update. I have to get back to the bridge."

I returned to the bridge and as I walked in, everyone was at their assigned positions. It was the scientists' turn to be nervous, excited, even a bit scared. Today, they play archeologists and planetary science experts. Most of the world does not know what we are doing. Theo told me that today is a pivotal moment for all mankind. It may stand head and shoulders with the first humans to set foot on the moon. Depending on what we find, even the fabric of philosophy may need to be reviewed. In the spirit of full disclosure, I have to admit, I was a bit antsy. My forehead and palms were damp with sweat, not the kind following a long run, but from apprehension. It seemed I'm not alone. Today, we will deploy a shuttle to emplace the first ever, deep Lunar sub-surface probe. All aboard Angels Landing and selected partners in rooms across the U.S. and the world sit in near silence, sipping tepid coffee or tea watching patched-in video as the NEXT BIG THING begins a quarter million miles away.

"Captain on the bridge."

I didn't respond this time, just walked up the steps onto the command island. Ever since we lifted off from our cradles in Wyoming, there have been people with expensive high-resolution video cameras in every significant location on Seraphim chronicling every moment for posterity. I couldn't move without being followed by someone with a camera. Well, I suppose it is necessary for history sake. I gave mom a call and asked if she were free, could she meet me in my quarters. She agreed following some work she needed to do. I asked dad, too.

Alone in my quarters and with the earth in proper alignment for a line-of-sight transmission, I accessed the internet and Amazon.com. In the book section I looked up what was new. I found two books by the same author as the one I had just completed. I liked his style, detail and attention to character development. I ordered both to be delivered to

Meredith Ames in Angels Landing theme park security with a message to her that she hold them for me until we return. Darien's tales of the old west didn't interest me now. Although they are great classic novels of the American West and Canadian North, I had read most of them in my formative years. Reading was a distraction I needed and often used to help push aside my concerns and responsibilities even for just a few minutes. I also wanted some personal time with my parents just to talk without the pressure of responsibilities and command. In my residence I opened the door following a knock and a smiling mom and more serious dad came in. I had the video screen on watching the events taking place in the hangar as preparations were on-going. I had coffee and tea ready along with some goodies delivered by Pauline Baxter, my housekeeper.

"Hey, mom, dad. Thanks for coming. I hope I didn't take you away from anything important."

"No, we're glad to come by. It's been awhile. Is everything alright Hannah?"

"I'm fine... or maybe not. I think I'm getting overwhelmed on occasion with so many activities to be monitored and considered. People are constantly needing support and guidance in areas none of us have experience in. Anyway, let's sit in the living room. I have coffee made, tea water is hot and a tray of goodies. I wanted to remember those times when I came home on leave to the house I grew up in. An R&R of sorts. Is that strange?"

"Not at all." said dad. "In fact, I am kinda surprised you have gone this long without it. I have served under several command structures, all of them with critical missions, some very dangerous. That's why the military has 'home-leave', R&R and shore-leave. There needs to be some personal time for us to unwind and reset our ability to cope. By the way, we received another e-mail from Evie Candalerie, wondering why she hasn't heard from you. She sent several and thinks that because of your position aboard Seraphim you don't care anymore. She was your best friend since you were kids. You stayed in touch even when you were on the submarine."

I thought I was going to cry. This must be part of the love-hate relationship we have with jobs like this. We love the work, the challenge and the people we work with. But we hate what it can do to us. How could I have forsaken my best friend?

"I haven't checked my mailbox in months. I have friends from Annapolis and crew members on the Lindstrom that I used to email regularly. Now? Not even my own sister, Amanda. What's wrong with me?" Tears ran down my face. I held my hand out in front of me, and it was shaking.

"Am I having a breakdown?"

"No." said Mom. "I suspect you are, as you said, just overwhelmed. You take your responsibilities very seriously and you probably fear you will miss something, something that could possibly harm the crew. You need to find a way to mitigate that emotional burden. This ship needs you... YOU, not a basket case. I'm your mom but I am also the ships' doctor. As such, I have the responsibility to ensure that each member of the crew is fit for duty. That includes to be mentally, physically, and emotionally able to safely perform necessary work tasks. In the armed services a program called the Integrated Disability Evaluation System (IDES) was developed in 2009 to review whether a service member develops a condition that may make him or her unfit for duty. You are **not** unfit for duty, but you are showing symptoms that could lead in that direction. As we often do, we compare our experience aboard Seraphim to the crew of the Enterprise. You may remember episodes when Dr. McCoy...

'Bones', would get on Captain Kirk for showing signs of fatigue and threatening him with a mandatory removal from duty until he gets his shit together. Well, I want you to step back, and use the facilities on this ship. That's what Darien and Symphony put them here for. Swim laps in the pool, run laps around deck 10, work out on the fitness machines. Read your fiction novels. You are the one who insisted on the proper training of each and every crewmember on board. The scientists saw this. They started a physical fitness club which you can join. They even invented a fun game... Zero-Golf. You forgot maybe the most important crewmember on Seraphim, the Captain. Now, be responsible and take charge of this or I will have no choice but to put you on medical leave. The XO can easily move to the center chair until you get better."

"I agree with your mother. They used to call it battle fatigue, now it's called PTSD. I've seen a lot worse than what you are feeling. Listen to her. Do what you need to do to get your energy and focus back. Seraphim needs you as much or more than any other person on this ship."

I looked at myself in the mirror. My face was somewhat drawn and wrinkles seemed more obvious. It scared me.

"You're right, both of you." I paused and just stood there staring at myself.

"I see I am my own problem. I've lost discipline. I will fix it. It might help if I got more sleep, too. I'll do better."

"Of course, you will. Start now." She smiled and they both left.

I had pledged myself to making Seraphim and her crew able to function in the most safe and best possible way. And now they are. But focusing so intensely on that made me miss something important... ME!

Me? I had to fix... me.

I worked out a regime of both physical activities, as suggested, more quality sleep and even added some TV movies and reading as a diversion. It was working.

Oh! And the pools were great. I never really paid much attention to them. There are two. Each, side by side, 60' long x 8' wide and 5' deep, set across the beam of the ship. Each lane was separated by a near waterline wall with baffles the full length that reduce wave action. I found out later that the baffling included counter-gravity functionality that kept the water in the pool during ship acceleration or turns. Symphony thought of everything. What great minds they have. My bathing suit was old but functional. I'll get another when we get home. Mom was right (as usual) and after three days, I began to feel a whole lot better. And, I kept at it. Theo had commented that I had lost weight and looked tired. Now I'm not tired and am eating and sleeping better, too. Mom asked me to come to Med bay for a physical and she noticed the difference. People saw me there and wondered about my health. They were told that everyone in command is required to have routine checkups. For military officers they are called fitness reports. They saw me running around deck 10 perimeter track, working out in the fitness center, going one-on-one with a bad-ass SEAL doing full-contact mixed martial arts training, and I had the bruises to prove it. I could tell that the level of respect for their Captain was growing. The scientists stood back and watched as I got the shit kicked out of me. Although I did hold my own and slammed him once or twice. I hurt but it was a good-hurt (if there is such a thing) as my body began returning to my post Navy condition. Deck 10's perimeter track was no longer exclusively my domain as

I found myself setting the pace for others following my example. The amazing thing was... it was fun.

I was wondering if they would find anything useful in the holes. No matter! It was thrilling and the scientists were excited. I was curious about the communications dish that lay ensconced in the vertical tube leading to the back-bone surface of Seraphim. I had never seen it work and wondered if it still did. Maybe we'll get a chance someday.

In the meantime, maybe, I could get the magicians down in Engineering to check it out. I got the key to the padlock on the vertical air-lock and requested a complete checkout.

Head Guru was my pal, Fred Mooney. It only took 3 days. I learned that it was incredible technology but needed some simple up-grades. I would get a full briefing in a few days.

In the meantime, I checked e-mail. OMG! I read them all, with a tear in my eye. Then I started typing. I wrote a letter to Evie with apologies for my lack of concern. It was a long letter. *'SEND'.*

Overall, I spent nearly two days typing away. One after another I sent out twenty-two emails. In all of them, I promised to do better. I will keep that promise. It was labor intensive and I was glad when I finished. Now it's back to work.

Going deep

Once again, the shuttle *Raphael* exited airlock 1. On board were Jake Maxwell, pilot, Scott Randal, co-pilot and the team from the Jet Propulsion Laboratory (JPL) with their new toys code named *Sonobuoys* 1, 2, 3 and 4, ready for the second deployment. We now had four *Sonobuoys* as the folks in JPL finished the last one. Last, because they didn't have the materials to make any more. It didn't matter that much anyway because the night terminator was moving inexorably toward our position. Soon it will not just be dark, but near black outside. That forced our decision to pack up and return to our ancestral home... Earth.

Results from the many scientific studies were being reviewed, collated, studied again and again. Reports were written. Studies examined over and over. I was told that some incredible findings will likely alter the accepted belief system to the origin of the moon, its age, and its history. There were things that I became privy to that may shake the very foundation of understanding about who we, humans, have about our origin and that of others who share the galaxy. That will not be shared with the world right away because of the harm and dissention that it could cause.

It is time to go home. Now I am looking forward to it, with a content smile on my face, and shrinking wrinkles.

But... we will be back. We have to... We aren't done, yet.

But there is also talk of another destination. Now we're getting serious... Very!

Part III
A New Danger

Good news! The Counter Insurgency part of Tactical report nothing on the horizon that will interfere with our return to our dusty home in the Wyoming desert. We didn't release the exact date of our arrival and kinda hinted that the return might be in another month or so. Yea! A white lie. A necessary one. But, there was another reason. Jerry Dickson, *Angels Landing* security was concerned over a major influx of guests welcoming us home that might overwhelm the facilities.

I had just finished my morning run and was heading back to my quarters and a shower when Mr.Scott apprised me of an urgent meeting in the Council Chambers already on progress. Still in my snug two-piece workout clothes for yoga, gym, and run and with gym bag in hand and towel around my neck, I walked in, obviously out of uniform, my hair wet with perspiration. Who cares. I'm the captain.

"Good morning, Captain. Sorry to interrupt your workout."

"Not a problem. I was just headed back for a shower when I got your message. What's up? Theo responded with a concerned look...

"Hannah, instrumentation from Site 1 seismometers have recorded a major seismic shock wave at maximum recordable levels. It was like a bomb was exploded somewhere on the surface of the moon. The tremors are reverberating throughout the moon. We don't feel it because we are not in physical contact with it."

"We have another conundrum. It has to do with the results from one of our *sonobuoys*. It was giving us some really surprising readings. This hole is on the 78° south latitude, reporting a lot of heat radiation. Then we found more holes in the vicinity of the south pole. Our South team found them. Now we have a problem. They are different. Shallow and filled with... liquid water. We don't think we can just drop one of our instrument packages in there. We tested their functionality in everything we could think of... accept immersion in water... something we didn't expect. Our geologists believe there is a geological hot-spot down there. That's what is melting the ice." said Joseph Lindquist, Environmental Studies Laboratory. Then it was Jody Lynn Sampson, geologist also from Environmental Studies Laboratory that took us over the edge.

"Something is going on down there. We have been seeing changes to things that shouldn't change. Gravitational waves are reverberating through the rock strata and suddenly we are showing a growing magnetosphere. The moon has suddenly become alive geologically."

There was a knock on the door. Theo opened it and saw an excited Mary Pipkin from Navigation, seemingly in good health but very upset, with Naveen Patel from Gravity in trail.

"Captain" said Mary. "Something is happening. We were doing some mapping adjustments to our existing Lunar database when a computer algorithm suddenly went crazy."

"Same thing in Gravity, Ma'am. We monitor gravitational waves from off-ship and adapt our controls to compensate for outside influences. Ma'am... the moon is moving."

"Everybody... Bridge, NOW"... I yelled

"**XO:** status"
"Nothing going on, just some people feeling a little dizzy.
"**Helm:** Are we moving?

"Yes, we are. We are now floating south-west at about 17 knots. Oops! Make that 18 knots. Our speed is increasing, captain."

"No, that's not what's happening. We are not moving. The moon is moving under us in the other direction.

Tactical: is everyone aboard?"

"Yes, Ma'am, all shuttles and personnel are aboard.

"Take a count, please. Lock down the hangars. Lock all pressure doors between the ship and hangars. Exception, leave personnel access to ship through the small airlocks, closed but unlocked. Then set all shuttles, Valkyrie and Pocket Rockets into alert configuration in all Hangars."

"Aye captain, all access to the ship is tight. Utility vessels are being moved into alert configuration."

"Theo, what's happening on your instruments."

"Hannah, the moon's rotation rate has increased. It is no longer in sync with Earth. The tidal forces are no longer locked. This is going to cause monstrous storms and tectonic activity on Earth."

"Copy that. XO *Sound General Quarters*. All personnel to duty stations and belted down.

"**Tactical:** perform a full spherical sweep. Report any anomalies to bridge only, even if asked."

"Copy that Captain."

"**Helm**: with full power on thrusters, take us up 200 meters and float.

"**Navigation**: lock onto Earth center mass and moon center mass and record comparative deviations. Lock in your navigation pulsars. That will be our position standard and baseline."

"Copy that. Nav Pulsars locked in. We're already showing changes. The moon is moving out of its normal orbit. What's happening Captain?"

Suddenly I felt motion and grasped a handrail for stability, remembering I had Gravity lower counter gravity effort to .9 G on the bridge. The scientists and bridge crew could all feel the shifts in perceived gravity, too.

Theo yelled...

"Captain, if this movement continues, the moon will move out of earth orbit and go on its own. That would be devastating to our planet. The moon has several vital effects on the earth: it provides the tidal force which causes ocean circulation, wind and weather patterns, it affects our seasons, provides nighttime illumination, has cultural impact (mythology, religion, etc.), effects the earth's solar orbit and rotational speed, and it plays an important role for stabilizing tectonic plates. It could change life on our planet and be devastating to the entire ecosystem and even habitability."

"We aren't going anywhere. We are going to extend our stay here and find out what the hell is causing this."

I turned to the scientists.

"You just became musicians in our *Symphony* orchestra. Darien, we need every brain on this one. Choose your venue. I suggest the big theater. Theo, you're with me. Here's a starter question, could the drilled holes have anything to do with this? By investigating them, did we set off a booby-trap? A signal?

Admiral Holder, would you remain here please.

Everyone had a look of panic. I suppose I did too.

"We are going to circumnavigate the moon at the equator then on a polar orbit. We will be looking for anything unusual. Meanwhile you get started with all collected data, find out what the hell is going on with the moon."

Darien had Sarah make available the large conference room/theater. All left to their respective laboratories to get copies of the findings from the emplaced science hardware and find some correlation to the anomalies. Now it was my turn.

"**Comm**: open a channel to bridge and ship departments only."

"Aye, you're on."

"This is the captain. We will be delaying our return to Angels Landing due to some disturbing activity discovered by our deployed instrumentation packages. You may feel some odd gravimetric affects: dizziness, minor changes in equilibrium. Anything you discover that seems odd, call the bridge. This is all close-hold and cannot be discussed outside your department. Parish out.

Tactical: Silence the ship, close the observation deck and lock-down. Comm, block all outgoing communication. We are going dark. Only monitor incoming comm but don't respond unless it's an emergency and advise command.

"**Helm**: make our heading 270°, climb to 1-0 thousand feet and maintain. On thrusters only, set speed to 2-0-0 knots relative.

"XO, you have the Conn. I'm going to take a shower and change clothes."

I didn't take long in the shower. I was out, into my slacks and yellow blouse. Then walked onto the bridge still forming my ponytail with a band.

"Captain on the bridge"

"As you were"

"**Helm**: report."

"We are westbound, heading 270° at 10,000 feet, speed 200 knots."

"Very well. Have Lory Amundsen, Jake Maxwell, Gus Mayer, Scott Randal and Richard Daniels, come to the bridge, please. Admiral, join us, please... and you too, dad."

In less than 10 minutes, all requested stood in a circle in the middle of the bridge deck.

I rolled up my sleeve and held my arm out in front of me.

"All of you do the same." Puzzled, they bared their arms.

"All of you are ex-military. Some of you may have special skills you may not even be aware of. The hair on my arms is standing at attention. Admiral, would you hazard a guess why that is?"

"Damn! I don't believe this. I was an observer on an *Ohio*-class ballistic missile submarine out of Faslane, Scotland. We were on maneuvers with a U.S destroyer and our British counterparts, when suddenly the captain called *'Full Stop, rig for silent running.'* He was looking at his arm like you are now, Captain. He knew there was another sub close by, he felt it. You were on a submarine, weren't you." throughout the bridge you could hear a pin drop. The admiral had a look of fear... and said...

"We are not alone out here, are we?" I smiled...

"No, we are not. Francine, shoot the ship. Full Stop, set conditions ultra-quiet. All decks nobody move. Shut down anything that shakes, rattles or rolls."

Dad quickly turned to the bridge tactical position, Theo ran to the science position and sat down. I called out...

"Theo, passive only. You too, Tactical. No radar, laser ranging, no transmissions of any sort. Helm, set main screen view 360°. No lights. Status:"

"Holding position 10,000 feet. Not moving."

"Let her float. Do not compensate with thrusters. See if we have GMI. We were just told that the moon suddenly has some more gravity and a magnetosphere. Then move us ahead at 10 knots. And check operation of the collars."

"It's working, Captain. Collars working fine."

"Ok, now we coast."

"Aye, GMI at station keeping."

"**Gravity**: return bridge gravity to full Counter Gravity."

"Aye, Counter Gravity now full, ship wide."

"Very well. Jake, is the *Dragon Slayer* complete?"

"It is. We haven't tested it outside but all systems have tested functional."

"Excellent. Jake, as quietly as you can, gather up your best and make the beast ready to launch but with these modifications: First, move it to the deployment position at the portside airlock. Power-off the search detection array. I want it silent, too. Put the on-board ACPU at station keeping, stand by to purge the VASIMR engines, place at station keeping as well. Do we have any sentinels on board?"

"We do, but only the block 2 variants. We have all six. The block 1s are on perimeter duty at Angels Landing."

"Very well! Do a pre-launch check list and load all six into launch tubes: 3 portside and 3 starboard, ready to launch, Very quietly."

"Aye Captain. Why are we so quiet? Sound does not carry in space."

"Correct, but a laser microphone can detect minor vibrations in our hull, although I doubt it would be very effective. Engineering, fire up all 5 ACPUs and both reactors. Stand by to purge VASIMERs 1,2,3 and 4."

"Copy that, Captain. Ready in 10."

The Kraken

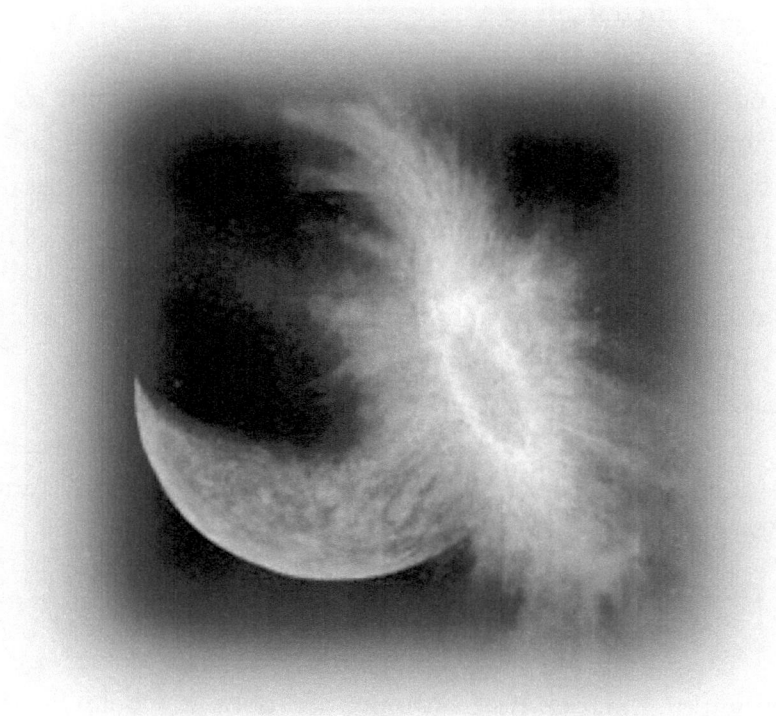

"Holy crap! Look!" yelled Josh Whitmore at the helm. He was pointing to the main screen. He continued...

"What the hell is that?"

I screamed...

"Helm on GMI and nose thrusters at max, back us away fast, give us everything you've got. Engage NOW.

That's debris. Purge VASIMR engines. When clear, point us toward earth, set all four VASIMRs ahead flank for 10 seconds... then flip the ship... on my mark."

"Looks like we're clear, Captain."

"Shut down thrusters and GMI and *'PUNCH IT'* Mr. Whitmore." Only moments passed...

"Flip the ship, Mr. Whitmore with all four VASIMRs engage flank for 10 seconds. HIT IT!"

We really tossed the Seraphim around but now we were facing the moon once again and saw the sun side and an enormous impact crater. Most of the debris was still falling back into the moon but not all. Some very large pieces seemed to be continuing outward from the moon's gravitational grasp and might soon get caught up by earth's more substantial attraction. People from Symphony were running back onto the bridge. It was getting crowded.

"Commander Parish, could you manage these folks, we need room here."

"All non-bridge personnel, please return to your science stations. We will mirror our view-screen and bridge view direct via video comm. Now please step off the bridge. We will keep all of you apprised." I was focused on the incredible sight before me. I turned...

"Mr. Remington, your thoughts."

"I'm still trying to put it together but here is what I know. The moon was hit by a sizeable meteor, comet or asteroid. I'm still working on the approximate size and speed. It appears to have impacted at about a 60° angle to the surface. That's what caused the moon to rotate slightly on its axis. There was enough direct energy to give the moon a nudge that potentially can move it off orbit. Something else, if that space rock hadn't hit the moon, it would have hit Earth. Its size is smaller than the Chicxulub impactor 66 million years ago, but big enough. It might have caused another extinction level event. The moon saved us.

Now! Are you ready for this? You know when you were chatting about that hair-raising moment. Well Captain, you were not wrong. **We are not alone**, and here it is."

On the main view-screen was the moon and debris cloud on the right still falling back. But on the left side of the moon, opposite the new crater was a ship, a huge ship. Many times, larger than Seraphim, moving closer to the moon or was the moon moving closer to it?

"What the hell." Exclaimed dad. I called out.

"Helm: Hold position. No movement at all. Resume condition ultra-quiet."

"Copy that." Then dad said...

"Hannah, I called Laurie Zoloth. On her way."

"Why?"

"Ah! We shall see. She deserves to see this" A few minutes went by and...

"Ms. Zoloth, I hope you weren't too busy. My dad thought you might want to join us as the Firmi Paradox no longer exists."

"My God. What happened?" she asked staring at the apocalyptic vision on the screen.

"Theo, would you brief Ms. Zoloth on what happened?"

"Sure, Laurie, come over here and all will be explained, at least as much as we know."

I stood and watched as the last of the debris fell back onto the moon. The few pieces that had escaped the moon's gravity, began accelerating under the increased pull of earth's gravity. Soon they will enter the atmosphere and most likely burn up.

"**Nav:** what is the status of the moon's movement?"

"Captain, the rotational motion has slowed, then stopped, although doing it slowly, the rotation reversed and is slowly, and I mean slowly, returning to its normal orbital alignment position facing earth. This doesn't make any sense. I have no idea how it's doing that. It is still quite a few miles off its ecliptic but that too, is slowing. Might take a month or two."

"Captain, our guest has retreated and is now holding position about 200 kilometers perpendicular from the lunar surface. Not moving relative to the moon, which is moving. Nothing coming from that ship, either. It is as quiet as we are."

"Copy that. Everybody, stay frosty."

Darien came in, his eyes glued to the video screen. With him was Rear Admiral Bascom Holder retired.

"Hey Darien, Admiral, welcome to *'Star Trek - Wrath of Kahn'*.

So, Laurie. Are you still glad you came along on Seraphim's first Star Trek episode?"

"That depends on the outcome, I guess. You don't seem too ruffled. What's the plan?"

"Oh! Am I supposed to have a plan? How much influence do you think this itsy-bitsy little ship might have out there?"

"How big is that thing?" she asked.

"Tactical, would you care to answer that?"

"We make her out to be over 2 kilometers long, at least .25 kilometers wide. Big son-of-bitch. What do you think, captain?"

"Interesting! When the lunar regolith settles we should take a run over to the new crater and assess the damage. I'd like to hear a report about the status of all our deployed devices. Are they still reporting and if so, what are the readings? Please have a report ready in 30 minutes here on the bridge. That is all. I'm going for a hamburger."

Someone yelled...

"Wait! What about the alien spaceship?" I stopped... turned, and looked curious...

"Which one?" everybody stared at me like I had lost my mind.

"Perhaps you haven't noticed but we are not on earth anymore. They are not at their home planet, either. Out here... we are both aliens. At least we have something in common. And... that, my friends, is a start. Back in 20." I left.

Laurie Zoloth burst out laughing, then everybody chimed in. They sat down wherever there was space and stared at the view-screen. They looked at our moon with a hole in it and a spaceship nearly the size of Manhattan. Someone said...

"We are aliens."

Laurie looked at Darien.

"So... Darien, how's your dream coming along?"

"Doesn't this bother you? You seem to be awfully calm."

"Look, sooner or later something like this was bound to happen. We have been waiting, speculating and imagining this for centuries. Now, here we are. At least we're in a comfortable space ship close to the action in a front row seat. Imagine being in Angels Landing with a cloudy sky, unable to see anything and wondering what's going on. Or in Washington DC in full panic mode, unable to do anything. You can be pretty sure that everyone down there is scared stiff as all they have are ill-conceived reports from radio and TV. Be glad Seraphim's captain has her head on straight and isn't losing it. This would terrify even captains Kirk and Picard. She's functioning like a submarine captain at war. And, in situations like this there is no-one better than a submariner." Admiral Bascom Holder looking on smiling, offered...

"That is so very true. And here I offer a quote from Winston Churchill...

'Of all the branches of men in the forces there is none which shows more devotion and faces grimmer perils than the submariners.'

Be glad you have someone like her in that chair. She will not be blindsided by people, aliens or circumstance."

Everyone on the bridge turned and looked at the admiral standing straight and tall, eyes on the main view-screen, tear in his eye, prepared to follow someone who was the same age as his daughter, yet seemed to have all the right stuff. He looked around at the bridge crew and saw the most professional group of men and women he had ever served with. They really knew their jobs and were absolutely devoted to her, trusted her and would march, lock step into whatever situation they were put into. There was no denying it, she commanded a very tight ship. He wondered what would have happened in this situation had the chair been occupied by someone else.

The main access to the bridge opened and five people walked in followed by the captain.

"Put them along the edge, here. Thank you."

Various bags with names of fast food shops were put in a row on the edge of the raised command deck along with water bottles.

"This is your only lunch break for a while. Starting at tactical, come over and grab a bag, water and plan to clean up any mess you make. No crumbs in the equipment." I looked over at Comm and pointed to the ceiling.

"You're on, Captain."

"This is the Captain. We are going to be here for a while. I suggest you get some food. Bring it to your work station but keep it clean. I might come through and check that you are shipshape and Bristol fashion, meaning if your position is messy, you could be assisting the good folks in the restaurants on KP duty. Parish out."

The delivery people left and returned to their restaurant duties.

"Where's ours?" yelled Darien.

"Up one deck." I responded. "The crew before guests."

I could see Admiral Bascom Holder and Darien smiling discreetly. They waved and left the bridge. Mr.Scott...

"Have the XO and Lory Amundsen report to the bridge."

"Message sent and acknowledged, Captain." I grabbed a bottle of water and climbed onto the raised deck and sat in the Captain's Chair munching on my hamburger. Both came in and climbed up onto the command deck.

"Grab a chair. They swing this way. We need to have a chat. Take a close look at the main view-screen. There is our romantic moon. On the right, we see a new impact crater. We believe the meteor, comet or asteroid was about 6 to 30 kilometers in diameter. That makes it similar in size to the one that hit Mexico's Yucatan Peninsula 66 million years ago. The people of earth are fortunate that the meteor slammed into the moon and didn't continue on a path that could have begun a sixth extinction of most all life on earth. The impact has also caused a slight change in the moon's orbital dynamics. The good news is the tidal forces between earth and the moon may be self-correcting the lunar orbit around earth, returning it (hopefully) to its original position. But as science officer Remington has pointed out, it may take months.

Now, over on the left we see a ship... a very big one. It seems to be hovering about 200 kilometers from the moon surface... just sitting there. It has been there quite a while, maybe a few days, weeks. We didn't see it because it was over the horizon when we were near the surface. It is silent. We're silent. Obviously, they know we are here. So... what do you think we should do, if anything?"

"Damn. You're asking us?" remarked Lori

"Sure, why not. This is new territory. I might have some ideas. I'm going to call a meeting with Tactical and members from the council. I'm interested in all ideas. What do you think?"

"I'd like to hear some of your ideas."

"Well... We should first take a look at our lunar companion. Tactical... set single view on the main view-screen. Zoom in on the nose of our friend, then pan very slowly down the side of the fuselage. Everybody, look carefully at the image. Does anyone see anything that even barely resembles a munition; gun or missile? Does it have positioning thrusters anywhere? Are there any view ports?" To all questions, the answers were no.

"So, am I to presume that the ship we see is a threat? Is it pointed at us? No! Has it made any move what-so-ever in our direction? No! SO... I guess we should go about our business and ignore them. Anyone disagree?" No one spoke. The bridge door hissed open and a group of scientists entered.

"Captain, you asked for a report on the status of equipment out in the craters."

"Yes. How did they fare with the moon quakes?"

"We are happy to report that all systems are still functioning and have continued to send data to earth. We are still in business. What's going on with that thing?" asked a scientist from NASA looking at the telephoto close up of the alien vessel.

"Nothing. It's just sitting there, like us."

"Captain, a word please." said Darien standing with my dad at Tactical. I walked over and...

"Comm has been keeping tabs on all transmissions from earth. They are in a tizzy, mostly concerned with our status and with our friendly alien from out of town."

"They can see us and it?"

"Yes! The cloud layer has broken and everyone with a home telescope in their back-yards are looking at the moon's new crater and some can just barely see the alien ship. The big telescopes all over the world are trained on us. Since we've been quiet for quite a while they are concerned. Maybe we should break radio silence and report." I looked sternly at him, then looked around and walked to Comm.

"Oh, something else, Captain." Began Lieutenant Calder our comm expert "I have been hearing some talk that the moon has wobbled."

"Define, 'wobbled', Lieutenant."

"Ground based huge telescopes have registered odd movement. They said the moon slowed in its orbit, then speeded up.

"Darien, your thoughts?"

"I really think we should talk to them."

"We are missing something. We don't have the whole story. Dad?"

"I believe we should call in."

I walked away deep in thought. I didn't want to do it. Not yet. But... why not? I looked around at those standing and sitting talking. I walked over to the science station and Theo Remington. He looked at me.

"Why don't you want to talk to the people on earth?" he asked.

"Do you think we should?"

"Yes, I do. I agree with them."

"OK! But I can't do it. Something else is happening here, Theo, that should not be happening. We need to know. It's important. I need to know what it is."

"Would you like me to do it?" asked Darien now standing beside me. I thought about it.

"OK, if you want to. But you must understand, there is more at play here. Something else that we don't yet understand that I personally don't want eluded to. So, go ahead and check in. Tell them we are fine and intend to look at our new impact crater." He walked away deep in thought.

Lory walked over.

"Why are you so reticent? You are very good speaker. Something is bothering you, isn't it?"

"Yea... I'm not sure why, but I have an odd feeling about all this. How is it possible that the moon just slowed in its orbit? I have concerns about this whole thing. I know, Darien is a good speaker and knows his stuff. Perhaps he can find a way to keep it lite, that everything is OK. Everyone aboard is happy and excited and we have done a lot of good science. Everyone has performed well and deserves praise. Do you think they will get it from those back on earth?"

"I guess we'll see.

"What are you going to do, Hannah?"

Let's get the lead scientists and gather in the Council Chambers. XO, you have the Conn."

"Aye, captain."

I walked over to tactical CIC where all positions were studying some readings and were in serious chatter. Dad saw me and walked over. He began...

"We are in a kind of standoff. There is something strange about the moon's new orbital dynamics. In the past several days, maybe weeks, the moon has slowed in its earth-orbital speed. It is now speeding up."

"Speeding up? Really? That confirms some chatter overheard by comm. I need to go to Nav. I'll be along in an hour or so. Help me out here. Would you gather all the lead scientists and department heads in the council chambers say, in 1 to 2 hours? If I'm right, this is going to blow their minds."

"OK, Let's make it 2 hours."

"2 hours is good, I'll be along shortly. There is something I need to do." I walked into the Navigation department and looked for Aldus Franklin, senior astrophysics professor, Pamela Martin, Astrometrics specialist, David Pierce-Watson, planetary geosciences and a much healthier Mary Pipkin, senior cartographer. I gathered them around and explained the situation. They looked shocked... and a bit scared. I told them what I needed and invited them to the meeting with the Council when they completed the tasks I asked for.

I walked back to the bridge and spoke to all there.

"XO, you have the Conn and keep the ship at General Quarters and in position. Everyone, stay at your posts and stay frosty. I'll be in a meeting with the Council. Lory, Darien and Admiral Holder, please join us. Oh, and I need Theo with us. Laurie if you want to join us... please do."

I went into my quarters for a bathroom break and took the time to freshen up. Then dropped onto the bed and considered what was to come. What I was about to share with them will be one of those 'knock-your-socks-off' moments. They want science... they are going to get it in spades. Their professional lives are about to change forever. I can't believe it myself. You can't make this stuff up. I was laughing like I had lost my mind. Talk about shaking things up!

Sarah made up seven name cards folded in half for myself at the head of the table, Theo to my right, Laurie beside him, and the four from Nav to my left on the table. Since the last time we had a 'big' meeting here, several more chairs were added and placed along the walls after the small tables with nice flower arrangements were moved out. We now had seating for about 60 people. I would have liked to have NASA and others tied in, but the earth was pointed in the wrong direction for comm.

Not in any Books

Pauline Baxter, from housekeeping at my request assisted Sarah Michaels with two push carts of drinks, finger food and other delicacies. I had a feeling this could be a lengthy meeting. Mr.Scott alerted me to a message from Nav. The team had completed their study and were prepared for a presentation to the council. One they called a 'blockbuster' of a revelation. I knew it was, now I had backup. Theo was brought up to speed. He was as shocked as I had ever seen him, and I think he couldn't believe it was even possible.

My group was the last to enter. It was wise that seating cards were placed for us. The room was filling fast. I grabbed two diet cokes from the cart and gave one to Theo. He was looking around with a kind of fearful expression. He wasn't alone with that. Dad looked incredulously at me and stopped by my chair.

"Hannah, what's happening? Everyone is wound up tight. And I mean everyone on Seraphim."

"I know. But there is nothing to worry about. We will be fine. However, the very foundation of science is about to be rocked to its core. This is going to be epic. Sit over here next to Laurie. Hey Darien. You decided to join us."

"I called home with a brief message saying we are all fine and doing the serious science stuff, but would be in touch soon with a more complete update. I decided to wait until after this meeting. As usual, you have everyone wondering what the hell is going on. You know something, don't you? Does this have something to do with the alien ship?"

"You are going to love it Darien. When this meeting is over, the revelations will rock the very foundation of science. Then as things calm down, we can take a trip to the new crater and check it out. These kinds of things are what you built this ship for. You have no idea what we are capable of. Let this wet your whistle. *I know why the alien ship is here.*" Darien looked shocked, scared. But, he needed to have faith in the science and the Captain.

I walked out to the hallway and stood still while others started filling the remaining seats at the table.

I watched as David Pierce-Watson connected a laptop to the input of the digital projector. Mary Pipkin said...

"Pamela Martin put together a video, a show-and-tell simulation that will diagram what happened. I'm glad I'm well enough to do this. And I am proud to be side by side with you, Hannah."

"I'm glad you're here, too. I was worried about you. By the way... Happy Birthday."

"Thank you, Hannah. You are like the daughter I never had. This is the proudest moment of my life."

"That you Mary, and I am proud to be your adopted daughter." I addressed the members present.

"We have quite a crowd here this evening. Thanks to Pauline Baxter and Sarah Michaels we even have coffee, tea, soft drinks and goodies. Feel free to come up and indulge your sweet tooth. So... let's get started, shall we? First the news. I'm told the instrumentation we set out onto the moon is still functioning and sending back data that they will pour over for years. That's good news. Many here busted their butts to rig up the cool equipment, some of which still remains below ground learning new things and sending the data back to us. I know all of you received a complete outline of what happened. The moon received a hell-of-a shock. We are planning to do at least a flyby of the crater in Seraphim, sometime in the future. I heard requests to put together an away-team to do a closeup, possibly even a walk inside the crater. If we do, we will use one shuttle for EVA activity, but we will also bring the big shuttle, Peregrine. It will tag along, set up in a rescue configuration with volunteers from Medical and engineers. We don't know the condition of the crater itself. The surface may be unstable so we will take every possible precaution. Lloyd Zimmerman from JPL, Theoretical Sciences Group, has agreed to take the lead in the planning phase. So, any volunteers should report to him or his team.

"Now we get to the main subject and the reason this meeting was called. We are going to discuss two events; the impact of a sizeable meteor, asteroid or comet, and the arrival of a large spaceship from outside our solar system. Then I will have some final notes. To give you all the facts in the case regarding the impact, I turn the meeting over to Seraphim's Science Officer, Theo Remington."

"Thanks Hannah. It was quite a thrill for all of us I can tell you that, when the huge rock slammed into our moon. It was somewhat of a miracle that we were not harmed. We didn't immediately know what happened until we backed away from falling regolith ejected by the impact. When we were far enough away, we saw the result of the impact. Quite impressive. The first thing we needed to know was its size. Well, we now have a pretty good idea of the impactor. The object was between 6 and 30 kilometers in diameter. That makes it smaller or maybe similar in size as the event a long time ago. Since it didn't have the erosion effects of an atmosphere, it was completely intact. Now the heavy-duty science.

We are pretty sure it hit the moon on an angle of about 57 degrees from vertical, with a resulting impact similar to the impactor that hit Mexico's Yucatan Peninsula 66 million years ago. It was also in line with the plane of the ecliptic. Which means, if it hadn't hit the moon, it would have had line of sight for an impact on the earth... just like 66 million years ago. The speed at impact cannot be compared to the earlier hit not knowing the specific mass of each. Since their material is usually categorized as iron, stones or stony-irons, each are different in weight, affecting its kinetic energy. Soon we will be able to work up an approximation of the delivered kinetic energy. Now here is where there is shocking news. As a result of the size, speed of the impact and angle it came in on, we now see some disturbing effects on the moons ecliptic. The moon has for 50 billion years been rotating on its axis only once for every revolution around earth. That is called 'tidal lock'. We only see one side of the moon from earth all the time. Earth observation on the big telescopes noticed that the moon seemed to wobble. Needless to say, that was disturbing news. Our own navigation department has plotted something else. And to tell you about it, our Nav people have put together a moment by moment simulation with more surprises. Here to narrate the simulation is Pamela Martin, Astrometrics Specialist from Navigation."

"We didn't have much time to put this together so it might be a little raw. Others back in Nav are working to put together a more comprehensive simulation. What you see here is a perpendicular overhead view of the lunar ecliptic with the earth in the center. You can see that the moon is facing earth from the same point as it goes around in its orbit. The orbit itself stretches and becomes slightly elongated over time, a natural occurrence. Now from the right side of the screen we see the asteroid coming towards the moon's orbital path. The moon is directly in the path of the asteroid, and they collide. Now if the moon had been in a different position in its orbit, this would have happened." The moon simulation was moved ahead on the ecliptic. The view-screen now showed the asteroid flying through the lunar ecliptic and slamming into the earth with a monstrous explosion (simulation).

"Say hello to the 6th extinction of nearly 90% of all life on earth. *We* would be the dinosaurs. The moon's position saved us."

The members' expressions showed masks of horror and 'thank God', all at the same time. Pamela Martin continued...

"Yea! We lucked out... but we're not out of the woods yet. The effect of the shifted rotation dynamics of the moon included a speed-up in orbital velocity, causing the orbit to extend away from the earth. It would soon define a new ecliptic, more oval in shape and probably would change the orbital month by maybe... well, instead of 27.32 days with respect to the fixed stars, it might become 33 – 35 days. The synodic month is the *time* it takes the *Moon* to reach the same visual phase from earth next time around. This varies notably throughout the year, but averages around 29.53 days. Now, due to the impact, these figures could change adding as much as 3 or 4 days to our lunar calendar. Take a breath, people, it gets worse. Professor Remington, would you like to jump in here."

"Impressive imagery, there, Pamela. Gives me the heebie-jeebies just watching that. OK! We Earthlings have come to accept and depend on various physical formalities in our daily lives which gives us a sense of security that things are all right. The moon contributes to the normality because it has several effects on the earth: it provides the tidal force which causes ocean circulation, wind and weather patterns, it affects our seasons, provides nighttime illumination, has cultural impact (mythological, religious, etc.), it effects the earth's solar orbit and rotational speed, and it plays an important role for stabilizing Earth's tectonic plates. For many animals, particularly birds, the moon is essential to migration and navigation. It could change life on our planet and be devastating to the entire ecosystem and even habitability. It's amazing how we accept the day-to-day normalcy of gravity, air, random but tolerable weather changes. Captain?"

"Thanks Theo. Important considerations, the lack of sleep variety. Let's take a break. Let's say 20 minutes. And grab something off one of these carts."

I darted out the door and down the hall to the bridge. Nothing had changed. Our visitor remained still. I made a quick stop to my quarters. Staring at the figure in the mirror, I began to theorize the effect the next presentation was going to have on the members and eventually the whole world. I was scared to death for the first time in my life and certainly as Captain of the Seraphim. OK! Let's do this."

As I moved toward the Council Chambers, there was a pile up of people clambering to get into the room. My dad was congenially attempting to sort out who was returning from the break to return to their seats from those who truly wanted to know what was going on. These were scientists, engineers, and techs from non-ship departments. I just stood there fascinated by the first in-space flash-mob. Then... my super-cool dad went solid military. I will never forget it. Very loudly and in the deepest baritone voice he could muster, he thundered...

"ATTEENNNNNNN-SHUN, CAPTAIN ON DECK. STAND ASIDE."

Boy did they move. I smiled as I walked past and into the Council Chambers. Live video captured the whole thing and as I would learn later, was broadcast throughout Seraphim and on to the entire Blue Marble. I guess you don't mess with 32-years of exemplary service Naval Aviator.

As I managed entry, everyone was standing, I guess not daring to be complacent to the call for respect. I had all I could do to keep from laughing but after all was said and done, it was damn effective. And... I did appreciate it. That one will go into the books. I love my family. I began...

"Welcome back. I hope you had a good break. Interesting times, these. During the break I took a few moments with someone that is among the most talented crew members on Seraphim. Please welcome Seraphim's premier Navigation Guru: celestial cartographer and astrophysicist and dear friend, Mary Pipkin."

Everyone in the room and outside stood and clapped for the 68-year-old sweet, kind and just plain wonderful lady at my side. She looked up at me with moisture filled eyes and a smile that could melt moon ice. They were about to find out just how brilliant she was and with it will come an astonishing revelation that will rock everyone in the room to their core.

"Are you sure you want me to deliver this?"

I nodded. She began...

"OK, here we go folks, put on your seat belts and sit straight up in your chairs." She said doing an elderly lady version of me.

"Yesterday, Hannah.... sorry, Captain Parish came to us and asked us in Nav to perform some extraordinary tasks. The captain has these hunches, ideas that inspire her to ask questions, seek answers. Boy did she make the right call this time. She asked us to plot the movement of Earth, exactly, against the millisecond pulsars we use for celestial navigation. Then asked to do the same with the moon. Then take that data and adapt it to what we already know that gives us the ability to accurately provide Seraphim with super accurate charts when Seraphim is in space. Once we had a specific motion plotted for each, we were able to run them backwards to plot a history, or forward to project the future position over time. Once we had the locations of each celestial body plotted, she asked us to look for any anomalies in that motion. As a matter of routine, we use typically 4 to 6 known pulsars to vector our positions. They are extraordinarily accurate, plus or minus maybe a half mile over billions. What we discovered was disturbing. First, we needed to show the exact relationship of the Earth and the moons position over the last 72 hours. We imported both data onto a time-line and into our simulation, so it is very accurate. With Professor Remington's help, we applied relationship algorithms to plot the exact position and movement of the asteroid at any moment in time relative to the Earth and Moon and then add that onto the time-line and into the simulation. You saw the raw reproduction earlier. This time, it is exact. We needed you to understand the dynamics of this event first. Now you will see it essentially second by second. The first scenario is the one you saw earlier but with more precision. You will now see it in run-time. The moon and earth will not appear to be moving, but of course they are. Then we will speed it up and you will see the motion of both. Here we go."

During the time leading up to this moment, people in Nav had updated the original simulation file with the precise position data and had replaced the earth and moon flat circles with 3d depictions of each. Run fast, the earth rotated on its axis as it moved along it's ecliptic. Same with the moon, but their rotations were barely visible. The asteroid depiction was upgraded to look like a rock with the approximate size and speed as well as could be known. But the timing was precise.

The simulation was run in real time. Nothing seemed to move until from the upper right came the asteroid. The impact was more shocking to watch as parts of the moon were blasted into space, most of which could be seen falling back by the moon's gravity. Then you could see it. The moon actually moved... In real time. It started to rotate clockwise very slowly, opposite its normal counter-clockwise slow rotation as it circled the earth. It also seemed to move forward ever so slightly.

Again, the scientists were, at once fascinated, but still shocked by the visuals before them. But Mary had more...

"That was real time. Here we speed up times 10."

The earth and moon moved so we could see them, but not the asteroid. On the now compressed time-line, it just happened and was over. But even at that rate the visual was stunning. Mary continued...

"I told you earlier, Captain Parish asked us to look for anomalies. Somehow, she knew something was off. She was right and it gets even better and better. Are you strapped in? You're going to need it. First, something about the moon's velocity on its ecliptic wasn't right. On the screen here, we show the position of the moon yesterday and as we advance slowly toward the impact, we found that the moon was proceeding slower than it should. Much slower. We already knew what the moon's orbital velocity should be and it was down to about 97 percent of its normal orbital velocity of 1.022 kilometers per second or 0.635 miles per second. None of this could be seen by the naked eye, but technology saw it. Some higher end home telescopes have computer controlled motorized mounts that find and track the objects in the sky. They precess the scope mount so the object image like a star or moon doesn't wander out of view, as the earth rotates underneath it.

That's when some star gazers noticed the moon didn't stay centered in the view. The moon was lagging the telescope mount precession movement. Something was wrong. Phone calls were made. Big telescopes took notice. The world could see it. The moon seemed to be slowing on its travel around earth. That's when we heard about it and it confirmed our finding. Then the impact. The reaction moved the moon but suddenly the change in movement stopped. The moon rotated back on its axis to its tidal position around earth and then sped up for 3 hours, finally reaching its normal orbital speed and position on the ecliptic, as if nothing had happened. Before I close, we'll run the sim again as if no slowing had taken place and using our projection analysis, this is what would have happened."

The sim was started this time but the moon was much farther along on the ecliptic when the asteroid came by, not hitting anything on its path, but continued on, ultimately causing the earth's destruction.

"Nobody would have seen it coming. In 10,000 years, the earth would be as desolate as Mars." Mary looked at me.

"Are you really going to tell them?" she asked with a kind of solemn look. "Be careful, this is hard on them."

"Yes! But, they have a right to know. And thank you Mary. That was amazing. You are our 'Katherine Johnson'."

My turn... but, be careful of what? I wondered.

"They nailed it. We have incredible talent in our departments aboard Seraphim. I am proud to serve with them. Now it's my turn. You still ain't seen nothing yet. I hope you brought a lot of additional underwear. Here we go. You all are aware of the away-missions we have been doing while at our location on the moon. We found some odd, possibly ancient holes that appeared to have been drilled somehow and we were studying them with technology trying to date when they were drilled. But, they also afforded us an unexpected opportunity to see into the moon's interior. The analysis of the investigation is still on-going and will be made available shortly. We had just completed all our extravehicular activities and all shuttles and personnel were returned on board safe and sound, and we were preparing to head on toward home, when the asteroid smashed into the moon halfway around to the west. We backed away as fast as we could, then climbed to a position to see what was happening. You have seen the pictures, I'm sure. We discovered, in the process, we were not alone. And to the left at the edge of the screen is a ship. A very big one. Many times larger than Seraphim It has been there for a few months I imagine. Being close to the surface we couldn't see it because it was far below the eastern horizon, possibly a quarter way around the east side of the moon.

We just sat here in our position watching impact debris fall back into the new crater. We also saw the ship start moving slowly toward the moon. Then I realized it wasn't the ship moving toward the moon but the moon moving toward the ship. The ship then slowly backed away but did not change position or attitude. They could see us as well as we could see them. Then, I had the ultimate epiphany. In my mind lay some extraordinary questions. Among the most profound were, why were they here?

In order for the asteroid to hit the moon so precisely and exactly when it did, could it really have been an incredible coincidence, divine intervention, pure damn luck... or could it have been something else?"

Could it be we have friends in far off places?

"I have been fumbling around trying to find the right way to tell this story... and decided on an old favorite of mine. 'Going Rogue'.

What if... What if you were a highly intelligent forward-thinking civilization, a race of people with enormous intellectual capacity and resources that over the millennia allowed you to search the galaxy for other intelligent life using spaceships with near-light or full light-speed capability. When a matching civilization is found, you study that new civilization getting to know a lot about them. What if... as part of your civilization's development, one of your cautions is to not get involved in the workings of that civilization, like Star-Trek's Prime Directive. But, what if, you have another obligation, too. As part of this... other prime directive, you have the obligation to protect a civilization from annihilation like an Extinction Level Event if you KNEW it was going to happen. What could you do?

Take a breath, folks.

On earth, NASA has a program that monitors near-earth objects (NEOs), and can forecast time and distance when the object passes earth. They identify, study them, catalog them, even name them, and follow their paths all the time.

What if our friends do something similar. For instance, they discover a rogue asteroid that has been whizzing around the galaxy for thousands, millions of years and suddenly at a precise moment in time, on an exact date, they discover that it will plummet into an inhabited planet on the Milky Way Galaxy outer rim, a planet called Earth, creating an extinction level event.... over time effectively killing every living thing. Following their own Prime Directive, how do they stop that from happening... They **Block it.**

Mary. Using that scenario, is it possible if given the exact time of the asteroid arrival as it cuts across the orbital path of both moon and earth to know where the moon will be in its orbit on that exact date and time in the future?"

"Yes. There's a lot of math involved but computers do that now. In fact, I can tell you, not only where the moon will be in its ecliptic but where earth will be around the sun and where our solar system will be in our galaxy 10,000 years from now."

"OK, you know the date of the impact. You know how fast the asteroid is moving and where it will be crossing the moons ecliptic, but the moon won't be there will it? It will have passed that point some days earlier." Mary nodded her head in agreement. I looked around the room, waited... then added...

"But... that is not what really happened is it?

This... is what actually happened, folks. Many days ago, that ship out there, somehow slowed the moons orbital velocity just enough, starting at a precise moment in time so it delayed the moons crossing of the inbound path of the asteroid, and at the precise moment, forced the asteroid to impact the moon. That action protected the Earth from sure annihilation. Immediately following the impact, the moons orbital speed increased to catch up to where its original position on the ecliptic would have been had they not intervened, and settled at its normal orbital speed. The moons attitude was then adjusted to fit the tidal lock profile." I stepped back waiting for a reaction. Everyone in the room was mesmerized, terrified, yet amazed... I could go on and on.

Mary grasped my arm and squeezed with a smile. She stood and whispered, 'slow down'. Then said out-loud...

"That would definitely work. I can run the numbers again if you like and can, in time, tell you when each of those milestones needed to occur, or in this case DID occur. I can tell you the velocity the moon would need to be slowed to, mindful that too slow would cause it to shrink the orbit. Not good. A balance needed to be met. Then once the event was over, the velocity needed to catch up. Like a time-machine. It's only math."

The people in the room and standing outside were in utter shock. Could it be possible? Did an alien race actually intercede on behalf of the earth and enabled our survival? Some in the room were openly shedding tears. Darien looked at me, his complexion was pale, but he said nothing. Theo just shook his head slowly, silently from side to side. Everybody aboard, watched the whole dramatic event live on video screens throughout Seraphim. An epiphany grabbed us all. My head was spinning, throbbed. I'm glad it was over.

But it wasn't, not completely... there was something else. Something was wrong, I could feel it. But that will have to wait until things on board settle down.

I walked over to Laurie Zoloth.

"Are you going to put that in your book?"

"Your damn right, I am. That was the most amazing thing I have ever seen or heard. This ship is amazing. Her crew is amazing. You are amazing. It's going to be difficult to get to sleep tonight."

"Me, too, I think. Good night Laurie."

"Good night, Hannah."

I walked back to where Mary was chatting with Darien. He was asking questions.

"Mary, did you figure all this out?"

"No, I just did the math. Hannah came to us very disturbed about something. She asked to speak to us and we all got in a circle squatting on the deck. Then she told us a short version of what she told everyone in there. We were asked if it were even possible. She was asking us to prove it mathematically. Well... We did. She had seen the whole scenario in her head but couldn't find a way to prove it. Some of it didn't make sense to her because it seemed so outrageous, incomprehensible. But it was Hannah alone that solved the puzzle. I'm sorry, but I'm going to have to say good-night, and go back to my residence. I'm beat. I have an appointment tomorrow morning for some tests in Med-bay. Good night, Darien."

"Good night Mary. You were amazing. Thank you."

"So, Darien. Can we talk tomorrow? I'm going to walk Mary back to her home. She isn't feeling well. I'll see you tomorrow. Then I'll tell you what the holes were really for." He frowned... and I smiled.

The ship was alive with intellectual activity. Some did not believe any of it, others just pondered it. Still others were in open intellectual combat debating the incredible event. This would go on for days on Seraphim. But it was not all shared with earth. The comm was still in quiet mode. However, ...

The guys down on earth with the big telescopes, began to realize what did happen and started to run the numbers, too. Many observers did. And they all concurred. The little old lady from Austin, Texas had nailed it. It was all true.

Very soon now, we will be going home. But now? I needed some serious down time. Off to bed. Before resting my head on the pillow, I called the bridge via Mr.Scott.

"XO, when you are able, please bring Seraphim back to Point-Bravo and float at 100 feet and point her south... a heading of 180° as exactly as possible. Go to station-keeping. There is something that needs to be done. See you in the morning."

"Aye, Captain. Have a good rest."

No Little Green Men

I finished a nice breakfast in the Captains Mess prepared to attack the day with renewed enthusiasm. Only a few people were there enjoying a similar morning repast. Most were in quiet conversation but I did notice the occasional glance in my direction. Yesterday's meeting had raised the eyebrows of everyone on board. But I paid little attention. Something about the mood of the crew had changed. I thought they would be elated. They weren't... Why? Time to go.

There was no, Captain on the Bridge.

"Good morning everyone. Hope all are ready for another day of crazy revelations. Good morning COB. I hope you weren't on all night."

"I came in at about midnight and relieved the XO who was sitting in for a while. Jessica is recuperating from revelation-madness. Seems to be a common malady, today. But it has been a long night."

"Anything happening?"

"We are back at Point-Bravo, headed 180° and floating at 100 feet as requested."

"Very well."

"Tactical: Status of our Visitor?"

"Just sitting quietly, Captain. Our friend is still out there. It moved away from the ecliptic and positioned as you see it and is quiet. Interestingly, it has re-oriented itself due north, 360°, exactly parallel to us. Nothing else on any horizon. Some seismic activity has been recorded by our sensors out there but Professor Remington believes it could just be the moon shaking off some of the trauma it received. After-shocks, he said."

"Very well."

"XO won't be in right away. Oh, Darien Hunter, and Professor Remington would like to meet with you this morning sometime."

"Copy that. Tactical. Are the shuttles ready in case we need to go outside?"

"Aye, Captain. Seraphim is ready to rock and roll."

"Very well."

"Ma'am, did they really save Earth?"

"Yes, Josh. It appears they did."

"How? Why?"

"Now those are two questions we may never know the answer to. We need to be thankful they did."

"Yes, Ma'am."

I was sitting on the stairs leading up to the command level when the door to the bridge swished open. Professor Theo Remington, Seraphim's science officer was grumbling to himself as he came around to the stairs. He just stared at me. Not a good sign. I just looked back at him and smiled.

"*Jesus, Hannah,*" he turned and walked to his station, sat down and said nothing more.

"What? You don't believe me?" I yelled over.

"I don't know what to believe any more. I'm a scientist. Theoretical science. I study books and papers by others doing the same thing. Its peaceful. It's something I can count on day to day. THIS... this whole thing is upsetting beyond belief. Others are feeling it, too."

I watched as my best friend, my mentor was collapsing before my eyes. Theo is a humble, peaceful man who wouldn't hurt anyone. We kidded about the box... that damn metaphorical box. Inside or outside. He was safe inside. I dragged him out and it's tearing him up. It's my fault. I didn't understand that insisting he explore the more chaotic world outside the box how devastating it was to his comfort level. We needed to go home, and I needed to go with him.

"Captain?" my dad called. "Darien, Sarah and Jessica would like you to join them in your Day Room, please. Bring Theo, too. I'll get COB to mind the store.

"OK, on our way. I followed behind Theo as we entered the Day Room. Carl Ledbetter, Senior member, Ships Council was there, too. It was very quiet. I moved to one of the side chairs. I did not feel comfortable sitting in the traditional Captain's position at the table. Theo sat opposite and was stifling tears. I was, too. Did I do something wrong? Was I so wrapped up in what had happened that I did not consider the feelings of the crew. What was happening to me? I looked around at the faces at the table. None were looking at me. They seemed to just stare at the table before them, perhaps not knowing what to say. I stumbled forward...

"I just found out that I hurt my most loyal and trusted friend by jumping headlong into solving a major scientific riddle. I did it with good intentions but without considering the effect it might have on everyone around me. It's always *damn the torpedo's, full speed ahead,* for me isn't it? My old CO, Captain Freeman always considered the crew. We had our tough moments where things got really tight, but never once was it shoved down our throats and always, he somehow found a way to relax the moment and smile, talk in low tones and inspire confidence in all of us. I guess I didn't learn that side of command. Maybe I lack the wisdom that more senior officers have cultivated over the years, and I believe now, is a necessary requirement to be a complete commanding officer. Perhaps I'm really not fully qualified for this job." I stared at the table ready to cry my eyes out. I didn't... but wished I could.

"STOP!" it was Carl Ledbetter. "This get-together was not to lay blame on you for not including a more sensitive element on recent events. How could you? How could anyone? That was a gigantic monster out there that nearly wiped out the entire human race... our entire planet. It scared us to death, Hannah. We are all fairly smart people on this ship and that... thing, a natural occurrence, to be sure, rallied our darkest fears and for many of us pushed us right to the edge with terror and hopelessness. Some even wonder now if being out here is biting off more than we can chew.

Yet, there you stood, majestically on the bow of this ship, sword held high, ready to do battle with the Kraken. I can't do that, Hannah. I'm not strong enough. *I'm just not strong enough.*" And he broke into tears. He wasn't alone. The moment was long and difficult. No one moved, other than to wipe a tear away. I was shocked. Then, I realized something...

"I see now, it really wasn't necessary to lay out all the dynamics of what happened in such detail. I look at you and see the most amazing people, so smart, spending years studying an intriguing possibility, fussing over details. I really look up to you, unable to see and understand what you do. I feel inadequate and realize I'm simply a bus driver trying to be something maybe I'm not yet qualified to do. I was wrong... all wrong. I should not have expected anyone to..." and I stopped, then continued...

"It was, what it was. And it was over. Time to go home and appreciate what we have. I realized how vulnerable we are and I felt inadequate at that moment. I didn't do anything, other than move the ship out of the way so that ET over there in the big ship could save us." then I did go one step further.

"I had another hunch. I asked the XO last night to return Seraphim to Point Bravo at 100-foot level facing exactly 180°... south. Why did I do that? Then guess what? This morning I looked over at ET and that ship is now facing 360° at 100-foot altitude exactly parallel with us. It is a message.

I was fully prepared to put on the blue suit, hop in a Valkyrie, and park out on the lunar plain, grab 2 lawn chairs, set them 10 feet apart facing each other, then sit out in the silence of our moon and wait. I believe even now, I would have been joined out there, alone, defenseless, away from our ships, face to face so that I could find a way to say, thank you. I do care about every living soul on this ship and all the life on earth. But I do apologize for my lack of empathy for the feelings as people had to deal with the horror. I just didn't see it. Mary actually cautioned me before I spoke. She saw that I went too far. I'm so sorry." Darien quietly began...

"The intent of this meeting was not to strip you of your position or reprimand you in any way. In fact, it may be an opportunity, at least for me, to say thank you for standing on that bow doing the right thing, while we helplessly watched. So... you would really go out there and meet one of them alone?"

"I would."

"Do you still want to."

"I do."

"Why?"

"It's first contact. It's the right thing to do."

"Why lawn chairs?"

"Laurie Zoloth, in her book on the *Lewis and Clark expedition*, described the part played by the Shoshone Indian girl, Sacagawea, baby in her arms, when hostile tribes bent on killing everyone in the expedition were stopped because no one with hostile intent would journey into Indian territory with an Indian woman with a baby. Sacagawea acted as translator, too. She was quoted once as saying...

'Everything I do is for my people.' I was genuinely moved by that, and... it is the right thing to do."

"Why, lawn chairs?"

"Simplicity in a complex and chaotic universe."

There was complete silence for several minutes.

"May I be excused, please?" I was ready to break down.

"Yes, of course."

I walked out and onto the bridge but no-one said anything. The view-screen had a full broadside view of the other ship still sitting motionless a mile away. I sat for another 5 minutes on the stairs. Then, I decided, and walked slowly to Hangar 1.

The Right Thing to Do
Objective view...

W"here's the Captain?" asked Theo returning to his position as Science Officer. He looked at the full screen view of the alien ship sitting quietly. Others from the meeting and more, entered the bridge staring at the ship that the civilization had used to save human lives.

"Where's the Captain?" asked Theo again.

"There." said Lt. Jeffrey Lancaster quietly at the Helm.

"She just loaded up two lawn chairs and has gone to put on her space suit."

"There she is."

They all watched as the door on the Valkyrie closed and sealed. The inner door to the hangar opened and the sleek little fighter moved effortlessly into the air lock.

"Shouldn't we stop her?"

"No." said Theo emphatically with a touch of a smile on his face but still... he had a tear in his eye.

"Why?"

"Because, it's the right thing to do."

It became absolutely quiet on the bridge. They watched as the Val moved very slowly toward the center of an open area a few kilometers west of the Copernicus crater and south of Eratosthenes. She stopped and in about 10 minutes the side door opened, hinged from the bottom with stairs like on some business jets. She slowly walked to a point about one hundred meters from the Val, shook one chair until it opened, placed it on the surface facing east, then walked about ten feet further, flopped the second chair open and placed it facing the first. She walked back to the first and calmly sat down, folded her arms in front of her and waited.

Eyes were glued to the view-screen on the bridge, nervously watching the bravest thing anyone could imagine. Laurie Zoloth had arrived after a call invited her to the bridge.

"Who is that?" she asked.

"Hannah. She seems to think the alien ship will send someone over." Theo added...

Then Jeffrey Lancaster at the helm said...

"Something is happening on the ship. Looks like an airlock door is opening."

From the opening came a small ship.

"That's a shuttlecraft. It's heading toward Hannah." All watched as the ship, only slightly larger than the Valkyrie, set down oriented exactly parallel in the same north-south orientation as the Valkyrie. Hannah remained seated.

A door opened on the alien shuttle and a tall figure emerged, looked around before stepping down onto the grey powdery surface. The figure was wearing a white spacesuit, covering details of the tall slender being. Hannah stood, moved one step forward and stopped. The other figure didn't move any further, just seemed to watch Hannah. Hannah raised both arms outstretched to each side. Then slowly pivoted a full 360° showing the alien that she was wearing no weapons.

The figure stepped forward several paces, stopped and repeated Hannah's action showing her he wore no weapons, either. Then slowly he moved forward in slow steps toward the human in the blue space suit. She remained standing as the alien moved beside the other chair. Now only 10 feet apart they seemed to just look at each other.

"That's right, Hannah. Easy does it. No fast moves." Laurie was enchanted. She was watching a First-Contact live, as it was happening. Tears rolled down the elderly face and stopped at the big smile.

Hannah turned a quarter turn to her left looking up at our blue planet Earth. She raised both her arms toward Earth palms up then slowly brought them to her chest like holding a baby, bowing slightly as she did. She turned to the alien, pointed to the Earth with her left arm and again brought it together with her right arm across her chest. Looking straight at the alien she took one step closer, grasped her hands together in front of her, intertwining her fingers and bowed to him, slowly down then up.

"That was a thank-you gesture. But will he understand it?"

He made a step closer, turned, looked into the sky to the north, extended his left arm with finger outstretched and straight pointing to a position in the sky. He then brought both arms up parallel with palms up and quickly brought them to his chest and bowing slightly.

"He pointed to his home world. This is amazing."

Hannah reached behind her and rattled her chair, then sat down. She pointed to his chair and motioned for him to sit down, too. He carefully reached for the chair and moved it gently, then slowly sat. He looked around then back at her. They remained sitting, looking intently at each other for several minutes. He suddenly looked surprised and tapped his ear. He had just gotten a message from his ship. He leaned forward, turned to his right and pointed to the ship. He pointed at himself and then to the ship. He was being called back. Hannah stood but the alien was having difficulty standing up out of the chair. Hannah moved forward, extended her right hand to the alien and moved backward like she was pulling. She moved forward again with arm extended and nodded to her arm. This time he took her hand, she pulled and helped him to his feet. Then backed away just a bit giving him space. The people on the bridge were amazed at the interplay. Then the alien did something that blew everyone's minds. He stood straight and tall facing Hannah, looked up and to his left with left arm raised and again pointed, held that pose, then with his right arm he pointed to Earth. He was pointing to both home worlds. Then slowly he brought both arms together in front of him, locking his fingers and nodded to his locked hands. Hannah pointed to Earth, then pointed to the same point in the northern sky, brought her hands together locking fingers bowing to them. He turned and began walking toward his shuttle. She remained still watching him go. He stopped and turned to look at her. Hannah brought both hands together once again and held them up for him to see. He did the same. They stood facing each other, fingers inter-locked, both raised above their heads. He turned returning to his ship, she did the same, but stopped. She went back to the chairs and placed them closer together... as a marker for first contact of two civilizations. Like the flag placed on Tranquility Base by earlier Astronauts in 1969. She sat in the Valkyrie with gravity set to normal and pressurized for nearly an hour. Then lifted off and returned to her home on Seraphim. Alone in the Personal Equipment room, she changed into her uniform, washed her hands, splashed water on her tear stained face, set her pony tail, then, with some trepidation turned to the door to return to the bridge. The walk was slow. She felt no rush. People stepped aside as she padded slowly through the hall. They had seen it all. Here is our Captain. Here is the most courageous person anyone had ever seen. No one spoke as she passed, just looked. Hannah kept her eyes forward and down looking at the pattern of the carpet as she got closer to the bridge. The door opened to utter silence. There were maybe thirty people there looking on. Many faces were marked with tears running freely. She climbed the three stairs to the command deck, sat in the center chair and said only one thing. ***"Let's go home."***

Part IV
Parting Thoughts

Commander Ed Parish (Dad) stepped up onto the command platform and stood in front of his daughter and asked...

"I wonder if you considered the idea of making a flyby of the crater before turning toward home."

"Who wants the flyby?"

"Let's go back into the Council Chambers. It's a good deal larger and more people may show up. There are a few more things we need to discuss."

"Keep all systems at station keeping. We'll be on our way in a few minutes." She said.

Commander Hannah Parish, AKA, *The Captain*, followed her dad into the Council Chambers where several more people now stood. She was nervous.

"What's going on?"

"Please sit down, Hannah." Said someone.

"Why did you do that... out there?" asked the same someone.

"I had to. For myself, I had to. When I came aboard Seraphim and was offered a position among you. I was overwhelmed and wanted to succeed by making Seraphim and her crew ready to take on an adventure that has never been done before. I don't have your background in science, but I do have some skills I learned as a sailor. I tried very hard to understand the science that you all know and the part that science plays in the places we were going to go. As a navigator I began to feel comfortable in my job. I messed up a few times... going rogue trying to add, or improve what Angels

Landing and Seraphim were. But then, when the top two people in the chain of command suddenly disappeared, I was thrust into a position I really was not prepared for. But Seraphim needed a Captain. My dad said "Your next on the succession roster so 'Suck it up'." And I did, yet still hoping Darien and Sarah would come back so I could move back into a position I felt I WAS qualified for, and felt competent to do. That didn't happen, so I Sucked it Up and took charge of my insecurities and learned to be... a captain. In the process, I lost sight of something even as important as being a ship's Master. I had forsaken my best friend, Evie, my sister, Amanda, friends from the Lindstrom, and Annapolis, and the feelings of my own shipmates here on Seraphim. I forgot we are all human with concerns, fears and dreams. And a need to love. That chair out there, the center chair is not a throne of power, it's the seat of respect so that the crew has someone to believe in, lead them, protect them. That person must be strong enough and able enough to ensure the physical integrity of the ship, ensure all personnel are properly trained to do incredibly complex tasks, to join each together as a cohesive team. That person must be the personification of trust; must be a father, a mother, sister and brother to all on board, never flinching when times get tough. To be a symbol of strength that others may follow confident in the outcome because he or she says there will be one. Well, it is good we head on home. We were tested and with the help of some far-off friends, we are able to go back to a lush, familiar place, and for some of us live out the rest of our lives in peace. I suggest you ask the XO to move to the center seat, go see the crater and then take us home. Is there anything else...?"

She didn't realize it, but XO, Jessica Pearson was present for the entire meeting.

"Yes, there is, if I may be allowed to speak. For those who don't know me, I am Jessica Pearson, presently the XO she just spoke of. I'm wondering if any of our learned scientists have ever held a command level position. None, huh? I'm not surprised. Personally, I think Seraphim is very fortunate. You have several experienced commanders among the top-tier bridge officers and in your engineering ranks. Her father, Edward Parish came aboard Seraphim with his wife Lorraine at the behest of Hannah and invited by Darien Hunter for a tour as their daughter was being hired on as a crew member.

Ed was a decorated Navy veteran during the Vietnam conflict flying RF-4 Reconnaissance Phantoms over North Vietnam, dodging SAMs and chased by Mig-21s. Later he served aboard several aircraft carriers flying the F-14 Tomcat and later the FA-18 Super Hornet. He served as an FA-18 squadron commander on his last carrier assignment until assigned a new job as Tactical Advisor aboard the brand-new Carrier Gerald R Ford, again serving with distinction. He retired as a Navy Captain, O6.

Lorraine Parish was an Air Force Captain assigned as a medic and served under fire in Afghanistan and Iraq. Eight years later she resigned her commission to continue her education and became a full medical doctor.

During their tour here, Ed was studying the so-called tactical position on Seraphim and found it profoundly lacking. Once again, he raised his right hand and became chief of security. He rebuilt Tactical into what it is today with dual purpose utility shuttles doubling as fighters if necessary. He collaborated with teams of former SEALS, Spec-Ops, and former Secret Service Personnel on-board and in politically hot spots in the eastern United States. His teams have the pulse of those determined to do us harm. Did any of you think of that? No, of course not.

Lorraine Parish found Seraphim's hospital, called Med-Bay without any doctors and only a handful of duty nurses. What did she do? She stepped forward, raised her right hand and hired on as Medical Administrator, overseeing the entire Seraphim medical division. With her knowledge and contacts, Seraphim now has a working hospital that can do anything that an off-ship hospital can do and even includes a surgical center and a cancer ward, fully staffed with medical professionals. Did any of you think of that? No, of course not.

That tall woman standing there is Lory Amundsen. An honor graduate of the United States Air Force Academy, she has spent her entire career flying two of the F-15 Eagle variants. One of the most powerful air superiority fighters in the world with a top speed in excess of mach 2.5 and with several assignment in the U.S and overseas she finished up her 23 years of service as squadron Commander of an Aggressor squadron, part of the Air Force Warfare Center teaching adversary fighter tactics at Nellis Air Force Base. She retired from the Air Force as an O6.

Another; Augustus (Augie) Lincoln, Lieutenant-Commander, Chief of the Boat (COB) aboard Seraphim, is #3 in succession. Former British Royal Navy. Last assignment aboard *HMS Iron Duke (F234)* a Guided-Missile Frigate. Left the Royal Navy as a Commander O4.

Me? I graduated from the Air Force Academy, I'm a twenty-year Air Force veteran having been a C-130 Command Pilot and squadron executive officer? I retired as a Colonel O6"

There are others in positions all throughout Seraphim. We have everything covered. And who tied it all together? That courageous young woman there. From my perspective and that of others, she is the finest Commanding Officer any of us have ever served under.

Seraphim has some of the best, most learned scientists anywhere. All of us respect and salute your knowledge and understanding of the universe. I am privileged to work with and for you as we reach out and explore. But you have to be aware of something. This is a very rough playground out here. We don't understand all the rules. We can get seriously hurt.

Who was it that prepared everyone aboard for space flight by instituting two Boot Camps?

Was it you? No! It was her.

Who trained virtually everyone on the bridge and departments to be ready for anything by challenging them with her famous 'What-Ifs?"

Was it you? No! It was her.

Who took the time with a mastery of the craft to run drills without warning that created the finest, most competent crew anyone has ever seen?

Was it you? No! It was her.

Speaking of science. Here is something maybe you should ponder. Who was one of the first to put boots on the Lunar soil? On this trip?

Was it you? No! It was her.

Who was it that took a romp out there in a shuttle and found holes dug by extraterrestrials?

Was it you? No! It was her.

Who was it who insisted on what to do in the face of a possible first contact?

Was it you? No! It was her. You never even considered it.

Who was it that suddenly knew we were not alone out here?

Was it you? No! It was her.

As Professor Ledbetter said... Who was it that *stood majestically on the bow of this ship, sword held high, ready to do battle with the Kraken?*

Was it you? No! It was her.

Who was it that instantly moved this ship out of harm's way when thousands of tons of impact ejecta were tossed far out into space. Then backed us far enough to be able to understand what befell the moon. Did you step forward as scientists to inquire what happened and how the earth would be affected. No, you didn't. Hannah collaborated with the Navigation department and Seraphim's Science Officer. Together, with the extraordinary talent serving there, told us what happened so she could brief you. She felt you would want to know. Why? Because you are scientists. With her extraordinary team, did they nail every nuance of the event and succinctly relay it bit by bit so you would understand? Yes! Why? Because you are scientists and you would want to know. But, did you really want to know? NO! Apparently not. Instead you shunned her. Even from the walk from the Personal Equipment room to the bridge. People she passed... She felt shunned. Were you afraid? Yes of course you were. Did she immediately see your pain? No, she didn't and she feels very bad about that. But how far does her responsibility go? Is she responsible for your fear? No, she is not. You are. Maybe the next time you are washing your face, look into the eyes of your image in the mirror and ask yourself, 'am I tough enough to handle space exploration?' Or should I call it a day and return to the musty and boring halls of academia, drink tepid coffee, and just read other peoples' findings in periodicals with your feet up on the desk. And...

'Oh! The game is on tonight. I don't want to miss it.'

No! Space flight is not for the faint of heart. Exploration of any sort has always had its down side. It can be dangerous.

But, throughout history, men and women have walked out into the night, explored the north polar region, the south pole, western migration and more recently the age of flight flying rickety-wood and muslin covered airplanes. Then came exploration of space. Pilots aboard thundering missiles with tremendous noise, vibration, high 'G' loads and marginal hope for getting home. Yet, here you are, aboard a vessel that is silent, warm, one 'G' of gravity, has incredible capabilities for the advancement of science. Too bad we don't have scientists on this ship that mirror the pioneers of the past. I'm sad that it appears that era in our journeys has gone.

You know what? It's OK. Because, we **will** find replacements that have what it takes to open a new book. You should be thankful; this ship has an amazing crew, cruise ship amenities and a dedicated commander. I guess we left ... *'that's one small step for man...'* gone into legend and history."

The members sat in quiet personal reflection as the articulate and well considered admonishment began to sink in. Hannah sat to the side wondering if she was really up to the task and responsibility of her position. But... she thought, who else could have done what she did? She realized she didn't do anything wrong except maybe could have been a little less forceful with the explanation of events.

Jessica Pearson moved toward the door. Hannah Parish and Lori Amundsen followed. The door closed behind them... CLOSED.

The Bus Driver

You were pretty hard on them in there?"
"Yea, well. I don't care how damn intelligent they are. Those are grown men and women. They need to 'suck it up', too. You are not a baby-sitter, Hannah. You are the only human-being EVER, in the history of our species to walk out onto a lifeless and airless world to meet a representative of an alien civilization that saved all of humanity, and you humbly thanked them. Did our resident scientists even suggest that? Hell-no. My God, Hannah. That was magnificent. That's going to go down in the history books... *First contact...* *Lawn Chair Diplomacy*. Who'd a-thunk-it?"

'Clap', 'Clap', 'Clap', 'Clap'

"Way to go, Jessica."

"How long have you guys been standing there?"

"Long enough."

Darien, Theo, Laurie, Sarah and Ed Parish were leaning against the wall watching... and smiling.

"Yea, she was pretty hard on them." Said Darien. "But they kinda deserved it." Then it was Theo's turn...

"We call ourselves scientists. But somehow, we got complacent. Maybe we sit most of the time in squeaky, revolving desk chairs, or sit in laboratories that are comfortable, with foldup chairs in convenient locations so we can sit. It's really no different here. It's comfortable. I suspect we could lose over half of them when we get back. On the other hand, they will be doing a lot of talking to one another. Jessica's extremely succinct admonishment may have a more powerful and positive outcome. They are scientists and do knock on the door of exploration, but they did seem to forget that it's a very rough playground out here. We can trip and fall, scaring a knee, get stung by insects, bit by a snake, beat up by the neighborhood bully, hit be a car. But in deference to their seeming lack of involvement, they WERE scared to death. So was I. But I had an advantage. I went joy-riding out across that wasteland with Hannah when we found those holes. That is not something I could have done a year ago. I would have been like them. But I have learned to have implicit faith in Hannah Parish. I trusted that I would be OK. Frightened, yes. But confident, too."

My turn...

"I'm waiting to hear if we are supposed to go to the new crater or go home. Please advise. I will wait on the bridge."

I entered the bridge, walked up in the raised deck and sat down in my chair. Theo took up his position as science officer. I asked Sarah to check with Lloyd Zimmerman from JPL who was going to head up a surveillance team to investigate the new impact crater. Did they still want to do it... or pass? Jeff Lancaster at helm was looking at me expectantly. I think he wanted to talk. I stepped off the command island and moved to an empty seat beside him.

"What's the matter, Jeff?"

"Ma'am, we heard what happened in that meeting. We, here on the bridge talked about it and we think you got a raw deal. You didn't do anything wrong. We are still behind you 100%. The XO has some serious Moxie, too. I really think most of the ship thinks you were dealt a bad hand."

"Thank you, Jeff. That means a lot. I really don't think there is anything to worry about. I'm still captain. The scientists just got frightened... terrified actually. I didn't need to spell it all out like I did. We could have waited to explain things to them. There really was no rush. That was the mistake on my part. I was caught up in the moment."

"We all watched you out there alone with the alien. Were you scared?"

"A bit... yes, of course, but, it needed to be done. They saved us... everyone. They saved Earth. I felt it only right to try to say thank-you."

"Do you think they got the message?"

"I do. It was a hell of a moment."

"Yes, Ma'am. You are still the most *Bad-Ass-Female-Starship-Captain... Ooh-Rah, Captain Parish*". And all on the bridge repeated it. The bridge door hissed open and Darien walked in, just in time to hear the salute. He nodded to the Day-Room. I followed. Darien began...

"Listen, I was meandering around the halls of science and I heard a few things. I think they got the hint. Jessica's admonishment hit home. Damn, she was good. She slammed them. Broke them out of their malaise. I think they realize how good they have it and what a great Commanding Officer you really are. You need to keep doing exactly what you have been doing. Show them the way, Hannah. They are now, more than ever, watching. You set the standard. They DO want to do the science. You may be surprised to hear this, but they compared the results of Mary's, Theo's and your findings against about 35 results from some of the most prestigious telescopes around the world. 28 agreed exactly with your data when they ran the numbers you presented to our people. That hit home, to all of them. You are not a scientist, yet you presented some serious truths out there. Sometimes scientists compete for the latest scientific breakthroughs. Our folks had a ring-side seat, and didn't realize the opportunity they had. Then, the world saw your walk of fame, out there. '*Lawn Chair Diplomacy*' has gone viral as a model for its simplicity and effective non-intimidation across alien frontiers. I'm not sure we will lose very many scientists after all. They work for many of the major Aerospace companies that pay their salary. Those companies will still want representation on Seraphim. I think they are ready for a stop at *Acidalia Planitia* even if it means getting caught up in one of Mars's famous dust devils. Oh! You should know. Laurie Zoloth has begun her new book. She said she may call it '*Lawn Chair Diplomacy in the Limitless Void of Space*'."

"Wow. That's a mouthful."

"And... one of the scientists that was most outspoken during that meeting, also happens to be a writer. He had an epiphany. He intends to write a book... you're going to love this...

'*The Bus Driver*', a story about the first Starship Captain who happens to be female and the journeys through space and enlightenment. You are going to be famous. Don't be surprised if he asks to interview you."

"You know, that's a damn good name for a science book. I like it." Sarah came through the door.

"They would like to go to the crater, no stop, just a visual... then home. The view from the observation deck should be good enough. There was also a request, if we had room on the bridge, could a few stand and watch the best captain ever."

"Wow! That was a switch."

"Yes, they are very apologetic. They said, *you didn't fail... they did.*"

"My, My! OK, let's get on with it then. Sarah, no more than twenty may come in but must remain along the back wall. No food or drink."

I lead the way into the bridge.

"*Captain on the bridge*" yelled the XO now back in her seat.

"As you were." I pointed to the ceiling.

"This is the Captain. We are about to cast off lines, fore and aft and go for a peek into the new chasm for the first time. We will not be doing an EVA. The observation deck is open and will give you the best view. We will pivot around the crater wall for maybe an hour. Then, folks, we are going home. Enjoy this while it lasts. Parish, out."

Sarah held the door as eighteen scientists migrated onto the bridge deck. She herded them along the rear wall and they looked wide eyed at the Captain's work place... her office. The place from where the magic came. None of them present had been on the bridge. I didn't pay any attention to them. Sooner or later they might start asking questions but I suspect Theo would relieve me of that task. We'll see. Time to get underway.

"**XO**: report."

"Captain, all departments report ready. By your command."

"Very well."

"**Engineering**: report."

"Two ACPUs are powered up and standing by, the other two are primed and in standby mode but ready at your call. Gravity ACPU online and stable.

"Very well."

"**Gravity:** report."

Ships gravity at 1.000G all decks. Counter Gravity at station keeping and stable.

"Copy that"

"**Environment:** Report."

"All is well Captain, ships atmosphere at optimum balance. We're ready to go home, Captain. It's been fun."

"It has. Great work, folks."

"**Navigation:** Report."

"First nav point set in for south rim of our new lunar feature. Per your request, second nav point upon leaving for home, call it tangential point alpha for orbit of the home world. Atmosphere insertion point over Great Falls, Montana. Nice easy ride into Wyoming and Angels Landing."

"As usual, superb work, Nav"

"Mr. Lancaster. Float the boat to 2000 feet AGL. Rotate on center mass counter clockwise. Stop rotation when facing 270° heading. If our friends haven't moved, dip the nose 30° and hold position. Wait for a response."

"Aye Captain, here we go. There's the ship. She lifted off and turning toward us. they're matching altitude and exactly the reciprocal of our heading. "

"Hold firm Mr. Lancaster. Wait"

"They're dropping their nose, too."

"Hold that pose, Jeff. Don't move. Let that be a beautiful picture for the rotunda wall."

"Copy that." The view from our screen was monumental. Those in the observation deck watched as two alien ships acknowledged each other with a sign of friendship and respect. Live video was sending it, and the activity on the bridge in split screen to our home. Those on the bridge were suddenly very emotional. I was, too.

"Captain, did you know they would do that?"

"Not sure, but I thought they might. I hoped."

"They are turning away Captain, heading north-north-east, climbing fast. Whoa! They are gone. Your '*Lawn Chair Diplomacy*' really worked. That was magnificent. No one else could ever have done that."

"Tactical, recover the Sentinel."

"Coming in, Captain. We got the shot."

"Helm turn to port, heading 103°, maintain 2000 feet AGL, and make our speed 200 knots relative."

"ENGAGE"

"Heading 103°, 2000 feet, 200 knots, Aye"

Going Home... but first...

Seraphim approached the looming crater. It was huge but not quite as big as I thought it would be. It was, however, deep.

"Mr. Lancaster. Pivot the ship to port stopping when pointing at the crater center. Now here's your challenge. Keeping the nose focused on the crater center, slip sideways to starboard at no more than 10 knots. Stay outside the crater walls but scribe a circle around the rim until we come back here. Think you can do that, Jeff?"

"You bet, Captain."

"Keep in mind, Jeff, the asteroid came in on about a 60° degree angle at impact. That means the crater walls will be taller on the west side where the moon's surface was piled higher. The east will be somewhat shallow."

"Copy-that. Am monitoring the keel line. No scratched paint today."

"We are taking a lot of high res pictures for you folks back there to study. Tactical, launch second Sentinel. Fly into the crater at about 10 feet. Let's see what it can tell us."

"Hannah, the center of the crater is very hot. We may want to back up some."

"Agreed. Jeff, back us away 200 meters. Widen our radius but keep pivoting on the center."

"Copy that. Backing off."

"Ma'am, that surface is very thin dust. It is quick-sand. It also may be a dust covered lava lake. It would not support an EVA. Besides it may melt our suits. We prefer to stay inside, thank you very much."

"Excellent idea. Recover the Sentinels. Let's go home. Jeff, continue backing until my call. That's good. Pivot to port, line up on the Earth east side."

The hair was up again on my arm.

"Jeff with VASIMRs 1 and 2, all ahead full for 5 seconds, do it now..."

"ENGAGE"

"Screen to the rear, tactical."

"What the hell was that? Is that another asteroid?"

"No, part of the old one. Some of the big rocks got kicked further out away from the surface. Got stuck in a kind of La Grange point. Couldn't make up its mind whether to continue and be burned up in the earth-atmosphere. The moon won that tug of war.

Helm, status."

"On our way home, Captain. Good timing on that one, Ma'am. Just in time." I was walking around behind the control console watching my crew. Boy are they good!

"Jeff, skip in at 150K feet, slow to subsonic before entering the atmosphere. Then hold at 150K feet until you get to... this point here. That's Great Falls, Montana. From there, go on GMI."

"Copy that. Then a slow descent? About 800 feet a minute?"

"You keep this up, you are going to be a captain one day. Proceed per your suggestion."

"Beginning descent"

"Copy that"

Tactical: report."

"All clear all the way to Angels Landing. They report sky clear, light breeze, 78°. Inner gates around the landing area cleared and available." Darien, near the door had a thumbs-up and a big smile.

"Take her in Jeff. Nice and smooth. You got this."

"Nice and smooth, copy that. Here we go." I was scanning everything, watched for anything out of sorts. He was doing a great job. Only a few hundred feet to go. Seraphim matched position with the cradles, alignment perfect. Descent rate no more than 1 foot per second. Then... stopped. The clamps closed. Seraphim was home.

"All ships functions at station-keeping,

Set GMI to off.

VASIMR engines shut down.

ACPUs as necessary.

Gravity to normal, disengage Counter Gravity.

Make all thrusters safe.

Bring in the jetway and lock.

All departments in shut-down mode."

"Captain we have a call from Angels Landing."

"On speaker"

"Welcome home, Seraphim. We have a lot of people that have been here since early this morning. They set up a tailgate party with nearly 500 cars. Come on in."

"Ship only, Lieutenant Calder." She threw a couple of switches then pointed at me.

"This is the Captain. We are back home, secure on the cradles. I want to thank everyone aboard Seraphim for the amazing jobs you all did; whether you were engineers, technicians, food service, housekeeping, medical professionals, scientists and all ships departments. We learned a lot on our first official shake-down cruise. We have a lot of reports to write, stories to tell, excitement to share with people. Each and every one of you make me proud to be your captain. Enjoy your vacation. Maybe we will have another adventure sometime in the future.

Hannah Parish, out."

Fresh air and home

I know we should have anticipated this, but the news media was all over the place. I decided I didn't want to put myself through that. Everyone was asking, *Where's the Captain? Where's the Captain.? Where's the Captain?* I just holed up in my quarters. I hoped someone would quelle the crazies. After seeing the horde of clamoring people and news media, some of the crew quickly came back aboard. Even some of the scientists. It was mayhem out there. I don't blame them. The media is sent out to get a story, however accurate they choose to spin it. The rest are regular folks who probably have visited before. There are 30 plus or minus hotels and motels in the greater Rawlins area not the least of which is our own. Right now, I'm told... they are all full.

Well, it won't be long before the gates will close for the night. Security and cameras have been watching the movement and will walk the area with dogs, in case someone or many, will try to hide inside until gates are closed and pad-locked. I was tired. That seems to be the norm for me, these days.

Two meetings are scheduled.

A general meeting of ship's crew (all officers of the deck), department heads and supervisors to go over lessons learned following our Sea-Trial. Then a meeting with the Ships Council. That may be interesting given how the last one worked out. The gates closed and guests rumbled down the road to their respective hotels.

'Knock, Knock'
"Come in. Oh! Hey. The main team. Dad, Mom, Darien and Theo. My favorite people. Coffee is on. Sorry, Darien.

I'm out of Earl Grey. If you want tea, try the Jasmine Oolong. My second favorite."

"I'll try it."

"Mom, how's things in the hospital?"

"Good. Everyone is happy to be home. Some are going on vacation to visit family. A lot of folks are doing that. I have everybody trained and my second is staying on board with a few nurses. So, Dad and I are thinking of going home and visit Amanda and family. If you can break away, maybe you should consider coming along. You know, Evie moved back to Norfolk. We won't be leaving for a couple of weeks, so you have some time to decide."

"Actually, I have been thinking about something like that. I have some things to get in order here, so, that may work out." Theo added...

"We are going over to our new hotel. We have reservations at the Hotel's *Captain's Mess*, for everyone here plus a show-up. Dress is civvies. C'mon, it will be fun."

"When is the reservation? I need a shower and prettify a little. Can I meet you in the rotunda in 20?"

"Sure, don't be late."

They left and I immediately began getting ready. The uniform was set aside to be cleaned. The shower was hot, steamy and great. After drying, I brushed out my hair, left it long over my shoulders, did some mascara, eyeshadow, lipstick and blush. Wow! What a change. I had a nice black pant-suit I hadn't worn in a couple of years. Perfect! Bedecked with a necklace of pearls, my Annapolis ring and low heels, I was ready for a night out... on Earth. The ship was quiet as I walked to the elevator. It never was noisy, but the quiet sounds of industry were missing. The rotunda was still busy. A few hosts stood in small groups laughing and talking. When they saw me, they did a double-take almost not recognizing me. But, they smiled big and waved. I returned the wave. A shuttle bus met us at the Visitor Center entry. In five minutes, we were dropped off at the hotel entrance. It was gorgeous. With Theo on my left arm and Darien on my right, we entered the Captains Mess. It was beautiful, too. It was very similar to the on-ship version, but much larger. The décor was the same. It had similar views out the windows of ocean, and town. A digital freighter made a pass but the room did not appear to move like on Seraphim, but it was fine, anyway.

People looked at our group, I think trying to identify who was in our group, over there. '*Is that the Captain?*'

The menu was better, with more choices than ours but our chefs do just fine. I did order a cocktail, a classy *double-pear martini* in a tall slender martini glass. Oh! That was good. I wasn't the only one with a spirited imbibement. There were no spirits served on Seraphim as a matter of protocol, only wine with dinner. Darien selected an *Old Fashioned* with genuine Kentucky Bourbon from Buffalo Trace. Theo stayed with a light *Cabernet* wine from California. Mom, a *Moscow Mule,* Dad... a *Manhattan* . Dinner was scrumptious. Everyone looked tired. I certainly was.

We all managed to get a little tipsy and it showed as each told an anecdote from our recent travels. Time to go home. I walked back preferring to enjoy the light breeze of summer in the Wyoming desert. And there, high in the sky was 'The Moon', clear in the desert sky. It was the same 239,000 miles away as earth was, when looking this way. The walk did me good as I was unaccustomed to the effects of alcohol. I stopped at the rotunda café for my favorite latte when I noticed some workers putting up a huge picture on the wall. It was the photograph taken by the Block II Sentinel in our last hours on the moon. It was a magnificent picture with the moon's surface in the foreground, Earth high above, Seraphim to the left, the alien ship on the right facing each other, both bowing. It brought tears to my eyes, as I remembered that moment.

"Amazing picture. People have already commented on it." Said Darien. "First, they asked, 'did that really happen?' yes it did, we said. There were five other pictures. These taken from a Seraphim starboard-side high resolution camera. The first is you, Hannah, sitting alone in your lawn chair facing the other one empty. The next one with the alien facing you with you pointing at Earth. Then the alien pointing at the northern sky in the direction of his home world. The fourth picture with both of you appearing to shake hands, but we know you were helping him out of the lawn chair. The last is of both of you facing each other your right and left hands fingers interlaced. The alien doing the same. Five magnificent pictures of First Contact."

"The Angels Landing management are going to create a floor level montage of all our pictures, crater, bore-hole instrumentation package deployment and a lot more. Our first time out not saving astronauts. That has a section, too. OK! I'm heading up to my quarters. Great meal, great company. Good night."

"Good night Darien. Sweet dreams."

"I'm heading up, too." I said. "See you in the morning."

I slept until noon. Showered, and attacked some reports in my Day Room. Lory and Jessica agreed to help but not right now. I fussed with the paperwork for a while longer then... just gave up. Mr.Scott pinged my communicator and said.

"Lassie, yer mom and dad and others are having a late lunch in the Captain's Mess, with several bridge officers and Council members. They are wearing jackets. Will start in 30 minutes."

Will start in 30 minutes... start what? Well, I better go. I finished primping, fit my signature pony-tail and slipped on my dress jacket.

"Why the jacket?" We really should review the dress code. Maybe make it more distinctive. I'll run it by Theo. He has a sense for that. Dad has been pestering me to upgrade to full Navy Captain O6. I have been reluctant to do that and I'm not sure why. OK! Off to lunch.

The Captain's Mess

I came through the doorway to the Captains Mess and shook hands with the stewards at the entry which I normally did. The place was full. Some of the tables and chairs had been moved aside in the center of the seating area. There was now a fairly wide walkway that went to the back where I saw our table was. Actually, two large tables were put together allowing for the Seraphim hierarchy, I guess. As I began to walk down the new aisle, you could hear a pin drop. Then from the side, someone bellowed...

"Ladies and gentlemen, please welcome Commander Hannah Parish, Captain of the Seraphim." I stopped as everyone rose facing me and began clapping. Then...

"*Ooh-Rah*, Captain Parish." I was overwhelmed. Then it suddenly quieted to a whisper. All sat, except two from the head table. As two uniformed men turned to face me. I was in a state of shock and almost fainted. There stood Captain... wait, two-star, Rear-Admiral Douglas Freeman and to his side Command Master Chief Petty Officer Perry Newcomb my COB from the Lindstrom. I was dumbfounded. Then I remembered my time in the Navy. I was maybe 8 feet from the pair. I stiffened, stood straight, then snapped my best hand salute. The first and second fingers of my right hand just touching my eyebrow, my hand to elbow perfectly straight, and barely a smile. The two moved forward a little, waited a moment then both rendered a hand salute.

"At ease, Commander." I lowered my hand but remained straight. He stepped forward and extended his hand. Slowly I accepted his hand and looked into my Captain's eyes and managed to say...

"Sir, Welcome to Seraphim" I turned to the COB and extended my hand...

"COB. Damn good to see you again. Welcome to Seraphim."

"The XO and his wife are here, too."

"I waved, then walked to an adjoining table and shook hands with him and his wife. I was overwhelmed, said a few words then returned to the table where I was offered a seat between my parents and Theo Remington along the back wall. I was sitting directly opposite, the Admiral and COB.

"Well, Hannah, things have sure changed for you. Captain of the only interstellar starship in existence. One that really works."

"How long have you been here?"

"We've been at Angels Landing for nearly two weeks. They told us you and Seraphim were on the moon, making history. We decided to wait for Seraphim's return. This is our first-time inside Seraphim. We have been going to seminars, movies, and listening to stories about Seraphim's famous and perhaps the worlds' Captain. I have heard you don't particularly like the fame this has brought you, but it seems people all over the world know and respect this ship's master." I smiled...

"Have you met my folks and our science officer, Theo Remington?"

"Only for a few minutes. I met Darien Hunter and some of the members of your Council down in the rotunda.

"How long are you going to be here? I hope you can hang around for a while."

"Maybe two weeks more. If we don't bother you."

"I'd love it if all in your party can stay. Are you staying, down in Rawlins? How many in your party?"

"Yes, we're staying in Rawlins, and we have four in our group."

I pulled out Mr.Scott and requested Sarah meet me in the Captains Mess. She showed up 15 minutes later. I stood, excused myself, and met her by the door.

"Sarah, would you check with housekeeping and see if we have two of the two-bed apartments available for the Admiral, Perry Newcomb , and Jimmie Burque and his wife starting tomorrow?"

"Right away, Captain."

"Thank you, Sarah. Are you glad to be back?"

"Yes and no. I found it fascinating and frightening, but I look forward to our next adventure." I returned to my seat.

We ordered and while waiting I managed to introduce everyone else at the table. My dad piped in...

"Admiral, Hannah virtually transformed this ship into a model of Nuke Sub efficiency. She adopted many of the ways you did things on the Lindstrom. So now, we use the same call-outs, jargon, drill schedules and challenges you used on your ship. She watched every move you made for the 3 ½ years she was with you."

"You know...?" I said. "I'm sitting right here while you embarrass me. Can we set that aside for a bit so we, or at least so I can finish my plate?"

"Well, it's true." ...dad said.

"I didn't assume this position by choice, but by succession. I didn't move up through the ranks as is normal in the Navy. I adopted the only thing I knew and that was my experience on the Lindstrom. So, yes, I did model how I do things from... you. It works and that is the only thing I care about."

Theo asked if the Admiral had had a tour of the ship. He said no, but, would it be possible? Theo said yes of course. I was looking down at Mr.Scott, then Theo added...

"Hannah, you look concerned, what's happening?"

"I just got a message. Something is wrong. I have to go to the bridge. Anyone want to come? This is as a good time as any to begin your tour."

Everyone was done, and the plates were being removed. Dad signed the bill at the desk and caught up with me. I was near the exit when I said to him.

"You may want to have your team meet us there."

Most of us fit in the elevator down to '8'. I guess I was walking pretty fast with most of the head table in trail.

"Bring them in, I have to stop in my Day Room to pick something up."

Five minutes later I stepped onto the bridge with a pad in my hand.

"Captain on the bridge" yelled Jessica Pearson who had the Conn.

"As you were." I responded. I slowly walked up onto the raised command deck and stopped, still reading.

"XO: Report." She was looking at the fairly large group of people standing near the door.

"Captain, we have two things of concern. Our ops in the DC area have reported movement in our direction. They know we are back and it appears they want to negotiate the takeover of Angels Landing the hard way."

"... and the other?"

"NASA is in a tizzy over something. Says it's urgent we talk with them. Something to do with the ISS... and I just called general quarters."

"Very well. Comm. Call NASA and tell them we'll get back to them in an hour."

"Copy that."

"Tactical: Report"

"Do you have the status report, Captain?"

"I do. Right here."

"The XO is recommending we go to DEFCON 2. We are at General Quarters, now."

"Excellent. Go to DEFCON 2. Status in the hangars?"

"All shuttles prepped and ready.

"The Valkyrie?"

"Ready to go Captain. They're fitted out for fun and games."

"Sentinels?"

"We have 12 block-I's on perimeter watch down in the brush. What do you want to do with the Block-IIs?"

"Load three in port launch tubes, three in starboard tubes. On my call send them up on a perch at 15,000 feet, quarter-mile separation, facing east."

"Copy that."

"Engineering: Report."

"All four ACPUs ready to go... at station keeping. Do you want the reactors fired up?

"Not at this time. Status of ACPU #five?"

"Exclusive to Gravity. System has it at 100% availability."

"Copy that."

"Nav: Report crew compliment?"

"Everyone at their station. Pulsars locked in, just in case. Are we going topside?"

"We might, but not 'til later."

"We're ready Captain, make the call."

"Gravity: Report."

"Gravity at 1.000 Gs, ship wide. Counter Gravity at station keeping."

"Put CG at .9 G, bridge only and operational now."

"Set in, Captain."

"Environment: Report.

"Ran all post-flight system checks, Ma'am. We did an air recirculation protocol which includes microbial contamination monitoring protocols and microbial detection filtration systems checks throughout the ship. All water and food stuffs have been restocked.

"Very well, Keep up the good work."

Med-Bay: Report

"We have a few nurses on vacation. Should be back in a few days. We restocked but didn't need much. All systems functional. Don't let anyone get hurt, Hannah."

"That's my goal in life, Mom."

I gestured to dad to move into my Day Room. I spent a few minutes talking with crew members who were concerned we would be heading out so soon. I told them that nothing has been decided, yet. But stay frosty. I knew they would.

The Day Room:

As I came through the door, I motioned to Theo to join me in the private part of my quarters.

"Theo, it is worse than I thought. Two things are happening simultaneously that has me concerned. I think they are linked somehow."

"Are you thinking that NASA may have an interest in taking over Seraphim and Angels Landing?"

"I have been wondering the same thing but it doesn't make sense. But... there is another side that has me equally concerned. If there is collusion between NASA and the MiB, the 'why' doesn't make sense. Anyway, keep your eyes and ears open for anything weird. Let's get back in there."

Theo returned to his seat and just stared straight ahead. Dad saw it and knew something serious was going on. I tried to be cheerful.

"Admiral Freeman and crew of the once great Andrew Lindstrom, you have billets on board Seraphim waiting for you. I would like you to join us in the one and only Interstellar Starship. If you agree, you should check out of your hotel rooms and come back." I kept my smile but dad knew it was forced. "I would really like to catch up with all of you. It has been too long."

"Sounds good. If we all agree, we will be back."

"Excellent."

"Captain you have a call coming in from NASA, Houston"

"In here, Francine."

"They're on."

"Hello?" the voice in the speaker box said...

"*Hi, this is Lieutenant Atkinson, military liaison, to the ISS Project Manager. Is this Commander Hannah Parish?*"

"It is. What can I do for you, Lieutenant?"

"*Your shuttle pilot just left with 14 NASA people. Some are administrators, scientists, and board members.*"

"OK. We are expecting them. By the way, how's the weather in Houston?"

"*Beautiful weather outside. But a storm is brewing, inside. I have to go. Bye.*" I looked at Theo and he had his hand over his mouth. I called Lori in *Gabriel*.

"Hey Lory. How's the flight?"

"*Good, everybody seems to be enjoying the ride. What's up?*"

"Go internal." She switched to headset.

"We may have a problem. I have been alerted that not everyone you have on board may be who they say they are."

Everyone in the Day Room was listening to the speaker phone and had a serious look. They looked at Theo still looking scared.

"Lory, fly as smoothly as you can and quietly shut off Counter Gravity. Then, make sure your belt and harness are tight. If anyone does anything stupid, slam hard Gs. Also, if you sense trouble, overfly us and go out to Riverton. We will join you there with back-up. Are they listening?

"*Yes, of course, Mom. I'm always ready to do that. Of course. I look forward to seeing you, Bye, Bye.*"

"What are you thinking, Hannah?" Inquired my dad.

"Is it just a coincidence that we get an alert from our operatives in the East, and something sneaky is going on inside NASA?"

"You have better instincts than I do."

"Well, Lieutenant Atkinson seems to have his suspicions, too. We seem prepared. A lot of well-trained eyes are watching."

"By the way, I'm curious, why did you salute the admiral?"

"Oh! C'mon, you know why."

"He wondered why, since it's not protocol."

"Back in a minute, I have to go to the bridge. Come along. Did he ask? What did you tell him?"

"I told him the truth. I said, *'you may be the most influential person in my daughter's life. The amount of respect she has for you has made her what she is today'*. Since Seraphim bears some resemblance to a submarine, minus screw and sail, Hannah adapts her training in the Navy to this paradigm. It works. The crew loves it... loves her for it. They know from whom her skills come. I'm glad you and COB wore your uniforms. Now everybody knows, and their respect follows hers."

"I'm still active duty so I can wear it but I think I would rather wear civvies, if that's OK?"

"That's fine. But, I think she may prefer the uniform... not formal but maybe what you wore at work. I don't know. Ask her if you like."

"For now, we'll wear the uniforms. Are we going to be in the way if this thing she was talking about goes south?"

"No, definitely not. She would definitely prefer that you stay. Hell, she might just put both of you to work. That would be a kick. If you have got some time, I would like to show you something. Do you have a laptop with you?"

"Not here, but at the hotel."

"Good. Have the COB and your XO watch this." ...and handed him a flash drive.

"Oh, do you know Admiral Bascom Holder?"

"Yea, we've met. Been awhile. Is he here?"

"He is a friend of Darien Hunter. Well that's a stretch, but yea, we know him. He's around here somewhere. He was with us on the moon. So, he may show up."

"Does he work here?"

"No. Technically, he is a guest. I think the whole asteroid thing kinda did him in as far as space flight is concerned. He may have returned to Houston. You should get going, they're going to close the gates in half an hour. I'll walk you down. See you in the morning."

"Thanks, Ed. We appreciate the hospitality. Good night."

The Rotunda

I slept in late again but at least I received no distress calls. I had checked with Tactical and things sort of died down, so I took us back to DEFCON 5, but kept up the surveillance. Lori was back following drop-off of all NASA people in Rawlins at the *Best Western Cottontree Inn*. Hmmm! The same hotel Theo and Sarah were kept at. Augie had the Conn, so I met Lori at the Rotunda Café for a quick breakfast. I asked about the flight up and the people at NASA. She said there were no incidents and everyone seemed professional. I was glad to hear that. Maybe I had just been paranoid. I told her about my old boss from the submarine.

"He's here?"

"Yea, what a shock. I was meeting my folks in the Captains mess and there he was, along with my old XO and COB. They were wearing their uniforms. Captain Freeman is now a Rear-Admiral, two-star. They will be staying on board for a couple of weeks."

"Does that make you nervous, having your old CO here?"

"Not at all. I hope I have some down time to sit and just talk."

"I don't miss my old Commanding Officers, they were jerks. This place is filling up fast. They're staring at your pictures."

"Did we actually do that?"

"We didn't... you did. Those pictures will be in every scientific publication around the world. And why shouldn't they. That was a monumental achievement. Uh-oh, we have company."

I stood, as someone that looked familiar but I did not know, came forward.

"Captain Parish. It is such a privilege to meet you in person. You are the most amazing person. The whole world watched you meet face to face with that alien."

"I was as much an alien as he was, given we both were not on our home planets. His people saved Earth. We owe them a debt of gratitude we will never be able to repay. Thank you for stopping by. I have to go to work now. Have a wonderful time at Angels Landing." Then Lory observed...

"For the life of me, I will never understand how you manage to stay an 'ordinary person' with all this."

"It's easy... because, I am an ordinary person. My latte is cold. I'm going to get another and bring it with me. Do you want one?"

"No thanks. I'll wait until you get yours then I'll walk up with you."

"OK. Just a minute."

"Here comes Darien and your dad."

"Hey, good morning. Hanging with the hosts, huh?"

"No, she just likes the café's latte."

"They really have done a fine job with the pictures. At most, all science-oriented theme parks and museums, the exhibits are theoretical... artificial. Here, it's for real. These pictures are not artists impressions, these are real-life photographs, and the people coming through those doors, know it. They go outside and look at Seraphim lying in her cradles and tears come to their eyes. Then they look at the crew pictures over here and the top most picture, and, more tears."

"That's you..." said a woman looking up at the picture, then at me standing with friends. A crowd began to gather. "and... that, too" looking at the picture of me sitting opposite the alien in lawn chairs on the moon. Then they wanted pictures. Me with her and the kids, Mom and Dad with me in between, and so on for over 15 minutes. I must have been shaking hands with over 50 people that day in the rotunda. I did manage to smile through it all.

...*from Ed Parish's perspective...*

"Good morning, Ed. What is all this?"

"Good morning, Admiral, COB. Did you sign out at the hotel, yet?"

"We did, and came over here just as the gates opened. Then we found housekeeping and they showed us to our rooms on deck 10, I think it is. Then they brought our luggage. Someone named Sarah Michaels came in too. She left a lot of reading material, then gave us these... communicators."

"Good, you're going to need them. Did she show you how they worked?"

"Yes. A short manual came with them. And we were given directions to turn them in at security check-points if we leave the ship."

"Where is your XO?"

"Oh! They won't be joining us. He and the missus had to return home. He wanted to stay on for a while but Marsha had enough, he said. They have been gone for over three weeks. Her mom is in a bad way at home. They wanted to be there for her."

"Sorry to hear that. That's too bad. I think Hannah would have liked to spend more time with all of you."

"Lori, did you meet our guests? This is Admiral Douglas Freeman, former Captain of the hunter/killer Attack submarine USS Andrew Lindstrom, and Command Master Chief Petty Officer Perry Newcomb, former Chief of the

Boat on the Lindstrom. Admiral, COB, this is Lori Amundsen, graduate of the Air Force Academy, and former USAF F-15E Strike Eagle pilot. She works with us in Tactical and is qualified in all our utility craft. Also, is Valkyrie 2s pilot."

"You were her CO. She seems glad you're here. But, we need to get her out of here. The guests will crowd her. Maybe you should start walking toward the elevator. She will see you moving and will break away from her adoring crowd. We'll be right with you."

"We had heard about Angels Landing a few years ago. Then someone who had visited here said it was the new Epcot. Then a few months ago Perry started looking into it. He came to my office and said. 'You aren't going to believe this, but do you remember the Navigation officer on the Lindstrom, Lieutenant Hannah Parish?'

'Who? Oh wait, yea. She was the one putting some of our horney sailors in to see the doctor. She was also the one that found that Russian Akula trying to sneak into our baffles when our sonar team didn't even know it was there. She did."

"Well, she is the Captain of the Seraphim, the starship out in Angels Landing."

"What?" That's when we decided to come out here. Meanwhile, you folks are sitting on the moon doing things never been done before and were even there for the big event with the asteroid. And who was in the center seat controlling everything? Lieutenant..., now, Commander Hannah Parish. She would have had my chair on the Lindstrom in only two or three more years. By the way, we watched the videos on that flash drive. She is scary good, isn't she?"

"Oh yea." Lori said... "You don't know the half of it."

"Since we are down here, I want to show you something. See that part of the rotunda that has that big tarp on the wall?

They are expanding out toward the back of the property almost to the barns, creating a museum. Look here." She pulled back the tarp enough that each could get through.

"We need to go through here." The sign above a door said 'Enter' the other door to the right said 'Exit'.

"Oh, my God! Look at that."

The whole area was a work in progress but one thing seemed complete. The room contained a magnificent diorama of the surface of the moon and had only two things set onto the artificial lunar surface; Two worn green lawn chairs, facing one another. The set was large with little else on the beautiful rendering of a real place so far away. The black sky above the grey surface to the horizon was offset only by the chairs. Worn green color against only grey and black. The room itself was an anechoic room/chamber with 99% of all sound was absorbed, it was absolutely silent, uncomfortably so. The designers had a single light shining down from the ceiling from the side, just like the single source on the moon... the sun. A sign in front of the diorama read simply, *"First Contact, Lawn Chair Diplomacy"* The simplicity of the message was as powerful as anyone could imagine. Later it would become the cornerstone of an immense museum with room for expansion that will include items and dioramas from Seraphim's future journeys. In the shadows behind the group stood someone standing alone, looking on.

"Hannah, come over here." She slowly shook her head, turned and walked out and disappeared. Doug Freeman asked...

"Why did she walk out?" Her dad responded.

"What she did on the moon with all the scientists looking on, but never once participating in, was all her own doing. I doubt anyone attempting to talk with another race of beings, never mind from another planet could have felt lonelier than she felt as she sat in one of those chairs by herself doing the right thing with no other humans out there with her. Maybe if we go back there, take a walk, by yourself and you will be overwhelmed by the sheer loneliness in a lifeless, airless, desolation in which there is no sound or movement or indigenous life. She must have been devastated sitting alone out there, yet still had the presence of mind to continue with the meeting. Then when she returned to Seraphim, she felt shunned by everyone except her bridge crew and family. I can understand why this diorama brings back those feelings. As wonderful and accurate as it is, it just doesn't compare to the real thing. On the flash drive, you saw the meeting with the scientists and Jessica Pearson's, admonishment. Hannah knows who has her back, and we always will, but, it was she alone that had the fortitude to step out, into the void because it must be done. Carl Ledbetter, senior member Ships' Council and good friend, said of Hannah and I quote, *"Yet, there you stood, majestically on the bow of this ship, sword held high, ready to do battle with the Kraken. I can't do that, Hannah. I'm not strong enough. I'm just not strong enough."* And he broke into tears. That was a turning point for all of them. They let their Captain... the captain of the Seraphim down in the presence of the most devastating natural event in human history. How she still holds it together, I have no idea. But she is my and Lorraine's daughter and we will forever stand by her side.

"So, will I." said Lori

"Me, too." Said everyone else.

Then spoke Admiral Freeman...

"Ed, I wonder if I might have a word with her... just us two. Would she agree to that?"

"She might, we can ask."

Hannah's Isolation

I am actually feeling ashamed. I walked out on my dad and people important to me, but that diorama, though accurate and beautifully rendered, suddenly made me feel the same alone-ness that I felt going out in the Valkyrie to sit and wait for something that might not happen. But... it did, and it worked out fine. I was able to return to my duties. But why did I feel that people didn't approve of my choice to go out there, or didn't want my contribution to science following the asteroid impact. I am still alone and it scares me. Lately, I only feel comfortable in my residence... the Captains Quarters. I now have my two new books I ordered from Amazon and was sitting in my favorite reading chair when there was a knock on my door. I had locked it, so I got up, unlocked and partially opened it.

"I wonder if we could have a chat. I'm alone. If you don't want me to come in I understand. Your dad suggested I ask." I waited a moment then stood back as my old sub-captain entered.

"I opened a bottle of Merlot if you want a glass. Or I can make coffee or tea. He motioned to the Merlot and I poured him a glass. Then I walked to my chair and motioned him to the other.

"You don't seem very happy, Hannah. Do you mind if I ask why?"

"No. I think I'm a bit down. It has been a rough month. I am wondering why things seemed to get out of hand. I do feel we accomplished a lot. We certainly proved the abilities of Seraphim and her crew. They are truly amazing. The crew IS this ship."

"Do you feel the scientists let Seraphim down?"

"Yes! I think they did. And that bothers me the most. I wanted to do the good science. It is what Seraphim was built for. It is why I agreed to take this position and believed that the scientists were here for that, too. Then, it seemed they backed away when the asteroid hit the moon. I responded properly and quickly, saving the ship and parked it about 500 miles from the impact point with ejecta still falling back. Here was the greatest scientific opportunity of a life-time and they cowardly stepped back. At least that is how I viewed it. I tried to inspire them to take an interest by relaying what I... we, knew about the event. They didn't seem to want to hear it. As far as the science goes, I am not a scientist and was in way over my head, trying my best to understand the dynamics of the event so that I could succinctly help them understand, too. As for me, I had a zany idea and decided there was only one thing left for me to do. I had to go out there on the off-chance one of the other ship's crew might come out. Their action saved our planet and all the life-forms that live here. I felt compelled to find a way to thank them. At least that worked out. When I came back in, people seemed to turn away, as though I was being shunned. I never felt so alone in my life. So, I went back to the bridge where people there do like and respect me. And I kinda vegged for a while.

Well that's my story, what's yours?"

"First, what you did out there boggles my mind. I don't know of anyone, myself included, who would have or could have performed so bravely and with the presence of mind, as you did. I have to tell you, Hannah, that was the most amazing thing I have ever heard or seen. Little by little, people are beginning to understand and look upon you as a hero. I know you don't like that kind of adoration, but we can't alter the fact that what happened out there was heroic. Which brings me to... I'm curious, why did you salute me earlier?"

"You should know why."

"Yes, I believe I do. And I feel honored by the action. So, after you left the Lindstrom and resigned your commission, we went back out two more times for extended missions. The new hardware additions to our navigation capabilities performed flawlessly. I found myself occasionally looking over at your old station on the bridge at an empty chair. I felt sad. I lost my best and most reliable crew member. But I've also learned that people come and go in the military and the rest of us have to move on. That's when we got word that this was to be our last mission. When we got back to Norfolk, the Lindstrom was to be decommissioned. I was transferred to Groton as an instructor. I was able to bring both the XO and COB with me to assist. They were both getting older and were afraid they would get some hole-in-the-wall office duty. So, we stayed together. They both got rank and I got my first star. That lost me any possibility of getting another sea-command. I did get an advisory position aboard an *Arleigh Burke* guided missile destroyer for a year, providing insight from a sub-captain's evasion techniques. When we got back to port, I spent time at another do-nothing job at the Pentagon and was given my second star. When I got back to Norfolk, I started thinking about retiring. My wife had left me for someone more geographically and emotionally available. Then I heard about Angels Landing, the Seraphim and her captain. The three of us decided to see what mischief you were up to. None of us expected what we found in Angels Landing. We started taking as many seminars and lectures as were offered. Then we studied Seraphim: how it came to be, what its capabilities were, then learned of the proprietary technologies. The two biggies being the VASIMR engines that no-one else has, and Gravity. That's the one everybody wants. Darien said he was scared stiff he would lose his dream to those who would try to take it. You promised to not allow that to happen. What was it you said? *'Not on my watch, they won't'."* And that turned out to be a very big mistake by those who would do you harm. Some pretty serious people became terrified of you. Every time they tried something, you blocked them at every turn. Then you built the infrastructure for self-protection. It is magnificent."

"I suppose dad gave you a tour of Tactical and CIC. He supported my promise to protect what geniuses built here and created a rather formidable team of experienced SEALS, and Special Operations folks. Then we were joined by a pack of disgruntled Secret Service people that got dismissed from their presidential detail for political reasons. Not one of them is under 50 years old. Then there are the ones back east that were part of the same fraternities, mostly retirees, that now sit out on their front porches watching and listening for tell-tale movement headed our way. They are our underground network of spies. They love it... Sometimes they sneak around the Halls of Power listening at doors and buying coffee for a friend for information. We do have some serious talent here."

"He said you also have some interesting local help, too."

"Yea, we do. Colonel Paul Bradford of the Colorado Air National Guard, with some available F-16s. We even got nine AIM-9X Sidewinder missiles through some discreet, and I suspect illegal channels which we adapted to our Valkyries. We only have two missiles left, following a real air battle. Then received ten more so all three Valkyries are now well armed. Our own people laid in the weapons control cabling and control systems. Then there is Colonel Jake Hanover, Wyoming National Guard with a division of kick-ass weekend warriors. The local police have been very helpful, too. So, yeah, we seem to have some resources, if necessary. We don't get many surprises."

"Perry is amazed. He said if he retires he might just hit you up for a job."

"He would be most welcome. You would be, too. I sometimes have to remind Darien that we have some of the best talent running and protecting this ship. We all work closely together and trust each other. We are a family. I'm just a kid from back east that finally got a job."

"Well as jobs go, none could be as exciting and prestigious as this one. The only Star-Ship captain in the world. You are known world-wide. And, after they learned about your first foray into space saving those two astronauts and one Cosmonaut on the ISS, then the moon and what happened there, you and the people aboard Seraphim are rock-stars. I heard about your reluctance to stand in the lime-light. I understand... I doubt I would want that either. The crew... and the diversity of skills they have, are unlike anywhere else in the world. Even NASA is awed."

"Have you seen NGE?"

"No. What's NGE?"

"NGE is a multi-departmental work area: Navigation, Gravity and Environment. Come, let's go see it. You think the bridge is something, wait 'til you see NGE." We walked to the long corridor on deck 8 and turned into NGE.

"Oh, my God!"

"Yea, I said the same thing the first time I came here. OK! This area over here is Navigation, over there is Gravity and on the other side is Environment."

"This is amazing. What's that center island, there?" a voice from environment chimed in...

"That's where the *Most-Bad-Ass-Female-Starship-Captain* sits when she isn't fraternizing with aliens on the moon." yelled Lieutenant, Daryl Plumber, Environment group supervisor.

"OK! Now I know what I'm going to do. I have a drill planned that will melt your brains, and with one of my famous surprises, you'll wish you were flipping burgers up in the Burger Shack on Deck 9. Laughter followed our joking. Now, if you would, please, all of you come over here, I want you to meet someone." Those that weren't at critical positions gathered around.

"If you ever wondered where I came up with all the fun 'What-Ifs' and fancy drills. Blame him. This is Admiral Douglas Freeman, my old boss, then-Captain of the Hunter/Killer nuclear submarine, Andrew Lindstrom. It's all his fault. There was instant quiet, then everyone began clapping, then, "*Hear, Hear.*" ... more clapping.

My old boss was overwhelmed. He smiled and his eyes glazed with moisture.

"If you have any questions, now is the time. We will be coming around to each section and I would like you to explain what you do and how you do things, and please answer any questions he might have. OK! We start at Gravity."

For nearly two hours the former submarine captain engaged the extraordinary people that made Seraphim function like a well-oiled machine. I sat in my chair on the raised deck watching and listening. A much-improved Mary Pipkin joined me sitting in an adjacent chair. We watched as he was enthralled as each department shared things he had never heard about or believed could be possible. They were very serious in their talk. When he finally came around to Navigation, Mary joined the others on the main floor as he learned about our Stellar-Lighthouses: millisecond pulsars, X-ray pulsars or accretion-powered pulsars, neutron stars, random stellar anomalies, short and long-distance flight planning, object avoidance, then how space-time was factored into their planning. I thanked everyone for their cooperation.

We left to go to lunch in the Captains Mess. Along the way he commented.

"That was amazing... they are amazing. I thought our sonar people were great. They told me you are the supervisor of the whole department... and Captain, too?"

"Yea, so it seems. That's a long story... for another time."

"They really like and respect you. They said you challenge them to think of things they might not have thought of, and in the process, they developed confidence they thought they would never have had. That was amazing and speaks directly to who you are. They feel a sense of family. Hannah, you have done some wonderous things here. The people I have met through your dad honestly do not believe Seraphim would do as well with anyone else in that chair on the bridge."

"Thank you. That is extremely reassuring coming from you. I'm really glad you came out here and it is really good to get to talk without the military over-tones. I'm hungry. Up to deck 9?"

"Yup, sounds good."

The Captains Mess was busy but not packed. We saw the COB sitting with the COB. That even sounded funny.

"Is one of those yours?"

"Might be yours, I don't think so."

"Oh my. We may have COB-be-Cats. I think mine is British."

They both rose as we approached.

"As you were gentlemen." I said as we moved to the remaining two chairs.

"Have you ordered?"

"No, not yet." said Augie

"Oh! You were waiting for us... how sweet." I joked.

"Of course. Oh, look. Doppelgangers. Two captains. Which one is in charge?" wondered Augie.

"The submarine guy, of course." responded Perry.

"Yea! But her ship is bigger than his ship and goes faster." Augie countered.

"Ok, guys. Moving on... I just want a tuna-melt with potato salad. You?" I inquired.

"I'll go with the BLT and fries." said Boss. (his new nickname)

"I'll get what she's getting." added Perry.

"It's the soup du jour for me." advised Augie.

"Hey COB. I hear you are retiring."

"Well... I'm considering it seriously. I have twenty-eight years in. I'm still young enough to try something new."

"Do you have anything in mind?"

"Nope! Not yet."

"Well, if you need a job, I have some sway with the Council. Same for you, Boss."

"Are you serious?"

"Would you rather I not be? Hey, this sandwich is good. Mmmmmmm! Potato salad, too"

"Captain, you are wanted in the Council Chambers." Stated Mr.Scott.

"Sorry folks, I have to go. Come along if you like. Bring your sandwich." I signed the bill at the desk, hopped onto the elevator, then walked the rest of the way to the Council Chambers. It was almost full. Some were Ships Symphony members. The rest were scientists from upstairs. I sat in an available chair next to Theo. I hadn't seen him for a while and wondered if he was alright. He nodded and smiled. I want to spend more time with him and I guess I've spent a lot of my free time with my old boss. I will change that, in favor of my teacher and mentor.

"Thanks for coming, Captain. We have some news. NASA would like to return to the moon if that is possible and as soon as possible. Some of the instrumentation left on the moon are sending some interesting data. The Lunar Rover is running around responding to what appears to be calls for help by some of the emplaced instrumentation. The built in AI programming does this when there is a problem."

"Do you know what the 'call' is all about?" asked Robert Kleinberg from RJ Robotics, AI Science. "We did the initial programming."

"The 'Call' is not known at this time. There appears to be no malfunction on the part of the instruments because more than one is making the call for help. Some, are not even in the same crater. We believe something new is happening deep inside the moon. So, we would like to investigate it, if you are willing." I responded...

"If the Council authorizes the trip, I will check our manifests and insure we have proper staffing. I'll also start the process of making the ship ready. Let me know your decision. Theo could you join me on the bridge?"

"Of course."

"Is there something they aren't telling us?"

"I think they are sincere. But I do think whatever it is, it is more than what they think it is."

"That's ominous given our recent track history."

"Hannah, you need to stay frosty on this one, too. I think they are not completely forthcoming. Apparently, some have suspicions, but aren't sharing. They trust you now, and have had their own epiphany following their last moon trip. I think they will now step up to the plate when needed."

"Let's hope so."

Concentric Circles

And so, it begins once again. I called the Ships Council. I asked them to join me in the Council Chambers in a half-hour. The first to arrive was Carl Ledbetter, Senior member, Ships Council. He asked if we could speak in private. We retired to the private part of the Captains Quarters. He began...

"I've been meaning to get together with you. So much has happened since our bout with the Kraken. I wanted to apologize for my behavior out there. It wasn't professional or fitting for a scientist to act that way. It is a potentially dangerous world out there. We had the chance of a lifetime to do the good science and we botched it. That won't ever happen again."

"It seems that I have very little time to catch up with the less official duties of a captain, but they are no less important. I need to work on my priorities. You are a very important member of the Council and I have always respected your work and help. You are one of five special people that have been there for me since day-1 of my arrival on Seraphim. There was Darien Hunter, Theo Remington, Porter Williams and Paul Conway who I don't see much, and you. I was insensitive to your feelings. That was a very scary situation we were in out there. Tensions were high. I apologize for my lack of consideration for your feelings."

"Wait! Yes, I was scared, but you did nothing wrong. I need to muster the courage to join you when times get tough. I know you will be headed back there, soon. I just wanted to tell you, I will be going with you and do the good science, as you put it. Oh, there are more of the people coming in now. We should start."

"Yes, we should. I'm glad you will be coming along. Sometimes I need a more mature point of view. And you are my council." We walked back to the Council Chambers.

NASA had emailed me a schedule of activities they would like to include and asked for comments.

Everyone invited showed up as requested and was briefed on a possible return to our Lunar neighbor. I had made copies of the NASA letter and handed them out to all present. Then I asked for comments per NASA's request. We went around the room and listened to suggestions. We also heard concerns that maybe something will go wrong, again.

"Of course, it's possible something could go wrong. That is the nature of exploration of any kind. We got a reminder of that on our last trip. It is how we handle surprises that puts our faces on a cereal box." I was getting frustrated with the whole thing. This was not working. There was too much difference of opinion and we were not accomplishing much. Disappointed, I was about to adjourn the meeting and head for the bridge. I wondered if I was going around and around in circles with my thinking that scientists cannot agree on anything. In their world, research is done in a proprietary neighborhood of cloistered thinking, not often sharing or agreeing to things. Niels Boer and Albert Einstein were cases in point. It was amazing that some things actually do get done. Then I got pissed.

"OK! Listen up. If you cannot agree on the goals of the mission and don't seem to understand and accept that space exploration is not without risk, perhaps you should do your exploration in the comfort and security of your home office at work. You know what Seraphim is capable of. You know what I and my crew are capable of. You know that you have the best chances for success with us, or, you can grab the next flight out of Cape Canaveral on an Atlas V. Your personal problems are not my concern. I'm only the Bus Driver. I'm wondering if you are ready to look beyond parochial thinking and see things not yet considered. People use the term 'think outside the box'. Personally, I hate the over-used term. Can you do that? Can you look beyond and into the unknown? If we agree to another lunar visit, I need to be at the top of my game and have the crew as alert as they have ever been. The secret to our success, and ultimately, our survival is group interaction. I know you are all gifted scientists or you wouldn't have been selected for this mission, so what's it going to be? Are you going to work together and plan a fruitful mission to the moon? If not, I will scrub this flight in a heartbeat. I await your decision and look forward to see your work.

This meeting is adjourned."

I did have a concern that this might be a game-changer. What if another monster does lurk deep in the moon's interior. That was a speculation I did not want to consider. But, I must... I have to. I am responsible for this ship and all those in it.

I need to gather a few non-scientists, but gifted people... NOW!

I messaged Mom and Dad to see what their lunch plans were. Mom returned my message saying they were having a lunch over at the new Captains Mess in the hotel and I was welcome to join them. I did. And, they were not alone. Theo Remington, Darien Hunter, Carl Ledbetter, Adm Douglas Freeman, Perry Newcomb (COB), Jessica Pearson (XO) were there. I was surprised. These were among the very people I wanted to meet with.

"Well, surprise, surprise. Talk about gifted people. This is perfect. May I join you?" Mom responded...

"Absolutely. Carl said he had a chat with you earlier said you and were not satisfied with the demeaner of scientists that had wanted to return to the moon. He knows you better than you know. He alerted us that you might want to talk with the right people about this very thing. And... here you are."

"Have you ordered yet?"

"No, we were waiting for you."

I didn't know how to start, and just fidgeted with my knife, looking out over the synthetic ocean. I guess I had a troubled look on my face and it was well noticed.

"You seem troubled, Hannah. What's the problem?" The table was quiet with all looking at me.

"I wonder, do you sense anything a little off by the request by NASA for another moon trip?"

"I don't understand what you mean?" said Dad.

"Well, just a while ago I was trying to get the science team to define the flight parameters per the request by NASA. They seemed to be obsessed with a probability that something will go wrong. They seemed almost, well... scared. I acknowledged to them that in all endeavors of exploration there are risks. Then I told them that if they can't settle down and work according to the NASA request, I will scrub the mission. Of the 500 or so people on Seraphim, only 73 are scientists. My responsibility includes protecting everyone on board. If I am not comfortable in my ability to do that, it's time to close up shop and go on vacation."

"I agree with that." Said Carl.

"Me too, Hannah." offered Darien. "The lives of everyone on board come first. The science can wait."

"Yes, it can." Then I added...

"We should call Houston and apprise them of our doubts and why. We need to speak to key people. People with decision making power. But there is more, just a feeling, perhaps. Can you get me numbers, or make the calls yourself?"

"Sure can."

"Good, I have to take a quick power-nap. Stop by when you have the numbers."

I went to my residence fully prepared to let them fight with the NASA planners. Functionally I'm wasn't up to it. Instead I laid down with one of my new books and proceeded to drop it as I fell sound asleep. A knock on my door roused me. Several hours had passed as I groggily made my way to the door.

"Hi Carl, C'mon in. Coffee?"

"Sure."

"There is still hot coffee in the carafe. What time is it?"

"3 pm. You racked out in fine style. Your dad dropped by and found you sound asleep, so he left. I have news. You'll love this. We had a conference call with Houston. Your old pal Admiral Bascom Holder was part of the Houston team. I guess the people you met with here this morning were put off by your 'attitude', they said. They had heard a recording of the meeting. It was Admiral Holder that came to your defense saying that everything you had said that irritated the scientists was spot on. He decried the call that you were wrong for the position and should be replaced with someone who was more tech-savvy and followed a more corporate mind-set. He railed on them. He is definitely in your corner. Your mom and dad were furious.

Then another Navy guy stepped forward and in a quiet and professional way, slam-dunked the entire NASA team. It was your old boss. Admiral Freeman laid into them, condemning the whole concept of 'corporate mindset in space travel' saying that the center seat in a nuclear submarine or an interstellar starship requires someone who can put aside the manuals and engage a world that does not play by any known rules, and does not march to convention or political expediency. There are no rules in that world. We fly by the seat of our pants.'

He was brilliant. Even I took them on by reminding them of the total lack of support you received during a time when nothing was pre-determined and how brilliantly you performed during that difficult time.

Then Theo lambasted them for even considering removing you as our chosen captain. Darien followed up by saying they should 'go take over SpaceX or Blue Origin. We in Seraphim don't work for you. We work for Captain Hannah Parish'. Yea! Darien actually said that."

"Wow! And here I was, entertaining really depressing thoughts. Trying to find a way of making things right. I was not successful at all, but what you just told me makes me feel 100% better. I truly am not alone."

"No, you are definitely not alone. But it gets even better. Barely an hour later we got another call from Houston, this time from Lonnie Portman and astronaut Derick Jameson in a private call. I guess they had sat in at the other meeting but did not contribute. They were furious as well. So, they went in and made an ultimatum. They and about 15 other managers and astronauts will no longer participate in the, as they put it, 'Bull-Shit' maneuvering of 'Corporate' mindsets. They reminded the people in the meeting that if it weren't for you and your team's quick thinking we would have lost three of our astronauts in a very dangerous situation at the ISS. They demanded that apologies be made to Angels Landing, Seraphim and especially to Captain Hannah Parish. And... guess what? We got the apologies."

"Holy crap! What now."

"I would recommend you do what you are most comfortable with. Go sit in that center chair on the bridge with the people that respect you more than anyone."

"Carl, I have wonderful people around me that support and care for me. I am so glad you are one of them. Thank you. Now, I think I will go to the bridge."

From now on, we will plan the missions as a group. We have done this before. We select the route, site locations, how to get there and continue the drills and procedural protocols. We will do it our way.

"Captain, got a minute?"

"Of course, Jeff. What's up?"

"Why do you think they are picking on you? The NASA people, I mean."

"Well... there could be a number of reasons, I suppose. One, we have something they would love to have. But, we have it and it's completely under our control. Corporate types seem not to like independent organizations muscling in on what they believe is their territory. I understand that. I have to wonder how NASA organizations get along with SpaceX and Blue Origin. They are independent too, and have made great strides with their hardware development and launches. The thing is, their technology is not revolutionary, it is evolutionary, it is simply a new take on older, more conventional ideas. Perhaps that is why they seem to be getting along... for now. We have some extraordinary technology available to us exclusively. Nothing like it exists outside Seraphim. Maybe someday, some of it will be shared, but we are more concerned about its mis-use than who actually has it. For now, we hold on to it. I hold no animosity towards NASA. They have brought the wonders of space travel forward with incredible new technologies."

... *and that*... gave me an idea. I asked Mr.Scott to find Sarah Ann Michaels and ask her if she can join us on the bridge. Mr.Scott reported that Sarah was off ship and, on a trip to visit family in upstate New York. She would be gone for another week. I went to my Day-Room, grabbed a blank letter size piece of paper and with a pen, sat down and jotted a series of names, folded it, then, walked to CIC and the TAE group. I found Lory sitting with others laughing over some jokes. She saw me come in and rose to meet me. I quietly told her what I wanted and she had a surprised look. I then handed her the folded page. She glanced through it, her I eyebrows lifted. She looked at me with my serious look and a small smile. She nodded and said...

"We really do need this. I'll get right on it." I asked her to keep this between TAE members only. She nodded. I left and went back to the bridge and made another call. Twenty minutes later, Susan Richards met me in my Day-Room. I needed her legal opinion and support in preparation for something I feared might happen. I told her my ideas. She, too, nodded and smiled a mischievous smile. I reminded her of the sensitive nature of this. I told her...

"I *WILL* not be blindsided. I will be prepared." She nodded with a smile.

I totally forgot supper and stayed on the bridge, my new book open in my lap. I finally felt at ease and could concentrate. I would occasionally look up, into the distance. In my mind I saw situations brewing and as I thought of them, I moved chess pieces around on a virtual board. I really do know how to play chess.

"It's their move."

Moves and Counter Moves...

I hadn't eaten anything since the small breakfast in my quarters. Fortunately, Theo came by and wondered if I would like to join him and others at the new *Saturnian* Restaurant and bar on *"Deck 9"*, of the raised restaurant platform in the hotel. It was recently added following a shut-down of operations of two small fast-food restaurants that chose to move to new digs along i80 near Rawlins. The space was consolidated into a small but very quiet chique meeting place for those seeking a more upscale dining experience. With that came a higher price point, too. It somehow melded a classical western ranch-house motif with a spacy ceiling with subdued rings of Saturn looping over the seating areas. It was very clever and comfortable.

Two 4-chair tables were put together to accommodate the seven people that had just arrived. It was a nice atmosphere with just the right friends in attendance. The concerns I had were mostly abated following development of a new strategy for the future of Seraphim's cosmic journeys. I suspected that everyone present, now knew of my mindset. All seemed to smile as Seraphim's captain will no longer tolerate bull-shit from outsiders.

For my meal, I selected a prime-rib with a side of fried mashed potatoes and gourmet mushroom risotto. Oh yea, and a glass of 7-year-old French Cabernet Sauvignon. I was in heaven.

The selections made by the others had similar intent with very exciting plates served... just right.

Conversation was minimal and subdued. That was fine. Then Darien made a quiet announcement.

"I received a call from Dorothy Williams, NASA in Houston. She is a flight director and assistant program manager of the lunar probe development program. She works closely with some of our friends from Jet Propulsion Laboratory that created your Sonobuoys. She was one of the engineers studying the anomalous readings from their lunar instrumentation. She knows about the row we had with their planning group. She and Philip Nordgren from JPL would like to visit us here for a chat. Would that be possible?" Darien looked around the tables waiting for a reaction when he noticed most all were looking at me, waiting for my reaction.

"Where?" I asked.

"Here." He said.

"If you handle it, then... OK."

"You don't want to be part of it?"

"No! I really don't. I think she and Nordgren are fine. So... you do it, but watch your backs. My trust in Houston has taken a furlough. Anyone having desert?"

The subdued conversations continued. Most sitting here were aware that anything could happen and that I was very uncomfortable with visits by people who I now feel might be looking to annex some of our proprietary stuff. I'm glad I put a series of protections in place. Darien had not been informed, only TAE and legal.

We all commented on how good the meal was and prepared to call it a night. Time for my book.

As I sat in my favorite reading chair I was getting 'into' the book when I knock on the door interrupted my focus. "Come in."

"Hey COB, what do I owe the pleasure."

"I wonder if you could spare a few minutes."

"Sure, what's on your mind?"

"I've decided to put in my retirement papers. So, I will be heading back to Norfolk and make the big change."

"Is there anything I can help with?"

"I'm wondering if I can come back to Angels Landing. You said maybe I could get a job here. Is that idea still viable?"

I looked at my old Master-Chief COB, Perry Newcomb. Here was the USS Andrew Lindstrom's most trusted NCO and friend to all service members on that submarine. I really liked Perry. I will find him a job aboard Seraphim.

"Do you like the idea of going into space?"

"Yea, actually I do."

"OK! Go get detached and start collecting your retirement pay. I'll have a job for you when you get back. By the way. We have no NCOs in our ranks. How do you feel about starting out as a Lieutenant-Commander?"

"I could handle that, Ma'am."

"Good. Come back here tomorrow morning, please."

"Thank you, Captain. See you in the morning."

Back to the book. About an hour had passed and I was up to page 54, and was getting ready to turn in, when... '*Knock, Knock, Knock,*'

"What now?"

I opened the door and I saw a smiling Admiral Douglas Freeman.

"Got a minute?"

"Yea, sure. C'mon in."

"Have you seen Perry?

"Yea, he was just here."

"By any chance did he tell you he is retiring?"

"He did, yes. I offered him a job."

"Wow! I knew he was thinking about it. That was quick."

"He didn't tell me his motives but seemed excited about joining our motley crew. I offered him a Lieutenant-Commander rating since we don't have any non-coms. He accepted. I'm happy. Now, what's on your mind?"

"When is he going home?"

"He didn't tell me, but I think, soon. I'm thinking of having either me, or Lory, or Jessica fly him home in a shuttle or maybe a Valkyrie. Then we'll go back and get him when he is ready."

"This would be really good for him. He loves it here and really cares for you and what you do."

"I'm happy to have him. Now! What about you? What're your plans?"

"I don't know. I told you I am thinking of retiring but I have nothing planned beyond that. We both put in our letters of intent a year ago, so everything should go fairly quickly."

"You know..." I glanced around like I was deep in thought. "I could use an experienced advisor on the bridge. You know, someone who has been around the deck of ships most of his life and brings with him an understanding of the diverse world under the sea or... out in space. Someone who relates well with people under his command. Someone that could establish trust with the crew and stand as a model for others to follow in their pursuit of a challenging career. Someone who would continue at his present rank and wear it proudly on the black collar of a yellow shirt, like this one. Two Stars. Hmmmmm! We would have to put two more pictures on the wall of fame in the rotunda. Hmmmmm! Not too shabby. So... what do you think?"

"What? I would work for you?"

"Nope. You would work... **with** me." I smiled big and hopeful.

"Can I hitch a ride back to Norfolk with Perry?"

"Of course. So, will you be coming back with him... to your retirement job."

"Yes, I believe I will. Hannah, thank you. Thank you very much. I'll catch up with Perry and see you in the morning."

"Sleep well."

"That is absolute. Enjoy your book."

"Well that ended the day on a perfect note. I didn't get much further in the book as I would soon pass out and sleep 'til next week. (Not!). But, finally I was happy.

It was 8am when the first knock came. I had gotten up but hadn't taken my shower yet.

"Hey, dad. I just made fresh coffee. Have a cup."

"I heard you had guests last night."

"I did. Did you know about that?"

"I found out this morning. I think you made a fine choice there. Mom and I are both excited about it. Douglas was a bit taken aback when he asked you if he worked for you and you said 'no you work *with* me'. That thoroughly surprised him and sealed the deal."

"Tell me what you think of this. What if he were to work parallel with our science officer. Theo is my science advisor, much like Spock for Kirk. Then In a kind of parallel role the Admiral could be a tactics advisor and a sort of a psychologist, providing insight as things happen. It would be an extension of the Tactical department but not redundant any way. He would more or less be independent. Your group would handle the big stuff. His position would look at, and evaluate the smaller things, perhaps tied in with the science officers' observations, not security issues. but lessor things that happen in the periphery of our vision and thought processes. What do you think?"

"You may have something there. That position could evolve over time just like ours has. He is liked by all those he has met in Tactical. Having a Flag-Officer on staff may have other benefits, too. You should consider an upgrade, too. At least to Navy Captain, O6."

"I don't have time-in-grade."

"Jesus, Hannah. What difference does that make?"

"It makes a difference to me. I'm content with remaining a Commander, O5, in fact I prefer it." He went on...

"You know, I was taking a walk through the rotunda and I noticed something different, the hosts had new uniforms. They now have different ranks, or ratings, and colors like ours. I asked about it and one of the administrators said that the hosts wanted some differentiation between responsibility levels. Some have been here 5 or more years, others relatively new. So, they began reviewing how best to present themselves to our guests coming through the doors. I think they got it right. We need to take a lesson from that philosophy. I would like to see a more formal uniform standard, and redo our casual dress as well. That includes our grade structure. Many of us are tired of people in outside organizations not taking you seriously at meetings because you are only an O5 when some of them were flag officers."

"OK! I'll think about it. Here's a thought, since it is your idea, you take point by creating a task force consisting of former military and upper level management. I am a bit tired of these adopted early Star Trek uniforms, anyway."

"Will do."

"Mom and I sat and talked about the various activities that we planned for, or others planned for us."

Mr.Scott chimed.

"Mr. Freeman and Mr. Newcomb are arriving, Captain."

"Send them in."

"Good morning Admiral, COB. I hope you slept well."

"We did indeed. Have you had breakfast, yet?"

"Dad, have you had breakfast?"

"No, your mom will meet us in the Captains Mess at 10 am if all are willing." We nodded and they left me alone to take a shower.

Promptly at 10, I entered the Captains Mess, chatted for a moment pointing to something on a menu with the mess stewards and moved to our usual table.

"Good morning, all. Have you ordered."

"Yup! You better get your order in, Hannah."

"Already did, at the desk. So, what's the plan?"

"Well... Perry and I already have appointments with our respective organizations and we can finish paperwork and sign-out sometime next week, about 6 to 10 working days, Max. Maybe sooner. Most of the paperwork has already been done. Our COs are aware of our retirements, but not our intentions. It's just a matter of going there and running around to offices."

"Sounds like a plan." ... said Mom."

"Hannah, dad and I talked about the trip back to visit Amanda and friends. We were wondering if we could all fly out together, for maybe a week, then fly back when our two new officers of the deck complete their retirement paperwork. Then we can arrange for the shuttle to come back to get us. Hannah, you should come, too."

Then the doodoo hit the air recirculation device.

"Captain to the bridge" signaled Mr.Scott.

"Sorry, gotta go." ...and I didn't get a chance to eat my breakfast.

"Captain on the bridge." Wailed the XO as I came through the door.

"Over here." Hailed Science Officer Remington.

"Listen, Hannah. We may have a serious problem. Two things are evident. First, something is happening on the moon and I don't think its natural. Second, if you check with Tactical, you may find some movement originating dark and deep back east."

"OK, back up. What do you mean 'not natural'?"

"Darien is working with some of his off-the-charts whiz-kids working the problem. It appears for what-ever reason, some people within NASA may have booby-trapped the moon."

"WHAT??? What the hell for?"

"Possibly to destroy Seraphim or render it inoperable."

I walked into CIC and saw people in disarray with troubled expressions. Donna Singleton saw me standing by the door and ran over.

"Where is your dad? We have a real problem."

I pulled out my trusty Scottish companion and made a call. Dad and Mom were in their quarters preparing for the trip east. He answered immediately. I gave him a short update to what I was told and said I would not be going with them, and asked him to reconsider also. I waved at Lory and she came running, too.

As they came onto the bridge, I motioned to my quarters. All followed including our two Navy Submariners. While Theo and Donna were briefing dad, I spoke with Admiral Freeman and Perry Newcomb.

"Listen I think it best, as active military, you not be around here when the shit hits the fan. Politically it could go badly for you. So, I am asking Jake Maxwell and Lory to fly you to a secure area near Norfolk right away. I don't want either of you hurt."

"If it's all right with you, I think we'll stay."

"Are you sure about that? It could get gnarly."

"So, be it."

"OK."

The XO came through the door...

"Captain, I put us at DEFCON 2 but didn't call GQ. All shuttles and Valkyries are on alert, locked and loaded. We have 12 Block 1s on 360° perimeter duty. Colonel Hanover has been alerted at the Wyoming Nat'l Guard. We also sent a heads up to Colonel Bradford at the Colorado Air Nat'l Guard. I suggested they stay frosty but don't launch. We have nothing to work from yet."

"Tactical, do not deploy the Block II Sentinels!"

"Very well, I'm coming in." Freeman and Newcomb followed along behind. Dad was at Tactical getting a briefing.

"Captain on the bridge."

"Comm, shoot the ship. Ship's crew only." Francine just took her seat responding to the call to DEFCON 2, and pointed at me.

"The is the Captain, General Quarters, General Quarters, this is not a drill. I say again, this is not a drill. Engineering light the fires on the ACPUs, purge the VASIMR engines. Navigation, plot a course off planet to L1 ASAP and clear of space debris. Tactical, keep a weather eye and plot any intruders. Hangar two, prepare the Dragon Slayer for launch. All other departments, assist non-ship's personnel and scientists for immediate departure. Clear guests from the restaurant areas and theatres to the rotunda. Security, assist all guests to the parking areas. Have all shuttle-buses available at the door. Prepare to close down Angels Landing. Make it safe. Parish out."

Crew members were still running to their stations on the bridge and setting their stations active. My concentration was laser sharp. My soon to be tactical flag officers had never seen me become this serious.

"Helm: Report."

"Helm at station keeping Captain, initial headings set in and awaiting float."

"Very well"

"Gravity: Report."

"ACPU 5 is by our control, 100% Captain. Ships gravity at 1.000 G, Counter Gravity evaluable at 100% and steady ship-wide."

"Very well."

"Navigation: We need an initial heading to a safe egress point for on-top. Plot initial point at L1."

"Initial heading 305° and sent to helm. Ready, on your call.

"Very well."

"Environment: Report."

"Seraphim breathing atmosphere at optimum levels, O2 at 21%, Carbon dioxide scrubbed to 3%. Water and filtration systems all optimum, Captain."

"Copy that."

Tactical: Report." ... dad answered...

"Still evaluating, Captain. Our folks back east are in a huddle going over all the alerts. There is activity throughout the inner sanctum. They are watching closely. We are in a secure comm loop with six of our organizations. All the rest finished their beers, put away their double-barreled 12-gauge shotguns and just came down off their porches and are moving around the halls of power. We have a couple of Navy guys watching for deployments out in the bay. To the best of our knowledge there have been no military alerts."

"Very well. Stay frosty. Mr. Remington, can you find out if there have been any unscheduled launches from Florida or California?"

Right away, Captain."

I moved to the center seat on the bridge, XO Jessica Pearson standing to my right. COB Augie Lincoln to my left.

Suddenly it was whisper quiet. I continued scanning the screens and watched the lights. Then... from Tactical

"Captain, we have incoming. High altitude over Canada. Heading 2-3-0°. Coming right for us. ETA, 35 minutes at current speed. They are not USA or Canadian. Best we can make out they are Sukhoi jets, possibly Su27s or Su35s. and two Backfire bombers. All supersonic."

"Copy that. Call the Colorado air guard. We have some un-friendlies inbound. Helm is the jetway retracted?"

"Aye Captain, the ship is closed tight. You have the ship, by your command."

"Helm, release clamps. On GMI climb to 60,000 feet as fast as she'll go. Stay level. On the way up, pivot to port to new heading 050° and hold position. Warm up the FFP. Hangar 2 launch Dragon Slayer... at my control." I stepped off the bridge and sat beside Josh Whitmore at the control console for the Dragon Slayer. I brought up the forward view camera on the split screen. "

"Put the FFP at station keeping on both the Dragon, and Seraphim." I sat, my feet on the yaw pedals, my left hand on the Mode II power quadrant, my right on the F-16 style joy stick.

Dad was looking over my shoulder.

"Are you sure you want to do this?"

"What choice do we have? We need to send a message. Captain Freeman, Sir. Would you join me here, please?"

My old sub-captain stood alongside my dad.

"OK, here is a scenario, you have an Akula head-on with active sonar and torpedo doors open. What would you do?"

"I would close the range between us head-on and be ready to fire all forward tubes."

"Sounds good to me. Helm?"

"Steady at 60,000 feet and level."

"Good, I'm going to pull the Dragon Slayer ahead of Seraphim, you follow and match speed. Have the FFP set at 10° spread, power max. dead ahead."

"Copy that."

"OK, I'm going head-on with that flight, Josh. Then, I'm going to sidestep hard to port. When I'm clear, light 'em up. The Su27s will swing hard-over. I'll deal with them. You take out the Blackjacks. Here we go, on VASIMRs 1 and 2, ahead 2/3. Wait...wait...wait...

Punch it.

I slammed the power quadrant forward and kicked the rudder pedals to port.

Both ships leaped forward ahead of bright blue streams of plasma. I focused the crosshairs on two of the SUs and engaged the FFP. As they disintegrated into dust, I slid under Seraphim and dusted two more SUs. Then the Blackjacks disappeared amid clouds of dust... and it was over.

"Jeff, do you have an egress point we can use? We're over Canada."

"Right here is good."

"Copy that. Hangar 2. Dragon Slayer, is your control for recovery. Report recovered."

"Hangar 2 has control and bringing her in. Nice shooting Captain. OK, Dragon Slayer is in and locked down."

"Very well. Jeff point Seraphim to the stars. Good shooting, Josh.

"OK, Josh, on VASIMRs 1, 2, 3 and 4, all ahead 2/3 for 10 seconds.

ENGAGE

As before, Seraphim raced upward into open space. The moon was on the other side of earth.

"Josh, flip the ship and with VASIMRs 1, 2, 3 and 4 ahead 2/3 for 10 seconds. NOW! We were effectively stopped in position and pointed at earth. The main view-screen was reset to forward view full screen and there in the center was our home-world. People all over the ship began shouting and enjoying the view. Then came the chant. *"Ooh-Rah, Seraphim"*, *"Ooh-Rah, Hannah Parish"*

"XO, you have the conn, we're going to my quarters for a few minutes."

"Take your time, Hannah or should it be *the most Bad-Ass-Female-Starship-Captain?"*

"Your choice Jessica." We all gathered in the captain's meeting space called the Day Room.

"OK! I have diet coke, ginger ale, coffee, Jasmine Oolong tea, an open Merlot and a fresh un-opened Cabernet." Each made a choice and soon we were sitting or standing reflecting on our most recent encounter.

The door opened and Lory poked her head in.

"All quiet on the Eastern Front. We're getting post game narrative from the losers. Whoever they really are, we wiped out all their fighters and both bombers. Feedback has us so bad-ass, that they don't want to play anymore. *You go, girl. Ooh-Rah, Seraphim."* She closed the door and returned to Tactical.

Perry and Doug were shaking their heads and smiling.

"Since we are already out here, perhaps we should check to see if the instrumentation we placed on the moon, is still functional."

"You mean go back to the moon."

"Sure, why not? We're out here."

"Jeez, it seems we just left, and now, here we go again."

"Hey! We don't want to get bored, now do we, Theo?"

"Hannah, we lucked out on that one. They seem to be getting serious again. Does it never end?"

"Doesn't seem so, does it? I suspect they are going to run out of hardware if they keep this silliness up. And... luck has nothing to do with it." I was beginning to feel the onset of a giddy mood.

Dimensions...

If we meander back to the moon, people with big telescopes will see us and give who-ever a heads-up, and prepare whatever greeting they have for us." ... remarked Theo. "Not a good idea." I thought about that and a smile formed. More than just a smile.

"What if they can't see us? What if we were invisible?"

"What? More Hannah Parish magic?"

"More like *Legerdemain*. Sleight of hand." I was smiling broadly and it had everyone's attention.

"C'mon Hannah, this ship is huge and can be seen even by smaller telescopes in back-yards."

"Would you like to know how we are going to do it?"

"Are you thinking outside the box, again?"

"It's where I live, Theo, you know that. So....

consider... **DIMENSIONS.**"

"What??"

First, here is the Wikipedia definition of Sleight of hand: *"Sleight of hand (also known as prestidigitation or legerdemain) refers to fine motor skills when used by performing artists in different art forms to entertain or manipulate. It is closely associated with close-up magic, card magic, card flourishing and stealing."* I was walking around stopping momentarily in front of each person in my Day Room, then moving on to the next, smiling, my eyes glowing as I continued my thoughts. In my best Rod Serling voice...

"It is the middle ground between light and shadow, between science and superstition, and it lies between the pit of man's fears and the summit of his knowledge. This is the **dimension** *of imagination. It is an area which we call... the* **Twilight Zone.**" I moved quickly to the head of the table with a kind of skip in my step, stopped and looked casually around at all the faces.

"In order to venture into this new dimension, we must consider how to find the *middle ground*. So therefore, first, we must know the audience. To whom do we apply the *Legerdemain*. What do we know about them? Where do they live? How do they see the world? Where do they look to find things?

Well... first, they live on a flat world, more or less, a two-dimensional world from their perspective. They look upon the moon that faces them the same way throughout an entire month's time, changing only with the phases of sun light. But it is always there. That moon rotates around the earth on an ecliptic that is also flat. The earth and its moon travel around the sun on a similar but much larger ecliptic... also flat. All things in their world are flat. So, if we went to the moon, we would surely be seen by those looking and they would see us on the moon because it is a on the same ecliptic." I waited, still walking a kind of cat's walk, slowly... slinking, eyeing each with a curious eye. Then...

"What if they can't see us? What if we... just... aren't... there. Why? They are looking out across the flat, two-dimensional ecliptic and earth's flat surface. They think in two-dimensions, too. Of course, they won't see us. Because we will fly straight... DOWN. 90° from the ecliptic. Then, after turning away from earth in a kind of artificial orbit with the moon as center. We come around until the moon is precisely between us and earth... on the far side. Then we turn directly toward the moon and take a position 100 feet above the surface and do our tests. They will never see us. They will never even know we are there." I grinned.

Theo and Darien were looking at me laughing out loud. Others joined in. Soon the room was filled with laughter. Some were shaking their heads in disbelief. Their **crazy-as-a-loon** captain had done it again. I finally sat down, smiling.

"Nobody sneaks up on Captain Hannah Parish. Nobody gets to play chess with the goddess of celestial determination. My God, Hannah. You take down an attacking force of first-line Russian aircraft, bolt into space and devise the sneakiest maneuver to remain invisible in a ship a ¼ mile long, in a crystal-clear sky. Then go to the moon. All in under three hours." Said XO Jessica Pearson.

"Let me have the Conn, Captain. I'll brief the crew." ... she waited. Dad walked over.

"Where do you come up with this stuff?"

"It's his fault." I said pointing to Admiral Douglas Freeman, soon to be formally US Navy. He responded...

"Wait a minute. When you asked me what I would do with an Akula in an attack mode head-on. You knew the answer all along, didn't you? You knew that if we closed the distance head-on, their torpedoes wouldn't have time to arm. Same with the aircraft. They expected us to turn and run. Instead they had no time to adjust their strategy with such a high closure rate. It was brilliant. Oh, yea. If I had doubts about shipping aboard, I don't any more. Thanks for asking my advice even if you already knew what to do." I smiled a knowing grin.

"Jessica, you have Conn, let's make a stop on the moon."

"Aye Captain. We'll do it the sneaky-way."

Lory approached Admiral Freeman...

"Admiral, remember when, after you saw the contents of that USB drive, you said, 'She is scary good, isn't she?' and I said, 'You don't know the half of it.' Well, now you know what I meant."

"No wonder she's Captain." Said COB Perry Newcomb.

"Amen."

An hour later...

"Captain, do you have some place in mind to do the studies?"... asked Jessica.

"See that crater at 1 o'clock high? It has plenty of sunlight and is big enough to set Seraphim in. Josh, just a reminder, watch your keel line, keep the ship high until fully inside the crater walls, then descend vertically to, oh... make it 50 feet."

"Copy that. Coming in slow. We have functional GMI, it's slow. But, it's good enough."

"Excellent. Keep your hand on the maneuvering thrusters... just in case."

"Copy that."

"Tactical. Deploy two Block II sentinels, one for a close-up reconnaissance of the inner crater. Have the other skim the perimeter of the crater, along the walls. By the way is Charlie Parker from JPL still aboard?" Theo looked up...

"Yes, he is."

"See if he would join us on the bridge, please."

15 minutes later he came in the door with two of his engineers. They looked at the main view-screen in wonder.

"Captain!"

"Hey Charlie. Been awhile."

"This is a surprise; didn't figure you would be back here so soon. I'm glad I stayed aboard. What can I do for you?"

"Do you have any more of those seismometers we deployed from the rover?"

"Aaah! I'm not sure."

"We have two, Charlie." Said Pete Jackson, engineer.

"Good. Could you check them out and prepare them for deployment? And... prepare a receiver to capture the data on-board the ship. You will have to tap into the comm panel down in Engineering. See a guy named Fred Mooney. He may just be the best hacker in the known universe. He can do anything. Wait, I'll see if he is here." I pulled out Mr.Scott and made the call.

"Aye, Lassie, the wizard be here."

"Mr.Scott would you ask him if he would join us on the bridge?" a few moments passed.

"Aye. The fine gentleman is on his way, Captain."

"Thank you, Mr. Scott."

"Who is that?"

"Why, that is Chief Engineer Montgomery Scott of the United Federation of Planets, Starship Enterprise. *Do ya not r-r-r-recognize the voice, laddie?"* I mimicked rolling my Rs. In minutes...

The bridge door opened and LCDR Gus Mayer, First Engineer and Lt. Fred Mooney, Engineering entered.

"My God." Exclaimed Fred Mooney. Seeing the moon from this vantage point was quite startling for poor Fred.

"What's up, Hannah?" asked Gus.

"Gus, this is Charlie Parker from JPL, one of the resident scientists. We are going to deploy two remote seismometers onto the surface out there and we need to be able to listen to the results. Is there a way to install a receiver on board to monitor the readings?" asked Pete Jackson, engineer. Then....

"Captain, guess what? Sentinel *Sierra6alpha* has located another bore hole along the rim."

"Let's see it. Yup, same as the others."

"Captain, we have one of your Sonobuoys left over that wasn't complete when the shit hit the fan on the other side. We completed it later on, so if you need it, someone could go out there and send it down. It transmits on a collateral frequency so the one receiver can monitor both." said a wide-eyed Pete Jackson. I looked at Darien, Theo and dad with a huge smile. "Boy, did we just get lucky?"

"Pete, go back upstairs, do some checks, make sure it is functional, battery charged, then bring it to Hangar 1 and see Jake Maxwell. You will need a low-gravity gurney."

"I'll go with him." said Charlie.

"Oh, before you go. Are the frequencies on the seismometers and Sonobuoys selectable?"

"Yes, they are. What do you have in mind?"

"Can you select frequencies outside the assigned band for these things, and can the receiver tune to that band?"

"Yea, we can do that. May I ask why?"

"Because, I don't want anyone else listening in."

Smiles formed on all the faces.

"No worries there. They can't hear anything on this side of the moon. It blocks all RF signals."

"Yes, but there is the Lunar Reconnaissance Orbiter in polar orbit right now. It comes by every 2 hours."

"Oh! Right. Good call, Captain. We will have all three ready for deployment in an hour, or sooner."

"Carry-on gentlemen."

"Now, my dad told me, you Navy guys are Boot-Camp qualified and have even been assigned space-suits. So, Perry, how about you join our engineers down in hangar 1 and prepare to get your boots covered in moon dust. By the way, the first person to step out of the shuttle onto the surface will be the first Human Being from the planet Earth to ever step onto the surface of the backside of the moon. You will be the first. Congratulations." The shock on his face was palpable. But, slowly a smile formed.

"Dad, please have Valkyrie 1 ready for a trip. I'm going for a drive." I turned toward my old boss.

"Rear Admiral Douglas Freeman, since Perry is leaving now to make history for which we are all immensely proud. Perhaps you would join me in a short journey. There is something I need to check and it may require some help on your part. Would you follow me please?"

Everyone on the bridge was smiling. A right-of-passage was about to be administered.

Taking a stroll with Demons

We stopped at the personal equipment room with its multiple rows of lockers. Two assistants helped us with the blue space suits. Once each was checked for function, we walked to the main hangar where my Valkyrie waited, its door open. A technician exited after completing the required pre-flight systems checks. He stood to the side in a semi-attention position.

"Is everything good?"

"Yes, Ma'am. Have a good flight."

"Thank you." Admiral Freeman climbed aboard and waited inside, bent over a little due to the low ceiling. I followed and closed and secured the door.

"You sit here please." pointing to the co-pilots seat. I sat in the pilot's seat, snapped my safety belt and shoulder harness and began the pre-flight. Using the printed check-list, I stepped through each system test requirement. As I finished the last on the list, I placed the 8 x 10 plastic-coated card into the center console folder between the two seats. I heard the snap of his seat belt and harness, and, watched as he scanned the instruments, then turned checking out the little ship's accommodations. I waved to the Hangar Chief. He engaged a lever, and the inside airlock door began to open. On GMI, I moved the Mode 2 control lever forward a small amount and the Val moved silently toward the airlock tunnel.

"Lower your pressure shield. That's good, now pressurize your suit. Good!" I did the same. Once inside the airlock, the inner door closed and sealed. We could hear the air being evacuated from the tunnel to a vacuum. Silent once again. It showed no leaks in the Val and I signaled the outer door tech that we were ready. Slowly the outer door opened and we floated out.

"How are you doing?"

"I'm fine. Where are we going?"

"Around to the other side."

"Of the moon?"

"Yup." A voice sounded in our helmets.

"Val 1, radio check, over."

"Val 1, Loud and clear, Tac."

"Copy that. Have a good flight. Tac out"

"OK! Here we go. We are going east around the equator. I'm climbing now to about 2000 feet AGL. Then we'll accelerate to about 2500 kilometers per hour, still on GMI, but will accelerate using the VASIMR engines. GMI is not very effective on the moon because of its far less gravity and lacks a magnetosphere necessary for good GMI operation. We have 1 G of artificial gravity and Counter Gravity on so you shouldn't feel any acceleration forces. How do you feel?"

"Fine, go for it." I set the GMI control forward enough to provide vertical control for level flight, then pushed the twin VASIMR throttle controls forward. The Valkyrie leaped forward and in less than a minute was skimming across the Lunar surface at 2500 KPH. Upon reaching, shut them down to coast the rest of the way.

"What is that? It's black. I can't see the moon. How can you see where we are going?"

"That is the night terminator. We are moving from the sun side to the night side. Since there is no atmosphere, there is no light diffusion, so if the sun does not illuminate the surface directly, nothing does. Disconcerting, isn't it? See these instruments, they show us the way ahead using a combination of radar, lasers, and synthetic imagery. Cool, huh?"

"How do you know all this?"

"How did you know how to drive a submarine? You know, that was much harder to do than this. What you and your crew did was much more complex than any of this."

"I don't know about that. But, I can see why the people on Seraphim have so much faith in you. You stay on top of everything. As the XO said, you won't be blindsided, and you stay alert to every nuance the ship telegraphs to you. The Lindstrom did the same thing. You learned well.

There is something I've been meaning to ask you that has had me troubled ever since I was captain of the submarine. How did you know that an Akula had tried to slip into our baffles? Passive sonar didn't pick it up. Then you strongly suggested I pull a Crazy-Ivan. You knew... how?"

"Actually, I don't know. I did learn very young to be open to feelings. A sort of intuition. It's not a gender thing. The hair on my arms stands out straight, like goose-bumps. They did, that day on the sub. It happened again right here on the moon when I 'knew' that the alien ship was out there. I trust those intuitions. OK! in a few seconds you are going to see something wonderful. Stand-by for Earth-Rise."

In 20 seconds, it happened.

"Oh my GOD. Earth. Oh, is that a beautiful sight? Oh! I'm beginning to see the moon surface."

"That's Earth-Light. The reciprocal of Moon-light."

I saw hints of tears on his face.

"Worth the trip?"

"Oh yea. My God, it's amazing."

"I'm going to slow in few more minutes. Soon the morning terminator will hit us and it will be super bright. So, lower the sun shade in your helmut. You'll be glad you did."

He did. Then the sun hit us from the west.

"Wow! Oh, that is bright."

"On earth we have a great filter... our atmosphere. Here, none."

I had accelerated to cruising speed for only a minute then shut down the VASIMR engines and had been coasting until now. I unlocked the maneuvering thruster lever... like a joy stick that was in the center position. Slowly I pulled it back and the nose thrusters began slowing the ship. I saw our destination but said nothing to my co-pilot. My heart began to beat faster, my blood pressure was going up. My nerves were interfering with my motor reflexes. Part of me did not want to do this. But I felt... I knew I had to face my demons. The ship stopped and I lowered it until we felt the slight jar of the struts making contact, then set the GMI to push down holding the Valkyrie against the moon.

"Well, we are stopped. Please close your pressure shield and seal it. Check your gauges. All good? Excellent." I did the same then...

"OK, I'm going to depressurize the ship, then I'm going to shut down artificial gravity. We will be going to 1/6 earth gravity. You ready? You already did this in boot-camp. No surprises here." I remained seated and waited a minute as our suits expanded in the airless environment.

"Release your seat belt and get used to the feeling. Good. Now standup slowly, don't launch yourself into the ceiling. You only weigh about 30 – 40 pounds. I got up and moved to the door slowly.

"As you walk down here try not to make any sudden moves and don't turn your head fast. Your inner ear mechanism is expecting heavier gravity. You will get used to it. I'm going to open the door now and will step down to the surface, then you follow. OK?"

I waited on the lunar surface as Rear Admiral Douglas Freeman, former submarine Captain stepped onto the dusty surface, straightened and stood waiting for his stability to return to normal. Then he saw the Earth. He shuddered in his space suit.

"Please, don't say it."

"Say what?"

"That's one small step for man..."

He laughed but also realized this was the same kind of moment. It certainly was for him.

Then I spoke.

"There is something I would like you to do. Please walk over this way, slowly, and sit down in that chair."

"What?" then he saw it, he was standing 20 feet from two green lawn chairs facing each other. Another shiver raged through his body. This was where it happened... first contact.

"Please." He moved forward taking short steps. I followed behind but moved toward the opposite chair, the one the alien sat in. He stopped beside the chair, reached down and touched the arm. Then he looked to his left and saw the second chair, 10 feet away. I walked into his line of sight and stopped by that chair. We looked at each other and I motioned him to sit. He did, but I could hear his hard breathing. Mine was rapid, too. I was fighting my demons. This was an epiphany for me, something I had to get passed and why I was here. We sat that way for about 10 minutes. Then he stood, looked around, up at our home planet, then the Valkyrie, then at me still sitting. He started walking away. Away from the Val, me and earth in the black sky. He walked about 30 feet, stopped and just stood there looking a little to the left and a little to the right surveying the moonscape. He turned and looked at me. I stood and motioned to the Val. He remained motionless for almost a minute, then began walking slowly in the direction of the little ship. I followed, climbing the stairs into the cabin of the Valkyrie, sealed the door and pushed the ***Pressurize*** button, then walked to my seat. He was already in his seat and had secured his seat belt and harness. The gravity slowly increased to normal 1 G. The pressure now normal, I flipped my sunscreen up and then unsealed the pressure shield with a slight whoosh of air as the suit equalized with the cabin. He did the same. Now we were in a normal human atmosphere and gravity. We sat without saying anything for several minutes, then he spoke.

"Why did you want to come here, Hannah? Wasn't it traumatic enough, the first time?"

"Yes, it was. But what I did then, I did because I felt I needed to do, not only for me but for Seraphim, and people of Earth. It was the right thing to do. I still believe that. But I wasn't prepared for how it affected me. I was hoping this trip would help me find a way through my fears and night terrors. I needed to move past my demons so I could be a Captain, others could count on... feel safe with. But this time... I did not want to be alone. Thank you for agreeing to come along."

"Your dad said something to me that day in the museum part of the rotunda with that diorama that had spooked you. He said,

I doubt anyone attempting to talk with another race of beings, never mind from another planet could have felt more alone than she felt as she sat in one of those chairs by herself doing the right thing with no other humans out there with her. Maybe if we go back there, take a walk, by yourself and you will be overwhelmed by the sheer loneliness in a lifeless, airless, desolation in which there is no sound or movement or indigenous life. She must have been devastated sitting alone out there, then still having the presence of mind to continue with the meeting." Oh my God!

Then he burst into tears.

"Now I think I have some idea what you felt. How could you have sat out here all by yourself. My God, Hannah. Why didn't those bastards go with you? You were right. I see it now, you needed to do it, it was the right thing to do. But at what cost to you? When we get back home, I'm going to visit that diorama again. Can we go back to the ship now?"

"Of course."

Fifty-five minutes later the Valkyrie floated into the hangar bay. In another ten minutes we were back in our 'street' clothes walking toward the bridge. Neither said anything.

"Captain on the bridge."

"Welcome back Captain. I trust your trip went well." I nodded with a smile. Then went directly to my quarters. My lawn chair partner left the bridge.

I stood in front of my mirror. I saw a tired, grief-stricken woman fighting to keep her sanity. It was finally over now, completely over. I met my demons and vanquished them. Now I just need to find Hannah Parish. The real one.

The subdued sound of harp and cello sounded from the bedroom. A message from Mom. I was invited to a private gathering of a few people in the Council Chambers. First, I needed to resurrect Hannah Parish. I stood under the liquid warmth of a refreshing shower, feeling the bad things wash away, standing unmoving in the gentle spray. Who am I? Can I go back to our home in Norfolk, now? Minutes passed by. Somehow, I mustered up enough energy to put on a black slacks/white blouse combo, a simple gold necklace and Annapolis ring, brushed out my hair leaving it untethered, down past my shoulders.

I really didn't want to go. But... I persevered. Everyone was wearing casual uniforms or informal street clothes. They all stood as I entered. I smiled, shook my head (no) and patted the air in front of me implying... sit down. They did. A chair was available between my parents, which I took. I tried to smile but was having difficulty. Among those present was the two-person delegation from Houston. That did not please me, but I continued a limp smile.

My dad sensed the awkwardness of the situation as did my mom. I would soon find out that he, Mom, Darien and Theo had a lengthy conversation with Doug Freeman following our trip to the lawn chairs. They knew the depth of my pain. Dad spoke up first...

"XO Jessica Pearson has the Conn and has set sail for Angels Landing, via a 'sneaky-route'. Her words. We should be home in about two hours. The JPL science team successfully deployed two seismometers into the crater and deployed a sonobuoy into the only bore hole we found in the area. I'd like Charlie Parker from JPL to explain the results. Charlie?"

"Thanks, Ed. Well the deployment went well and we immediately began to receive data. We started seeing low level seismic activity on the order of magnitude 1.5 to 2.8. It is a steady rumbling that on earth would mean, essentially, nothing. The bore site was more interesting. We are still analyzing the data, but we can say the data is quite different from the earlier tests around Site-One. The one thing that stands out is the temperature. Over time it fluctuates up and down about 6 degrees C and averaging 34°C. It's quite warm. The moon is not doing anything exciting from our perspective. However, it would be extremely helpful if we could lay down some instrumentation in the middle of the new crater. But we know that is unlikely any time in the near future due to the crater's instability. That's all I have."

Dad spoke...

"Thanks, Charlie and your team. Now! We have a presentation to make. Perry Newcomb, would you please rise. It is my understanding that you were first to exit the shuttle onto the lunar surface during the deployment. That makes you the first Human Being ever to set foot on the far-side of the moon. In recognition of that, we would like to present you with this Plaque, signed by the entire bridge crew of the Seraphim as an acknowledgment of that achievement. Captain would you do the honors?"

('My name... is Hannah.') I didn't say it... I thought it. Dead silence filled the room.

I stood and walked around the table with the award in hand. As I approached, everyone stood and turned toward a smiling COB. I wish I could have enjoyed this more. The COB, my friend, deserved it.

"Perry, we have been to the bottom of the sea together and now to the far side of the moon. This is to commemorate this moment. I am proud to present this to you in honor of your devotion to duty on a submarine on which we both served and to your *courage* to step out *alone* onto an alien world, Earth's only natural satellite, The Moon. Congratulations."

Everyone was standing and clapping. Then, they all raised their left hands in the Vulcan Salute. Perry was having trouble keeping his emotions in check. The impact was overwhelming... but he was as happy as he could ever remember being.

The two words 'courage' and 'alone' were significant and my only way to jab at the Houston scientists. It was noted by some, possibly all.

Dad, Darien, Theo and Admiral Freeman understood the meaning.

Then the pizza arrived. Mom said...

"We got your favorite, Hannah, sausage and pepperoni. There are others, too."

"Thanks, mom." A cart with a large bowl of prepared Caesars Salad and another large bowl of soft drinks and a coffee urn were placed along the wall. I hadn't eaten anything since before our trip to the far side. I watched as people assembled into an informal line at the impromptu buffet. When most had returned to the table I got up and spooned up a generous helping of Caesar salad. I slam-dunked the salad and two pieces of pizza. I guess I was over-hungry. A diet coke provided the wash-down medium. The chatter volume was way up, as people competed for air-time. I think the now jovial atmosphere began to side-step my morose demeaner, because it seemed I was smiling more and contributing to the banter. I know Mom was concerned about me especially when she found out I had returned to the First Contact Lawn Chairs. I told her, and dad, that I could not go alone and needed someone with me I could trust implicitly. It was difficult enough but doable and helped me identify my demons and usher them away. I knew that the Admiral was deeply moved by his own exposure to that kind of incredible isolation away from all things familiar. But, I could not have done it without his being there. The fear and isolation of that experience came slamming back again into my psyche, but frankly, it did not have the impact the first experience had. Was I getting used to it? Was I adjusting to this world?

The group began to break up and left the room. Mom and dad remained with Adm Freeman, Perry Newcomb, Theo and Darien. I cleaned up my mess and prepared to leave when a voice stopped me. I turned to a tall middle-age brunette I had never met before. She asked if I could spare her a moment. She had a pleasant demeaner so I agreed and sat down. I was then introduced to another person I hadn't met before, but I remembered the name, Philip Nordgren from JPL. He was the intermediary in Houston when we extracted the two astronauts and one cosmonaut from the ISS.

"Hannah, my name is Dorothy Williams, I am a flight director and assistant program manager of the lunar probe development program in Houston. Phil works with our group as a senior development engineer and supervisor. We are here to offer an olive branch on behalf of all the good people in Houston and other laboratories who support a continued collaboration with Seraphim and her people. Before this meeting, Phil and I met with your mom and dad, Darien Hunter, Theo Remington, your two Navy guys and a few others. They briefed us that you may not be interested in a discussion, but, that is the only reason we came here. May I continue?" I hesitated, then...nodded, but said nothing. I noticed her hand was occasionally shaking slightly. She was nervous. I suspected a lot must be riding on the outcome of this meeting so I mellowed a little, but continued to remain silent. Phil Nordgren spoke...

"A lot of people in Houston and beyond have watched the videos from the moon. The meetings with our people when you explained the event in detail and saw the lack of response by our scientists. We watched in amazement the now famous *Lawn Chair Diplomacy.* Then, the follow-on meetings with our people and how they totally let you down. Your XO, Jessica Pearson is one tough lady. Her admonishment, though directed at the people that were in this room at the time, was also an admonishment to everyone in Houston and perhaps the world. If we are going out there, with the goal to advance the science and our understanding of our universe, we better be prepared to offer up our swords in support of those who would show us the way."

Dorothy Williams spoke next...

"When we came here, two weeks ago we were given tours of Angels Landing. We were wondering if we would get to see more of Seraphim before we have to leave, but what stopped me in my tracks... was the diorama down in the museum. Built into an anechoic chamber, it was absolutely soundless, disturbingly so. The effect was nothing short of incredible. It was cold in there as though the air-conditioning was turned on high. I have never been so consumed with emotion as I was then, as I looked at those two chairs and the desolation around them, the silence, the shear loneliness that it represented.

I understand that recently, Admiral Freeman went with you, back to the real lawn chairs and he told us from his perspective. What happened that day when you went out alone to a meeting with those that saved our planet, will be a monument and example to future explorers. It is the stuff of legend. I don't want to lose the connection we have with you and Seraphim. Please accept our apology on behalf of people back home for the treatment our scientists gave you. It was a disgrace to our profession. You showed us the humanity side of space exploration." Her eyes were watering up and her hands were shaking. This was very difficult for her and Philip Nordgren. I had to admit that I was consumed by my own feelings that still lingered. I sat listening and weighing what I was going to say. But, slowly...

"I'm not sure I'm ready to jump into any agreements any time soon even though that event is now well in our past. It was the disappointment I felt in people I admire so much. The people that designed and built this ship are like gods to me. Even though I have a rudimentary understanding of the technology and the science, I don't really know how it works. I bow to the incredible minds that did this. A one-of-kind ship, beloved by us all who fly her, and millions world-wide, who look on in wonder and hope for the future of the human spirit. I looked at your people with similar respect and admiration. Knowing that the crew of Seraphim is contributing something to science and the understanding of the universe was a point of pride for us. We worked feverishly to provide the tools for you to work your magic.

Then, the gods fell from glory. I can't tell you how badly that hurt. How it hurt us all. What do we do now? I wondered. As Captain, what do I do? It is my job to keep everybody aboard safe from harm, but also to provide access to whatever mission is decided upon. In the face of an incredible natural event like the impact of an asteroid into our moon, I did not see one scientist step forward and recommend anything. So, I did, I had to... somebody had to. With the collaboration of some brilliant crew members, we parsed the event. We sorted through the findings in order to construct an overview of the dynamics as they took place. Then came the revelation that someone out there actually saved us... saved our world. The question that baffled me most was why you didn't step forward and help? It was cowardly. You have PHDs, Nobel Laureates... some of the best minds on the planet. I'm just a pilot, a bus driver, it's what I do. Why couldn't you have just helped?"

I guess I am still angry. Why were smart people so disappointing? I turned and left the room and returned to my quarters. I don't want to do this job anymore.

Terminus

W e arrived home safe and secure on the cradles at Angels Landing. It felt good to breath the desert air of home. Maybe I preferred the salt air of the Atlantic Ocean better, or the forest and fresh water lake smells. But this was good.

We are working to put things in order aboard the ship. I was told that Dorothy Williams and Philip Nordgren had not yet left the ship. I decided to bite the bullet and visit the diorama, and then find a way to repair issues.

Two long bench seats had been placed along the inner wall between the entry door and exit, with all the sound-absorbing Pyramidal Foam Absorption material on all walls, ceilings, and doors. In the dark, barely visible, I saw a figure sitting alone. It was Captain Freeman.

"Can't get enough of it, huh?" I asked as I sat on the bench seat also covered with sound absorbing material.

"You know, those two were just trying to set things right. I think they realize the error of Houston's ways. I really think they were looking for assurances that the collaboration has not failed. You made your point and I heartily agree. I came down here to feel what I felt up there. We haven't talked about it but I have a pretty good idea of how the combined fear, loneliness, and disappointment affected you. Your dad was right. It was devastating to you. But you did rise above it, and continued on. That is special, in my mind. That experience could have sent you into a spiral of PTSD. But it didn't. And, here you are. Why did you come down here?"

"I don't know. There are moments I think about going home and finding a normal job. But then I have to remind myself of how much effort I put into this... and... how much

I really love it. I love everyone aboard Seraphim. I really do. When you were a sub captain, did you ever doubt yourself, your knowledge, your understanding of the environment you were in?"

"Yes. Every day. Sometimes it did scare me. Am I right for the job? Does the crew respect me enough to respond to the needs of the boat, the mission or danger? I think they did, but I understand the weight of responsibility can give me second thoughts. I was both sad and relieved when the Navy no longer wanted the Lindstrom. I felt I was getting too old for the job anyway. I look at those two chairs, nearly identical to the ones we sat in, the real ones. I sat in the green lawn chair you dragged out onto the most desolate environment I have ever seen, by yourself, with no support and you waited. I tried to imagine what that must have been like, when the alien walked toward you, neither of you knowing how to greet each other and you trying to find a way to thank someone from light-years away. I look at you now, and realize you may be the only human from our planet to be able to pull something like that off. The only one out of 7.7 billion. You say you are only a 'bus-driver'. Well those people with all those smarts you admire so much, don't have anything close to your ability to rise to a crisis situation like you do. They do not hold a candle to that. I personally watched you in a combat situation, not ruffled at all, then on the fly figured how to get to the moon without anyone knowing it. Who can do that? I hope you don't give this up. I know you have been thinking about it. I must tell you, I will not take the job here if you are not the Captain...

C'mon, let's go to lunch, but first, go put on your uniform...*Captain*. I'll meet you in the Captains Mess."

The restaurant was not as full as I imagined it would be. In the back sat Doug Freeman, Perry Newcomb, Mom and Dad, Darien and Theo. I was glad they were there. I sat at the head of the table. I ordered something and it was good but I don't even remember what it was. I was deep in thought while around me there were cheerful discussions going on. I did not actively participate but smiled and laughed when something was funny. I know what I needed to do.

"Darien, could I talk to you for a moment in private?" He joined me out in the corridor... just us.

"Darien, would you do something for me?" He nodded... "Of course." I explained what I wanted and we went back to the table. I wasn't my usual bubbly self but I wasn't remote, either. I joined in to an energetic conversation about our first paying jobs so long ago. It was funny and we laughed. Darien had gone somewhere for a moment. When he came back he looked at me with a smile, bent down and whispered.

"15 minutes, your Day Room." I nodded and mouthed... 'Thank you.'

We had all finished a nice lunch and were heading out. I moved quickly and outpaced everyone else, on my way to my quarters. Darien told everyone I had an appointment and wished to be alone.

Two people were standing near the raised command deck on the bridge talking with the XO. She saw me and pointed my way. I smiled and nodded toward my quarters.

I held the door as Dorothy Williams and Philip Nordgren entered. I followed, closed the door and offered them seats at the table. I turned the water on for coffee and also uncorked the chardonnay. They agreed on the wine. I partially filled three stemmed wine glasses and placed them on the table... and sat.

"Please, just relax. I didn't know you were on board for this last flight. That was not planned. Circumstance forced the flight. What did you think of your first flight into space?"

"This ship, it's amazing. We had heard all the stories and we were on the comm-link when Seraphim saved the ISS crew's lives. We didn't know there are people out there that jealously want Seraphim's technologies or destroy it if they can't have it. You certainly have been faced with challenges." My turn.

"I have been doing some thinking, asking myself if I would undersign a resumption of partnerships with outside companies or organizations. Then I sat with my... call it, my inner circle to discuss whether it benefited us, and, do we really want outsiders with us.

By the end of the meeting it was resolved; we would consider entering into a contractual collaboration but with some added terms. We agreed that we would accept proposals that outlined the interest areas in generalities only. It would include a list of possible destinations for your science studies, what the mission goals are. The proposal should detail compensation for our participation, a complete list of personnel assignments, with an overview of each's qualifications.

The last thing I am absolutely firm on. If, for instance you want to start planning a mission to Saturn's moon, *'Enceladus'*, then Seraphim crew personnel will plan the route, departure date, time on site, return dates and would execute by the captain's orders only. No non-Ship personnel will, at any time, attempt to assume or influence control of Seraphim. Access to the bridge will be limited to approved requests or by invitation only. Other ships control departments are off-limits to non-Ship personnel except by invitation by department managers only.

You are aware that we have resident science departments on board from other companies like JPL, Boeing, Lockheed-Martin, Raytheon, etc. The activities of the resident departments have priority over any short-term organizations like NASA in science related matters. Join with them if you like and enjoy the usual repartee you have at home.

We have a strict chain of command aboard Seraphim with relief qualified people. Whomever is sitting in the center seat on the command island on the bridge is the captain, whether it is me, the XO, or COB, if given a directive or order by any one of us, you must follow it to the letter. Yellow shirts, like this one are command personnel. Red are engineering, Blue are non-ship personnel, like Med-Bay, Environment, Gravity and so on.

If this meets with your approval so far, then I will continue." They nodded...

"I would like you to meet with your people and give them this overview. Then put together a team with authority to join us here for a meeting with our planners and Council members across the table. I may, or may not, sit in at that meeting. We will discuss the terms as we have discussed here. You should be prepared to hear detailed briefings by Security, Tactical, Command, Legal, and Hangar personnel, regarding hardware you may wish to bring along, and advice from our Council members.

I will tell you, we already have our next trip planned. We have been discussing it for a few months now. This is an in-house project. We are going to Mars. Date not set, but in the not-too-distant future. The resident scientists are already detailing their own requirements. During your up-coming meeting with us, we might be open to NASA as guests on that flight. However, remember, our resident scientists have priority for instrumentation deployments and site selections.

So, I suggest you get busy. If you need a ride back to Houston, I'm sure we can have one of our shuttles available.

"I look forward to your call with a time/date certain for a meeting. Again, we can come get you unless you prefer your own transportation."

"Thank you, Captain. I was worried we may have lost something incredibly important. We will see you soon, hopefully." They were escorted to hangar 1 where Jake Maxwell waited to fly them to Houston. I was wondering how our two Navy submariners were making out since Lory Amundsen dropped them off outside Norfolk. I looked forward to their call. I would like them here when the NASA meetings kick off. Anyway...

I took a couple days off and did very little of consequence. I spent time doing laps in the pool, running around deck 10 and getting the crap kicked out of me by my Martial Arts instructor. However, I was getting better and it wasn't as easy for him. He got laid down firmly a couple of times. I put on a little weight... mostly muscle, I think.

I asked Mr. Scott where Theo Remington was. I was directed to his office.

'Knock, knock, knock'

"Anyone home?"

"Who dares knock upon my door? Speak now knave."

"Please, oh exalted one! Mayest I have audience?"

"Then step forward and sit."... we laughed.

"It's been quite a while since we sat in this office. Those were the days. I miss them, Hannah. Little did I know what you would become. Or me, for that matter. Science Officer!"

"Yea! Doo-doo happens doesn't it. Those were heady days for me. You wondered if you could find a way to instruct me since I alternate between inside and outside the box. You wondered if you had the talent to do that. I had confidence in you and your ability to find a way. You did, didn't you. Or I wouldn't be where or what I am today."

"I think the thing I miss most is our chats. And, perhaps I learned as much from you as you did from me. How did your meeting go? I sensed you would have preferred not to do it."

"True, enough. I am fighting to remain objective, but it is difficult. Part of me wants nothing to do with working with NASA. But, I also realize the charter of this vessel, is scientific exploration, and that can take many forms. It seemed reasonable to join with elements outside this ship for help as well as offer them a portal into space. For science sake, it makes sense. Yet, I am still thoroughly angry with them for destroying my faith in them. Shall I go on?"

"It's not necessary. I am disappointed, too."

"Then, what should we do?"

"I think you already started it by holding that meeting with the only two that were here."

"Yes, and I think I accomplished a few things. Here is a list of main points I shared with them, that I think need to be included in the negotiations." I handed Theo, basically the minutes of the meeting.

"you must have just typed this up."

"I did. Those aren't my recommendations, they are my minimum requirements."

"Oh! Indeed. What do you want to do with this?"

"Would you bring it to Carl Ledbetter? I think he is going to be Seraphim's contact when NASA decides what they want to do. Meanwhile I have some other tasks to do. We have to do this more often. I'm sure there is more that you can teach me."

"There is. We should plan on it. Where are your Navy buddies?"

"Jake brought them back to Norfolk to finish their retirement requirements. Then, they will be back. I have to go."

"See you later, Hannah."

I went down to my old workplace, Navigation. As I walked in, they waved at me and I waved back. I loved these guys. I walked around the room counter-clockwise, giving a high-five as I went but occasionally stopping to chat. I really hadn't been in NGE since before the moon thing. Not the most recent one, the one with the asteroid. I was peppered with questions... some about my *Space Walk of Fame*...Duh!

Mr.Scott, interrupted with news that The Admiral and COB had finished their retirement administration and had signed out. So, I should think about planning to retrieve them for the new assignments. I had a thought and visited Mom and Dad at the residence.

"Our two Navy guys are now retired. They had received their pre-retirement packages a year ago and began assembling necessary documents. Then Submitted Form DD 2656 and reviewed it with their personnel office. They received the usual briefings: retirement pay arrangements, accrued remaining leave and security briefings, blah, blah. So... they are all done. They both want to touch base with friends in the area before coming out here. So, I had a thought. How do you feel about the three of us taking a shuttle or Valkyrie back to Norfolk and combine visiting family and friends while they are doing the same? Then, all of us return together in the Val. What do you think?" Dad spoke first.

"That is an excellent idea. What do you think, Mom?"

'Great idea. I need to make sure the med-bay is set up, and personnel will be here. Same for you both."

We set a date three days hence. I sent a message to Freeman and Newcomb. We all agreed we would fly back here a week after we get there. That would give all of us time for visits. I had a mini-meeting with Lory, Jessica, Theo and Darien. Sarah helped make sure we had the necessary staffing on-board. I explained...

"Lory, who had worked at an FBO at Virginia Beach Airpark (Atlantic Airpark) has a friend there that owns a couple of warbirds and had built a new hangar. It's set off in the back of the airport property. She suggested we might want to hangar the Valkyrie there. She made the call."

"His name is Alfred Clark. He has a circa 1930s Stearman PT-17 Biplane and a WWII fighter which he keeps hangered there. But, we're in luck. He loaned out the Stearman to the Military Aviation Museum on the east end of the field. They are doing a fly-in of period bi-planes and requested Alfred let them show his plane. It's a beauty. That means his hangar, which is small, is able to hold two airplanes so it now has room for the Valkyrie. It is very secure with an 8-foot chain link fence around that part of the airport, considering the value of his airplanes. The little airport is a grass strip, so there is very little traffic. It's about 18 miles southeast of Norfolk center and 10 miles south of Oceana Naval Air Station. May I come along? I know people."

"Yes, of course. Sounds like we have a plan. So, you worked there?"

"Yes, when I left the Air Force, I went back home in the town of Chesapeake and stayed with my mom who was beginning to have problems... age-related. Dad passed away a few years back from a heart attack. She is preparing to move into a senior citizens community nearby. My sister is watching over her now. I might be able to give her a hand. Then, when everybody is ready, I'll come back with you."

"Now, that sounds excellent. I wondered what we would do with the Val. This is going to work out great."

It was decided. I sent a lengthy message to Freeman and Newcomb, and they were on board with all of it. Dates were established and all agreed to meet at Virginia Beach Airpark.

It was getting late in the afternoon and time for dinner. At the behest of Mr.Scott, our inner circle met in the Captains Mess. I laid out the plan and Lory explained how we were going to hangar Valkyrie-01. All seemed satisfied. Theo passed around copies of the minutes of my meeting with the Houston folks. Darien asked what I meant by minimum requirements. I smiled and nodded. I said quietly...

"It is the only way I will agree to take this ship into harm's way again with people that can't muster the courage to support their own agenda. Your call." ... and I looked intently at Darien.

"This is your bottom line? No room to negotiate?" I shook my head and I continued eating my salad.

Theo added...

"I have no problem with the minimums, but it is your and the Counsel's call." Carl Ledbetter added...

"Nor I, I don't have a problem with it either." Then Darien said...

"I don't know if the NASA folks will buy this." For this, I responded...

"...and if they don't? Look, Darien. Everybody was terrified out there, including me. But somebody had to take command and protect the ship. That's a captain's primary duty and responsibility. I did what was necessary, I moved the ship away from falling rocks and boulders. I found out what really happened and made that information available to people who did not seem to want to hear it. And then... I had to take a walk outside alone and... **by myself.** I do my job to the best of my ability and I think I do a pretty good job. Perhaps you should ask Jessica Pearson to take the Conn for that flight with NASA. I trained her. She is very good. I'm going to my quarters. Have a good evening folks."

I threw a $twenty on the table, turned and started walking toward my quarters. Lory caught up, but didn't say anything. We just walked.

"May I come in?" I held the door open for her.

"You get no rest from the challenges, do you? Maybe this mini vacation will help you sort things out."

"I hope so. I don't get it. Don't people know that Space is not a theme park ride, any more than guiding a submarine through a pitch-black water-world from a boat you can't even see out of. Why would anyone agree to come along, then cower in fear at their first real-world crisis?"

"Knock, knock, knock"

"Hey, Jessica. C'mon in. What's going on?"

"You know? I think that was the first time anyone went head to head with Darien and Council. I read over the minutes you wrote... a couple of times. If I were tasked with meeting Dorothy and Philip Nordgren alone, I might not have been as respectful. I agree with that paper 100%."

"Anyone like a glass of Cabernet?"

"Got any vodka or scotch?"

"Nope. Spirits are not allowed on board. Even beer. Well I'm going to have a small glass of wine."

"Me, too." Agreed Lory."

"OK! Me, too."

"Hannah, did you mean what you said in there about my being ready to sit in the middle chair?"

"Yes. You have twice now brought the ship home from the moon. You sit in the second chair and watch and listen and then apply that to running Seraphim. You did what I did and went to each major Ship's departments and learned how things work. So, yea. You are qualified to captain this ship."

"I'll wait on that, if you don't mind. I may not have the intuition or the fortitude you have, so, I prefer the #2 position. But thanks."

"You will have the Conn for the next couple of weeks, though."

"That's fine. Who is going?

"My folks, and Lory. Her mom lives nearby and is not doing well. At the end of the time there, Freeman and Newcomb will come back with us."

"What if Darien and company meet with the NASA people while you're gone, and gives up stuff you don't agree with?"

"Well then he either changes it or he can find another occupant for the center chair."

"You don't mean that."

"I don't? Ask around."

"Hannah...!"

"When are people going to take me seriously? If the wrong person is sitting in that chair when the shit hits the fan, and people on board won't or can't do the right thing, or make the right decisions instantly, then a lot of people will be hurt or worse. You know as well as anybody, I take my job as captain very seriously. If Darien doesn't understand or see my concern then it's on him if the ship and the entire crew is destroyed. I will not be party to stupidity."

"You need a vacation."

"Yes, I do." Then, Lory stepped in...

"I don't think Seraphim has anything to worry about. If the crew finds out, then there won't be anyone on the bridge or the other departments. I have to go. Hang in there Hannah."

"Captain on the bridge."

As I took my position in the center chair on the raised bridge deck, Augie leaned over and said something ominous.

"Unless you are in that chair, this ship 'int going anywhere." His British manner of speech was obvious. As he stepped down off the raised deck, I saw several crew members offer a thumbs up as he passed. They know! They all know. As much as that was a vote of confidence, it also made me sad. It made me even more angry that power hungry bureaucrats might try to intimidate us into allowing mostly well-intentioned NASA personnel control over decisions that might be harmful as we do what we were trained to do. That could be so easily remedied if the Council and Darien could muster the balls necessary to insist on our limitation clauses in my directive. Well, it hasn't happened yet and my family and I are going home to visit other family members and friends. It will give me some time away to think this through. If what I'm thinking and already putting together, I am going to need help, the right kind of help and now I know who that will be. What will be waiting for us when we come back? Time will tell.

I was packing the few things I felt I needed for this relatively short trip when I heard a knock on the door.

"Carl, nice to see you, come on in." He didn't look happy.

"I thought you should know. Darien sent a modified version of your minutes of the meeting to Houston. Along with the briefing with Dorothy Williams and Philip Nordgren. NASA administrators are not happy. Now I need to remind you, the administrators are not the scientists that would be joining us. Your old buddy, former Admiral Bascom Holder has point on this for planning purposes for the meeting with orders to make sure their directives are followed. On his behalf, he does not agree with his bosses. In a moment of clarity, he said that this, in the Navy, is kind of like... a coup. Very quietly he seemed to suggest that NASA may not be the top authority of this directive. Higher level people may be pulling the strings."

"Are you suggesting that after all the failed attempts to over-run us, they might now be trying to hit us from the inside?"

"Exactly!"

"When is this meeting supposed to be held and where?"

"Here, in three to four weeks. No sooner."

"Do you have a copy of the modified version of your minutes of the meeting Darien sent down there?

Yes, here, and there was this, sent back amending Darien's."

I looked it over and nearly started breaking stuff. I was major league pissed. Clearly it was a coup.

"Did Darien comment on it?"

"No, he just walked off."

"He doesn't know what to do." I growled. I thought for a few minutes...

"***But, I do.*** Carl, thank you. I guess you know, my mom and dad and I will be spending a few days back home visiting family. I'm not exactly sure when we will be back. Now, I have a tough question for you. Do you want Seraphim to remain under our full control or turned over to NASA?"

Carl looked carefully at me and I suppose he saw determination in my eyes. This was one of those moments when you step forward or you didn't. My eyes told him that. He remembered when he said that I *stood majestically on the bow of this ship, sword held high, ready to do battle with the Kraken.*

"Carl. The Kraken is back. And my sword is sharper than it has ever been." I held his stare... and then I saw it. He was not going to back away from this one.

"Hannah. You have my complete support. Whatever you need, I have your back." He smiled. He knew I was going to fight. He knew that I never lose.

"I need a sword." He said with a serious expression.

"Indeed, and, you shall have one." I said.

"Now... starting right now, I am formulating a plan which I will not share as yet. But I will be adding people. I need you to not say a word that the captain has a plan. That includes Darien, anybody. Actually, I'm just beginning to put something together. Please remember, '*Loose lips sink StarShips*'." I said paraphrasing propaganda posters during World War II.

"I will keep you in the loop as things gear up. And, no, I'm not throwing Darien under the bus. I just need him protected. And, the best way to do that is put him into a witness protection program... of sorts. If he doesn't know anything, they can't hurt him."

Carl Ledbetter, Senior Member, Ships Council is a brilliant scientist with a PHD in Astrophysics, but he is also a sensitive and caring person. He was not built for battle, but he needs to be prepared for one. I have faith he will rally-forth when the time comes. This is a battle worth winning.

There will be others that will join our ranks, with him. I'm going to build an Army... an *invincible* one.

Norfolk, Virginia

L ory expertly descended over the rural Virginia countryside to the small grass airstrip that is the Virginia Beach Airpark. Someone with a flashlight acting as a beacon, guided us down. I watched in wonder as she deftly coaxed the little grey-striped Valkyrie into a silent, effortless landing. The new but non-descript hangar sat in the back of the northern most end of the airport property. On the east side of the grass parking area sat a beautifully restored Junkers JU-52 and behind it, an olive-drab PBY Catalina. Oh, yea. I like this place already. Alfred Clark moved forward and greeted us as we descended the steps to the grass. At just under six-feet tall and slender, wearing a farmer's denim bib overalls over a flannel shirt and work boots, the grey-haired senior with a friendly approachable smile, greeted the four of us with solid handshakes. Lory received a warm hug from her old friend.

"Wow! That's quite the little rocket ship. OK! Let's get her inside. How do you do that?"

"Easy. I'll just back it in."

The double doors slid sideways revealing the interior. Several lights illuminated the freshly painted gloss grey floor. To the right was a beautifully restored P-51D Mustang with yellow and black checker-board nose paint. Beneath the six exhaust ports of the Roll-Royce Merlin, Packard built V1650-7 engine was the nose-art name of the aircraft.

Valkyrie

What a beautiful airplane. The plane that won the air war over the European Theater, in WWII. Some would argue that, but the statistics were definitely in the Mustang's favor. My dad loved this airplane but never got a chance to fly one. Through him, I got to know a lot about them. The most famous fighter of WWII. No argument there.

Lory returned to the cockpit of our Valkyrie. She hovered 2 feet off the ground, reversed the GMI slightly and it moved very slowly backwards into the hangar with Alfred guiding from in front. I checked space behind and there was plenty of room as the ship came back... and back. I crossed my arms high in front of me signifying stop. That was relayed by Alfred in front. A seldom used device on all Seraphim vehicles is a panel on the underside, that, when opened, exposes the vehicle to the effects of natural gravity. With the struts lowered, the little ship descended onto the concrete floor. All switches were turned off and Lory exited into the hangar. Alfred looked on in wonder

"Damn, that thing is neat." Headlights were coming down the access road.

"We should close the doors." both doors slowly closed sealing curious eyes from seeing in. The car pulled up just outside. Then another car. When both were side by side. My sister, Amanda and her husband climbed out and ran to me. I received generous hugs from both. She said the kids were home with a baby-sitter. The other car deposited our two retirees. Boy was I glad to see them. Mom and Dad received hugs and kisses from their other daughter and son-in-law. Alfred was introduced around, then suggested we go into his office. His office was really a work area, half as large as the hangar it was attached to. It had big tables, some clear of anything, others sporting aircraft parts like starters, carburetors, special tools, wing and tail panels that were to be covered, lay awaiting the fabric. Rolls of polyester fabrics Ceconite™, Stits/Polyfiber™, lay on an adjacent table still in their protective sleeves. Paint cans were lined up on wall shelves, with some power tools. It looked like an OK-equipped work shop. There was an air-compressor, shop-vacuum, table saw, drill press, etc. It may be too new to have had a lot of work done in it. A very large table and a bunch of chairs made up the opposite side of the room. He said he has periodic poker games and cookouts or cook-ins, when the weather was bad. He said there were a bunch of ex-GIs that would hang out here from time to time. Folks from the warbird museum would come by. As a surprise, I realized those from this group were now resident in Tactical on Seraphim. I remembered that was how Lory came to be with us.

"Is this room heated?" asked Perry.

"Can be. Wood stove over there. Wood outside. Couple of cord, I think." Then Lory suggested.

"This would be perfect for a private meeting, Hannah."

"Yes, it would. I'm beginning to put a plan together. We could do it here. Alfred, how many people can sit in here?"

"I have fold-up chairs for upwards of sixty. Can even cater dinners from a catering company close by. Good food." I was smiling now.

"Where's dad?"

"In the hanger caressing the Mustang."

"Figures!"

"Hannah, Evie was going to come with us today, but she came down sick and is home being cared for by her mom, but she really appreciated the e-mail."

"Amanda, why are you looking at me that way?"

"I'm sorry, but it seems everyone knows you are my sister, the Captain of the Seraphim. Sis, you are famous. And, mom and dad work for you."

"Well, that is not entirely true. Mom is top administrator in our on-board hospital... Med-Bay, and dad is head of Security, we call Tactical. They don't work for me. We all support the ship. I just run it. I'm the Bus-Driver."

"She's more than that." ... said dad.

"OK, I'm a fireman, too. I put fires out."

Mom, Dad and I spent the next two days with Amanda. Lory stayed with her mom, and Doug and Perry with friends. In three days, we would return to the little grass strip where grass roots planning would resume and a battle plan devised.

Before we left with our respective families/friends we spoke with Alfred about our problem back home. I had a sense that I could trust him and it was what he said next, convinced me I was right.

"Ya-know, I realize that many of us look like country-bumpkins by the way we dress and how we talk. But some of our people went out to Wyoming to give you a hand. When they came back, they told the rest of us about Seraphim and her beautiful, kick-ass captain. I see they were correct and am proud to assist in any way I can. The rest feel the same way. The Vets in this area are mostly ex-Navy. We still hold true to our vows when we held up our hands and took the pledge when we entered the Service. Most of us are retirees and collect our stipend once a month. We all own guns and go to church on Sunday. So, whatever you need, we'll make it available. We know how to keep quiet, too."

I like these guys.

Three Cornered Hats and Leather Helmets

When we arrived back at the hangar, the P-51 was sitting out in the sun near the two larger war-birds. A flurry of excitement enveloped the little airport as vintage airplanes arrived and parked in a line on both sides of the freshly mowed runway. The occasional sound of an arriving bi-plane with its two-speed rotary engine (all on, all off) *burrrrped, burrrrped, burrrrped* as it settled to the ground to join with others. It's leather-helmeted pilot needed help getting out of the little fabric covered plane. Then together with others, pushed the early 1900s flying machine into position with others. Women walked around in period dresses holding parasols in the morning sun. Some men were walking around carrying late 18th century black-powder muskets and wearing three-cornered hats of a time 130 years before WWI. Here we stood with a craft unimaginable to the real people of those times. Coming our way was a nearly-silent modern-day electric golf cart with two people sitting astride the 16-mph vehicle. Alfred and Lory pulled up beside us in the glory of the morning countryside. Lory excitedly said...

"They have food tents with all kinds of stuff: huge donuts, funnel-cakes, hot dogs, burgers, Italian sausages smothered in onions cooking on grills. It's great. Smells great. It reminds me of my childhood at the country fairs. The smells are all the same. We all need to take a walk down there. Even for only a few minutes. The sights, the sounds... Ah! So great. Alfred is one of the organizers here. You are having way too much fun, Alfred." He snickered. We took the walk Lory suggested and she was right. Two centuries of history were displayed with people in period costumes walking among the food venders, vintage aircraft and Patriots with their 3-cornered hats and muskets. Alfred's immaculate circa 1930s Stearman bi-plane sat in the corner of the field near one of the Museum's hangars. I was getting itchy to start making phone calls so I returned to the Valkyrie hangar and using a real cell phone, started making calls. The first was to...

Jerry Dickson, Dir of Internal Security in Angels Landing
I told Jerry what was happening and that I needed help.

From my travel bag, I retrieved some paper and pen. I wrote a list to myself in cursive...

From Security:

- *Susan Richards, Ship's Gen Council, legal affairs,*
- *Myron Campbell, Attorney, Contract Law,*
- *David Bradley, Legal Ass't to M. Campbell*
- *Felicia Cunningham, Attorney, Constitutional Law*
- *Constance Knowles, Paralegal.*

From Tactical:

- *Donna Singleton, Former Secret Service.*
- *Sam Lonegan, Counter Intelligence (retired)*

From the Executive Committee:

- *Carl Ledbetter, Chairman, Ships Council*
- *Porter Williams, Exec. Admin Ass't Science Divs*

Well, I had the people I needed. Should I bring them all here for a closed-door meeting? This was somewhere that nobody could crash the party. Two hours later...

"I wondered what happened to you." stated my dad coming through the hangar side door, followed by the rest of them.

"What are you doing?"

"Making phone calls."

"With Mr.Scott?" I held up my iPhone.

Lory and I told the story to those present. I said goodbye to Amanda and Brad Wagner, and they went home to be with their kids.

I reminded Mom and Dad who were at the table for our evening meal when Darien and I had a difference of opinion. Lory showed them the papers Darien sent to Houston that Carl Ledbetter thought I should know about.

"These are copies of a modified version of my minutes of the meeting sent to Houston, along with a briefing by Dorothy Williams and Philip Nordgren. NASA administrators are not happy."

"Hannah thinks something is happening. There may be a coup attempt."

I interjected...

"Remember when I was talking with Lieutenant Atkinson, military liaison, to the ISS Project Manager. I asked how's the weather in Houston? He responded..."

"Beautiful weather outside. But a storm is brewing, inside. I have to go. Bye."

"That was a warning. Carl told me Admiral Bascom Holder has point on this for planning purposes for the meeting with orders to make sure their directives are followed. I was told he does not agree with his bosses. He said that this sounds like... a coup. And, he seemed to suggest that NASA may not be the top authority of this directive. Higher level people may be pulling the strings. I asked if he was suggesting that after all the failed attempts to over-run us, they might now be trying to hit us from the inside?" and he said...

'Exactly!'"

"Do you have a copy of the modified version of your minutes of the meeting Darien sent down there?" asked dad.

Yes, and there was this, also, they sent back additional amendments to Darien's paper. Here."

Dad looked both pages over and reacted with anger. He stood up and said a few profane words, and realized it clearly was a coup.

"Did Darien comment on it?"

"No, he just walked off. Carl said. I don't think he knows what to do. That's when I decided on coming here. Show that to the others, please." Admiral Freeman picked the paper I had been compiling a list, and read it over carefully.

"What's this Hannah?" I didn't say anything...

"This looks like a list of personnel and advisors for a legal team... a dream-team. You're going to go into that meeting and mess them up, aren't you? You are the warrior."

"We have a lot of work to do, but this is my goal. I'll need help refining it and seek your approval on some elements. First, I would like to invite all the people on that list to come here to join us in this hangar, and join in a planning session away from scrutiny inside Seraphim. Please note, these are legal scholars from our own security department with paralegal help. There are some Council members whom I like and trust to provide thought and reason to make this work. Feel free to add personnel to that list as we hash out a war plan. I don't just want to free ourselves from the tyranny of outside control or influence by NASA, I want to crush the whole black projects, deep state involvement, once and for all. I have no desire to hurt NASA and their people. Maybe they can't find a way to extricate themselves from the outside influence. What if we worked from inside NASA, too? Sky's the limit, folks. Those evil folks will be safe and secure inside the box. We're going to burn it down from the outside.

Admiral Freeman and Perry Newcomb, I think I have a job for you. Do you mind working close together again like you did on the Lindstrom?"

"That would be great, what do you have in mind?"

I looked at Mom and Dad, Lory and Alfred. Then looking at our new crewmembers...

"At Annapolis I was on a sailboat racing team as the tactician. I watched the water, the wind, movement of our sails, the tell-tail on the mast-head. Doing so, I was able to suggest very slight course changes, sail settings. I learned to read the wind by watching the ripples and waves often a half-mile away, which told me the direction and strength of the wind well before it reached us. We would adjust sail settings and 1 to 2-degree course changes in anticipation of the approaching breeze. We were always ahead of our competition by making these incremental adjustments. It is an art-form. Our boat won every regatta we were in. So, I would like both of you to be Seraphim tacticians like that. Read the prevailing winds of those who would do us harm and suggest adjustments to strategies before they realize it. You will work closely with me, with Tactical, Helm, and wherever you feel the ship can do better. We will stay one step ahead of them at every turn. Then, when the proper time comes... we will sink them."

I looked around the room at those there... our new friends, as they looked at me. They sat quietly listening, their eyes bright as they saw the warrior rise to the occasion.

I was stoked. We can do this. We are going to take our ship back once and for all... and keep it.

"Do you accept this challenge, Admiral, COB?"

They looked at each other and nodded.

"You bet. It's perfect, Hannah. Nobody thinks this stuff up like you do."

"I am tired of constantly being on the defensive, and being the prey. An effective predator learns the ways of the forest and jungle. We will no longer be prey, but we must understand the savannah, too. So, what do you think? Should we have the Pow-Wow here as Alfred has been so kind to offer, or pick somewhere else?"

"It would be an honor to have your meeting here. I am ex-Navy, most of my friends are GIs. Build your team. Hell! You may even find some useful talent among some of our lost souls. I see now why you are the Captain of the Seraphim. I saw you out on that moonscape with your new pal from Andromeda or beyond. That was epic.

I am a partner with a couple who owns a cute little Bed & Breakfast less than a mile from here. We even have an old school bus that the museum uses to chauffeur people to the big airport. Another X-Navy guy that hangs around here was a cook on a destroyer. Sometimes he comes and caters during our games or air shows. We have all the things you need. Bring-um-on in,"

I walked over to My Captain and COB, put arms around both of them, pulling them close and said...

"Welcome Aboard"

The Raising of a Militia

Calls were made to Theo Remington and Carl Ledbetter who were updated to our plans. Carl was ecstatic, Theo, not so much. I understood why. He fears some of his dearest friends might be harmed. But, I reminded him that should Runestone or whoever gain control of the Seraphim/Angels Landing franchise, people would be hurt. I assured him we have no intention to start a physical battle. This time we are going in, fully prepared with legal artillery. I explained that some of our people would be coming here to Virginia for top-level meetings away from prying eyes. If he and Carl would like to join us, a shuttle would be leaving very soon. See Jake Maxwell." I added...

"Since many are taking legitimate vacations, your 'few days away' would not be noticed. Please do not speak with anyone about this. ANYONE! I have every intention of protecting Darien and every man and woman aboard Seraphim and Angels Landing."

Dad had coordinated with his people in Tactical, and Jerry Dickson in Legal.

The die was cast.

Amassing the Troops

On Seraphim, Jake prepared *Peregrine* for the trip being rather public about a problem with the navigation systems on board that only occurred once in a while during long distance flights. He would check it out with the help of a couple of engineers. He forgot to say he was bringing a large group of people along. He was airborne several hours later. The *Peregrine* was seen headed west and climbing. Once out of view, it turned east with the VASIMR engines at max acceleration for only 45 seconds. They arrived here an hour later.

XO Jessica Pearson was outside the rotunda, and smiled as she watched the vapor-trail disappear headed east. She was the only other person to know what was happening. She walked back through the rotunda with a smile on her face, then to the elevator to Deck 9 and met with others in the Captains Mess for a glorious meal. She did not speak of anything we were doing.

Peregrine set down silently behind the hangar at the Virginia Beach Airpark, in rural Virginia. Our friends from Seraphim came through the back door of the Hangar to a party like atmosphere. And... Theo and Carl came, too. I was elated and greeted both with hugs.

"What's with the hat?" asked Carl. He looked around and saw eleven of us wearing Revolutionary War period Colonial three-cornered hats.

"Getting into the spirit of the next revolution. Oh! This is Alfred Clark. He owns this hangar and two airplanes that reside inside. Alfred, this is Professor Theodore Remington,

Seraphim's Science Officer... our Mr. Spock, and this is Dr. Carl Ledbetter, physicist and Ships Council. "

"Pleased to meet you both. Welcome to our little refuge away from the crazies. We have fifty or more ex-military and wives, in our motley group. We put on aviation related open house activities and family-oriented picnics and cook-outs. Weather permitting, we take grand-kids for rides in a friend's J3 Piper-Cub. We just finished our annual vintage bi-plane fly-in. Please, come over here. We have a catered evening repast. Help yourselves. Drinks in the fridge. You have an amazing captain. In fact, I think she is about to speak."

"Good evening everyone and friends of Seraphim. Welcome to the sons and daughters of the New American Revolution. We do seem to be in part of the country that was present during that historic part of our nation's history, hence the hat and, oh wait. May I borrow that?" I was handed the very heavy *Kentucky long rifle,* one of the former Navy guys was carrying around during the fly-in.

"Now I'm ready." I stood tall looking high to my left, my hat properly perched on my head. Everyone laughed at their captain acting silly. But soon, that would end.

"Is this your war-party, Hannah?" asked Alfred.

"We'll see. Would you tell them about accommodations and transportation?"

"Yes, of course. Ladies and Gentlemen, it's late and I'm sure you would like to have a nice rest in preparation for tomorrow's serious planning meeting. We have a bus outside. It is a 1950s era military Navy bus. It's noisy, uncomfortable and cold. But it runs, like the rest of us from the same era. We and the bus, will not let you down. You will be staying at a cozy mid-south style Bed and Breakfast owned by these folks here. This is Betty and Floyd Cochran, also Navy veterans. He was a corpsman and she was a pilot flying C-47s and C-

54s. Now, if you would follow them to the yucky-green bus sitting outside, we will see you in the morning."

Bright and Early

"Sleep well?"

"Yes! What a nice B&B that is. Betty and Floyd made a great breakfast, this morning. They asked if it would be OK if they attended our meeting. We said fine. I hope that's OK?"

I thought about it and ...

"Yes, of course it's fine. All these people are Patriots and have served our country well. They don't like what is happening to our ship and theme park. Every one of them know us, who we are, and have followed our history since day-one. I see six of you. Where is everybody else?"

"Their looking at Alfred's Mustang outside. Your dad is sitting in the cockpit with Alfred giving him his first lesson, 'How to Start a Mustang'."

"That doesn't surprise me. He's been lusting over the P-51 since before he left home for the Navy. Given a choice between an FA-18 Super Hornet and P-51, he would take the Mustang, damned if I know why. Everybody has their passions, I guess.

Well, folks back in Wyoming have no idea where we are, if we are together, or any idea what we intend to do. So, with that in mind... let's begin. Let me get the rest of our folks in here." In minutes we had everyone present.

"Susan Richards, what do you make of this plot to take command of Seraphim?"

"I have here the papers from the communiques between Darien and Houston. First, I don't know why Darien would even consider accepting NASAs requirements. He would lose everything. The good thing is, he is not authorized to hand over the keys. The Council and the members of Symphony would have to co-sign, and my sense is... they won't. Myron, what are your thoughts?"

This memorandum from NASA is ambiguous. It has no legal authority. Felicia?"

"A Constitutional lawyer would tear this to ribbons. Let me ask a few questions. Has 'Angels Landing' as an entity been trademarked?"

"Oh yes." returned Susan. "Including Seraphim. Then we filed for copyright protection of all significant technologies on all vessels."

"What about patents?" asked Myron Campbell.

"No. We have to be very careful with that. If we file we have to describe the function of the science as well as the implementation hardware. An example is the discovery of Quantum Gravity and how we found we can use it. It is an intellectual property. We don't know how to protect that."

"I think all we have to do is form the patent application so it doesn't reveal much. I'll find some patent lawyers who do this for a living. No sweat, we'll have patents, too."

A voice came from the back of the room.

"I know somebody that could help. Works out of the Navy Judge Advocate Generals office, Region Legal Service Office, Mid-Atlantic (RLSO MIDLANT). Their jurisdiction is east coast. It would not cover Wyoming. Let me make a call."

"Who are you?"

"Elliot Brimley, I used to be a JAG officer before my retirement in 2012."

"Welcome aboard, Elliot."

"I don't like Government intrusion into civil activities. I have a thing about that, that really pisses me off."

"We need to get on this fast. They could slap us with a Cease and Desist Order. It's an official order handed down by a government agency or court directing a person or entity to stop doing something immediately which essentially keeps us from moving anything, including Seraphim, from the property. Such an order effectively places an injunction on the person or entity that prohibits the named activity as suspicious or illegal. That would essentially lock us down and stop all activity. They will claim they have some kind of right to the property until a court, in this case probably federal, rules on it. Of course, we know it is bogus, but it could give them more time to come up with more legal instruments that would shut us down." said Constance Knowles, Paralegal. Then... Elliot Brimley piped in...

"OK! Listen up. We do have someone out in the F. E. Warren Air Force Base Legal Services/JAG, located approximately 3 miles west of Cheyenne, Wyoming."

"What do they do there?"

"The base? It is one of three strategic-missile bases in the U.S., but they do have a functioning Jag office. They are willing to help Wyoming residents. They know Hannah. They know Seraphim. They talked with Colonel Jake Hanover, Wyoming National Guard. They were briefed about past intrusions by the bad-guys." Constance Knowles added...

"It may take them awhile to gather the legal support to make a case. Right now, they have a series of obstacles that can give us time." My mind was racing...

"Who owns Angels Landing? Is there a signed deed to the property?

"No." said Susan. "All that land is Wyoming State property. We were gifted the property to build the theme park. If we pulled up stakes and left, it would revert back to the State. I'll send an inquiry to the Wyoming State Attorney-

General's office to get their take on it. I have a long list here. But... it does give us action items we can work with. We can tie this all together, Captain... No worries!"

"Susan, remember when I was staring down Kensington and Furukawa in the rotunda that day they were feeding their handlers with information about us? I asked you, as Captain, what options do I have?"

"And I said 'Under Maritime Law, the captain has the option to render a judgement at his or her discretion'. Therefore, you could be judge, jury and executioner. But, then I followed with, 'but, it could be argued that since this ship is on U.S property, that option is limited."

Oh, did I have an idea. I smiled, all saw it...

"What if... Seraphim wasn't in the United States?"

"What are you thinking, Hannah?"

"This is going to be fun. You watch, we... are going to take back Seraphim. I'm going for quick walk."

Utter silence... but big smiles.

Mustang Sally

W here is Hannah?" asked Admiral Freeman. Dad answered.

"She is out sitting on the wing of the Mustang. Helps her think, I guess."

Theo and Carl joined Doug, Perry and dad and walked toward me. I was sitting on the starboard wing leaning against the fuselage with 16 swastikas painted under the canopy. This plane had seen action over Europe. I still had the 3-corner hat on. I felt comfortable out here smelling the fresh morning fragrance of trees, grasses and a frog pond nearby. I had detailed my plan in my head. Now, I was preparing to tell all of them how we can do it. But something was missing.

"Nice morning. Bugs eating you up?"

" No, they left me alone."

"What are you doing besides breathing fresh air."

"That and working out how we are going to win this. There is an imperative here. Seraphim is a flying machine. If they could muster up the talent, they could fly it to someplace of their choice. So... The first thing we do, we render it unflyable. That's rather easy, actually. With a little help from engineering, it won't go very far without the ACPUs since they also provide power for the GMI and gravity systems.

"Hannah, are you ever going to take that hat off."

"Maybe... when I shower."

" I have news from the bridge." Said Theo.

"It seems there are more people from Houston and somewhere around the DC area, coming to Angels Landing. It started with only five people from Houston. They are now all congregating in a hotel in Rawlins. Although they don't do much when they visit Angels Landing, they just walk around outside and everywhere they are allowed to go, checking it out. Tactical and Jessica have locked access to the bridge, CIC and NGE. The five objected and demanded access. Jessica politely said with a smile, it is always locked and off-limits to non-ships personnel. Engineering has been locked out, too."

"Excellent! She's on top of this. Doing just enough that the bad guys don't know that what she's doing isn't policy. We need to talk to Jessica, Gus Mayer, Augie Lincoln and Paddy Lewis." I stopped dead in my tracks... a thought fought its way to my attention.

"Maybe we are approaching the solution all wrong. I'm still having a problem understanding why Darien would sell out his life's dream. Then it hit me. He's running out of money. Theo, you are closer to him than anybody. Has he said anything about the state of Seraphim's operating costs?"

"He has. About a month ago he was all happy that Angels Landing has had its highest quarter ever. It more than covers its expenses even with the construction of the museum. The hotel is always a full sell-out. Angels Landing gets a pretty good kick-back from them, and the theme park is packed all the time. Food services are in the green. It's Seraphim that's running in the red." As the picture became clearer... I added...

"So, that became knowledge outside of Seraphim. They found out about the shortfall and made out a whopping big check as a bailout, but with provisos. Darien probably hates the idea, but he panicked. *He freakin' panicked!!!*" I jumped off the leading edge of the 70+ year old airplane wing and started walking really fast into the hangar and work room beyond.

"Theo. Would you please contact your friend and colleague, Darien Hunter, and tell him, flat out 'Do not sign the documents.' I don't know crap about high finance or cooperate this or that, but... we need to find an alternate source of financing. I'm a bus driver, what do I know?" and suddenly a thought hit me...

"Wait... or... a truck driver..." I grabbed the Kentucky Long rifle leaning against the wall and started pacing around the room, tri-cornered hat still in place on my head with a firearm used very effectively 300 hundred years ago to secure the freedom and forge a new country from despotic rule. My anger was abating, and a new idea was forming. I started walking again, now, with renewed energy and enthusiasm...

"*WHAT IF...*" I began... "we offer a trucking service... bus service to say... the Saturnian moons Titan, Rhea and Enceladus or any of Saturn's other 59 moons. Future missions might include the Jupiter world with its 79 known moons. Think of it this way, what if we offer this as incentive... We offer to take their scientists, rovers, orbital probes, instrumentation packages, trained deployment people, we will provide close proximity fly-bys of all the moons in the comfort of our shuttle craft."

I was parading around, the 10-pound flint-lock rifle going up and down as I paced the room, like I was marching...

"We'll tell them, walk on those moons if you dare, take close up pictures with your cell phones. Live aboard the spacious and luxurious inter-stellar star ship, the only one in existence. Live in full 1 G gravity throughout Seraphim and shuttles with closely monitored excellent air quality. Swim in our pools, use our putting ranges, play Zero-golf. Eat in our *Fábulas* restaurants. Watch movies. Be able to talk with loved-ones using our reliable two-way inter-planetary phone-call capability. Put on State-of-the-Art space suits and walk the surface of Titan, pick up rocks, sand, find peculiar other-worldly artifacts that will be securely placed in environmentally and biologically protected sealed containers to bring home for scientific studies in their own laboratories on Earth."

Out of breath... I stopped... and sat down. It was so quiet... had everyone left, bored with my diatribe? No, they were sitting quietly behind me. Then a voice from behind me said...

"We can do that. YES! We can do that." Susan Richards repeated." Then I heard Theo's voice...

"Hannah, that's it. What a great idea. We definitely need to follow up on that."

"Yes!" said Carl. "We need to get a team together. People with organizational and financial backgrounds in corporate matters. We need to start immediately." Carl got up and walked into the hangar, phone and notebook in hand. Others in the room began talking, soon a cacophony of voices rose talking over each other. Ideas were shared and amended, excitement was building.

The Militia was assembling.

I was on my feet again... walking... talking. All were looking at me.

"May I use that computer? Does it have access to the internet?"

"Yea, sure. High speed."

I opened the browser and was typing like a mad-woman. Then I found it. I was suddenly filled with exhileration.

"Y-Y-Y-E-E-E-E-E-SSS, *Yes, Yes*." I screamed. They all looked at me. Did I see hope on those faces?

"That's it. Look at this." I backed away so others saw what was on the screen. They gathered round.

"Look at those names. *Look, Look.* Everything we need to know is right there. We don't try to compete with big heavy lift companies like SpaceX that have already cornered the market. We carefully advertise our ability to bring stuff and people out there emphasizing safety, comfort, lower risk, perhaps lower cost, etcetera. C'mon, you folks are smarter than me. Do you see the opportunity here? We do the deep space stuff, the shortest being the moon. Double up... First stop, the moon, drop off, next stop Mars, and so forth. We don't try to compete with Low Earth Orbit stuff. We tell the world what is available to them and they will call us... *THEY WILL CALL US.*" I yelled. I heard cheers resonate through the hangar work room. I continued, on a roll...

"We already proved our ability when we saved those astronauts' lives on the ISS and we did it in less than six hours." I placed the rifle against the wall and with hat still on my head walked out into the early night. Damn it smelled good. I think I really like the country atmosphere. I remember as a kid, those days when the family would vacation near the mountains, swam in the warmth of summer lakes, fished off river and pond banks, catching mostly nothing, smelled the wood smoke of camp fires as other families enjoyed the same thing. I was the youngest. Mark and Amanda much older were not as enamored with camping. I loved it... and now miss it... a lot. I was sitting on the bank of the little frog pond when I sensed others behind me. I heard Theo's voice.

"That little speech you gave in there, lit the fires of imagination and inspiration. I've never seen more motivated people. We linked in to the Council, in chambers. With a secure tie line, we explained our plan and they were ecstatic. Darien all but cried with happiness. You should know that a 'just-formed' team of lawyers, marketing and advertising people are already building a program that we should be able to realize in less than a month. We should get back there soon, Hannah."

"I think you all should go. I need a little R&R. This whole thing has me worn out. But, I have some ideas I would like to play with. Theo, I'm going to make this EPIC. I'm going to stay at my sister's house or here for a while. Maybe see an old friend. Take the *Peregrine*. I'll keep the *Valkyrie*. I'll be back in a little while. I'm enjoying the peace and tranquility, and the smell of nature."

"OK! Will we be able to contact you?"

"Yes, of course. You have my cell number. I look forward to hearing your progress. I think this is going to work. When the big meeting takes place, send me a date/time. I'll be there."

"Take care of yourself, Hannah. We need you."

"Thanks. Have a good flight." His footsteps trailed off into the distance allowing the quiet of nature to again envelope this world. But, more steps were headed my way. It was dad. He sat on the grass beside me, saying nothing at first, just looking out over the water and listening to the occasional croak of a distant frog.

"It's nice here." He started... "May I ask why you chose to stay behind? The rest are leaving."

"They don't need me. I come up with crazy ideas they don't come up with on their own. That's OK. It's my job, but I feel a weight of responsibility that is overwhelming. I needed a break. Are you alone? Why didn't you go with them?"

"They don't need me, either. Tactical is fine. There are good people there. Same on the bridge. I wanted to spend some alone-time with my daughter. Mom returned because she loves it there and the challenge. She understands why you chose to stay here for a while. In fact, she thinks it is good therapy."

"You know... you and I have always pressed forward as we pursued our career goals. You, a decorated Naval aviator for 32 years. And, me just trying to survive, then low and behold I wind up the only person in the world that does what I do now. I wonder about people who don't have the drive to find their dream jobs and spend so much time in learning institutions making themselves eligible for good paying jobs.

I stumbled into a new world. Tagging along with a friend as she moved to a new job out west. In doing so, I meandered to a place that would change my life. What was wrong with the one I had? Going back to my early childhood, I remember going on camping trips... the five of us. Do you remember where we went?"

"When you were about six, and I was home on leave, we went up to Shenandoah Valley Campground, and next year to Cumberland State Forest, Bear Creek Lake, camping. Mark complained the whole time and Amanda didn't seem to enjoy it much. But you loved it. I remember the first time you caught a fish, you were so excited, but when you pulled it in,

you insisted we release it unharmed. Then there was the time
you had gone off by yourself, then you came running back to
the campsite screaming at the top of your lungs with a bunch
of wasps chasing. Your mom grabbed the can of spray and
walked around the campsite emptying the entire can. I threw
wet pine branches into the fire causing billows of smoke. The
bugs, bugged out and didn't come back. Mom checked you
over and found no bee-stings at all. You didn't stop crying for
the rest of the day, and wouldn't move further than 5-feet
from the fire and wanted to sleep near it."

"Yea, that day kinda sucked. How about the time you
wanted to swim in a mountain stream fed pond? Beautiful
crystal-clear water moving slowly to the out-flow of the pond.
It was nice and deep so we jumped in from the over-hanging
rocks. That was the coldest water ever. Damn that was cold."

Dad continued our reminiscence tour through time while
sitting side by side over-looking the little pond. Footsteps
caused me to turn as Alfred came alongside.

"There are a few of us in the hangar with a nice lunch set
up. Come on in. Some new folks arrived you should meet."

"OK! We'll be right there." We got up, brushed the pine
needles and grass off our butts and walked toward the
Hangar.

There were about 12 people moving around carrying
paper plates of fried chicken, corn bread, baked beans and a
canned drink taken from a really large galvanized wash tub
filled with ice on top of beer, soda, and chilled sun tea. Alfred
saw dad and I, the last remaining Seraphim crew members.
The rest had gone home. I was still wearing the tri-cornered
black hat when I heard Alfred yell...

"Ladies and Gentlemen, look who we have here? Please
welcome the only Starship captain in the world and the only

person to shake the hand of a real inter-galactic alien, Captain Hannah Parish."

The place was loud with clapping and 'welcome'. I smiled broadly as I walked around shaking hands with real Americans, real patriots. People I think in later years I could live with. Perhaps not here, but in a cabin someplace on a lake with the sound of loons calling in the morning.

"We've seen you on television confronting bad people who would try to steal your ship's secrets. Alfred told us about the NASA folks that are helping the same bad guys to take Seraphim for their own." My smile disappeared as a looked toward the ground suddenly sad. I said...

"That's never going to happen, any more than you would let your homes, farms, businesses fall into the hands of corporations or government people. You would fight for your freedoms like you did 245 years ago. I WILL NOT let them take our home either." I grabbed the flint lock rifle once more, and held it at the ready and said...

"Whatever it takes. No. I'm not going to use firearms. I have something else planned, something *SPECIAL*. Watch the news in a week or so. It will be EPIC. Dad and I will be leaving early tomorrow morning, I think."

"Are you flying out? In what?"

"Yup! Wanna see it?"

"I'll go open the hangar door." Said Alfred. I climbed in and powered up the Valkyrie, closed the gravity door and floated straight out and stopped on the concrete apron, hovering 2 feet above the surface, making no sound at all. They asked questions on top of questions as they walked around Valkyrie-1. I was happy to answer them all.

"Hey, your dad's going flying." Sure-enough he was sitting in the jump seat of the other Valkyrie... Alfred's P-51. Alfred strapped himself into the pilot seat. After a few moments, the big 12-foot 4 bladed propeller began to turn. Then with flames shooting out the exhausts, and with a loud pop, the big Merlin V-12 caught and roared to life.

I watched as the 70-year-old airplane moved, turned and bounced a little on the uneven ground and disappeared around the tree line taxying to the east end of the grass runway. The roar sounded again as the throttle of the mustang reached full takeoff power. In seconds, the sleek shape of WWIIs greatest fighter came by... gear folding into the wheel well and the gear doors closing on top of them. I watched with a tear in my eye as my dad was living a life-long dream. Too bad it wasn't dual control.

"Anyone want to go for a ride? I have room for 8 more." 6 entered. Then a wife of someone already on board, climbed in.

They sat and hooked their seat belts. I gave a quick briefing as I moved forward on GMI with no sound at all. The Mustang roared past barely 50 feet off the deck at 400 miles per hour, then went vertical for a half loop, staying inverted at the top. Alfred pulled positive Gs into a 45° inverted dive, then half-rolled to horizontal pulling out 100 feet from the ground. It's a good thing dad was accustomed to Gs because the little fighter was pulling upwards of 6-Gs in some of the maneuvers.

I turned my Valkyrie on its tail and climbed at full GMI. My guests couldn't understand the counter-gravity concept.

I called Nav on our secure line and was cleared through the debris cloud. Once above 150,000 feet I lit the two VASIMR-4 engines for 5 seconds. I flipped the ship and lit the VASIMRs for 5 seconds. We stopped pointing back at Earth. My guests were awe-struck. Again, I was peppered with questions. They wondered where the moon was. I explained that it was on the other side of earth. That's when I noticed something very odd. I took some pictures with the nose camera; wide angle, panoramic and several with different filters. Something was happening around the earth. I would wait until I returned to Seraphim where I would ask some questions of our ultra-smart scientists. I started down and leveled at 120,000 feet and engaged GMI. I made a nice slow descent so my guests could get pictures with their phones. As we approached the little airfield, I could see the mustang had returned and was parked where it had been earlier. I set down in the same configuration as before we left, shut everything down except position hold on GMI. Everyone disembarked and headed for the hangar meeting room. I saw dad standing with Alfred behind the food table. They both were laughing and talking at the same time. Meanwhile, the others were showing pictures they had taken with their phones from their first extraterrestrial journey. It was definitely a party mood. I joined dad and Alfred. I picked up a paper plate and placed some finger food on it.

"So, how was your flight in your favorite airplane?"

"Hannah, we are so spoiled with all the latest technologies, we forget the beauty of classical aviation. The mustang is cramped in the jump seat, smelly, very noisy and bouncy in turbulence. But it is also magic. I can't imagine those 6 to 8-hour flights from England to Berlin and back escorting the B-17s and B-24s all the way. Without the Mustang and its ability to protect our bomber streams, the second world war may have ended differently. Our flight was great and full of Gs, which I seem less comfortable with now. Must be age. Thank you, Alfred, for the opportunity to experience a wonderful airplane." I decided I should give a short speech...

"Ladies and Gentlemen, may I have a moment?" The room quieted and attention turned toward me, still sporting the tri-cornered hat.

"I want to thank all of you here at Virginia Beach Airpark for your gracious hospitality: the lovely B&B, food and use of this hat. We will be heading back to Wyoming in the early morning to confront our next challenge. Then... who knows what? It has been a pleasure meeting each of you. I will keep you all in my heart as we move into our next space adventure, hopefully without incident. No more asteroids, please. I love it here. Perhaps we will be back one day. Fishing sounds good, huh, dad?"

"You have an amazing daughter there, Ed. The world is watching as she and Seraphim's crew blaze into new frontiers bringing all of us with you in mind and spirit."

"God be with you all."

Renaissance (A Rebirth, Revival)
Theodore Benjamin Remington
His Story

There was a sense of urgency that permeated our souls. Each of the group at a place 1740 miles from our Wyoming home, feared what might happen if the NASA/Runestone consortium were to succeed in its bid to annex Seraphim. The phone call to Darien garnered some success. He seemed very happy I called. I was his partner and best supporter over the last 24 years. I explained our fears and was adamant that he not sign any documents. We have a plan to save Seraphim, I told him. He agreed. I told him we would be home soon. There was a long silence then he said...

"I'm not signing a damn thing. Hurry home. I feel alone like I never felt before. Hurry home."

"Just hang tough, Darien. We have your back and we have a plan. Sit with Jessica Pearson on the command deck and just open up a little. She can help. Take care."

We were leaving in a few minutes but I started walking. I left the hangar and walked toward the grass runway. I heard a sound to my right and followed it to an oddly shaped pond. Three ducks were swimming slowly across the slightly muddy, algae bound banks with an occasional stand of tall cattails, a circle of pink and white waterlilies and pickerel-pond plants. A very peaceful, serene scene. I sat down on a dry piece of the bank and just, smelled the fresh earthy aroma of wet earth and decaying plants. From a distance came the raspy call of a crow. Very few other sounds interrupted the moment.

In this place of peace and quiet, my mind wandered to the people that made up the crew of Seraphim. Foremost was the youngest of our group. I will never forget those early days when she sat in my office as I attempted to teach her the things she would need to know. Hannah Parish was, and still is, an exemplary student. She dove headfirst into the world I opened up to her. When you get to know her, she is not difficult to love. She has a saucy, childlike, humorous way about her, mixed with sarcasm and laced with intellectual-irony. She is tall, blond, slender, a bit tom-boyish, not quite beautiful like some models, but very attractive. But it's her expressive blue-grey eyes that can twist anyone either to her or terrify them. I watched in several meetings as she looked intently at someone across the table that she did not like. Very quickly that person would begin fidgeting in their seat, very uncomfortable. When she was required to move to the center chair on the bridge as Captain, initially she was reluctant, then she took charge. She was relentless in her pursuit of crew readiness, job skills and professionalism. There were bumps along the way, but she persevered and the Seraphim crew became a model of efficiency and preparedness. And now, we are again challenged. But, the group we have here are ready to join the fight and are doing most of the work this time.

Carl Ledbetter is the same age as me. We have been friends for years. He is a senior member on the Ships Council. Everybody likes Carl. An astrophysicist by trade, he is brilliant but very mellow and shy. He tends to frighten easily but yet, has a heart of gold.

Jessica Pearson is our XO, number two on our succession roster, now. She had the position when she first came aboard but was summarily replaced by Sarah Ann Michaels, much less qualified but a close friend of Darien Hunter, then captain of Seraphim. Due to circumstances beyond our control, Darien, Sarah and I were detained by not-so-nice people well away from Seraphim. Per the order of succession, Hannah Parish moved to the center seat. By an order from the new captain, Jessica was returned to the second seat on the bridge as XO. She is an easy replacement should Hannah not be available.

Darien Hunter is an *Anachronism*. I met him at a symposium on Quantum Theory vs Relativity, *Niels Bohr vs Albert Einstein*, titled *'Who is Right?'*. We met during intermission as many of the guests journeyed to the hall outside the auditorium for bathroom breaks and bar. He was listening to a debate between two young scientists on the same subject as inside. I stepped to the bar for a glass of wine when I bumped into Darien. He seemed tired of the verbal jousting and turned my way. I knew he had set himself apart from mainstream theoretical science by his propensity to adamantly disagree with others' point of view. That drew criticism and soon he would be excluded from invitations. He was eager to talk and, almost pointedly reflected on how smart he was. Well, the thing is... he is. That meeting was how I became his friend and his partner in the fabulous adventure yet to come. That was 24 years ago. Two years later we would form symphony, a gathering of like-minded scholars and scientists, all brilliant and eager to jump aboard a train of creative thought culminating in the first flight of Seraphim... the only functional Starship ever built. His brash, arrogant personality was overlooked in favor of his brilliant mind. These people have been the major players in our journey, but there are more. Not listed here but are no less important to the ship, others round out the list of remarkable, creative and highly intelligent members of Seraphim's crew. Now I'm concerned that due to some strategic planning on the part of our adversaries, we may lose what we all cherish so much... a Starship called Seraphim.

However, we have an ace in the hole...
The most unpredictable person ever... The Captain.

Taking Back, What is Ours

Before we headed home, we received a comm from our people in Legal, Tactical and Bridge, but no-one else. Not even Darien or the Council. I felt bad I couldn't include Theo, Carl, Doug Freeman or Perry Newcomb. Without this knowledge, Theo and Carl were unaware of our plans. We just asked them not to inform anyone that we were back, either. TOP SECRET we said. So, it was... we returned to Angels Landing arriving early in the AM, sliding silently into the hangar bay without fanfare. Only a few bridge and hangar crew knew we were back on board and sworn to secrecy. Dad checked in at Tactical, me, on the bridge. Dad and I had talked about the impending meeting with NASA and the interlopers. As far as the rest of the ship was concerned, we were still on vacation, 1700+ miles away in Norfolk, Virginia. Legal had arranged to have the meeting aboard Seraphim in the big auditorium. They were ready. Boy, were they ready. We had talked on the phone when I hatched the most complex plan I had ever concocted. Dad's and my entrance to the auditorium would be in disguise, because I wanted to scare the B-Jesus out of them... once and for all... and... it might even be fun.

With any luck, we were about to rid everyone associated with Runestone forever. At the same time, we would further protect Seraphim and Angels Landing. With the help of our friends from the Airpark, we were each given a pack with some interesting additions for the meeting which were moved from the Valkyrie with the help of some guys in the hangar. Each package was placed in dad's and my respective residences. If we can pull this off... it will be epic. Now, I needed to add a new phase to our planning. Select people from Tactical, Navigation, Helm crew, Command, Legal and Security met dad and I in my day-room. All were sworn to secrecy as I spelled out what was about to happen. Many just shook their heads while grinning to the point of laughing. The level of excitement was palpable. It was an extremely complex plan and required a very high degree of precision. But no-one felt this couldn't work and joined in the bizarre plan with a kind of joy few had ever experienced. We sat and created a time-line as events would take place. We practiced some hand signals I would use to direct things to happen. The hi-res video cameras in the auditorium were linked through a studio-like control room off-bridge and a script was written based on the agreed time-line. Jessica had Engineering prep the ACPUs and VASIMR systems for a potential lift off in the morning. Nav was put on alert for the early morning silent dust-off. Jessica agreed to help me in the morning with my outfit. Mom would help dad. We drew a map of the auditorium to be used and drew peoples' positions on it. The head table would have Darien, Susan Richards, as chairwoman. Then the rest of the legal team. Susan was the only one to know what we planned. She also received the time-line. She was really amused and excited but didn't show it. The map showed the approximate positions of the NASA people and Runestone. I asked Susan if she could find a way of separating the real NASA people from the rest. Thereby isolating the bad guys. Name cards were to be placed at all seating locations. Everyone left and I managed a short but welcome nap. It settled my nerves .

Then it was time. We went live...

The following is told by the people in the meeting. Each speaker is identified at the beginning of each line.

Susan Richards: "Good morning everyone. My name is Susan Richards. I am chief council for Angels Landing and Seraphim and am chair for this meeting. This is a sad day for all of us in Angels Landing. I hope we can move forward in a professional manner. I believe all at the head table and Seraphim management personnel have copies of the instruments to be discussed. So, let's begin."

For the next two hours each legal paper was read out loud and discussed. It wasn't long before the meeting got heated. Fists slammed the tables, people screamed at each other. Susan used a large gavel to try to gain control. Dad and I watched the screen in my day room identifying who we thought were the ring leaders among the bad guys. Some were quiet while others were more militant and getting cocky. Using Mr.Scott in text mode only, I could communicate with Susan. I asked who seemed to be the leader among the NASA group and among the MiB. She identified each with clothing colors. Now we knew the players. I sent a message to the XO on the bridge... it simply read...

'Begin...'

The gates were closed for the day, there were no guests aboard the ship. Slowly and quietly the Jetway was retracted, the clamps released. Counter Gravity AI anticipation-mode was set to zero-error. Helm had directions to use only the smallest inputs as Seraphim began a climb so slow and smooth, nobody knew or could feel what was happening. Any turning movements were at very low velocity so even the best pilots wouldn't feel the circular movement. As a result, no-one knew that Seraphim was no longer resting in her cradles. The bridge crew was letting the Earth rotate away beneath Seraphim. It wouldn't be long before we would be in space. Then the real fun begins. We had put on our spiffy Seraphim uniforms with the formal jackets. I polished my name tag and retied my pony-tail.

Our Colonial Williamsburg costumes fit well and again I would be wearing the same three-cornered hat. Dad looked great in his costume, wore a wig, but without a three-cornered hat. I curled my hair under the white wig, then put on the hat. With my uniform on underneath, the costume widened my usually slender figure. A stick-on mustache added to the ruse.

Time to go. It was agreed that one of Susan's legal team would be brought up to date at the last possible moment. He excused himself from the deliberations and left the room. David Bradley met us in the hallway and we chatted a bit. He laughed realizing the plot we had hatched. He was going to bring us into the auditorium with words from a written script that he memorized. With the door partially open, he started talking, loud enough for his voice to carry. He admonished us for being out of order bringing us in with period costumes from characters in an on-board play. But we told him in a loud voice we were members of the Senior Council so we deserved to be there. With a scowl he opened the door all the way still prattling on that we shouldn't be wearing costumes.

Dad in character: "Can't help it. We were supposed to start the play but no-one showed up and we didn't have time to change. We are senior members of the Council so we will be seated here regardless of the costume. C'mon Jim, let's sit down." I walked with a minor limp and wore spectacles and carried a cane, using it to steady my aging body. Everybody watched and snickered with humorous expressions and waited as we found two seats in the back near the wall.

Hannah in character: "Do you have more copies of that?" I asked in a semi-loud raspy voice. "Thanks."

Dad in character: "You're buying Seraphim? What the hell is this? Did you agree to this?" he said looking at the head table.

Darien: "We have no choice. Our financial state forces us to arrange a different source of financing and NASA has agreed to fund Seraphim operations with the caveat that we turn operations over to these folks here. They will be controlling partners. They are bailing us out. I'm sorry. Nobody is sadder about this than I am."

Hannah in character: I stood up and fumbled in my costume coat pocket and withdrew an old looking letter tube. From it I pulled a scroll, unrolled it, and walked to the head table facing Darien. There were two sheets. He read the top one...

"Read the second page carefully then pass it around. I'm about to raise holy hell upon these people. Play along... Rogue-One."

He looked into my eyes. He saw my baby-blues with the limbal rings as they bore into his. He saw my Annapolis ring, worn upside down. I raised up, feigning back pain and moved to return to my seat. NOW, he knows. He found it difficult NOT to smile, but a tear managed an appearance.

Dad in character: "You are very lucky the Captain isn't here or she would see to it, all of you would be breathing desert sand for all eternity.

1st MiB: "Yea, well now, she isn't here, now is she? Yea, I know she can be tough, but since she is out of town enjoying a vacation. When she gets back, if ever, she won't have a job anyway."

As I moved toward my seat I feigned losing my balance and fell to the side... in front of Admiral Douglas Freeman.

He looked into my eyes as I flipped my ring around showing the blue jewel of my Annapolis class ring, and he had immediate recognition. I said quietly...

"Ad-lib." He nodded. I sat down in the chair beside dad.

1st MiB: "May we proceed now?

Douglas Freeman: "Point of order, Madam Chairwoman."

Susan Richards: "The chair recognizes one of our newest members, Admiral Douglas Freeman."

Douglas Freeman: "I realize that I may be out of order, but I'm having trouble understanding how you can proceed without the Captain. It is her ship, is it not? No legal proceeding can continue without the Captain's participation. You need the Captain's concurrence."

1stMiB: "We don't need her agreement to proceed anyway. She isn't here. I demand we begin the signature cycle.

Douglas Freeman: "You seem to be in a rush here Mr... ah."

1st MiB: It's Davis, Now, my Lawyer is going to pass the articles to be signed... right now."

Outside, someone from NASA or Runestone watched in horror as Seraphim rose silently from her cradles, climbing higher and higher. He panicked, calling numbers on his cell phone to the people in the meeting. The skin of the Seraphim blocked the RF radiation and the people inside were not alerted to the Seraphim's departure from Angels Landing. To them, they were still in Wyoming. Well... not anymore.

I got up and limped to the center of the auditorium. All eyes curiously wondered what this elderly actor was up to. I looked around then quite suddenly jumped up with the athleticism of a 33-year-old onto the center table. Everybody except those who knew, all looked on in shock. Still in costume, I looked around. Legs set apart, then... with a flourish, I pulled my hat off, tossed it to the side, followed by the wig, releasing my blond pony-tail, then tossed off the big

Jacket, frock and vest revealing the formal uniform of the Captain of the Seraphim. Dad removed his costume, revealing his uniform with jacket. He stood beside me at floor level. Everybody in the room sat in a state of shock as we drove bolts of fear into the NASA-Runestone group. They sat dumbfounded as their worst night-mare appeared out of nowhere and was prepared to rid Angels Landing of the pestilence. I still held my cane that was really a sheathed sword. I paced to the left, turned and paced the other way. The MiB watched. Some had fear written on their faces. Head slightly down, glaring at the NASA-Runestone people, I drew the sword very slowly from the cane-sheath and dropped the cane to the floor. I continued walking, pointing the sword at each member of the opposing team. I looked down the length of the blade at each person.

"Who is first?" I said.

"These men here are federal Marshalls. You are under arrest." One began reading me my Maranda rights.

"**Stop**! Ms. Richards, can they arrest me? What about jurisdiction?"

"If they are Federal Marshals, they do have jurisdiction."

"You once told me I had jurisdiction and can apply whatever solution to the problem I want. Is that not correct?"

"Under maritime law the captain of the vessel may dole out whatever remedy he or she sees fit. In that case you are Judge, Jury and can issue whatever punishment you choose. But, I also said that we are sitting on Wyoming State property and in the United Stated, so your authority is limited."

"I understand." I nodded. "I can accept that."

On the bridge, the crew watched as the moon drew closer and closer.

The so-called Federal Marshals started walking my way. I waved the sword around making the swishing sound that swords make. I resumed pacing then asked...

"OK... but what if we weren't in Wyoming or the United States?"

"In that case, you would have full jurisdiction."

I turned and saw Theo, Carl and the rest of our team smiling and fidgeting in their seats all excited. Carl saw, once again, I was challenging the Kraken. His tear-filled eyes and cautious smile wondered what I was going to do next? I stared at the Federal Marshalls and Runestone.

"You folks should know by now, I am totally unpredictable and have destroyed your previous attempts to the demise of all who tried. Today will be no different. Draw the curtain, please." The large theater screen was revealed. I held up my left hand in a clenched fist. Instantly from behind and over the top of the screen, came an odd-looking ship. It floated silently forward and stopped 3 feet above me. I pointed at it with the sword.

"For those who haven't seen one. This is a Block II Sentinel. It is a semi-autonomous droid. It will do whatever I ask it to do. It has a very powerful Force-Field Projection array, using a high-powered quantum particle emission that disrupts and scatters the molecular structure of an object leaving nothing... but dust. Earlier this month the same technology was used to destroy your 5 SU-27 fighter aircraft and 2 Backfire Bombers. It destroyed your 2-stage Deep-Space Interceptor, and other military style assets, in an attempt to destroy us. Your plans didn't work, did they? There are 5 of these Sentinels deployed right now in the DC area at separate locations. Here is where they are."

I held up my hand with one finger pointed up. A live picture of a nice suburban house filled 1/5 of the screen.

"Who belongs to that?"

"That's my house... my wife and kids are in there."

I put up a second finger. Immediately a second live picture was side-by-side with the first. Then a third... a fourth... then a fifth.

"All I have to do is say the magic word and they are dust. Is that what you want?"

Seraphim was moving toward the backside of the moon.

"Please, Captain. Those are our homes." They screamed.

"That is true. But you fired on this ship with over 500 men, women and children in it. Why should I care who may be in those houses? And... just so you know that I mean business." I held up my left hand with my fist clenched, again. The five pictures were replaced by a full screen live picture of a nice office building.

That is your headquarters, isn't it?" They nodded.

"*Fire.*" I yelled. The entire building was replaced with a cloud of dust.

"You're going to jail forever said one of the Federal Marshals."

"Really? Susan Richards just said I could do whatever is necessary to render justice as the Captain of the Seraphim."

"But we are in Wyoming, USA."

"Oh! Didn't I tell you? We are no longer in Wyoming, USA. While we were playing show-and-tell, let me show you where we really are." I twirled my finger overhead. The live picture changed again. Seraphim had quietly travelled the distance and was moving across the moon's surface.

"Does anyone know where that is? How about you going for a stroll out there? It's really rather spectacular, isn't it? We are coming around the backside of our moon. This is live, by the way. In a moment we will witness Earth-Rise. I love this, everybody does. Ah! There it is. Beautiful, isn't it? So, you should realize we are around 238,000 miles from Angels Landing. We might stay here for a month or two. So... what do we do with you?" From the speakers came a voice from the Bridge Helm position.

"Captain, this is Helm."

"Go ahead."

"We've arrived, Captain. Same position as before. As exact as we can get it."

"Very well. OK! Let's see it." On the screen was the place that I met the alien. The two chairs were in the same place I had left them. They would probably be there for a million years. I stood in the center of the table, feet apart standing straight and tall, head lowered glaring into the eyes of the bad-guys. They knew it was all over for them. Those behind me sat in awe, with tear filled eyes and once again the Captain made all the bad things go away.

"We would think that after all your failed attempts to gain control of, or destroy Seraphim, you would quit. So here is my promise. I will rain the fires of hell upon you if you continue with more attempts. You have no idea what we are capable of... what power we can bring to bear on all of you. You tell your superiors that Seraphim will no longer be in defensive mode. Next time we will come and get you where you work... where you live... where you play. If you doubt me... do you recognize that place? See those foot prints in the Lunar sand? Those are mine. Do you really want to go One-on-One with me? Now, I'm going to give you a choice. I can kick you out the door right here and be done with you, or we can take you back to Earth and drop you off somewhere, not as yet decided. Your choice. What will it be?" There was a long silence.

"Please take us home. We will never bother you again." The men and women of security moved forward, preparing to escort them to Hangar bay 1.

Mr. Davis turned toward me, looking up from his position at floor level.

"Captain, may I have a moment to speak with you?"

I thought about it and said...

"OK. What do you want?"

"Ma'am, this is the first time this group has been involved in a confrontation with you. We are aware of some of the other teams' experiences. It did not go well for any of them. We were reluctant to take the assignment to partner with NASA to offer a take-over bid of Seraphim. We are not black-ops, we are administration, only. It didn't seem right. We knew your history, rising to the captain's chair on the bridge and the training of the crew. Then our black-ops people tried a more straight-forward approach and you kicked their ass. Then, we heard the whole moon story and we were awed by your courage and resolve. I tell you this, you will never see people in this group ever again. How you moved us from Wyoming to the moon without any of us knowing or feeling the trip was amazing... it was magic. The trip around the moon was amazing. We wish you and your crew safe journeys. I am very sorry this happened."

He turned away joining the others as security began escorting them to a waiting shuttle and return to their Rawlins hotel. The NASA people cringed. They didn't know what to do. Many just stared at me, asking themselves how they could fix this and work with us. But, soon, they began mingling with our Council members, hoping to remedy the relationship. One walked cautiously toward me. It was Dorothy Williams, from NASA in Houston. We had met here earlier following our return from the trip to the backside of the moon and the destruction of the frontal attack using Soviet era jet aircraft. I hopped off the table among the now milling crowd, picked up the sheath and carefully placed the sword's sharp point into the opening at the top and let it drop in. I began picking up the costume and placing the pieces on the table to be bagged later. Dad was talking with a group of mixed Council members, NASA people and the legal team from the head table. A complete list of all companies and organizations willing to pay for Seraphim's services was passed around by dad. Darien, Theo and Carl walked over to me. Darien began.

"That little charade scared the hell out all of us that didn't know what you and your dad were up to. I was terrified, too, but was shocked when you gave me those papers and looked me straight in the eye. Then I knew that we would win this and you had saved us... once again."

"Darien. I'm glad this is turning out to be a win, but I must tell you. You have to learn how to say 'NO', and have some faith in the people that work on Seraphim's behalf. We talked about this while in Norfolk. You, Carl, Theo and others need to participate more in the planning part . We need you. I use the Council more than you did. I need the help. So please, talk to us first before making decisions that can affect us all." I turned to the person nearby.

"Dorothy, I'm sorry I almost forgot you were still here. What can I do for you?"

"Hannah, I just wanted to say that all of the NASA scientists still want a collaboration with Angels Landing and Seraphim and were adamantly against the attempt to annex, Seraphim. I told them that in all likelihood every scientist and engineer that runs this ship would render the science unavailable or at least unusable, then would walk out. Of course, they didn't listen. They thought they were smarter than anyone here. But, they just now discovered there was one person no-one can blindside, anticipate, or bully, and that was you. That performance standing on the tables with the sword scared them. They don't know how to proceed. What you did this evening was classic Hannah Parish. Was it shown on the video feed?"

"Yes, it was. Everyone saw it from here on the moon to all of Earth. I have one more thing left to do, then we will head back home." I unsheathed the sword once more and jumped back up on the table. Everyone turned and watched as I laid down the gauntlet. I stood straight and tall, with a shallow smile of confidence, looked at the high-definition video camera on the back wall, pointed my sword at it and said...

My Name is Hannah Parish and I am the Captain of the Starship

Seraphim

And this... is my ship

Do you have any *doubt* that I will protect Angels Landing and Seraphim at your ultimate peril?

I suggest you consider your future very carefully

It was over. XO Jessica Pearson, sitting in the center chair on the bridge as acting Captain turned Seraphim toward Earth and home. On the way, our legal team made sure all paperwork was finalized showing the financial status with declarations verifying we are well funded. As we approached our home planet, the terrified Runestone folks were given one last caution that they were to pass on to their superiors. *'No quarter will be given in any further engagements.'* They were returned to DC via the shuttle *Michael* with security. The NASA people, still shaken by my theatrical admonishment, were dropped off in Houston by the shuttle *Gabriel*, saddened that they may have lost the opportunity to work together with Seraphim on future missions. But, nothing is forever and who knows how that might work out in the future.

Official letters were prepared to be sent to the appropriate NASA offices cancelling their offer to provide financial assistance to Seraphim. By the time Seraphim lay once again in her cradles in Angels Landing, all documents were completed and faxed to NASA with an additional proviso.

'In the future, any collaboration with outside organizations such as Runestone or other yet to be identified operatives, would render future cooperation with Angels Landing and Seraphim null and void.' The legal office in Angels Landing was abuzz with activity sifting through all existing Copyright, Trademark, and Intellectual Property protections to make sure we were covered, Patent applications covering our technical secrets were carefully worded and created for submittal to the United States Patent and Trademark Office (USPTO).

We heard through the space agency grapevine that NASA legal, successfully extricated itself completely from the dark side and began a series of requests to regain an affiliation with us. No decisions have been made as yet, but now a select team of legal, science and Council members was formed to review applications for possible future collaborations. Darien said in a get-together in my day-room with Theo and a few others, how remiss they had all been in the planning within the legal framework necessary for smooth continuing operations. He added with a sense of remorse that they had performed like amateurs. None of these challenges would have ever happened if they had done their homework first. But for us in operations and command, we were hard at work going through the myriad of applications for future flights by other organizations and companies. Our marketing and portfolio design people had opened the door for small companies to piggyback some of their smaller technologies with more distant voyages. We in command met with Ship's personnel from all major departments of our intention to extend our next voyage to Mars. They were thrilled and began working to make the ship able and safe for such a journey.

Our media department created some innovative documentaries around some of our Lunar trips and made them available to the Angels Landing film series given in their on-site theaters. I was asked for permission to begin video-recording the story of Seraphim, from the early days forward to the present including a non-sensitive overview of the technologies. It included short interviews with some of the scientists and engineers, short documentary called "*The Support Vessels of Seraphim,*" an overview of the shuttles and personnel carriers. Then came the request to do recorded one-on-one sit-down interviews with select scientists and crew members. A list was generated with the requested names. Lo and behold my name was on it. As part of that interview both Mom and Dad would sit together with the interviewer no doubt to begin a long essay of the now famous Captain of the Seraphim. I shuddered at the thought. But, that would have to wait. We have a planet to visit.

Professional Changes

Most of the planning was now complete. Only two more weeks and we will prove the worth of the Angel called Seraphim with the longest journey of any manned space-flight in the history of the world. I was busy checking and back-checking operations planning. It was amazing how little there was for me to do. Each department worked through the huge lists of checks, diagnostics, readiness criteria, logistics requirements. But the major activities were taking place away from Seraphim. Large and small research companies, some I had never heard of, were partnered now and under contract for the first *'feet on the ground'* of another planet. I sat in on several seminars held by people who had studied Mars from 34 to 60 million miles away using robotic rovers, orbiting satellites, and all the available technologies. I felt we needed to understand the 'lay of the land', so to speak. I wanted to know about the atmosphere, (what there was of it), gravity, weather, storms, the infamous dust-devils, temperature differentials, etc. In other words, I wanted to know as much as possible about the place from which more books and movies had been made than any other planetary system outside of Earth. I still had the same responsibility for the care of the ship and the people within, as I did on the moon or near Earth.

Major changes began throughout the ship. It started with Theo, Carl Ledbetter, Doug Freemen, Perry Newcomb, Dad, Lory, Jessica Pearson and even Darien Hunter joined me at these seminars. Darien gratefully understood the need for command personnel to become familiar with the world we will be going to. Parallel to what we were doing, a second team was formed that included a Navigation planning group and all

Bridge helm positions. That's when I wondered if we could establish a projects group who would compile all data and details around each singular destination. No two are the same. Why not have a mission-specific project library covering each venue that we could pull off the shelf and apply to the needs of the next mission so we don't have to re-invent the wheel each time we return to a given destination. We started with...

Theo Remington, Science officer, Carl Ledbetter and Paul Conway from the council would chair the start-up meetings. The major operatives would include:

Paddington Lewis, Gravity,

Jeff Lancaster, Steller Cartography, Helm operations

Aldus Franklin, Senior Astrophysics Professor,

Pamela Martin, Senior Astrometrics Specialist,

David Pierce-Watson, Planetary geosciences division.

They would begin creating individual programs and find willing professors with appropriate backgrounds. Then schedules and training syllabuses would be generated as mission profiles were created.

I stepped back and added another program. Borrowing from the earlier experience, I created an adjunct class to the standard Boot Camp, called *Planetary Physiological Dynamics - Mars* training. It covered all the in-space elements of the first Boot Camp but added the known realities of the Red Planet. All the new people planning to join us were required to take the basic Seraphim Boot Camp with the new Mars-specific Martian Dynamics training. Our training set the gravity to 38% of earth gravity, Atmosphere less than 1% of Earth's. Wind storms and occasional dust-devils occur but have little effect since the atmosphere is so thin, we didn't try to simulate it, but did have a Mars specialist give a seminar on it.

Other similar adjunct training would be required for other planetary or moon missions.

'Planetary Geophysical Research', an arm of NASA's International Information Library, provided a complete compendium of knowledge of the 4th planet in the Sol System. We were forwarded the latest photographs from the rovers as they slowly explored the red planet. These were uploaded into our on-board data Library that could be accessed by anyone on board with permission and a terminal.

"Hey Hannah. Guess who I saw down in the rotunda? Laurie Zoloth and Gordon Stanley, (not the actor), the two authors. I heard that both have asked security if they can come along on our next flight. The Council is reviewing their petition and will render an approval or denial in time for our departure. By the way, Laurie's book, *'Lawn Chair Diplomacy in the Limitless Void of Space'* has made it to #1 on the New York Times best seller list. And Gordon Stanley's *'The Bus Driver'* has received critical acclaim as well. There's talk of a movie. It's a docu-drama styled story of the first starship and its female Captain. He has copies of the pictures from the rotunda in the book. You are famous, Hannah."

"I'd rather just be the captain, but I appreciate the thought. I guess I'll have to read both to be sure they got their facts straight. By the way, when is the pre-flight Mars Project Management meeting? As I understand it, that meeting will be the last opportunity to finalize preparations."

"Next week... on Wednesday."

"Good. I'm going to Nav. You have the Conn, XO."

I stopped by my quarters to pick up some items, then walked into the NGE still wearing my formal attire, joined by Admiral Freeman and Master-Chief Newcomb, wearing Seraphim uniforms. Yellow uniforms. My old boss had two stars on his lapel per my request, Perry had a Lieutenant-Commander pin on his.

"I remember this place." I chided.

"I'm sorry, NGE is off limits to people who don't work here, anymore." called someone from Environment.

"Hmmm! And I thought I was still appreciated in some way." I pouted.

"Oh wait... you are that, what was it... Bad-Ass-Female-Star-Ship-Captain that once worked here. In that case... welcome back." A cheer gathered audible momentum and with hands held high in the Vulcan salute, I countered with a Vulcan Salute, accompanied with a smile.

"Gather around please. I have news. First, with me are two new members of the Seraphim fraternity. Rear-Admiral Douglas Freeman whom you met before, and Master Chief, Perry Newcomb, both formally of the nuclear submarine Andrew Lindstrom. Now retired, they have agreed to join us as ships Tacticians. This is a new position that works in parallel with science officer, Theo Remington in an advisory capacity assisting the captain, overseeing command decisions and offering alternative solutions as Seraphim plies the dark waters of the unknown in her quest for knowledge. Command feels that with Professor Remington's scientific knowledge and our two new tacticians, the bridge now has the right mix of talent to ensure a safe and accurate view going forward. They will come around to greet everyone in NGE since they may call upon you for guidance specific to your talents and skill sets.

Now, one more thing. Would Paddington Lewis, from Gravity, Daryl Plumber from Environment and Josh Whitmore from Navigation, please step forward." They moved to the front of the gathered group. I started...

"I've come to realize that my duty schedule even eclipses my sleep time. Worse, it has drawn my duties away from NGE, my first assignment aboard Seraphim. My time working with you has been inspirational and some of the best days I've had since my joining the Seraphim family. However, it is time to move forward. I must spend nearly all of my time as the...*Bad-Ass-* whatever. So, I have chosen to make a few things right based on promises I once made to you.

"Paddy: your work in Gravity, and supervision of all who work there, has not gone un-noticed. You are now *Chief of Gravity* with a promotion to Lieutenant-Commander and Bridge qualified." I handed him the gold-leaf pin to be worn on his lapel. I shook his hand saying...

"Welcome aboard, Commander." Next...

"Daryl: You have overseen one of the most under-appreciated departments on Seraphim. Proof of your department's skills are the fresh air we breathe, clean, clear water we drink and cleanliness of the environment. You are now *Chief of Environment* and raised to Lieutenant-Commander, Bridge qualified. Here is your gold-leaf lapel pin. Welcome aboard, Commander." And I shook his hand.

"Josh: your department keeps us from getting lost in the woods which we seem to be well-able to do. Your teams' support to the bridge has been exemplary, your knowledge of the Universe, remarkable. You are now *Chief of Navigation* and raised to Lieutenant-Commander, Bridge qualified. Here is your gold-leaf lapel pin. Welcome aboard, Commander." And I shook his hand.

"Now, all three departments in NGE have proper bridge support per my original promise to you. All three of you will now represent your departments in bridge staff meetings. Congratulations to you all. *Ooh-Rah, Seraphim, Ooh-Rah, NGE.*" Smiles were everywhere, the room noisy with adulation.

As personnel returned to their duty stations, I saw smiles on the faces of our new tacticians.

"You never fail to amaze me, Hannah." Said Perry...

"You pull off the most amazing take-down of a very bad group by scaring the hell out of them, then turn around and laud your own people for jobs-well-done. They saw you stand your ground, sword held high, putting the fear of God in anyone wanting to do us bad. When we came out here the first time when Seraphim was making history on the moon, we wondered about you as Captain. How does one learn the trade? What you were doing had no precedent. You did things never before done in human history. You were a navigator aboard the Lindstrom, sat quietly at your station, were friendly and un-assuming. We missed you when you resigned your commission feeling we lost a great naval officer and sailor. Little did we know your potential. Little did we know we would eventually work for you.

"I believe you work FOR Seraphim, you work WITH me."

"Only you would say something like that." Said Doug.

"You are most kind and I appreciate your support, but once again, into the breach, we go. So...

Perry, I wonder if you would consider working closely with Commander Augie Lincoln, our Chief of the Boat. He is a Brit, great sense of humor. Ask about his background in the Royal Navy. Be his second, and in time, work together. Call yourself a Master Chief and wear the anchor and star on the left side if you prefer along with your Lieutenant Commander pin on the right. In fact, that is a good idea. Let's think about that. I've been thinking about our uniforms lately and think they may be due for an up-grade. We need to look more professional. Perhaps you can adapt to the needs of Seraphim and her crew to the way you did on the Lindstrom. Be the intermediary with the non-command personnel (Non-yellow shirts). I suggest you both visit the main departments like Power, Gravity, Med-bay, Environment and Navigation. It's how I learned. Ask any questions you have. They love the attention and are anxious to demonstrate how smart they are. Learn how we do stuff. Right now, it is about gaining knowledge. And meeting the great people of Seraphim."

"I can do that. I look forward to it. Thanks for the opportunity."

"Admiral, in a similar capacity, I would like you to consider learning bridge operations. Be able to take over as ship's Master if necessary. Wear your two stars on your lapel. As I learned from you aboard the Lindstrom, you can learn how I do things. People already respect and like you and considering you were my mentor once upon a time, they are ready to follow your command if need be. My style of leadership is irrelevant, yours is your own. Someone a while back, looked upon the center seat on the bridge as the seat of power. I disagreed. I believe it represents a position of respect and responsibility. And, I think I have achieved that. When the XO or COB sit there in my stead, they don't assume a position of power, they know my feelings and significance of it and the crew does, too. Whoever sits there has the respect of everyone by default. If given the seat while one of us is gone, you would have command authority and the crew will follow your orders explicitly. It really is no different than on the bridge 300 feet under water. Maybe this is easier. I watched what you did and how you did it. It is the same here. It's a big boat, just like a submarine. You and Perry are ships tacticians, supporting whoever is in the center seat."

"You know, Hannah, when we were finishing our retirement paperwork and seeing old friends, everyone was shocked... in a good way, when we told them of our decision to be part of the Seraphim crew. They were thrilled and, I think, a little jealous. They asked about the Captain of the Seraphim. They had all seen the many videos of you from here in Wyoming, to saving lives at the ISS and then the incredible events on the moon. Some had met you when you were still crewing the Lindstrom as a feisty lieutenant with the dangerous knees."

"Really? They still remember that? Something I'm not particularly proud of." Doug added...

"As we moved through our checkout process, we were both inundated with questions about how a ship like Seraphim uses Navy command and control philosophies and performs so well. We told them that Seraphim has an amazing crew and is mastered by a most remarkable female captain who was once one of us. We had people of all ranks asking if they could come out, visit Angels Landing and see Seraphim and maybe meet the Captain. We said sure. It's a Theme park and a place of imagination and promise. And, a place of hope for our future. She believes that more than you can imagine. Maybe she would meet with some of you. She's very busy but perhaps she can make time."

"By the way, we had dinner with your mom and dad, Theo, Carl, and Darien. They really think that your latest crew assignments round out and fill a need previously non-existent on the bridge. And, of course, were never considered by anyone else. Darien, in a moment of reflection said that recent events have made everyone, especially himself, aware of the lack of detailed planning necessary for the operation of a ship like this. He followed with, 'damn good thing we have someone on board that understands the things we seem to lack.' We are blessed with her presence.' he said."

"Theo advised us that two of Navigation's finest and geniuses, will hold classes in Martian geography. Another on geology and weather. He said as the teams from outside join our ranks, they will be required to attend the expanded Boot-Camp and then will attend the planet specific seminars. You would like a team of 'off world' planners to build a library series of *'smart classes'*. These will be provided to guest science teams as they contract a mission profile of their choice. Carl recommended we organize a group of professors that would manage and teach. He called it 'Angels Landing University'. Once established, a direct copy could be provided to the folks in Angels Landing to augment their education series. Guests could experience the same planning programs in preparation for an actual flight."

For three days, the Governor of Wyoming and lots of staff were seen walking through the many displays, dioramas and taking seminars. The one that hit them hardest was the diorama of the Lawn-Chairs on the lunar surface. They were choked up realizing this was real and someone actually did that. Even I have come to appreciate it more, following my return there to find the real Hannah Parish once again.

As they walked around, the Governor and staff began hearing talk about the creation of a kind of university on the property. One dedicated to teaching interested future astronauts about... going out there.

Within a week the Wyoming legislature approved, and the Governor signed, a gift of nearly 700 acres of open land on which to extend the theme park and add large buildings with class rooms and lecture halls. The term 'Theme Park' was dropped in favor of ***Angels Landing Science Park.***

"Angels Landing University" is being built.

Going Topside

Two weeks later...

All was ready. Personnel (scientists), engineers and even some media reporters from scientific publications were on board. All had taken the requisite training. They provided their own space-suits tailored for each user. Boxes of hardware, packed instrumentation and even a couple of sophisticated rovers rested in Hangar 3, from two of the three organizations. There were also two large wheeled protective vehicles that would be lowered to the Martian surface via the forward vertical cargo elevators. These were self-contained habitat style mobile units. Each had most of their science/lab equipment built in.

All was ready, all ships personnel were at their duty stations.

Again, I was in my quarters reviewing some notes.

"Come in" I said responding to a knock.

"Hey, Carl, good to see you. I have something for you." I went into the bedroom and retrieved a gift.

"Some time ago during a discussion about fear and concern. You said you needed a sword to be able to face down the Kraken. And I said '...and you shall have one'. And here it is."

"That's the one from the meeting."

"Yes, it is. And, now it's yours."

"I don't know what I would do with it."

"Wave it around and frighten people. Be careful... it's sharp."

"Thank you, Hannah. I realize it is mostly symbolic but sometimes symbolism begets strength... something I need to find inside myself, and I will. Again, thank you. You know, it's almost time."

"Yes, it is. Are you going to stay on the bridge for lift-off?"

"I would like to, if you don't mind."

"There are new chairs along the back wall on either side of Theo, bolted down with seat belts. The two to his left are positions for the new Tacticians. They will have some new consoles installed in time, joined with Theo's science stuff. But the rest are open. Go on in, I'll be along in a minute." Carl left and I was alone.

I put on my complete uniform with jacket. This day was special. It deserves respect. I stopped in front of my door to the bridge and just took some deep breaths. I touched the button. The sliding door opened with a hiss. I stepped forward.

"Captain on the Bridge." Everyone on the bridge stood at attention. I casually looked around at the faces with all eyes forward.

"As you were." I winked at Doug Freeman and Perry Newcomb. They gave me a thumbs-up. I addressed the Ship.

"Attention Seraphim. Today marks a new day in the history of human exploration. We journey farther from our homes than ever before. In a month we will look back from whence we came and we will see a blue star, seemingly no larger than any star or planet around it against a black void. That tiny blue dot will be Earth, so small we won't even be able to discern the moon. We do this for the benefit of all man and woman-kind. We have never been more ready. As I look around I see my friends, and the best trained and most alert crew, in existence and I couldn't be prouder.

Today, we go to another planet. It's called Mars. It's where the Martians live. It's true... I've seen them in movies. Some say there is no life on Mars... What-say we go find out?" the crew laughed.

"Station!" I barked. "Prepare to cast off all lines fore and aft." Everyone immediately sat up at their positions.

"Engineering: Status."

"All systems ready and at station keeping. Five ACPUs purring like kittens. Maneuvering thruster fuel tank levels nominal. VASIMRs 1, 2, 3 and 4. Purged and awaiting your command."

"Very well"

"Gravity: Status."

"Ship's gravity steady at 1.000G. Counter-gravity standing by with AI anticipation mode at .001%. GMI standing by for initial heading and climb. Ready when you are Captain."

"Very well."

"Environment: Report."

"All systems optimum. Air quality; 21% - O_2, 3% - CO_2, scrubbers on line. Normal lesser gases. Water clean, tested, and all tanks full. We're ready to go."

"Navigation: Status."

"Nav computer has all plots loaded. On your call, we will be at Earth departure point-Alpha in low earth orbit in 4 minutes 21 seconds from lift-off. Delay at point-Alpha with 3-minute count-down for set-up heading lock. The initial heading to Mars is based on the latest information. Mars will be at perihelion in 8 hours, 19 minutes and that will put it 43.9 million miles or 70.65 million kilometers distant based on our present positions on our respective ecliptics, if we launch within 2 hours.

Initial terminal velocity will be based on 4x VASIMR burn at 80% for 7 hours and 50 minutes±. Time enroute to Flip Point-Bravo will be 15.72 days±. Distance to Mars surface from Bravo will be 1.2 million miles. Slow-down retro requirements at Bravo: 4 VASIMRs at 80% for 7 hours and 18 minutes. Terminal velocity at tangential Point-Charlie at 19.7 thousand miles per hour with a quarter-roll to starboard for surface-parallel alignment. Primary landing zone for the *Acidalia Planitia* plain option-1, requires half orbit, at 82,000 feet to stay well below moons, Deimos and Phobos and orbiting artificial satellites. Second flip occurs 12 minutes later for last speed reduction to 750 mph. That should put us over the initial point, *Schiaparelli crater*, about 2000 miles east of Acidalia Planitia. Will decide on approach to final destination on arrival over the crater."

"Very well. Are all parameters, as they are, uploaded into the Nav computer and verified?"

"Yes, they are Captain. Run-Time begins at your call. Following initial climb out, all activity will be in triple redundancy per your order. Confidence is high. Need for manual take-over probability, near zero."

"Excellent work, ladies and gentlemen... NOW

Are we GO for launch?"

"XO?"

"Aye, Captain, GO for launch."

"Chief of the Boat...?

"Go for launch.

"Science officer Remington?

"Go for launch"

"Comm"

"Go for launch"

"Tactical?"

"Go for launch"

"Navigation?"

"Go for launch"

"Angels Landing Security?"

"Go for launch"

I stepped up onto the raised command deck

"Helm. Sound external alarm. Verify all outside personnel clear of Seraphim cradles."

"Ground personnel report Seraphim cradle and surrounding area clear. All guest areas and jetway clear."

"Very well. Retract the jetway and seal all access doors. Disconnect shore power. Release clamps. On GMI climb to 140,000 feet. When clear of all obstacles, engage Navigation Flight Control system."

"ENGAGE"

The four VASIMER engines shut down as programmed following our timed acceleration burn and settled at our enroute speed. Now the long coast to our destination, Mars.

"Comm, shoot the ship." Janice opened a ship-wide channel and pointed at me.

"Soon we will be visiting our neighboring planet, MARS and begin using the Martian calendar. Defined in SOLs, day 1, of our arrival will be called SOL-1, differentiating it from the Gregorian calendar on Earth because days on the two planets are slightly different from each other and will diverge over time independent of Earth time and calendars.

A Mars year is almost twice as long as Earth's, at 687 earth days, and its orbital eccentricity is considerably larger, which means that the lengths of various Martian seasons differ considerably. Another thing to get used to. So, each day is computed as being in reference to the sun, or SOL. We now keep two clocks: Earth time clock with the Gregorian calendar, for communications reference, and a Martian clock and calendar, which better keeps track of activity schedules due to Mars' longer day. Welcome to another planet."

Acidalia Planitia
SOL-1

16 days later...

The rust colored planet loomed large in our forward view-screen. Our speed now reduced following the deceleration flip, then the flip back to normal forward flight configuration. Entering on a tangent, with thrusters, the flight control computers put us in a parallel quasi-orbit that would take us half-way around to the Mare Acidalium, (quadrangle MC-4), in which is Acidalia Planitia. It is a plain on Mars, centered at 49.8°N 339.3°E, located between the Tharsis volcanic province and Arabia Terra to the north of the huge Valles Marineris, the largest canyon in the Solar system, to the south. The plain also contains the famous Cydonia region at the contact with the heavily cratered highland terrain with a surface feature that looks like a human face from cameras in orbit. A favorite consideration for exploration, it will be the main focus for one of the science teams aboard. Because of its fairly central location, Acidalia Planitia will be the primary launch point for the shuttle deployments. All shuttle control will be by small and large reaction jet thrusters, since the GMI is ineffective on the planet without a magnetosphere. However, GMI vertical control seems to be functioning using only Martian gravity. The sun was still high but smaller than when viewed from the earth or moon. The added distance to the sun and the Martian ecliptic makes the surface cooler. The other disadvantage of a planet without a magnetosphere is the higher level of harmful radiation. On earth, our magnetosphere and ozone layer mostly shield earth and, as a result offers a view of the Aurora Borealis in the north and

Aurora Australis in the south caused by the ionization of the deferred radiation. Mars lacks all that. Suits and vehicles must be heavily protected. Our Boeing suits seemed better protected than earlier versions. Our guests were required to provide their own life-support suits, along with suit maintenance personnel similar to ours. Additional work-space was provided for this activity. All hanger and storage room protocols had been part of their required Seraphim training classes and would be monitored closely by Seraphim crew personnel. Slowly, life aboard Seraphim enjoying a full 1 G of gravity returned to normal following the nervousness associated with the sixteen-day flight.

SOL-2

It's Always Something...

M uch of the scientists' pre-deployment preparations were completed during the 16-day flight. The first of the two wheeled mobile units was staged in the long access tunnel at keel level, leading to the massive forward elevators. All shuttles were serviced for deployment and held the initial load-out of instrumentation. Bridge and Ships crew returned Seraphim function to pre-launch configurations.

Since no GPS or ground based navigation systems exists on Mars, our clever hacker, Fred Mooney with the help of a team of extraordinary technicians, had assembled an azimuth, elevation and ranging system that could be accessed by anyone with the system, and a mapping monitor thus providing location accuracy within a meter within 200 miles. The data is superimposed onto a virtual Martian topographical map. It always showed the current position of Seraphim. It was brilliant. Four units were constructed with the single master unit within Seraphim and a short retractable antenna on the dorsal line. You had to really screw up to get lost.

Well, here we are ten feet above the Martian soil and I'm hungry.

"Does anyone know of any Martian-Burger joints out there?" I got a few smiles for that one. But I was hungry and now was the time.

"Is the Captains Mess open?"

"Sure is, but not all fast-food joints, yet" Responded Donna Singleton passing in the opposite direction.

"Thanks, Donna" But they just couldn't wait. Now what?

"Captain, surface contact 1-3 miles bearing 247° moving toward Seraphim at... well... about 1 to 3 knots, Ma'am."

"On screen. Let's see it. Ahh! I don't see it. Can you point it out?"

"Right here Captain. That small black dot. You can see it move occasionally. We have no idea what it is."

"Send a Block II sentinel over there. Use only the small thrusters for control." In minutes...

"On its way, Captain."

"Let's see it from the sentinel POV (point of view). Climb to 100 meters. Focus on the target. Using only the small thrusters, the sentinel is moving at about 30 kph along the surface."

"Slowing now. I'm going to swing around to the backside."

"Copy that."

"It looks like a tarp or something, just blowing in the wind. Well at least we know this about it. It is made of very light-weight material or the wind in the scarce atmosphere wouldn't be able to move something heavy. It might have come from one of the early Mars explorer rovers. They have been on Mars since Pathfinder in 1997, that landed the first wheeled robotic rover named Sojourner on Ares Vallis."

"How do you remember all this stuff?"

"Hannah, you aren't the only smart non-scientist around here."

"Good to know. Where is Ares Vallis?"

"Not really sure, but I think it is located in the Oxia Palus quadrangle, at 10.4N and 25.8 W (334.2 E).

I think that cloth or tarp is caught on something. It isn't moving, just flapping."

"Maybe someone should go out there and bring a piece in for testing. OK, let's bring in the sentinel."

"Where are our tacticians, Theo?"

"I think one is down in Power learning about stuff, the other, I don't know."

"So, Theo, what do you think? Are you ready for another tour outside? I am." He looked at me.

"Not yet. I'm still getting used to the idea that we are on Mars. I have an AI program running, that evaluates several of the planet's parameters like current weather."

From Helm...

"Captain, there is something you ought to see."

"What do you have, Jeff?"

"On the main screen... dust devils." Everyone on the bridge turned to see. I exclaimed...

"Fascinating! That's the only thing moving out there. At least something adds a little life to this world. Are they dangerous if we walked around out there?" Theo answered...

"Actually, no. Other than getting a little dusty. The atmosphere is so thin that any wind would carry only the lightest of sand. Basically dust. So, no, there wouldn't be any real risk. The suits would require a good cleaning on return to Seraphim, though."

Scientists from the three guest organizations just stared at the view-screen with admiration.

"It's not red" said one

"There is more color on the landscape than I expected. And there are clouds." said another. One of our resident scientists added...

"The sky color during the day is what some call a butterscotch-color due to the dust particles carried aloft by the low-level breezes and thermal up-drafts. At night the dust settles and in the early morning and early evening as the sun rises or sets, the color changes to a violet color, thought to be caused by water molecules in the atmosphere."

"Do the dust devils form at night, too?"

"Not known, but we doubt it. Like on Earth, with the sun below the horizon, the surface cools and air currents dissipate, so there is not enough energy in the atmosphere to form rapid circulation and create a vortex. The only atmospheric concern we should consider seriously are the dust storms. They are not as vicious as stories and movies make them out to be, but it would be wise to respect them and they can often last for quite a long time. In the event of a dust storm, everybody should remain inside Seraphim or the shuttles, locked and sealed, should one develop. NASA orbiting satellites have provided us the ability to see dust storm development over the horizon, so we should have ample warning."

I remained sitting on the middle chair on the raised bridge deck when I heard the main entrance door to the bridge swish open then swish closed. Our two Tacticians stood gawking at the image on the main screen. They walked closer as though drawn by some un-seen force toward the first live image of the planet of myth and legend and star of books and movies.

"The observation deck is standing room only. You can hear a pin drop. People are fascinated, Captain."

"Jeff. Climb the ship slowly to 400 feet AGL. Then holding our geographical position, pivot the ship counter-clockwise on center-mass at one degree every three seconds or so, and keep rotating as smoothly as you can. Let's give the world a moving panoramic view."

"Aye, starting rotation." All bridge personnel watched in awe as the view slowly changed.

"Mr.Scott, play Hans Zimmer's *Blue Planet II*, volume at level 2 of 10."

More people entered the bridge. And stood enraptured by the view with several distant ropes of dust winding skyward. '*The Martian dust devils*', thought some in a kind of trance.

There was movement beside me, and a voice said...

"I was in the observation deck with a gazillion people watching breathlessly. Seraphim began slowly turning forming a panoramic view. Then the music. I saw people with tears in their eyes. Mine, too. Then I came up here. You have a romantic side to you, don't you, Hannah? This is amazing."

"Yea, maybe I do." I said to Laurie Zoloth who quietly watched.

"Darien and a few from his original team are standing spell-bound over there by the door. Some have tears of happiness as they see their dreams finally coming true in spectacular fashion. What an introduction to space flight. First the moon, now this. Everybody aboard Seraphim and millions on Earth are watching this in real-time, minus the 14-minutes distance delay, glued to their TV screens. Every scientific organization and university are watching. My god, Hannah, this is magnificent."

"I'm going to keep the ship this way until after night-fall. Maybe resume in the morning. Perhaps a very slow aerial tour might be appreciated, too, around the Mare Acidalium quadrangle. That's the larger general area in which we are now. On screen 5 is a map of most of the area with Acidalia Planitia in the center of this rendering.

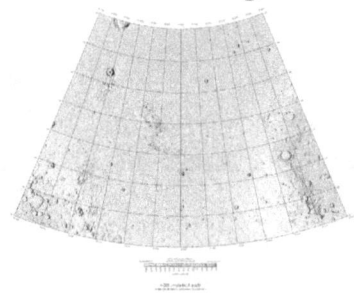

"You had this all worked out beforehand, Didn't you? You knew that this would spark the romance of adventure, the imagination of 'What's out there'. You wanted to put the traumas of the moon behind and open the door to imagination and excitement."

"Are you going to put that in your book, too, Laurie?"

"That one is done, I'm thinking about another one. Oh, it's going to be good."

"Do you have a name for it, yet?"

"No... not yet. But it will be appropriate."

Jessica Pearson stepped onto the raised command deck and asked me if I wanted a break.

"I would love one. So, to formalize it...

XO has the Conn."

"I have the Conn. Hannah, you should take a walk around the other decks, look at the people. See if you find one with a frown or unhappy? I bet you won't."

"I'll look. OK, here's what's happening: We are pivoting on center mass at a rate of 1° for every 3 seconds, at 400 feet. I would like to continue until maybe 8 pm. The music is Hans Zimmer's *Blue Planet II,* in case anyone asks. I haven't eaten since yesterday." I descended the steps to the main bridge deck, walked over toward two of the empty helm positions and just stood gazing for a moment at the slowly moving picture on the screen, with the distant dust devils. It felt like something inside me was updating my soul. My emotions were taking control as I smiled. Several minutes passed, then I turned and moved to my quarters. I needed a quick shower and primp which I finished in fifteen minutes. Mr.Scott had a message for me. Some were headed to the Captains Mess. 'Join us' it said. There weren't many people in the hallways. As I walked in and turned to the steward with a smile and asked if he had seen the video of outside. He pointed to my right, then to his left. Two very large flat-panel TV monitors had been installed near the walls for all to see. Each had the external view of the Martian plain with mountains in the background. As I turned to join the others at our regular table, hands from everyone in the room were raised in the Vulcan Salute. One person stood with tears in his eyes and said...

"Thank you, Captain... Thank you very much." I nodded with a big smile, and returned the salute. I approached the table. Mom, Dad, Theo, Darien, Sarah, Carl, Laurie, Lory, Doug and Perry all stood as I approached. The end chair to the right was empty and I guess was mine. Darien sat at the other end. Only one menu remained, one at my seat. The others had already ordered. The steward came over as I quickly glanced over the selections and chose a prime rib with baked potato, all up, and country style green beans.

"And, could I have some 'au jus' on the side, please?"

Darien was the first to speak as I was looking at one of the video monitors.

"Beautiful, isn't it? We are slowly turning with a live panoramic view of another world as we listen to beautiful music, 49 million miles from home, sitting in a glorious restaurant with our best friends... on Mars. It's magic. We did it, Theo." his voice was breaking up with emotion as he recalled the many years of imagining, then creating, and now seeing his dream before him. Personal pride was welling up and changing him. He wasn't alone. Millions, perhaps billions on the tiny blue dot felt it too.

Earlier, as I stood in front of the bridge view-screen, I didn't realize that someone with a camera, had set up a tripod about twenty feet behind me as I looked out at the Martian world turning slowly. That video clip and a single still-shot would soon become iconic across both our worlds.

I was told later that Angels Landing and the ships comm lines were deluged with calls from all over the Earthly world. The two video monitors view of the outside world were getting darker as Martian day transformed into Martian night. We finished our dinners and were preparing to leave when the picture on the screens changed. A still picture from the center of the bridge deck had a shot of me standing straight and tall with the Martian desert on the screen. Laurie Zoloth's introduction to her new book, yet to be named. She wrote the following:

In the halls and rotunda of Angels Landing, the offices and laboratories of the Jet Propulsion Laboratory, throughout all of NASA, Goddard Space Flight Center, Johnson Space Center, Kennedy Space Center, and a hundred international locations, and everywhere on planet Earth, one picture has become truly iconic. There stands the Captain of the Seraphim from behind, legs planted solidly, hands at her sides standing tall, her signature golden pony-tail resting against her back, looking out at the huge view-screen of the Seraphim bridge deck, and the first live vista of Mars. It represents all of human-kinds first journey into true space exploration. Never in the history of our race of beings does this better represent who we are as human beings as we reach out into the aether of the universe. There stands the magnificence of the human spirit.

I didn't know what to make of our guest author's view of things but it had served her well. I finally read her book, *Lawn Chair Diplomacy in the Limitless Void of Space*. It was excellent albeit somewhat romanticized. But I could see where it would hold regular readers' interest. As an avid reader myself, it held my attention. She is a really good writer, and it was accurate, though staying somewhat pedestrian with the science. At least the science wouldn't push the average reader away. A copy of the other book, Gordon Stanley's *'The Bus Driver'* was given to me by Theo, who had purchased two copies prior to our launch, at a kiosk outside the Angels Landing gift shop which also had Laurie's book. Copies of both books were sold out in a week, I was told, and more were ordered. I have to admit I was somewhat reluctant to read it. But, it was a well-researched biography of the Captain of the Seraphim. As it turned out, he was a hell of an author, too. It took me a week before I allowed myself time to begin reading his work, which I did during the passage from Earth or Mars. I only had two meetings with him as he interviewed me for the book months earlier. He is a resident theoretical scientist and psychologist aboard Seraphim studying physiological and psychological effects of prolonged space flight. He wrote an essay for *Scientific American*, a popular science magazine, and the oldest continuously published monthly magazine in the United States. He wrote that serving aboard Seraphim was an even better 'life-style choice' (his words) than working in a laboratory environment in Pasadena. And now he sits, holding his laptop in a comfortable chair on the observation deck looking out over the Martian desert. Someone said he was consumed by the grandeur of the experience; the slow-moving panorama, and celestial music. I received a message that he would like to schedule more interviews in the future. My celebrity status had risen to the point that we could use a fleet of three or more Seraphim's to satisfy future needs. We were in constant demand for a variety of projects in the future. We certainly don't have any more fiscal money problems. Alas! Tomorrow begins the real science.

Now... time to sleep.

SOL-3
Country Roads

There were four of us... Admiral Freeman, Perry Newcomb, Dad and me. We were all in our blue space suits, climbing aboard Valkerie-1. I ran through the checklist, fired up the single ACPU, waited for system self-tests to report ready. We were now prepared for our first flight on Sol's fourth planet. Also gearing up close by was *Raphael,* our newest and most functional standard shuttle. On board were Jake Maxwell and Lory Amundson as pilots, then an amalgam of 30+ scientists and managers from several offices of NASA, JPL and other mission teams. Theirs' was a familiarity / reconnaissance flight. Ours was strictly for... well because we could. We floated out the hangar-2 airlock following the pressure verification tests. As suspected, GMI barely functioned but did allow some control over our altitude getting some help from Mars gravity. We could go up or down without using the thrusters, but there was no acceleration in any direction. Thrusters did allow for this, plus I was prepared to use the 2 VASIMR-4 engines if we wanted to go really fast. First stop; we glided toward the bow of Seraphim. I wanted to watch the lowering of the two *Mars-Exploration-Vehicles (MEV):* A *Mobile-Lab* with an installed crane on the back, and the *Secure-Habitat.* I had a thought and called Jessica and helm.

"Just a thought, guys. When they lower the two forward equipment elevators, you may get a nose pitch-down from the exposure to normal Martian gravity since the gravitational neutral skin will not be complete in that area."

"We are prepared for that already, Hannah. Jeff anticipated that might happen and is standing by the nose thrusters just in case. We got this."

"Damn, you guys are great."

"We learned from the best."

I looked around at the others scanning in all directions, taking in the desert region through the clear wraparound canopy. Perry spoke up...

"My God, this is Mars. Look! Dust devils." I think he was really having a hard time believing this was real.

"Doug and Perry, what are you going to tell them back in Norfolk?" No answer.

As we approached the bow of this immense ship; 4-times that of the U.S.S Andrew Lindstrom, longer and with more internal room than the Gerald R Ford carrier, we watched as the forward elevator platform unsealed and began descending with its cargo, on cables to the surface. The first *Mars-Exploration-Vehicle (MEV)*, the *Secure-Habitat*, an all-electric vehicle, slowly drove off the elevator platform onto the mostly gravel surface with sparse groups of rocks of varying sizes.

Once clear, the platform slowly rose to its closed position under Seraphim's nose and sealed. The second elevator platform began its descent carrying the *Mobile-Lab*. Soon it was sitting beside the *Habitat*. The elevator raised the platform to its home position, locked and sealed into place. Seraphim returned to 400 feet AGL and began the slow rotation again. It was the first time my riders saw Seraphim rise silently from this close. Dad was equally impressed.

"And, I thought the carrier was big. Holy crap! And, that is your ship. You are that monster's master." I smiled.

"Yep!"

We watched from below as Seraphim, slowly, silently rotated. I was told by doing the slow rotation accompanied by the epic music, people became more settled and comfortable.

The two *Mars-Exploration-Vehicles* began moving slowly in-trail into the desert. A specially fitted Block-II Sentinel followed close behind the surface-bound duo taking still pictures and video of the activities of the scientists around the MEVs. It would stay close and provide additional support to the MEVs with reconnaissance and route suggestion provided by AI functionality. The MEVs were Jet Propulsion Laboratory creations. The Sentinels and shuttles were ours. It was one of three, assigned missions with support to the other two shuttle deployments. They would venture farther than the MEVs, to specific locations, and would return each evening to Seraphim, and resume the following morning. I felt each deserved a similar level of security. The shuttle crews were Seraphim crew members including two pilots and one engineer. The rest were scientists from their respective organizations. In the cargo area of each, were several instrumented fixed deployment packages and a rover, that would remain behind when we go home.

We got a call from the bridge saying that NASA would like to talk with us about doing a field repair of NASA's *Opportunity* rover that had stopped communicating with Earth when a severe planet-wide dust storm blanketed its location in June 2018. It had been doing continuas operations for 15 years. Darien, in a moment of benevolent cooperation had agreed. Prior to departure, a large box of repair parts and three rover engineers were placed aboard while at Angels Landing along with a sizable $compensation package. The repair will be done on site, undercover in a radiation protected tent erected over the sandy rover, in the field. They brought their own space suits, a solid-state field power package for power tools and air-tanks to clean dust and sand off the rover. I looked around at my colleagues and received affirmative nods from all.

"Seraphim, this VAL-1"

"Go ahead, Hannah."

"Jessica, you may advise NASA that we will schedule one of our shuttles to deliver the field package for the Opportunity rover in the near future. We have three teams in the field at this time. Will advise when one of the shuttles is available. We will need accurate location data of the rover. Be sure that the NASA team has complied with our Boot-Camp protocols. Give them whatever assistance they need that does not interfere with normal ships duties. On our dime, we would also like to dig *Spirit* out of the sand and see if we can bring it back to life? We might just bring it back to the '*Mars Rover Rehab Center*' in Hangar-3 for repairs. We'll need it's coordinates, too?"

"Copy all, Hannah. Will relay. *Rover Rehab Center*', huh? Something new, Cool! We'll assign someone to shepherd the Rover guys around while on board."

"Sounds good. Everything else OK on board?"

"Yes. People that don't have much to do are enjoying their first dips in our pools. Some find it hard to believe. When will you be back?"

"A couple of hours, I think. We are doing some sightseeing looking for some lakes to do some fishing. Damn shame. Mars has no lakes, so I guess, no fishing."

But, there were dust-devils. So, we went to investigate. We got close but didn't fly through any. It was funny that these were the only things we could find that were indigenous to the planet and moved. Nothing else did... except thin clouds.

Someone loitering outside the bridge suggested we should visit the tallest mountain in the solar system, *Olympus Mons*, a very large shield volcano at approximately 69,841 ft. AGL and located in the Tharsis volcanic region north-east of us. The volcano is located in Mars's western hemisphere at approximately 18.65°N 226.2°E, just off the northwestern edge of the Tharsis bulge. The eastern portions in the adjoining Tharsis, (quadrangle MC-9).

Olympus Mons is the tallest known volcano in the Solar System; it is 100 times larger than any volcano on Earth and spread out the size of Arizona. To our knowledge, it is dormant, but you know how volcanos are.

SOL-4
Places to go, Things to see

Josh Whitmore from Navigation was working with a couple of engineers from Ship to create a monitoring system that tied in with Fred Mooney's mapping monitor system to show a location map of the positions of all off-ship teams in real time. Of the four smaller video screens set two on each side of the main view-screen, video screen #1, upper left of the main view screen was assigned the task and would be available 24/7 and was closest to the consoles and viewable from the Tactical/Helm position and further back on the bridge. We could monitor the locations of each off-ship crew including each Sentinel. If one of the teams ran into trouble, we wanted to be able to find them. Their Sentinel tag-along was a backup. We were able to extract location data, and POV from the Sentinel. The MEV team would remain off-ship throughout their mission, living in the self-contained *Secure-Habitat*. The mapping monitor showed the MEVs about twenty miles west near some irregular hills, not moving. Last night, Fred Mooney's team installed a monitor repeater system aboard VAL-1. We now could see not only Seraphim but all the away-teams, too. We decided to see what the MEV team was doing and zipped to their location on the high-power thrusters. We could see the white vehicles easily contrasted against the red-ish color of the tundra. They saw us coming and waved. Five were hundred-twenty meters away in some jagged rock formations, tapping pieces off larger rocks, with geologist's tools. We decided to go for a walk. We sealed our face shields and dumped the internal air, set the auto pilot to force the Val down against the sand, holding it in place.

Dad was first out, the rest of us followed. I had parked about a hundred meters away from their camp. Doug looked at me with a big smile and said through the intercom...

"Are we having fun, yet? You know it is a lot easier here than on the moon." I responded...

"One main reason, there is twice the gravity here than on the moon, but is still just over 1/3 Earth gravity. The surface isn't as powdery either. More like gravel, although there are depressions that collect dust, walking should be easier." It was. We walked to the group by the rock formation. I looked at the tiny comm panel on the side of one's helmet. It was set to channel 2. I tapped the side of my helmet and held up my hand and two fingers. We changed our comm to channel 2.

"High guys. Do you hear me?"

"Yea, fine" said one. "Are you the Captain?" reading my *'Hannah Parish'* fabric name tag on my suit.

"Yes, it is. We just decided to do some reconnoitering. Can't let you guys have all the fun. I thought there were seven of you."

"There are. Paul and Becky are in the lab looking over some interesting samples. It looks like there was water here once upon a time. We're looking for anything that might indicate that life may have existed eons ago, too. We are looking for possible biosignatures. But so far, nothing. But we just started."

"How long do you anticipate being away from the ship?"

"A week, maybe two. The Habitat has food water, heat, air-conditioning for a month. It's a bit cramped but it is roomier than the ISS. It's also a proof of concept design for future long-term Martian studies."

"Well, good luck, then. We're going to head back."

"Thanks for stopping by, Captain. This is amazing. Thank you for giving us this opportunity."

"Your welcome." I turned away, joined the others who had already started back to the Val. I climbed in, sealed the door and engaged the 'Purge /Pressurize' switch. The green light came on completing the operation. We unsealed our pressure visors and pushed it up on our helmets.

"Yuk! What's that smell?" Asked Perry.

"You may be smelling a small amount of hydrogen sulfide gas in the Martian atmosphere. Like rotten eggs. It's similar to Yellowstone's smell around the geysers. The atmosphere is not thought to be harmful, other than there's very little of it and has no oxygen at all. It's too thin and won't support human life. It's getting darker. Might as well head home.

On the monitor, one of the shuttles was heading back to the ship. From a different location to the east, the other shuttle was headed back per instructions to recover each evening. The monitor was a great addition to our instrumentation. I will ask Fred Mooney if his team could outfit all shuttles and Valkyries with the same package as we have in VAL-1. Once inside, hangar personnel immediately began cleaning the shuttles and Valkyrie, while suit-maintenance from Boeing meticulously cleaned our four suits doing pressure tests and checking radiation dosimeter readings. All was OK. Engineers and technicians from NASA and JPL did the same for the two types of space suits used by our guest science teams. Meanwhile, following a shower and change of clothes, I went to the bridge, stopping first at CIC-Tactical. All was well. Most of the Ships' crew stations were quiet and at reduced staffing. Those that were at their station, monitored systems, that, for the most part were also monitored by AI subsystems. Both Jessica and Augie were on the bridge. I joined them on the raised command deck just to chat. Augie said quietly...

"Things have gotten so routine, Hannah, it's hard to believe we are on Mars. People all over the ship are getting bored, it seems. Maybe we should start taking tours of the planet."

"We could just take Seraphim. Contact our MEV team and advise of tomorrows tour."

Bridge view-screen, 2x magnified slowly rotating view of Acidalia Planitia.

As we entered the Martian night, people had dinner in one of the restaurants on deck 9, then retreated to their residences for family time, attempts at emailing or messaging recipients on Earth, mindful of the now 14-minute transmission delay each way. But, it still worked. People were happy and content.

Some decided to take advantage of the many activities that made Seraphim different. Little by little they were in the pools, playing regular and Zero-Golf. Darien and Carl organized a series of lectures in one of our smaller theaters on science subjects of all sorts. People attended a series on the planets, starting with Mars. All this was being coordinated with Angels Landing. What we did... they did, almost in unison. Comm with assistance from technicians, had raised the large communications dish on the dorsal line of the ship. With the help from Nav, they located Earth and locked in the signal. As the two planets moved, the dish precessed tracking the Earth.

SOL-5
Rescue

There seemed to be renewed enthusiasm as the crew prepared for a scenic tour. Sarah had anticipated doing this prior to launch and had some creative artists make brochures talking about the planet Mars, its history and its mythology. It included a pull-out topographical map of the entire planet. Forty-nine million miles away, these same brochures were being made available in the Rotunda kiosks in Angels Landing. A huge ultra-high resolution 20-foot video screen had been installed in one of the auditorium theaters, modelled after the bridge on Seraphim. It mirrored, in real-time, minus the now 15-minute delay, the view from Seraphim's bridge view screen. The dynamics of time wasn't difficult to understand but was simply another thing that set space-flight apart from the accepted routines on Earth. Mar's ecliptic around the sun was much larger than that of Earth resulting in a slower orbital velocity. Earth, therefore was moving faster than Mars. As each day past, the time delay for communications lengthened as the distance increased. Above the screen were two clocks. One Earth-time, the other Mars in SOL-time. People sitting on the observation deck on Seraphim had copies of the brochure explaining this and other unique realities of living on another planet. Jessica called the MEV team and advised them of our intentions. They will still have the Sentinel block II. For now, the shuttle away teams will stay in Seraphim depending on where we were and could leave the ship in the shuttles if we were close to something that was important. We certainly were.

"Captain..." said Theo. "We are approaching the last reported position of the *Spirit* rover. We could pick it up now, if you want."

"I do. Let's go get it. Bring it into Hangar 3. Find those Rover guys from JPL and see if they would give us a hand. I know it's not part of their contract but we can ask them."

"I found the JPL guys. They agreed to help us."

"OK you guys follow up and see if you can retrieve the rover. Take *Gabriel* to get it. Lory remain aboard, please. I have a feeling you may be needed elseware. Remain on the bridge, please."

"Copy that. Gabriel is headed out with Jake at the controls."

"Copy that. Good hunting guys." I left for my quarters. Following a good night's sleep, I was just finishing my morning shower when I got a call to go to the bridge. Something was happening.

I rushed to the bridge. I didn't like the sound of the call. People were nervous. As I entered, I immediately saw a large group standing in front of the main view screen.

"What's going on?" People moved out of the way.

"Captain look out there to the right of that jagged rock formation. Someone is walking this way and is having difficulty. He falls every so often, picks himself up and moves a few more feet. Then waves at us. See? He did it again."

"I don't recognize the space suit. Can you zoom in closer?"

"We are at max magnification. We estimate he's about 2 and a half miles away."

"Get a head count of our away-teams now. Janice call all the away teams and any still on board."

"On it." Minutes went by.

"Captain, everybody is accounted for in all three teams. We have no idea who that could be."

Dad, Doug, Perry and Theo were looking at me as I rolled up my sleeve. All saw the hair on my arms standing straight up.

"Holy shit, Hannah, is that what I think it is?" asked Perry.

In an excited voice... I yelled.

"Tactical, have Valkyrie-1 prepped for immediate departure. Jessica, when I leave Seraphim in the Val, follow along behind about a mile. Back off if I slow or stop. Dad, I need you at Tactical and stay frosty. Keep watch for other ships in the area. Theo, please keep an eye out for any activity. Janice keep tabs on any signals and note the frequencies. We have company folks and... I think I know who they are." I said with some trepidation.

"Permission to come along." Yelled Doug Freeman.

"Are you sure?"

"You shouldn't go out there alone... again" I smiled

"Permission granted." Others looked on with fascination. Do we have more aliens in our midst?

We hurried to the Personal Equipment room and as quickly as possible, put on our blue environment suits, otherwise known as space suits and did the tests.

He was hot on my heels as I jumped into the Val. He followed and closed and sealed the access door. I moved forward and quickly sat in the pilot's seat, strapped in. With Doug beside me in the right seat. I ran a quick but complete preflight while the systems warmed up. When everything was in the green I verified my space-suit was sealed and air was flowing. Doug mirrored my actions. I signaled the Hangar-Master to open the inner door. I was already floating toward the entry. I re-checked seatbelts and harnesses on and locked.

Following the required pressurization safety checks, the inner door closed and sealed, in moments, the outer door opened. We slid into the Martian atmosphere, and turned toward the sighting.

"Your initial heading should be 298° Hannah." Said Josh.

"Do you see him, Hannah?"

"No, not yet, too far. Lory, prepare Peregrine for departure. Outfit with a med-team with suits on and emergency kits, three Zero-Grav gurneys, Oh, and a mobile isolation chamber. OK, I see him. He is sitting down leaning against a rock. He waved but he is clearly hurt."

"Who is it, Hannah?"

"Someone I met before."

"On the moon?"

"Yes." An ominous silence fell over all listening.

"OK, I'm setting down. Mark my position. I'll leave the lights on. Leaving the Val, now."

"Do You know him?" asked Doug as I walked slowly up to the white suited being before us, kneeled down in front of him, then pointed at him with my right hand and pointed to myself with my left. Then brought my hands together locking my fingers of both hands and looked at him. He nodded up and down. He understood. Doug was having an epiphany as he watched the alien try to communicate. Then we heard a voice in our helmets. It was mechanical, sounded like a computer voice.

"I saw you before." It said. I smiled and said...

"Yes. I remember you. Are you hurt?"

"Tired. Legs hurt. Walked long time. Two... three Sol. Ship out of fuel. Saw your ship and tried to use skimmer and it failed. Was three of us. Others injured. Gone into sand. Help, help?"

"Yes, we will help you. My people are coming."

I could just barely make out his features with the available sun-light. He looked like us... a blue eyed human. I was shocked. Doug figured it out and put his hands together fingers intertwined and nodded. Then from Seraphim...

"Hannah, what's happening? I have two shuttles on the way and we are outfitting Peregrine."

"Good. He seems OK, just very tired. He has been walking for three Sols to reach us. His ship made an emergency landing... out of fuel, and his shuttle quit, too. He is asking for our help. I told him we would help him. There were two others from the shuttle craft that went down. The other two disappeared into the sand, he said. I'm guessing quick-sand. He will ride with us as we try to find the others. Tag along."

"He speaks English?"

"Yes, with the help of a universal translator of some kind. It seems to function both ways. Hold on..."

"What did he just say, Doug?"

"I think he is running out of air."

"Seraphim, find someone to get us an atmosphere analyzer. Our mixture may be harmful to them. We'll need a way to synthesize an atmosphere for him if he can't breathe ours. Theo, if you're listening, we need to save lives. These are lives of the people that saved all of ours. It's outside the box time folks. Use your imagination. Make Peregrine a hospital. Gotta go."

I pointed to myself and said...

"I am Hannah, he is Doug. We are from the planet Earth."

"I know." He said. I looked at Doug. He was as surprised as I was. Poor, Doug. He just signed on with us... now this?

"Find my friends. Under sand."

"Will you show us where they are?" He nodded

"Cannot walk. Go in that." Pointing to the Val.

"Yes. Let me help you up." He nodded. Doug and I got on either side of him and helped him stand.

"Seraphim, we are going to find the small shuttle, he's going with us. He will show us the way, in the Valkyrie."

I could only imagine what was happening on Seraphim. They could hear our comm. But, I knew that our ship was in good hands.

"Do you have a name?"

"Devian. I was the on Moon with you."

"Yes, I remember. We will take care of you and find your friends, Devian." He nodded up and down and seemed pleased.

"Hannah, this is dad. I sent a Sentinel high to find the big ship. It will start at 10,000 feet searching west of us."

"Copy that. Good idea."

Doug and I got Devian into the Val and loosely strapped in, closed and sealed the door. He sat in the right-front seat, Doug behind.

We coasted at about hundred meters AGL for nearly an hour when he pointed to our left. There it was. upright with the cabin door open. I set the Val down nearby, and equalized interior pressure with outside. Doug opened the door and hopped out, turned and helped Devian to the ground. I followed, then ran to the other shuttle and saw that it was empty. I looked around and saw a depression in the hard pack gravel. There was a flat surface of a lighter color level like water in a tiny dirty pond. That must be it. I walked over and dipped my foot into the dry powder of the quicksand. I looked at Devian and pointed to the pool of dust.

He nodded and tried to sit down but fell over from exhaustion. I turned and the two shuttles moved apart and let Peregrine come close and landed.

It was Lori in Peregrine. She waved through the windshield then said...

"We called the MEV Lab. They are on their way here with the winch crane in case we need it."

"Good call, Lori." Then I heard Mom,

"I'll be there in a second, Hannah. How is he doing?"

"I think he is suffering from hypoxia. His air is running out and he is exhausted. Hold on a second. Devian, can you talk to them?" pointing to the sand. He nodded then said...

"They are alive. They are tired trying to climb out of there nothing to hold on to."

"Lori, I need rope ½ inch or thicker. About 50 feet."

"Copy that." Mom said... "Hannah, did you say his name was Devian?"

"Yes, can we move him to the Peregrine?"

"Yes, of course. Devian, can we take you into that shuttle?" he nodded.

Doug helped Devian up and we walked him to the Peregrine ramp. Others were there to help.

"Mom, we need to talk for a moment. Privately." I turned a switch on her helmet and mine. A beep sounded in each helmet signifying a secure link had been established.

"Nobody can hear us now. I need you to select two people to work with you that you trust explicitly. We have a severe ethical problem. Devian appears to be human. Not from Earth but... somewhere else." I shrugged. "I don't know how you are going to do it but first you need to take a sample of his air and see if it is compatible with ours. Also, I don't want anyone to know what I just told you. The ethical considerations are enormous."

She looked at me, sighed, seemingly lost. Something was really bothering her, something deep within her.

"You can do this Mom. His people saved all of Earth. We owe them everything. You are the best. You can do this."

She said nothing, just nervously nodded.

"After we get Devian in, I'm going to get the others." She nodded again and climbed aboard Peregrine behind Doug and I holding Devian. She directed us to a room that had all kinds of medical equipment. We sat Devian in a chair. And he looked around.

"You have come a long way." ...and he wasn't talking about distance.

"Devian, this is my mother. Her name is Lorraine. She is a doctor and will take good care of you. OK?

"Hi Devian we are going to help you, OK?"

"Thank you. I cannot breathe."

"I need a sample of your air. I need to find out if you can breathe our air. If not, we will make some like yours. OK?"

He nodded.

"Hannah is going to get your friends."

"Hannah is a good person. She met me on the moon. She is very brave."

"Yes, she is. Now we will bleed a little of your air into this bag and test it."

"Dad. Are you still on Seraphim?"

"Yes."

"I want you to silence the ship. Nobody else hears or sees what we are doing out here."

"Already done, Hannah. All comm and video from your team out there was shut down when this started and is fully contained on the bridge. It is being recorded, though. We understand the ethical problem. Laurie Zoloth was here a few minutes ago and is concerned, too. She asked if she could join you, or at least Mom on Peregrine."

"OK with me. If she has a space suit."

"She has one and is checked out. Darien will bring her out in a Pocket-Rocket. I've never seen him so concerned, Theo too."

What happened next will be added to the Seraphim history books and talked about for years. Now told in the objective...

"OK, I have to go fetch two of Devian's ship mates at the bottom of a quick-sand pool. Out." Hannah walked back to the site. She said...

"I need the two shuttles moved back about fifty meters. All personnel not directly involved in this rescue mission, please return to your shuttle. Stand by in case we need you. We need more room here. Peregrine will stay where it is." Off in the distance they could see the MEV-Lab moving toward them, turning occasionally to miss a rock or boulder. In ten minutes, it arrived. They had heard the earlier call for rope and handed the team a coil of ½" rope from their Lab tool-box. Doug signaled them to back the MEV-Lab to the very edge of the quick-sand pool. A Pocket-Rocket arrived. Darien and Laurie stepped out and walked toward the sand pool. Darien bent down and ran his gloved hand through the surface of the quick-sand, feeling almost nothing. He didn't say anything, just stepped back as the rope was securely tied around Hannah's legs. Doug made a loop and attached it to the hook on the MEV- Lab's winch system.

Laurie looked on with curiosity and amazement as Hannah lowered herself into the sand-pool. When up to her waist, she jumped up and forward disappearing head first into the quicksand.

"Can you hear me, Hannah?"

"Yea, barely, this sand is blocking some of the signal. I found one. Feeling for the other. *TH*y6t mkjkd Alive. Mln er #@ you m*& copy*" noise and crackle sounds

"You 're breaking up. Can you see anything?"

"No 3#4ight.. &^ up."

"What did she say?"

"No idea."

"Pu&(up"

Doug waved at the winch operator.

"Pull her up, very slowly."

People on the shoreline watched as the steel cable slowly reeled in, the moments felt like days as the cable continued to rise. Then the hook rose from the dust. On it was the rope. Darien and Laurie watched fearful the rope was empty. But it wasn't. The first to break the dusty surface were blue boots and legs. Slowly Hannah's body completely emerged from the quicksand, her arms hanging taught below her. In each hand was an arm of each alien. The cable kept winding in until all three space suits, one blue and two white, hung just above the surface of the pool. The driver of the MEV-Lab slowly drove forward, away from the pool with Hannah hanging upside down still holding the two in white. Again, a moment of extreme emotion rocked all who witnessed it.

Three low-gravity gurneys were placed on the ground under the hanging trio.

The winch slowly unwound and the feet of the two aliens were directed to the foot of the gurneys. Slowly they were both helped to a prone position. Hannah released the hands but couldn't move her arms. A gurney was moved beneath her. Her arms were not moving and needed to be directed beside her as her body slowly was laid flat. She didn't move. The rope was removed from her legs.

"Hannah, can you hear me?..............Hannah?" No answer.

"Let's get them into the Peregrine."

Walking toward the three gurneys still on the ground was Lorraine Parish and a nurse. Between them, walking with difficulty was Devian. People backed away with suspicion as the alien who had met Hannah on the lunar tundra that fateful day on the moon, watched as he approached the three lying on the ground. He first went to his ship mates. Each held up an arm and he held it. They were alive. Then he moved to the gurney with the blue suited human on it. He bent down and held her hand for several minutes realizing she seemed to go in and out of consciousness. He raised one of her hands and clasped it with fingers intertwined with hers. Her eyes opened.

"Are they OK?" she asked.

"Yes. Yes, they are. Thank you." responded the translator.

Kneeling beside Hannah, and Devian, Admiral Freeman looked down at his former submarine crewmember. She is now the Captain of the Seraphim and perhaps the most important and revered Seraphim crew member. She shouldn't be doing this. Why is it she is the only one that does the dirty-work? He knew she would say, 'because it is the right thing to do.' Regardless of age, or her subordinate position when he was her commanding officer, she was now his commanding officer, and would be as faithful to her as she was to him in a different time and place. His sight was muddled by the emotions that raged through his body accompanied by an overflow of tears. This was a strange new world. It scared him, but it also was amazingly exciting.

Extraordinary Revelations

A flurry of activity replaced the slow-motion drama of the recovery of the two sand-trapped aliens and one dusty Captain. Five engineers from the Seraphim Hangar bays walked to the little fallen shuttle-craft to see what might have brought it down. The MEV-LAB pulled away to rejoin the MEV-Habitat and the on-going science activity. Laurie Zoloth and Darien Hunter stood to the side almost oblivious of their Martian surroundings, consumed by their fears for Hannah and the people she had saved. Others were puzzling over the depression in the ground into which dust had been trapped during a dust storm. Of some concern were muddy pieces that had fallen off the white environment suits of the two trapped. Was it liquid water, or something else. Samples were taken. Darien and Laurie were quietly talking when two unexpected people joined them. Theo Remington and Carl Ledbetter had actually left the comfort of the big space-ship, hovering silently a hundred meters away. They both walked to the edge of the quick-sand pool and tested the very flat pool-like surface.

"I wonder how deep it is." Said Theo.

"Deep enough to cover three people," added Carl.

"We should go to the field hospital and see how they are making out." All four walked slowly into a pressurized room from the airlock with the three prone bodies still wearing their environment suits lying on gurneys. Hannah's helmet had been removed. Her face was sweaty and her eyes closed. The two aliens still had their helmets on, but were awake waiting to get some more air. They knew it needed to be tested first.

"Hi Theo, Carl. I'm surprised to see you out here."

"We were worried about Hannah." The chief of the Seraphim med-bay pulled off her nitrile gloves and said...

"She will be fine. Both shoulders were dis-located pulling them out of the mud. I have her mildly sedated for the pain, but she is fine. She should wake up in just a few minutes."

"What about them?"

"Well... we tested both suit atmospheres and they are very similar to ours. They are exhausted and their metabolism has slowed severely. So, we are bringing their vitals up and they seem to be responding. Devian rallied quickly and is walking around with our breathing mixture."

"What did you mean... mud?

"The way the scientists are talking about it, Acidalia Planitia seems to have densely occurring mounds they think could be mud volcanoes. A mud volcano is a geological structure formed when a mixture of gas, liquid and fine-grained rock (or mud) is forced to the surface from several meters to kilometers underground. Scientists are interested in these mud volcanoes because the sediments, brought from depth, could contain organic materials that might provide evidence for possible past and present microbial life on Mars.

There may be many depressions in the Martian topography that become filled with light particles of sand following sand/dust storms, forming quick-sand. It is very fine and dry. But, if it is deep enough and you fell in, it could be very difficult to climb out. That depression out there, is fairly deep. The scientists are right now trying to figure out if an eruption of material from a small mud volcano joined with the dust at the bottom of the pit could make a shallow layer of mud with elastic properties. It becomes really sticky and difficult to pull away from. You can see it on the boots of these guys here. There is one more thing... but you need to keep it to yourselves right now. OK?"

Theo and Carl were really nervous. At the same time, the big shuttle slowly moved to enter Seraphim's main hangar. The three gurneys and the space-suited aliens were moved to the Seraphim Med-Bay.

"We drew blood from all three and checked it for anything that we might need to be concerned about. We discovered that they have identical DNA to... us. They are human."

"What??? You can't be serious."

"I'm very serious. When she was awake, Hannah became aware of this and said that was why they protected us. She said...

'We are kindred souls. We just evolved on two different planets.' It's also another reason she had to go out on the moon with those chairs. She wasn't sure why at the time, but she seemed to know all along. Now, are you ready for another shocker? The alien she met on the moon... was Devian."

"Oh, my God."

"This can't be happening."

"That is why she had to rescue them. As usual, nobody else stepped forward and volunteered. So, someone had to do it, and once again, it was my daughter that did. As she puts it, 'it is the right thing to do'. But now, we are faced with an enormous dilemma, an ethical problem of epic proportions. You remember her speaking of the Prime Directive from Star Trek?"

"Yes. She referred to it when she suggested that the reason they came to move the moon was, that part of the alien culture's adherence to a two-part prime directive. Everyone else thought she was nuts. Turns out, it seems, she wasn't."

"Who else knows about this?"

"Devian, of course, and was silenced by his own Prime directive. Now Admiral Freeman, Laurie Zoloth and Darien know, too. The ship's crew, do not. It would be wise to respect the Prime Directive, at least until we figure this all out. Hold on, I'll be right back. It looks like Hannah is up and moving around." She moved into the adjacent room. Theo asked...

"Does this keep getting better and better, or what?"

You know?" said Carl. "This has a huge case of weird wrapped around it. Why does it always have to be Hannah? She doesn't ask for this. Are the rest of us, that cowardly?"

In moments, a groggy but smiling Hannah Parish came from the same room, joining the group. She was wrapped in flexible netting around her shoulders, holding her arms from moving too much. Her hair was disconnected from her ponytail but looked like someone had brushed it out. All were glad to see her and she seemed to be much better. They were joined by Admiral Freeman, Perry Newcomb, Ed parish and Darien Hunter and Laurie Zoloth. Doug Freeman began with...

"Hannah, you never fail to amaze me. Why are these aliens so important to you?"

"They saved Earth. We would do the same if the roles were reversed. At least I hope we would."

"How are your shoulders? That must have been a heavy load."

"It wasn't the weight, they weigh 1/3 earth weight. It was something in the sand pit holding them down. Mom says it is some kind of sticky mud. Damn, that... hurt. Devian is fine. But, he walked for two, maybe three Sols to find us, walking through the night, without stopping, hoping we would help. The thing is... I'm not sure of what kind of help they are seeking."

Lorraine Parish returned and said...

"Hannah, would you come in here. There is someone who would like to see you. The rest of you, please remain in here."

Hannah followed her mom into the operating room. Nearly an hour passed.

Laurie Zoloth paced around the small waiting room, deeply concerned. There was more to this, she knew it, she could feel it. This whole first contact thing had her totally confused. She knew that Hannah has perceptions she had never seen in all her years at the University, and also seems to have an extraordinary level of dedication to the service of others. Learning that the alien named Devian was the same alien that joined Hannah in the green lawn chairs, first contact has taken an amazing turn. Laurie approached Theo, Darien and Doug Freeman. They were standing in a loose group, not saying much of anything.

"This whole thing is scaring me. Who are these people that care so much about... essentially, another species?"

It was Carl Ledbetter that offered a philosophical observation.

"Whatever happens, I have a feeling this 'first-contact' thing will have profound considerations beyond anything we can possibly imagine. Darien, I suspect it is these kinds of surprises that could not have been factored into our planning, and will continue far into our future in space. There is life out here. Intelligent life. And we didn't seek it out. It came to us and saved every man, women and child on Earth. All 7.7 billion of us. And those people from a far distant planet, sit in our ship, in Seraphim. I have never been in such a loss for words. I'm running out of tears, too."

Hannah returned to the room, stood still with an odd smile, looked around the room, and dropped the bombshell of all bombshells.

"You are about to have everything you think you know about life, science and imagination tested. Our whole future in space may depend on how we handle what you are about to see and hear. Open your mind, find your ultimate humanity. There is someone I would like you to meet." From the other room stepped a very attractive, tall blond woman with pale skin and blue-grey eyes with limbal rings. She stood close beside Hannah. They were nearly a double of each other. Like Sisters?

"Hello, I am Devian."

Shock radiated through the room. Some fell to the floor, losing control of their equilibrium. The white-suited alien from another planet was a human female. She bore an uncanny resemblance to the Captain of the Seraphim. If that weren't enough the door opened once again and two more tall elegant women joined the group. Devian offered, speaking near perfect English...

"This is T'merin, Lead Guider and Navigator of S'mparder. This is P'rtavin, the third Guider and Healer. I am Second Guider, Teller of S'mparder. All stood in wonder. Was this possible? All human endeavors in space had at its root, the discovery of extra-terrestrial life. Single cell life, micro-organisms... but this?

"S'mparder is your ship?" fumbled Darien, his voice quavering, trying to assimilate the profound event that was taking place. T'merin answered...

"Yes. It is a Journey-Class Jumper. Our home world is K'hfatoria-Prime in the Pr'ydorin Binary Star System. We came here to help, and keep Earth from being destroyed."

Laurie was beyond her ability to comprehend the amazing situation standing before her. Her entire life's work exploded before her.

Doug Freeman was choked up, but managed...

"Where is the rest of your crew?" Devian responded...

"S'mparder had a crew of seven. The others, have moved forward and begun their journey. They suffered from severe radiation poisoning. You would say, 'They died'."

"I'm very sorry. Is there anything we can do to help?"

"You already have. You saved us, we are the last of the S'mparder crew. The ship is no longer flyable. It is also the last functioning Journey-Class Jumper. We have no more. We sent a message to K'hfatoria-Prime. Sometimes it takes a time to communicate."

"How far away is your home-world?"

"You would say, 23 light years."

All stood shocked, trying to absorb the realities of the moment.

"Such a big ship and it only has a crew of seven?"

"Yes, *'Thinker'* controls everything. We control *Thinker*. We tell it what to do."

"What is Thinker?"

"A Non-Sentient." Said Devian. Hannah added...

"The best I can tell it's like a huge AI. Only the 'Guiders' can control it. T'merin, Devian and P'rtavin are the only Guiders left. Devian says T'merin is the equivalent to a Captain and Devian is the XO. The ship is fully automated and the three of them simply oversea its function adding a human element to *Thinker*. Here's one for all of you. Females are the only flyers. Men have technical duties, and have no... well... have little power."

"Oh, my. That will rock the very fabric of our culture." Said Theo. "What the hell are we going to tell people?"

Hannah smiled, looked around the small room, at her friends, comrades and advisors.

"Perhaps you should say nothing. I think it is time for Ships Council to bite the bullet and find a path forward for Seraphim to navigate. I have a proviso first and foremost, whatever you decide, there will be no exploitation or spotlights on our sisters here." Darien continued, coughing through his words...

"T'merin, does Thinker know what is wrong with the ship? Can it self-diagnose the problem? and lastly are there any diagrams of the ship's function we can refer to?"

"It doesn't really matter. We will not be returning to K'hfatoria. There is nothing technically wrong with S'mparder. The ship is without fuel. That is why we set down on the planet you call Mars. We used most of the fuel just getting to the moon and using the C'mpressr systems to control the moon's position. Our computations were correct, the rock hit the moon, not Earth. We knew we wouldn't have enough crystal even before we left K'hfatoria. We knew it would be a one-way trip."

"Why did the others die... move forward?"

"Without an atmosphere and magnetic force, K'hfatoria is exposed to the radiation from Pr'ydorin, and was too much for them. It was their time. We did not receive the radiation while in S'mparder and are the only ones left. We, too, have journeys to take." Said T'merin. She continued...

"For us and S'mparder, our job is done. This was a one-way trip for us. We believe the ship is functional, but it will still not be able to return to K'hfatoria-Prime. It does not have enough energy crystals to return home.

"Won't the people on K'hfatoria come and get you?"

"No, as we said, S'mparder, is the last of the Journey-Class Jumpers that was operational. There are no more with fuel enough to make the trip. It was agreed that it would not be necessary to come to our aid. Recently, our Council has stepped back from the Prime-Directive as you call it. It was not favored by most K'hfatorians. Our time searching the universe for similar civilizations is at an end. We documented all found locations. It is known." Then Devian added more.

"We had one last duty that was not in the original mission. It is why I needed to come along. We needed to find the Earth-Guider, join with her and pass our knowledge on to her. We were very lucky to find her. Or maybe she found us. Hannah Parish is the Earth-Guider. Now we are four."

"WHAT? Me? How can that be?"

"There is more to your story that you do not yet know. We are in Seraphim, if you allow us, we will join you, and in the privacy of only your favored, we will tell you the rest. I am a Teller and keeper of knowledge. You will know."

"There is more?" Hannah asked obviously in much distress.

"Yes, much."

"Strangers in a Strange Land"

Knock, Knock

"Hannah..."

Knock, Knock

"Hannah, please open the door. It's mom. We need to talk, honey." ... no answer.

"Ed, you try. She has me worried."

Knock, Knock

There was a sound, then a hiss. The door opened. Their daughter was walking away toward the private residence part of the Captains Quarters. She sat down in her favorite reading chair, a Kleenex box by her side, used tissue tossed haphazardly to the floor. Several books also lay on the floor. Two empty bottles of wine were on the kitchen counter. She is a young woman in mourning... and scared.

"You lied to me... both of you."

"We let you believe what was obvious. You were an infant baby and we raised you as our own, provided for you. You ARE our daughter."

"But what is Devian saying?"

"Come, we will get something to eat and we will fill you in. Then later Devian will tell you everything. It is why she is here. That is why I was very uncomfortable when you brought her in and said her name was Devian."

"But she is an alien from another planet."

"Yes, but she is Earth-Born, just as you are."

"What???"

"We should go now. A group will meet us in the Council chamber after we get something to eat."

"I have to stop in to NGE and the bridge first. I'll meet you down in the Captains Mess."

"OK."

This was driving me nuts. What the hell are they talking about. I am just the Bus Driver. What's so special about me?

I walked onto the bridge to a *Captain on the Bridge*.

"Captain, are you, all right?" asked josh at the helm.

"Getting better. What's happening?" Jessica answered.

"Everybody is back on-board captain. Except the MEV science team. Do we really have the alien on board?"

"Three aliens. Listen. We might cut this field trip off starting tomorrow noon. Comm tell the MEV team to pack up and be back here by close of business tomorrow. I haven't eaten since yesterday. I'm going to the Captains Mess. XO please alternate with Augie. Just so you know, the aliens are us. They are human and don't mean us any harm. They are the ones that re-oriented the moon so the asteroid would hit it, not Earth. They saved all of humanity. But now we have some serious ethical problems to solve. We are working them out now. You will be kept informed."

As I walked into the Captains Mess, I saw Mom and Dad and Lory at our usual table. With them was the brunette named T'merin. People around the room were staring at her... and us.

"Sorry I'm late. I stopped at the bridge. I'm considering ending all EVAs as of tomorrow until we sort this out and I feel comfortable. Did you eat?"

"Yes, we did. T'merin liked the food. Now you should eat something, Hannah. Your energy is low."

"T'merin, as captain of the S'mparder, what would you like to do next?" She answered...

"We would like to return to S'mparder, tomorrow. Can you bring us there?"

"Of course. It is your home. Your things are there: clothes, personal stuff. Does the ship have enough power to provide air, heat and electricity?"

"Oh, yes, it does. As long as we don't try to use the Jump power, we can last a long time. We can move the ship, too. It has plenty of power as long as we don't use the jump engines."

"Then what?"

"We don't know, yet."

"Hannah, S'mparder has three primary power systems to move the ship, like Seraphim." Dad reported.

"The jump engines are off-line and will not function as long as there is insufficient power. They have a secondary system, more like our VASIMR drives, that don't use a huge amount of power. And, thrusters for attitude control. By the way, with T'merin's permission, we brought the small shuttle into hangar 3 and it is being checked out in the hope we can get it functional again. They call it a *skimmer*."

"Excellent. I understand we are supposed to meet in the Council chambers."

"When you're done. You eat first."

"T'merin, Devian's name is pronounced differently than yours or P'rtaven's. Why is that?"

"Devian is not a K'hfatorian name, it is an Earth name given to her by her K'hfatorian biological mother while on Earth, thirty-four Terran years ago. We know you are very confused by all this. This will all be explained."

"OK, I'm done. We can go. Where is P'rtaven ?"

"She will meet us in the Council room with Devian and others." My hair was still hanging free. At least someone brushed it.

T'merin and P'rtaven were tall, very attractive women in their late forties, early 50s, I guessed. T'merin had long brown hair and brown eyes. P'rtaven had fairly short light brown hair and hazel eyes. Devian was younger and had blond hair much like mine.

I wondered if all K'hfatorian women were this attractive. They were smart and capable and all spoke surprisingly good English. I hope to learn more about their world and its history.

Before we walked into the Council Chambers, I made a stop in the bridge. I was surprised to see Admiral Freeman and Chief Newcomb chatting with Theo and Carl. Talking with Jessica and Lory was Devian. Everyone was smiling and the crew were all looking at Devian, the alien I had met out on the lunar tundra. I made a tour around the bridge stopping first at comm, then Tactical and Helm saying hi before joining the rest by the raised deck steps. Josh called me back to Helm.

"Hannah, she is gorgeous. You two look like twin sisters."

"Oh, does that make me gorgeous, too?" I chided.

"We're headed to the Council Chambers for a talk. Is everything doing OK here?"

"Yea, we're fine. Did you know that the XO ran a couple of 'What-If' drills while you were saving aliens from quicksand. You know, she is very good, professional, and knows her stuff."

"I'm glad she's doing well. She seems to enjoy it.

"I remember when Darien moved her out. That was a shame."

"Yea, well. I fixed that. Hey gotta go. I miss you guys. Uh-oh!" Walking over was Devian.

"Hannah. You have more really nice friends. Who are these?"

These handsome gentlemen are part of the Navigation team. This is Josh and Jeff."

"Very pleased to meet you both." And she shook hands with both.

"Is it true? You were the one who met Hannah at the lawn chairs on the moon? You didn't know each other, did you? Were you afraid walking out there?"

Devian answered...

"When the Terran in the blue environment suit walked out onto the lunar plain by herself holding two chairs. We didn't know what to make of it. Something inside told me, I had to go out there, and, yes, I was scared. But, it was the best thing I could have done."

"Was it you that moved the moon and saved Earth?"

"Yes, we did. Just seven of us. I think we have to go. We have a meeting in a few minutes. Nice meeting you, bye."

I gave Josh and Jeff a thumbs-up and a wink, and walked with Devian to the door. At some point today or tomorrow, we will go to the S'mparder. I'm not exactly sure why. The question I have, will our new friends prefer to stay in their ship or ours? But first the meeting.

We walked into the room that had a few people standing around talking. The other two K'hfatorians were already there when Devian and I entered. I didn't count, but it looked like 20+ people. Dad called me over.

"T'merin would like to begin the talk relating facts about their home world and their travels to other planets. This is an open forum so if people wish to speak they need only raise their hand."

"Are you moderator for this meeting?"

"I guess you could say that."

"Why am I very nervous about this. What am I going to learn that has me, well... scared?"

"There may be a few things you and others may have difficulty accepting. Hannah this is part of a first contact. Even Laurie is nervous. Let's get started. Would you like to open the meeting?"

"OK"

I stepped to the head seat at the table, remained standing and began...

"Good morning. I have to say, this is the first meeting I have ever hosted where I don't know what to say. This is an unusual time for all of us. For anyone here whom I have not met, I am Hannah Parish, Captain of Seraphim. We have some very special guests with us that will help us understand who they are and what their relationship is to us. Most of us are Terrans, from our home planet Earth. Our guests are from their home planet 'K'hfatoria, quite a distance from here, I'm told, about 23 light years or about 135 trillion miles, but still in our galaxy. Their ship is the S'mparder, a faster-than-light capable ship called a *Journey-Class Jumper*. So, I wonder if the Captain of the S'mparder would like to tell us about their home-world and why S'mparder is here. T'merin, you have our attention." I sat down.

"Captain Parish and people of Seraphim. Thank you for allowing us to speak to you. First, I would like to thank Hannah for saving our lives from a sand pool we fell into. She is very brave and resourceful. We would also like to thank the doctors of Seraphim who took care of us when we were near beginning the journey, which is our way of saying 'dying'. I think we may have been as afraid to meet Terrans as you may have been meeting us. But I... we, have learned something extremely valuable which I will get to in time. First let me tell you who we are and what our home world is like. Perhaps the best way is comparing our two planetary systems.

You have one star you call Sol and eight planets; four rocky and four gas giants. Earth has one moon, Mars two, Jupiter has 67, Saturn 62, Uranus 27, Neptune 14. You have a lot of moons, but none are habitable, nor are your planets, although this one, Mars, comes close.

We have a binary star system; two stars that are in orbit around each other. One is a large bright-yellow star like yours, called Pr'ydorin Major. The other is a red dwarf star called Pr'ydorin Minor. It is in orbit around 'Major with an orbital rate of about 97 earth-days.

The Pr'ydorin system has 12 planets and an assortment of small moons. The exception is the planetary system called K'hfatoria. Our home world planet is K'hfatoria Prime or KP and is .9 Earth Mass, slightly smaller than your home world. We are actually a moon of K'hfatoria B or KB and we rotate around it once every 20 earth-days. KB is about 3 time the size of Earth and is a rocky, desolate, and an uninhabitable place. The high gravity would not be healthy and it has no atmosphere. Prime has a thick atmosphere. It is highly affected by the twin stars and the high gravity from KB. Pr'ydorin, both stars, are often shaded by KB as we orbit around it. This happens once very 18 days and lasts 3 days. We go black. Prime has a surface similar to Earth. We have rivers and lakes and small oceans. All water is heavily affected by the tidal forces of KB. The water in a lake will flow to one end of the lake and then flow back. Pr'ydorin Major and Minor produce high amounts of gamma radiation that causes serious health problems for our people and shortens our life. Children are often born with defects caused by the radiation. It is chaotic living there.

Many of your years ago, we developed jump capability for our ships. We started to search the galaxy for any life, then intelligent life. Over many, many years, we found over 23 such planets. We began to realize that any interference with the cultures of those planets could cause damage to them. We backed away. That was when our cultural advisors devised protections in the form of directives. You called them Prime Directives. There were two main directives. One prohibited us from affecting the balance of the other culture's future. The second allowed us to watch over the world from afar and provide protection to them if we saw an impending danger. The asteroid that hit your moon was based on the second directive and forced us to intervene.

"Our people favored Earth because we had been there many times in the past, long past, hundreds of years. It is a beautiful planet without the chaos of companion stars or planets. Your moon is benign yet functional to keep a balance of nature on your world. Ours was dying. We needed to venture out to locate a possible new home world. We did not find one, so we stayed on K'hfatoria-Prime. After many years past, some decided they wanted to try living somewhere else. The first Prime directive was ignored and several partnerships went to Earth. Since we are essentially identical to Terrans, our early colonists weren't seen as aliens. Several generations past. The K'hfatorians began going to schools and universities, had children and seemed to thrive. Some had taken up residence in Norway, others in America in a place now called Norfolk. Then all were called back to K'hfatoria Prime. Most did not want to go but were forced to by threats that their relatives would take the journey. The most outspoken came from Norfolk. Horst and Victoria Benholt, their Terran names, were also threatened, but Victoria was pregnant... with twins. K'hfatoria has a one-child rule and Horst and Victoria had a difficult choice to make. They had many Terran friends and wanted their children the opportunity to grow up on Earth. But both children could not. It was known to the Council that Victoria would soon have a child. But, the Council was not told that she was expecting twins. If they went back to K'hfatoria..." she paused and took a deep breath...

"...one would be sent on its journey... eliminated. This was horrible news to them. Days went by. Victoria and Horst had two good friends that they trusted completely. Victoria told this story to them. They were shocked. A few days later the Terran couple came to Victoria and Horst with a proposition. They offered to take one of the children and raise him or her as their own. A few days later, Victoria birthed two beautiful female babies. Both were healthy and alert. Victoria chose to take their first born back to K'hfatoria. The second child was born only a few Earth minutes later. She was legally adopted by Lorraine and Edward Parish who raised her along with their other two children. Hannah Parish was never told of this at the request of Victoria Benholt. The other girl-child was named... Devian and was not told of this either. This is the first time either of them knows their true story."

T'merin was on the verge of crying. It was obvious this was very difficult for her. I was overwhelmed, and wasn't the only one. Devian was also beginning to put everything together. She is my blood sister. DNA confirmed that. I still felt I was lied to, until I realized, if it weren't for my adoption by my parents, real or not,... I wouldn't be here today. Circumstances made me the daughter of Lorraine and Edward Parish. The dark cloud of realization lifted. I am their daughter and will never allow the shock of this revelation to alter that.

I stood and walked to my mom and dad. I held them close, apologized for my outcry earlier. I said...

"You are my parents that I have always loved. I cherish you both. It must have been difficult to hear this and it probably brought back memories from so long ago when two couples had to make a terrible decision. You both made the right ones. I love you."

Devian walked over and stood beside us.

"My parents died when I was 16 years old from radiation poisoning from our two stars. 16 Terran years ago. I find out now, Hannah is my blood sister. Can you be my mom and dad, too?"

The whole room was in a state of emotional epiphany. A lot of Kleenex was used that day.

The Qualities of Leadership

Talk about things going viral. Things that happen in or around Seraphim have a way of migrating across the cosmos. It was almost as if a sub-space communication was sent out to the universe. Everyone now knew, the Captain of the Seraphim was born of extra-terrestrials. I wondered, would the Navy department yank my retirement status because they hired an extraterrestrial alien who had falsified who she was, who my parents were, and ... *MY HOME PLANET?*

I apologized to those at the meeting and stood to leave. Darien Hunter was first to ask...

"Where are you going? We were going to ask some questions. Don't you think you should stay, Hannah?"

"I have no answers to even un-asked questions. I just need a few minutes."

Devian left the meeting, too, and caught up.

"Are you not happy with this knowledge?" she asked.

"In part... I am very happy. It was just a shock, that's all. I realize now that when we brought you to the doctor... my mother... immediately knew who you were when she heard your name. That was why she wasn't saying anything. She remembered the other beautiful baby, Devian, who left Earth to go back to K'hfatoria. All this time she wondered what happened to you. It was a shock to her, too. I am very glad you are here now, with me. Mom and Dad are glad, too. What's going to happen, now? Will you return to the S'mparder and disappear from our life? What did T'merin mean when she said, *We, too, have journeys to take.* ?"

"T'merin and P'rtaven are approaching their end cycle. Our people have short life spans compared to yours. We live about 45 to 52 of your years. They are 51 and 52."

I was shocked and ...

"Come with me." I sent a message to Mom and Dad. Meet me in my day-room, bring T'merin and P'rtaven. **Emergency.**

The door swished open, Mom, T'merin and P'rtaven entered.

There were more knocks on the door. Darien opened the door. In walked Theo, Carl, Lory, Doug Freeman, Perry Newcomb, even Laurie Zoloth.

"What's happening?" asked Doug. The rest looked on in horror.

I was pacing. Devian was sitting at the table, head in her hands.

"What's the matter, Hannah. You look like you saw a ghost."

"Please sit."

They all did.

"How old were the others: S'nofer, I'odinn, D'rmin and X'orvkk?" T'merin answered.

"They were beyond their time."

"Mom, K'hfatorians have a life span of up to 50 years and then the accumulation of radiation poisoning... ends their lives. T'merin and P'rtaven are approaching their end cycle."

T'merin continued...

"Our people have short life spans compared to yours. We live about 45 to 52 of your years. We are 51 and 52."

"T'merin you told Darien explaining your use of the word 'journey' instead of 'died, you added *We, too, have journeys to take*'. You also said, *This was a one-way trip for us.*' What did you mean by that?" P'rtaven began crying, then wailing. She was terrified. She was next. I stomped around the room, screaming at the injustice. Angry at the audacity of the Gods to allow this to happen. I was livid. I have to do something. But, I can't. I just don't know how. I looked over and mom already had her communicator in hand.

It was Mom who took charge...

"Yes... I want you to do a complete panel on the blood we drew from our three guests. Yes, them. I want you to run every possible test as often as necessary to have a complete workup. Prepare three bed cubes side by side. Bring in the fancy diagnostic equipment. Also apprise the team headed by the Fellow from *Memorial Sloan Kettering* (MSK) Cancer Center. We're looking for the effects of poisoning from Gamma or similar radiation. I want the best doctors and nurses to form into a team, exclusive to this problem. Yes... yes... we will be there as quickly as we can. NOW! STAT! OK! We're going to my work room."

"Why are you doing this?" asked T'merin

"Because it is the right thing to do."

"You're daughter said that when she saved us."

"Well, it's my turn, now. T'merin, P'rtaven, come with me. You, too, Devian. The rest of you stay here. I will get back to you as soon as I know anything." That from the resident physician and former Air Force medic who treated wounded in a war zone, under fire. We would be apprised as soon as they had done the tests. I went and sat in my reading chair.

Each of those remaining had masks of horror and concern. Do the shocking revelations just keep on coming? I decided it was time for the Captain of Seraphim to join this oh-so-real world. I straightened up and walked to the day room. I tried to smile but couldn't find the right muscles. I began quietly...

"OK! We have another challenge, it seems. This ship is an exploration vessel. So, let's explore. I mentioned earlier that we might cut short our science studies and return home. I would like to amend that.

We are on MARS. Our species has been admiring, fearing and imagining more things about this planet than any other in the universe. Well, here we are. let's make our time count. I ask that you talk with our guest scientists and ask what they would like to do. They paid for this trip. I don't want it known that Seraphim and Angels Landing Science Park reneged on our pledge. If anything, maybe we should expand it. I just heard from Hangar-3 that the Opportunity Rover has been repaired and upgraded for another 15 years of exploration. Also, the *Spirit* rover was dug out of the sand, tested and upgraded. It has been given some new technology that makes it more capable, thanks to our friends from JPL.

"The 'A' team is preparing to deploy a new, huge rover in an area about 1900 miles from here in a crater that has had NASA curious for years. I don't remember the name of it, but they are excited about it. 'B' team is doing some geological studies with some sophisticated drilling equipment, almost like the bore-holes on the moon. Unless you can convince me otherwise... we stay here. Any questions?"

"Are you OK, Hannah? You had quite a shock, in there. Now this, with your new sister and friends."

"I have to be OK. I don't have the luxury of disregarding my responsibilities as Captain. I will never do that."

There were smiles all across the table. The warrior has awakened and she never loses, coursed through the minds of the people sitting quietly.

Then, came a knock on the door. I answered. Mom walked in followed by Devian.

"I'm OK" said my smiling sister and hugged me close. Without my permission, tears welled up in my eyes. Happiness took occupancy in my soul.

"My turn, daughters. I have an update. First Devian has only minor accumulation of radiation that should dissipate completely with the half-life of the absorbed isotopes.

T'merin and P'rtaven, have more serious problems. I would like to give you my observation and over-view of their situation. This won't be medical and, I am not a scientist, but I will do my best. I think K'hfatoria is dying. The entire race of people is in serious decline and won't last much longer. T'merin told me that the orbit of the two stars in the Pr'ydorin binary system are slowing in their mutual orbit. Soon they will fall into one-another and may, according to T'merin, go super-nova. The blast will encompass the entire inner system of planets. That includes K'hfatoria. She says that the K'hfatorian Council is scrambling to make three, old Journey-Class-Jumpers flight worthy. The problem is lack of fuel. The last remaining volcanic basalt-glass that was extracted from our moon, was given to T'merin's ship to come to save Earth from the asteroid. There is more, but I'm completely out of my league here. I can't give you an assurance that T'merin and P'rtaven will survive. But, we are doing everything we can, including reaching out to the best medical expert's humanity has to offer on Earth. We are challenging them to find the best minds that, at the very edge of scientific understanding, that can provide ideas and procedures. I should know more in a couple of days. For now, they are resting comfortably. I better get back."

"Thanks Mom. We have a lot to think about."

I had a thought... I started pacing, again. I wish I had my three-cornered hat. I paced some more. Each of those present saw the return of the real Hannah Parish, the Rogue, the Crazy-one...

"Darien, I have a suggestion." He looked at me with tear-soaked eyes. But, he saw resolve in mine. The ships master is back. They all saw it.

"It is time to reconvene 'Symphony'. We have some of the best scientists and thinkers in the world. It's time to light the fires in the forges of intellectual industry. No one is one thing. No one can hide behind their diplomas or PHD thesis. I'm calling on all of you to believe... *believe* you have PHD's in everything. You will stand together as a family, circulate ideas, arrive at conclusions, test your results. I want JPL, NASA and every department on Earth who graduated from the third grade, on this, folks. Seraphim is an amazing machine. Her crew is amazing. We stand together. The first thing we do, is locate and dig up all the crystal we can find, on Earth, the moon, where-ever. Second, we go to S'mparder. We study, we evaluate, we find out how the Jumper engines work. Then... We fix S'mparder. Then we pack up all the crystal into S'mparder and go to K'hfatoria, make their remaining Journey-Class Jumpers functional and we save their lives like they saved ours.

So, now. Create teams in all the necessary disciplines of science. Create new science, explore old visions and meld it with the new. We start by saving two lives, then we save more... then we save an entire civilization as they saved ours.

"This is the moment, when we all stand on the bow of this ship, swords held high, and do battle with the Kraken."

"This... is our Covenant."

...and so, it began

Epilogue

My name is Carl Ledbetter. I am a senior member of the Seraphim Ships Council. I joined the group of scientists 23 years ago, barely out of school. I have a Doctorate in Astro-Physics and was excited about the possibility we could build a space ship and maybe even get to go into space. I am not a philosopher or psychologist but I have been a watcher of people, and as the years went by, I was proud of the work done when the final configuration of the Seraphim took form. Being theoretical scientists, we rarely discussed the thought about extra-terrestrial life, or how we would deal with a first-encounter. It was too science-fiction-ish. The ship itself was incredibly complex. The early planning stages realized the need for a lot of group participation.

We started with about 50 people of which most were scientists. They were the thinkers, the designers. Then came the engineers, technicians, fabrication people, graphic artists, lots of electricians and LOIS (Lab of Impossible Stuff). Similar to Lockheed's Skunk Works. In that rarified atmosphere were people that were certifiably crazy, savants with a variety of syndromes, but all geniuses in some field or other. Some didn't even have a field. These were Graduates with Doctorates from universities at age 17 or 18 in the theoretical sciences. I remember one time when I was at a project meeting with Darien Hunter, the door flew open and this 23-year-old kid named Pauly ran in and slammed what looked like kitchen linoleum, only thicker, onto the table, sending papers flying. He leaned on the mat and picked things off the table and placed them on the mat. Then he backed away. The mat with three books, a coffee cup and a stapler, rose very slowly, vertically. No sound, just silent motion. He just smiled and said... "You don't need big rockets." Then he grabbed a lap-top computer and added it to the pile on the mat. It still floated. Everyone at the table was in a state of shock. What he invented would become the basis for **GMI:** *Planet Generated Gravity and Magnetosphere Interferometry*, one of the backbones of Seraphim's capabilities. There were many such innovations to come, in propulsion, gravity control, counter gravity, and, well, I could go on and on.

The crew seemed the most difficult nut to crack. Nobody, except a few astronauts had ever been in space. How do we staff a ship with just the right people to fly this thing to the moon? We didn't know how to do that. We had to eat, sleep and take showers. All that seemed secondary to the science. Fortunately, some people looking for work discovered they could help build the world's first Star-Ship. It took an additional four years... and it was complete. But it lacked qualified bridge officers. Some were just picked, put in a spot and we hoped for the best. Then one day, Theo was asked to mentor a new hire. I was skeptical. An ex-Navy type with no knowledge of space flight or the physical sciences. But, she learned. Did she ever? Later, due to some unusual circumstances, she became Captain of the ship and everything changed. We became a professional and capable crew.

Now we are faced with a conundrum of epic proportions. We are going to apply everything we know, everything we have learned, everything we are, to a project that could take us 135+ trillion miles from home. 23 LY (light years) and, save a planet, and its people. Sure! We can do that. It's going to be a real challenge, but...

I have a sword...

...And an amazing Captain.

Carl Ledbetter, Seraphim Ships Council

The Science of Seraphim
Testament

A Primer to the Origin of an Angel

The People of Seraphim

Initial Characters

Hannah Parish	LCDR, Ex-Navy Lieutenant
Edward Parish	Hannah's father, ex-navy fighter-pilot
Lorraine Parish	Hannah's mother, Med. Doctor
Amanda (Parish) Wagner	Hannah's sister
Mark Parish	Hannah's brother
Evelyn (Evie) Candalerie	Close friend

Seraphim Bridge Officers & Crew

Darien Hunter	Chief Scientist, Creator of Seraphim
Hannah Parish	CDR, Captain of the Seraphim #1
Douglas Freeman	ADM, Bridge Tactician & Advisor
Jessica Pearson	CDR, Executive Officer (XO) #2
Augustus (Augie) Lincoln	LCDR, Chief of the Boat (COB) #3
Perry Newcomb	LCDR, Master Chief (COB)
Sarah Ann Michaels	CDR, Captain's Exec. Admin Ass't
Theodore Remington.	Civ, Professor, Science Officer
Gustaf (Gus) Mayer	LCDR First Engineer
Drew Pearson	Lt, Second Engineer
Fred Mooney	Lt, Engineering
Paddington Lewis	Lt, Head of Gravity Department
Naveen Patel	Lt, Associate Head of Gravity
Daryl Plumber	Lt. Environment group supervisor
Carolyn Dinsmore	Lt, Environment 2nd in Command
Josh Whitmore	Lt, Helm/Navigation grp supervisor
Jeffrey Lancaster	Lt, Helm/Stellar Cartography
Edward Parish	LCDR, Chief Tactical Officer
David Janssen	Lt, Tactical, 2nd in Command

Lorraine Parish	LCDR, Dr. Medical Supervisor
Pamela Bingham	Lt, Medical Doctor
Francine Calder	Lt, Communication
Douglas Freeman	Adm, USS Andrew Lindstrom (ret)
Perry Newcomb	COB, USS Andrew Lindstrom (ret
Jimmie Burque	XO, USS Andrew Lindstrom (ret)

Ship Support Personnel

Porter Williams	Civ, Exec. Admin Ass't Science Divs
Karen Pelitier	Civ, Announcer/Computer Voice
Frederick Mooney	Civ, Lead Technology Engineer
Jake Maxwell	Civ, Chief Pilot, Support craft
Susan Richards	Civ, Ship's Gen Council, legal affairs
Myron Campbell	Civ, Attorney, Contract Law
Joseph Patterson	Civ, Attorney, Data Analytics
Felicia Cunningham	Civ, Attorney, Constitutional Law
Constance Knowles	Civ, Paralegal
David Bradley	Civ, Legal Assistant to M. Campbell
Paul Conway	Civ, Chairman, Executive Committee
Carl Ledbetter,	Civ, Senior member, Ships Council
Jerry Dissinger	Civ, Admin Assistant, Ships Council
Sandra Davies	Civ, Chaplin - Non Dénomination
Laurie Zoloth	Civ, Ethicist, Professor, Writer
Elizabeth Reynolds	Civ, Human Resources, Supervisor
Anna Scarafini	Civ, Public Affairs Officer
Janice Devlin	Civ, Hospitality and Host Supervisor
Aldus Franklin	Civ, Senior Astrophysics Professor
Pamela Martin	Civ, Astrometrics Specialist
David Pierce-Watson	Civ, Planetary geosciences division
Mary Pipkin	Civ, Senior Cartographer
Rosemary Clark	Civ, Medical Doctor, Pediatrics.
Allen Richardson	Civ, Chief of Surgery
Alexander Broder	Civ, Anesthesiology
Emily Pierce	Civ, Head Nurse
Jerry Dickson	Civ, Director of Internal Security
Meredith Ames	Civ, Theme Park Security

Roger Davidson	Civ, Ex-Secret Svs, Seraphim, TAE
Benjamin (Ben) Crowder	Civ, Ex-Secret Svs, Seraphim, TAE
Donna Singleton	Civ, Ex-Secret Svs, Seraphim, TAE
Loretta (Lory) Amundsen	Civ, Ex-USAF Pilot, Seraphim, TAE
Sam Lonegan	Civ, Counter-Intelligence (retired)
Jimmie Baker	Civ, Counter-Intelligence (retired)
Lloyd Jeffrey	Civ, Counter-Intelligence (retired)
Joyce Gardner	Civ, Counter-Intelligence (retired)
Douglas Archer	Civ, Counter-Intelligence (retired)
Jennifer Palmer	Civ, Counter-Intelligence (retired)
Justice (Jake) Hanover	Col, Wyoming Nat'l Guard
Paul (Lucky) Bradford	Col, Colorado Air Nat'l Guard.
Pauline Baxter	Civ, Housekeeping, Captain's Qtrs.'
Elliot Brimley	Vet, Retired JAG officer
Alfred Clark	Vet, Hangar, Museum
Betty &Floyd Cochran	Vets, B&B owners

Science Department Leads

Robert Kleinberg	Civ, RJ Robotics, AI Science
Dominic Schlesien	Civ, JPL, Propulsion Systems, Inc.
Lloyd Zimmerman	Civ, JPL, Theoretical Sciences Grp
Charles Parker	Civ, JPL, Special Projects Manager
Phil Raisonner	Civ, Randolph Cummings Develop.
Robert Conrad Farmer	Civ, Hybrid Synthetics
Jody Lynn Sampson	Civ, Environmental Studies
Joseph Lindquist	Civ, Environmental Studies
Gregory Vasilyevich	Rus, Propulsion contractor to Boeing
Scott Randal	ISS, Astronaut
Richard Daniels	ISS, Astronaut
Sergey Kuznetsov	ISS, Cosmonaut.
Dmitry Vasiliev	ISS, Cosmonaut
Dorothy Williams	NASA, Houston
Lonnie Portman	NASA, Houston
Philip Nordgren	NASA-JPL, Astronaut
Jerry Carter	NASA-JPL, Astronaut

Derick Jameson	NASA-JPL, Astronaut
Bascom Holder	NASA, Rear Admiral (retired)
Harold Kensington	Civ, Kensington Int'l (Under Arrest)
Roberta Furukawa	Civ, Planetary Systems (Under Arrest)

Seraphim Command Crew Assignments

Captain

The captain is the ultimate commander of the spaceship. He/she is responsible for its safe and efficient operation and ensuring that the vessel complies with established policies. All persons on board, including officers, crew, passengers and guests are under the captain's authority and are his/her ultimate responsibility. For most situations, the captain has the final say in all matters.

Executive Officer (XO)

The Executive Officer (XO) or Chief Command Officer (CCO) is second-in-command after the captain and also the head of the Bridge Department on a vessel. The XO assumes command of the whole ship in the absence or incapacitation of the captain.

Chief of the Boat

The Chief of the Boat (COB). He/she is third-in-command and also head of the Engineering Department. The COB assumes command of the whole ship in the absence or incapacitation of both the captain and the Executive Officer.

Chief Engineer

The Lead Engineer (LE). He/she is fourth-in-succession and also the Lead of the Engineering Department. The Lead Engineer assumes command of the whole ship in the absence or incapacitation of the Captain, the Exec Officer and the COB. More details on the Chief Engineer under the Engineering section.

Executive Committee (ExCom) **Ships Council**	The Executive Committee or ExCom consists of representative Heads of Departments (HOD) from all ship departments (Bridge, Engineering, Tactical, Intelligence & Security, R&D, Medical, Finance & Operation Support & Stewarding). The captain, Executive Officer (XO), Chief of the Boat(COB) and Chief Engineer are also part of the Executive Committee. Although the captain has the final say in almost all matters, the Executive Committee has the power to veto the captain's decision if all members unanimously agree on a different course of action.
Executive Admin Assistant	An administrative role, the Executive Admin Assistant acts as a personal assistant to the captain, handling paperwork for the ExCom and acts as liaison between department heads and other departments, Maintains the Ship's Log.
Med-Bay Doctors / Nurses	Is staffed by professional Doctors, Nurses, and Specialists who may be medical officers or civilian personnel. On the Seraphim it is the primary work space of Doctor Lorraine Parish

K'hfatorian language

Binary Star System
Pr'ydorin
Pr'ydorin Major and Pr'ydorin Minor
Distance from **"Sol" Star System**   23 LY (light years)

K'hfatoria Binary planetary system:
Ecliptic is Tidal-Locked

K'hfatoria Prime   Home world planet   .9x Earth Mass
K'hfatoria B   partner planet   3.1x Earth Mass

Star Ship S'mparder: Journey-Class Jumper
K'hfatorian Guider: Pilot/Navigator/leader

K'hfatorian Pronunciation

Pr'ydorin:	(pree–DOR-in)	System Star
K'hfatoria	(kafa-TOR-ia)	Home planet
S'mparder:	(sem-PARder)	Journey-Class Jumper
T'merin	(ta-MERIN)	Lead Guider, Navigator
Devian	(DEV-ee-ANN)	Second Guider, Teller
P'rtaven	(per-TAH-vin)	Third Guider, Healer
S'nofer	(sen–OO-fer)	Pelidan Lead
I'odinn	(ee-OH-din)	1st C'mpressr
D'rmin	(DER-min)	2nd C'mpressr
X'orvkk	(ZOR-vik)	3rd C'mpressr
C'mpressr	(sem-PRES-sor)	Mass Mover
P'elidan	(PAY-lee-dann)	Mover controller
Victoria	Benholt	Mother
Horst	Benholt	Father

Boot Camp – Training
Syllabus

Physiological Training
- Physics of functioning in space.
- Respiration and Circulation
- Decompressions
- Stress
- Hypoxia
- Hyperventilation
- Decompression Sickness
- Pressure Equalization Difficulties
- Aerospace Oxygen Equipment
- Altitude Chamber Oxygen Equipment Familiarization
- Altitude Chamber Flight Profile & Flight
- Spatial Disorientation, including demonstrators

Gravitational Anomalies.
- Using the seat of your pants
- Exposure to zero gravity.
- G-forces above one-G
- Effects on the human body and equilibrium
- Ability to adapt
- Physical fitness
- Zero-G Flying safely in an enclosed area.

Planetary Physiological Dynamics - *Mars* training
- Gravity
- Radiation
- Days, Nights, Years
- Atmosphere
- Storms: Sand / Dust. Dust devils
- Quick-Sand / Dust

Definitions

ACPU: **A**nnihilation **C**hamber **P**ower **U**nit A system of power generation resulting from the collision of Matter and Antimatter in an airless and highly magnetic-field chamber.

AGL: Above Ground Level

BOAT: Nautical euphemism for a submarine. A historical holdover, it reflects the time it came to be, when submarines were actually boats.

CIC: **C**ommand **I**nformation **C**enter

CO: **C**ommanding **O**fficer

COB: **C**hief **O**f the **B**oat is an assigned position aboard Seraphim who serves as an advisor to the commanding officer and executive officer and is #3 in succession to the Captain.

CONN: is the watch that directly controls ships movements. When a ship is underway, a conning officer must always be stationed.

CTS: **C**ommunications **T**ransfer **S**tation

DCFS: **D**ata **C**ollection **F**orwarding **S**ystem

DEFCON: **Def**ence **Con**dition - ranked from 5 to 1, 1=highest

Delta-V: is the change in velocity for Seraphim, shuttles and Valkyries where VASIMR rockets are used. It is measured at maximum throttle, and is proportional to the thrust per unit mass and the burn time. Helm control must weigh the application of power to available fuel (argon).

DFC: Distinguished Flying Cross

EVA: Extra Vehicular Activity – Space walk outside a space ship where gravity and atmosphere do not exist.

Exfil: Exfiltration: The process of exiting or extracting personnel from an area.

Fermi Paradox: named after Italian-American physicist Enrico Fermi and refers to the apparent contradiction between the lack of evidence for, but high probability of, the existence of extraterrestrial civilizations, so... "where are they?"

FFP: Force-Field Projection array (emitter). A protection methodology aboard Seraphim, shuttles and Valkyrie that can beam a high-powered quantum particle emission that disrupts and scatters the molecular structure of an object leaving nothing but dust.

Flip-the-Ship: An operational maneuver reversing the orientation of the ship relative to its course while moving through space. The VASIMR engines are fired for a specific time and thrust to slow the ship.

FOX-1; A Call-out by a pilot, of the launch of a radar guided missile such as the AIM-120, (not used aboard Seraphim)

FOX-2; A Call-out by a pilot, of the launch of an infrared-guided missile (such as the AIM-9 Sidewinder)

FLOAT: Term used by Captain Parish that paraphrases a submarine command to bring the sub to the surface. In the context of Seraphim, to allow the ship to move upward, away from the Earth's surface to a height pre-set by the helm officer.

GMI: Planet Generated **G**ravity and **M**agnetosphere **I**nterferometry. Method of low power propulsion used only near a planet or moon effective only in the presence of strong planetary gravitational and magnetic fields. The moon and Mars do not have magnetic fields and far less gravity. There-fore this system will not work as effectively, or not at all. Control must be augmented with maneuvering thrusters.

HALO: A HALO jump (also known as MFF, Military Free Fall) is a military-style High Altitude, Low Open parachute jump, intended to get troops on the ground quickly and undetected.

ISOP: Incredibly-**S**mart-**O**ld-**P**erson

ISS: International Space Station

Lagrange Point: (Libration Point) A location in space where the combined gravitational forces of two large bodies, such as Earth and the sun or Earth and the moon, equal the centrifugal force felt by a much smaller third body. The interaction of the forces creates a point of equilibrium where a spacecraft may be "parked" to make observations.

Mach 2: Twice the speed of sound, approx. 1,552 miles per hour plus or minus depending on temperature and pressure.

MEP: **M**agnetic-**E**ncasement-**P**rotocol, a method for isolating anti-matter runaway in an ACPU

MiB: **M**en-**i**n-**B**lack - euphemism for Government bad guys in this storyline.

Mikes: Minutes

MPDSF: **M**agneto **P**lasma **D**ynamic **S**elf-**F**ield thruster. This *self*-induced *magnetic field* interacts with the electric current flowing from the anode to the cathode (through the *plasma*) to produce an electromagnetic (Lorentz) force that pushes the *plasma* out of the engine, creating *thrust.*

MSL: Mean Sea Level

Murphy's Law: The proposition that if something can go wrong, it will.

NASA: National Aeronautics and Space Administration. – USA

NDA: **N**on-**D**isclosure **A**greement

NGE: **N**avigation, **G**ravity, **E**nvironmental - Multidiscipline Work center

PDM: **P**ower **D**istribution **M**onitoring

Regolith: refers to any layer of material covering solid rock... Moon: On Earth, **regolith** takes the form of dirt, soil, sand, and other components

Roscosmos: State Corporation for Space Activities – Russia

RQPGD :   **R**efractive **A**ctive **Q**uantum-**P**article **G**ravity-**D**isplacement Polymer.   A multi-layer amalgam that absorbs dangerous
        radiation from the sun, radar, cell phones, radios and Earth's gravitational field. Seraphim's hull is very thick 37.9" and is able to absorb considerable damage from small asteroid hits. The shuttles, Valkyrie and Sentinels have similar but much thinner skin.

Station-Keeping: Usually associated with placing a vessel or satellite at the Lagrange Point or Libration Point. Keeping the vessel fixed, unmoving or in the case of control mechanisms, in stall mode, in preparation for a command.

TAE: Tactical Analysis and Evaluation

Tricky-Room: Phrase by main character in reference to an odd meeting room with unique gravitation options.

Two-stage deep space interceptor: A two-stage rocket design implementation to destroy an approaching asteroid, comet or foreign body that might impact Earth.

VAL-1: Call sign - Commander Hannah Parish, Valkyrie 1

VAL-2: Call sign - Commander Lory Amundson, Valkyrie 2

VASIMR: Variable Specific Impulse Magneto-Plasma Rocket is an electro-thermal thruster used in spacecraft propulsion. It uses radio waves to ionize and heat a propellant. Then a magnetic field accelerates the resulting plasma to generate thrust (plasma propulsion engine).

'What-If...' An intellectual challenge to subordinates to isolate and find solutions to theoretical problems

XO: eXecutive Officer

Seraphim Fleet Propulsion Systems

The Variable Specific Impulse Magneto-plasma Rocket (VASIMR) is the primary thrust engine design for in-Space high speed propulsion. Although several different inert fuels are available, argon was the choice for the -9, -4 and -5 VASIMR engines. High power radio waves ionize and heat the propellant. Then a magnetic field accelerates the resulting plasma to generate thrust (plasma propulsion engine). It is one of several types of spacecraft electric propulsion systems. The VASIMR method for heating plasma was originally developed from nuclear fusion research. It is intended to bridge the gap between high-thrust, low-specific impulse and low-thrust, high-specific impulse systems, and is capable of functioning in either mode.

In-space (exo-atmospheric) long-range, high-speed engines provide Seraphim extremely high impulse linear thrust and high delta-v along the ships longitudinal axis using four Variable Specific Impulse Magneto-plasma Rocket motors (VASIMR-9) through independently controlled plasma tube ports at the rear of the ship which resemble huge jet engines. These provide the potential for near light speed terminal velocity. Each of the -9 engines are the largest ever built and provide a throttle-able impulse of 12 million pounds of thrust or approx. 53 million newtons at full power. Two smaller -5 versions of the VASIMR design are used as primary propulsion for the smaller space capable Shuttle designs. A (-4) version variant will see use in the very small but space capable Valkyries. 6-axis attitude control for Seraphim is accomplished using *Magneto Plasma Dynamic Self-Field Thrusters* (MPDSF-5), that don't require the external high-power source that *Applied Field thrusters* do. They have a significantly lower impulse capability but very fast delta-v. They do pose increased maintenance requirements due to erosion of the central cathode so were not used as primary thrust engines. However, they function well as positioning jets on Seraphim.

Monopropellant Rocket Motors:

The Seraphim fleet design portfolio describes three methods of in-space 6-axis attitude and positioning control. Seraphim uses the MPDSF-5 for large effort maneuvering, and a second system of maneuvering thrusters with a low effort design for more precise maneuvering.

6-axis attitude and positioning control for the Shuttles, Valkyrie and Pocket-Rocket ships have two systems available; the low power one described above and a very low effort second system. Small hydrogen-peroxide monopropellant rocket motors are used on all shuttles that require low specific impulse for both orbital station-keeping and attitude control, as well as providing limited thrust to use for orbital maneuvers to better rendezvous with other spacecraft. Having both systems allows for small adjustments to position as well as rapid repositioning.

Hypergolic Liquid-Propellant Rocket

Purchased under contract from SpaceX, a private American aerospace manufacturer and space transportation services company, several of their *SuperDraco* rocket engines entered service for use in the *Pocket-Rocket* series of small 6 passenger, space capable, personnel carriers. Set in pairs, each of the two engines provide a throttleable thrust of 73,000 newtons (16,400 lbf) utilizing a storable (non-cryogenic) propellant which allows the engines to be fired many months after fueling and launch.

Ships of the Fleet

Ship	Type	Length	Beam	Crew	Propulsion Primary	Secondary

Seraphim, Starship 1331' 133' 500+ VASIMR-09 x4 GMI 5

Power is generated by 5 interlinked matter/antimatter Annihilation Chamber Power Units, 260 megawatt each, and two backup 140 megawatt each General Electric S4G nuclear reactors.

Hull: multi-layer Refractive Active Quantum-Particle Gravity-Displacement Polymer (RQPGD) hull design.

3 large Airlock Entries to Internal Hangars 1,2 and 3

24 Individual Sentinel Airlocks accessed from deck 6

...12 Port, 12 Starboard. Includes maintenance facilities

for Block 1 and Block 2 Sentinels.

Airlock 1 accessed from stern between main thrusters.

Hangar 1: Airlock tunnel 121.2' long, 29.7' wide, 29.8' high

Hangar 2: Airlock tunnel 80.25' long, 29.7' wide, 29.8' high

Hangar 3: Airlock tunnel 80.25' long, 29.7' wide, 13.8' high w/

4 utility access airlocks amidships on each side joining Hangar 3.

2 Portside, 2 Starboard at deck 1 level

2 large vertical equipment access elevators, one under the nose and one further aft, just forward of the first collar. Sealable but not used as an airlock. The Interior can be pressurized or a vacuum. The elevators rise into a large tunnel that runs nearly the length of the hull along the keel line through bilge level and decks 1 and 2 for moving large bulky equipment to storage or maintenance halls on each side. Each hall has a pressure door to the tunnel. Tunnel dimensions are 28' high, 39' wide and 680' long. It ends at Hangar bays in the stern. It includes a Loading Platform with a placement tug 60x22x15 (Useful 52x21x12)

Gravity systems are the same as the rest of the ship.

Michael **Shuttle** 47.5' 19' 12 VASIMR-05 x2 GMI 1

First addition: proof of concept design: The VASIMR-1 engines initially installed proved problematic and were replaced with newer VASIMR- 5 engines. Power: single matter/antimatter Annihilation Chamber Power Unit. Used as shuttle with GMI only. Upgraded GMI to GMI1. Added parallel wall seating for 10. RQPGD hull design, and FFP planned in future retrofit,

Gabriel **Shuttle** 46.1' 19' 30+ VASIMR-05 x2 GMI 1

Second generation: Power: single matter/antimatter Annihilation Chamber Power Unit. First functional RQPGD hull design. Later Counter Gravity added. FFP planned in retrofit.

Raphael Shuttle   46.1'   19'   30+   VASIMR-05 x2 GMI 1
          Same as Gabriel

Peregrine Shuttle: 63.7'   25'   55   VASIMR-05x3, GMI 1
Advanced large body shuttle with added automation. RQPGD hull design, GMI 1, FFP, Power: single matter/antimatter Annihilation Chamber Power Unit. first to add an on-board personnel airlock with bathroom facilities and bunks.

Valkyrie, Tactical: 26,1'   13'   9   VASIMR-4 x2, GMI 3
RQPGD hull design, Medium power FFP, Laser disrupter. Power: single ACPU matter/antimatter Annihilation Chamber Power Unit.

Pocket -Rocket: 21.9' 8'   7.9'   6   SuperDraco x2, GMI 1
Small 6-passenger, short term, space capable, run-about, RQPGD hull design.

Dragon-Slayer: A Large autonomous drone operated as a shield well ahead of Seraphim during high speed travel through space. Equipped with a latest generation high-power, wide-beam version of the Force-Field Projection emitter. It clears the way ahead to prevent Seraphim from a catastrophic collision with an asteroid, comet or any other threat. Patrol distance ahead of Seraphim is predicated on Seraphim's relative speed, and can be guided by Seraphim helm control. The high-power requirements for both the VASIMR-5 engines and FFP requires the use of a single nuclear reactor often used in submarines. The fuel used in these reactors is a metal-zirconium alloy. The reactor is designed for long core life, enabled by the relatively high enrichment of the uranium. Command and Control comes from a purpose-built automatic and A.I computer array tied in with tactical and helm guidance. Manual override is available at both bridge helm and tactical positions. Feedback exists from Dragon-slayer sensors to bridge stations.

Science Departments and Definitions

Anthropometrics: *The study of human body measurement for use in anthropological classification and comparison.*
extravehicular mobility unit (EMU),
Extravehicular suits
intravehicular suit
Final Frontier Design
ascent-descent suits
NASA's "Biomimicry" Z-2 spacesuit

Facts:
Earth rotates once in about 24 hours with respect to the Sun, but once every 23 hours, 56 minutes, and 4 seconds with respect to the stars (Sidereal) Earth's rotation is slowing slightly with time; thus, a day was shorter in the past. This is due to the tidal effects the Moon has on Earth's rotation.

Moon rotates once in about 27.32 days
The sidereal month is the time it takes to make one complete orbit around Earth with respect to the fixed stars. It is about 27.32 days. The **synodic** month is the time it takes the Moon to reach the same visual phase. This varies notably throughout the year, but averages around 29.53 days.

Astrometrics: is the branch of astronomy that involves precise measurements of the positions and movements of stars and other celestial bodies. The information obtained by astrometric measurements provides information on the kinematics and physical origin of the Solar System and our galaxy, the Milky Way.

Astrophysics: is the branch of astronomy that employs the principles of physics and chemistry "to ascertain the nature of the astronomical objects, rather than their positions or motions in space". Among the objects studied are the Sun, other stars, galaxies, extrasolar planets, the interstellar medium and the cosmic microwave background.

Geophysics: is a highly interdisciplinary subject, and geophysicists contribute to every area of the Earth sciences. To provide a clearer idea of what constitutes geophysics, this section describes phenomena that are studied in physics and how they relate to the Earth and its surroundings.

Planetary Geosciences: alternatively known as astrogeology or exogeology, is a planetary science discipline concerned with the geology of the celestial bodies such as the planets and their moons, asteroids, comets, and meteorites. Although the geo-prefix typically indicates topics of or relating to Earth, planetary geology is named as such for historical and convenience reasons; due to the types of investigations involved, it is closely linked with Earth-based geology

General relativity: is the geometric theory of gravitation published by Albert Einstein in 1915 and the current description of gravitation in modern physics. General relativity generalizes special relativity and Newton's law of universal gravitation, providing a unified description of gravity as a geometric property of space and time, or spacetime.

Quantum mechanics: (QM; also known as quantum physics, quantum theory, the wave mechanical model, or matrix mechanics), including quantum field theory, is a fundamental theory in physics which describes nature at the smallest scales of energy levels of atoms and subatomic particles.

Quantum gravity: (QG) is a field of theoretical physics that seeks to describe gravity according to the principles of quantum mechanics, and where quantum effects cannot be ignored, such as near compact astrophysical objects where the effects of gravity are strong.

Celestial / Stellar cartography: uranography, astrography or star cartography is the fringe of astronomy and branch of cartography concerned with mapping stars, galaxies, and other astronomical objects on the celestial sphere. Measuring the position and light of charted objects requires a variety of instruments and techniques.

X-ray pulsar-based navigation and timing (XNAV) is a navigation technique whereby the periodic X-ray signals emitted from pulsars are used to determine the location of a vehicle, such as a spacecraft in deep space. A vehicle using XNAV would compare received X-ray signals with a database of known pulsar frequencies and locations. Similar to GPS, this comparison would allow the vehicle to triangulate its position accurately (± 5 km). The advantage of using X-ray signals over radio waves is that X-ray telescopes can be made smaller and lighter.

Thermodynamics: is the branch of physics that deals with heat and temperature, and their relation to energy, work, radiation, and properties of matter. The behavior of these quantities is governed by the four laws of thermodynamics which convey a quantitative description using measurable macroscopic physical quantities.

Ephemerides: In astronomy and celestial navigation, an ephemeris (plural: ephemerides; from Latin ephemeris, meaning 'diary', from Greek, Modern (ephemeris), meaning 'diary, journal') gives the positions of naturally occurring astronomical objects as well as artificial satellites in the sky at a given time or times.

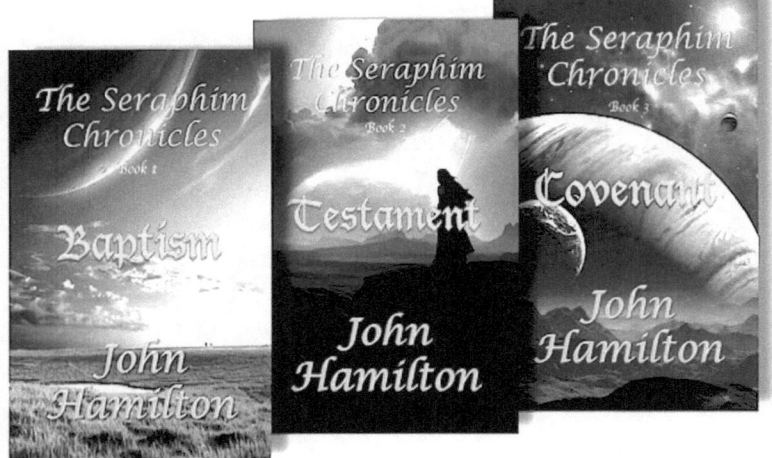

John Hamilton began writing fiction novels following retirement from a major U.S. defense contractor. He draws on his background in aviation as an Air Force veteran, a qualified commercial and instrument rated pilot, an employee of the Federal Aviation Administration, a qualified blue water sailor and tactician aboard a 39-foot yacht.

The Seraphim Chronicles Trilogy began his first true adventure into classic science fiction with an emphasis on real contemporary science and bold character development.

He now lives in rural Shelby County, Kentucky enjoying the peace and tranquility away from noise and city lights.

www.ingramcontent.com/pod-product-compliance
Lightning Source LLC
Chambersburg PA
CBHW051935240626
47153CB00005B/1503